MetalGhost

Kashif and the Echoes from a Past Life

Ali Mohammad Rizwan

Global Bookshelves International
Louisville, KY 40241

Printed in the United States of America.

Global Bookshelves International
Louisville, KY 40241
www.GlobalBookshelves.com

To comment on this book by email, email globalbookshelves@gmail.com.

MetalGhost: Kashif and the Echoes from a Past Life/Ali Mohammad Rizwan -- 1st ed.
ISBN 978-1-957242-10-1

Table of Contents

Dedicated to my Parents, Lubna and
Sikandar Ali.
My superheroes.

Dedicated to Palestine.
Insha'Allah Palestine will be free.
O Palestine, this book is for you.

Bismillahi Rahmani Raheem

"The strong man is not the one who wrestles others; rather, the strong man is the one who controls himself at times of anger." -Prophet Muhammad (ﷺ)

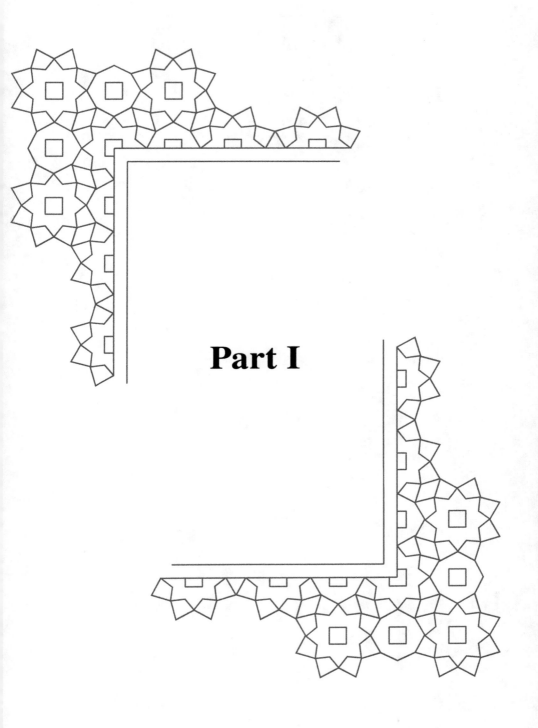

Part I

CHAPTER ONE

THE FALL

T he halls of the hospital echoed louder and louder as a nurse frantically ran through them, panic filled her face, and beads of sweat formed on her forehead. Out of breath as she reached the room filled with other staff, she froze at the doorway while staring at the TV screen, listening to the words being reported. In disbelief, she covered her mouth. The other staff members had their eyes glued to the screen, some with their faces paralyzed in shock, some in awe, and others crying in fear.

The hospital was louder than it had ever been. The buzz of anxious staff running back and forth; loud, nervous chatter and a palpable uneasiness in the air filled the entire building. Even though the clocks read midnight, the noise and commotion felt like peak hours during midday. People in every room were nervously chatting, attempting to get hold of the breaking news leaking out and trying to make sense of all the exploding events happening only a floor below them.

"Can you believe this?" a frightened voice gasped from a group huddled together near the TV in the waiting room to the nurse who rushed in.

"This can't be happening," another group of nervous-looking people whispered in disbelief.

The breaking news from reporters was heard from right outside the hospital, while some had made their way into the restricted areas inside, frantically reporting the same thing over and over again:

"We have shocking, breaking news as Ridgefield Park City's

vigilante, MetalGhost, was rushed into Ibn Sina City Hospital just moments ago with what is being reported as life-threatening injuries..."

"Famous Al-Fihriya University Professor Kashif Razvi has, in fact, been revealed as the masked hero, MetalGhost. According to sources, he is in critical condition..." blared from a screen in the next room.

"The city's controversial hero, MetalGhost, was found unconscious at the premises of the suspected mob leader known as the Mad Scientist..." blasted from the room across the hall as dozens of onlookers were glued to the TV set, gasping in awe and disbelief.

The scene on the hospital's ground floor quickly turned into chaos and panic as hospital staff, police officers, and press media all scattered around shouting over each other, desperately trying to get Chief of Police, Fahim Kazmi to answer questions. After every attempt to keep the unruly crowd of anxious journalists and reporters away, Chief Fahim finally made his way toward them. The wild crowd grew silent at once, ready to listen to Police Chief Fahim Kazmi, a man of a usually calm demeanor, but at that moment, he was visibly shaken. As he looked into what seemed like an ocean of camera lights and microphones pointed at him, he cleared his throat and carefully chose his words.

"At this time, I cannot give any official press release, and until we have more information, I can only tell you he is..." He paused before saying, "Being treated for severe injuries."

"Is he dead!?" shouted one reporter over him.

"Is it true he was found thrown from the top floor of the Mad Scientist's Lab?!" shouted another.

"Have you spoken to him at all?!" shouted a third.

He raised his arms in an attempt to calm the roaring crowd. Police Chief Fahim clearly became overwhelmed by the questions. Still, he tried his best to remain as calm as possible in such a turbulent and chaotic time, a truly momentous event for the entire city. He responded, "He is not dead. All I can say at this moment is the doctors are hoping he doesn't slip into a comatose state. Thank you." The voices roared even louder with questions and shouts, closing in on him as he was led away by Ridgefield Park City detectives into the police room they had set up across the hall.

"Had to pull you out of there. They were gonna eat you alive, Chief." Sergeant Rosser chuckled after having closed the door behind him. "What a show, huh?"

He analyzed Chief Fahim, a middle-aged man with green eyes, short black hair, and a sharp jaw of Afghan descent, who had just collapsed onto a chair, letting out a nervous sigh. He wore blue jeans paired with a white shirt and a black overcoat. He reached into his pocket to pull out and answer his buzzing phone. "Hasn't stopped buzzing for a single moment in the last hour," he anxiously commented.

"Wait till the mayor arrives," Sgt. Rosser carefully stated while looking at Chief Fahim, who stared back at him even more exasperated than before, realizing the mayor would be arriving soon.

"Have you secured all the floors of the hospital? Make sure no one comes and goes without it being known," instructed Chief Fahim with a stern face.

"On it, Chief. Estes is taking count of all the patients and staff as we speak," responded Rosser as he handed the chief a cup of hot coffee.

The door opened as Lieutenant Miller, a tall, dark man with a heavy build, approached the two with a tablet in hand. "They're already posting it everywhere. Amazing how fast news spreads," he said, swiping through the stories already posted by news agencies. Some read, *The MetalGhost is… Kashif Razvi, Famous Professor Revealed to be RP City's Vigilante,* and *Professor Kashif Razvi: Revealed to be Ridgefield Park's SuperHero, Currently in Coma.*

"Well, that was fast," said Chief Fahim, sighing resignedly at the two.

The realization of what was happening and what it could result in was slowly dawning on him; it weighed heavily on his shoulders like a burden almost impossible to shrug off. *The city is going to fall into chaos,* he thought to himself. *And it's all my fault.* He felt anxious, uncertain, and helpless, but mostly, he felt fearful. Chief Fahim was terrified. There was one man who was a barrier between stopping the crime mobs and keeping them from taking over the city, and that barrier was now shattered. *What now?* He knew the dam had been broken, and the criminals would burst out like firecrackers, holding their glitches for the perfect moment to shine. The city would be torn apart, and he knew his police force was not ready for what would happen next. *Ya Rabb,* "My God..." he whispered to himself.

"You okay, Chief?" Lt. Miller glanced at the coffee cup shaking in his hand.

Chief Fahim looked up, failing to hide the frightened expression in his eyes. He raised his cup to them, "Drink up, boys; we're going to be awake for a *long* time."

"Are you still going to call him a vigilante?" asked Lt. Miller. "It's Razvi; we know him."

"What else can I call him?" questioned Chief Fahim, genuinely unsure.

"A hero? The city's hero."

"He's been breaking the law and taking it into his own hands for years. Heroes don't break laws," responded Chief Fahim.

"Yeah... but... he's saved you more than once," Rosser responded. "And your family, Chief."

"And for that, I will thank Razvi... when he wakes up, and that's it," Chief Fahim quietly replied, staring into space, still deep in thought and worry.

"I just want to know how he kept his identity a secret for so many years," said Lt. Miller followed by a nervous laugh. "Now *that's* what's truly amazing: the one thing even Chief Fahim Kazmi couldn't figure out after all this time." He winked at Rosser and nudged him on the arm.

"No, but I'm going to find out," Chief Fahim muttered with a determined look across his face. He tightened his lips and rose up to make his way through the crowd of raucous reporters outside of the police room, ignoring the hundreds of questions, swiftly making his way in through the ER doors.

CHAPTER TWO

THE MAN
ON THE ROOF

A large hall on the top floor of a giant factory across the city was full of chatter, sinister laughter, and jubilation. A long rectangular table full of the most notorious criminals of the City of Ridgefield Park and its neighboring cities sat in awe, staring at the TV screens that blared the breaking news of the defeat of MetalGhost by none other than the man labeled by his peers as the Mad Scientist.

"Police Chief Fahim has just confirmed RP City's vigilante and hero, MetalGhost, is in a coma; however, the talk among the nurses is that he is in much worse condition. More updates coming up soon," boomed the news reporters' update. Cheers and applause erupted upon hearing the news on the TV. A few henchmen stood against the walls and began celebrating.

"Thank you! Thank you!" said the Mad Scientist, a large, broad-shouldered man in a white lab coat with slick reddish-dyed hair flowing back.

"You really did it, Boss," said one man standing in the back with a group holding guns. "The Ghost Killer!" quipped another as the celebration continued.

The men sitting at the table with the Mad Scientist, the leaders of the city's crime mobs, were less enthusiastic but gave their straight-faced congratulations to the man of the hour.

"So it's true what they're all reporting? You really did it, huh?" asked the Dealer with his heavy Spanish accent, with a half-smile, hoping not to sound too impressed. "And where's your boss, Iris Hill?"

At that moment, one of the Mad Scientist's men came up to him and whispered in his ear. He nodded while looking back at the table, "Looks like he wants to join the show." The TV image switched to a dark, bald man on screen.

"Ah, my good friend, Iris Hill," Mad Scientist greeted him. "Would you like to tell our friends how you tried to have me killed tonight?"

The men on the table shifted uneasily.

"I brought you MetalGhost, Dr. Daye, but you have truly lost your mind and are out of control," the man on the screen lashed out at the Mad Scientist in a slow and deep voice.

"You think you can manipulate me?" the Mad Scientist questioned.

He turned to the room. "My friends, Mr. Hill, here tried to have me killed tonight but failed. Your act of war will cost you dearly."

"You brought the war on yourself by not listening to me. And now you will face the consequences of Black Dread," Iris Hill hissed out.

"I look forward to it," the Mad Scientist turned off the TV.

The men on the table shifted uncomfortably, having just realized they had to take sides.

"They said he's in a coma; that's not dead," a loud, powerful voice boomed at the end of the table, which silenced all the commotion. "You're not a half measure, are you, Dr. Daye?" said the man dressed in a black pinstriped suit known as the Bone Collector, looking directly into the Mad Scientist's eyes.

The Mad Scientist locked his eyes with those of the Bone Collector's and shot him an emphatic smile. "If he makes the mistake of waking up, I'll be there to greet him to Hell." He laughed as if humming to a tune resembling "My Way" by Frank Sinatra.

"I'd like to be there for that," said a heavy, short man smoking a cigar. Mr. Hex continued with his beady eyes behind his round glasses, "mostly to make sure you finish the job."

"Trust me, if he wakes up and sees your ugly bald head, he'll immediately die from shock," the Mad Scientist maniacally laughed, causing an uproar of laughter around the room. "Don't worry about the GhostMan," he continued confidently, "I made *him* a deal…" He looked the Dealer in the eyes, "For his soul."

Reaching below the table, he pulled out the mask that once belonged to MetalGhost, which he had ripped off from the original suit. The whole room fell silent in disbelief at the sight of it. The Mad Scientist threw the mask on the table for all to see, causing palpable awe in the room. The mask was that of the man who had caused so much suffering to those around the table. It was the mask of the one man they could not catch or beat for so many years. Thus, the Mad Scientist cherished the moment of having the admiration and respect of each person in the room.

"I hear you all talking about me. I hear what you say behind my back. You all call me *mad* and *insane*," he said slowly, taking pleasure in each word. "And I say, *thank you*." He gave a menacing smile to each member sitting at the table. The occupants of the table eyed each other unsettlingly. "Now, let's get back to the plans, shall we?" The Mad Scientist continued. "Time for me to take this city once and for all. And I ask you all, my friends, does anyone now doubt me and my abilities?" he asked with a sinister smile. No one dared to question him.

Unknown to everyone in the hall, above the glass ceiling, was a man standing on the roof, looking down and listening to everything.

It's time, the man said to himself, wearing a long white cloak covering his body, leaving his arms bare, and a conical sedge hat on his head. His face was half-covered in silver armor wrapped around his torso under the white garment. Holstered on his back was his nodachi sword. As he peered down with raging eyes, the man stood up, one hand on his sword, ready to crash through the glass and make a grand entrance. He planned on leaving no one in the room alive. As the man waited, he breathed heavily with his nodachi in his fists.

Come on, he said to himself. He stood still, staring down, not moving.

Now's the time, Won. As his heart started beating more frantically, his hand on the sword started becoming shakier.

You've trained for three years for this very moment. They

must pay! Now! He thought to himself, attempting to refocus.

As his heart beat louder and faster in his chest, Won stood frozen on the spot. He slowly took his hand off his sword. After a minute, he took a deep breath, lowered his head, and took a step off the ledge, unable to make his move.

I can't. I'm...not ready.

Disappointed and angry with himself, he slowly walked back onto the roof, climbed down to a lower balcony, and jumped onto the next building's rooftop, disappearing into the night.

A few buildings away, a woman watched. She wore a black hijab, a yellow and gray suit, covering her entire body except for her face, a cape draped over her left arm, hiding her choice of weapon: the bow and arrow.

"Coward," she whispered, having zoomed in with her super lens in her eyes. Then, she quietly scaled the side of the building and jumped onto a motorcycle and rode off.

CHAPTER THREE

WAR WITH YOURSELF

G et out of the way!" yelled a doctor, whose usual slick combed-back black hair had become messy as he quickly led the gurney with the bleeding and unconscious man into the trauma bay. The other doctors tried to keep up with his fast pace as he stormed through double doors and hallways.

"Everyone to the trauma bay right now!" screamed Dr. Karim.

Inside, the doctors, nurses, and staff looked down at the body of the man known as MetalGhost, the Masked Protector of their city, a hero to some, and a vigilante of the law to others. The doctors, for the first time, were getting to see the face of the masked hero, for the metal facemask was torn off from the rest of the metal suit. The face was badly bruised and beaten, with blood dripping from his head. They were just finishing removing his dark blue flowing garment, a thobe covering his body that was torn and battered with blood stains. The doctors noticed that MetalGhost, now revealed to be the famous Professor Kashif Razvi, had a full metallic body armor under the blue cloak. The metal gray-colored armor was severely damaged with deep scratches, breaks, and clear signs of trauma.

The doctors were now staring at the highly advanced piece of armor which most had only seen in pictures from newspaper clippings but rarely in person because MetalGhost mostly worked in the shadows and stayed out of sight. Only one of the doctors in the room had seen the masked hero in his suit up close; the rest had only desired to. Gazing at the man and the suit now, the awe of the whole situation was still causing a shock to many of the staff. It was only the actual shocks of electricity whenever the doctors tried to touch the suit that snapped many of them back to reality. They saw a belt strapped around him containing different gadgets: a grappling hook of sorts, a holster for rope cuffs, and other gadgets they could not understand. Blasters forming a jetpack were on the back of the belt, which helped him float in the air. The smell from the blasters was still fresh as if he had used them recently.

What worried the doctors most was that the suit made a beeping noise. Unsure of what the sound meant, they stayed at a distance while noticing the entire suit was electronic, and it seemed…alive. As they stood back, unsure of how to get close to the body and remove the armor, the emergency room doors slammed open, and a tall, broad shouldered man wearing a black T-shirt and blue jeans accompanied Police Chief Fahim.

"The suit has to be disarmed!" Samir Khan frantically warned the doctors, "Don't take a step closer to the suit!" Samir was Kashif Razvi's best friend and colleague. He pressed a button on Kashif's wrist, but when nothing happened, he became more alarmed, whispering to himself, "No, no, no!" Samir proceeded to take out a device from his pocket and began typing commands into it. The doctors and Police Chief Fahim looked on in desperation as Samir took a closer look at his friend, lying on the table. He touched his arm and took Kashif's right hand's index and middle fingers and pressed them to his chest, a finger sensor. The armor stopped beeping.

"And how did you know this?" asked an astonished Chief Fahim.

"I know… because I designed this suit," Samir stated without looking back.

Clearly distraught, he lowered his face to Kashif's and touched his hair. With tears coming down his face, he whispered to him, "You can't leave us now, brother. I know you're at war with yourself, but it isn't over. Now, a new war has begun. Stay with us, please." Next to him, a disturbed Police Chief Fahim stared, raising his eyebrow. "There," Samir addressed the doctors in the room, "Now, take it off," Samir said, looking at

Kashif with tears in his eyes.

The doctors started removing the metal suit, revealing a strong, muscular body badly bruised. They were finally able to stabilize Kashif Razvi and determine the extent of his injuries. Afterward, the doctors confirmed severe head and body injuries and hesitantly reported that Kashif Razvi had slipped into a coma.

"We need to have a serious talk, Mr. Khan," Chief Fahim said to Samir, pulling back his arm and looking straight into his eyes. Taking him to the next room and motioning for a guard to stand watch at the door, Chief Fahim pulled out a chair. "Take a seat, and you better start talking. Time for you to tell me everything; let's start from the beginning," he demanded, folding his arms. Samir stood motionless for a minute in deep thought, then slowly accepted the seat in front of Chief Fahim.

"The beginning…" Samir looked up, searchingly. "I'll tell you everything. But for that, I have to take you back before it all began."

CHAPTER FOUR

BEFORE IT
ALL BEGAN

Five years before

I love you," Kashif whispered in a low voice to Aliya when the attention was off the newly-engaged couple as the room erupted in celebration.

As per the Islamic tradition, Kashif and his family visited Aliya's home, and his father had officially proposed by asking her father for her hand in marriage to his son. Aliya's father, Asif, had gladly accepted, and the celebration and festivities began between the families in the living room.

"Bold," she whispered back. Sitting next to him, she also kept her voice low from having anyone else notice her smile. Aliya lowered her head, trying to hide her happiness at Kashif's sudden proclamation, words they hadn't said to each other until that day. They had known each other since childhood, but since last year they started speaking with the intention of marrying.

It was a year ago that Kashif finally confessed his feelings and proposed to Aliya. "I have liked you since I first saw you."

"That's too bad. I never liked you and still don't," she had joked sarcastically.

"Ouch!" Kashif replied dramatically, wincing and holding his heart as if having a heart attack. "I guess I'll just ask some other girl for her hand. Hey, your friend Sara is single, right? Okay then, bye!" He responded while walking back off the rooftop of Aliya's home, where they would usually meet without anyone knowing or noticing.

"Kashif Muhammad Razvi!" She almost screamed, but

caught herself, as they always tried to be quiet, not to have anyone notice or hear them. "You will NOT be doing such things! We will get married and live together forever until we're old and you're wrinkly, and while I'm still beautiful, you hear me!"

"I'll take that as a yes then," he bantered back, smiling.

"Yes, fine," she folded her arms and tried not to smile. But it was only a few seconds later that they both started laughing, realizing that they had officially and verbally agreed to marry.

"Alhamdulillah," they both exhaled, smiling.

Kashif admired Aliya's dimples and honey-dew eyes that tried to hide behind the curtains of her long lashes.

"Alhamdulillah for the countless blessings. But I'm still mad it took you this long to ask to marry me. I mean, we've been talking for over a year now and our families are aware of our interest in each other and waiting for you to ask already," she said in a playful voice, but her point was fair.

"You and our families know I've been working on my project, and this is what will propel me to become the head of my Robotics Department."

"Robotics department," she repeated mockingly. "Nerd!" She fiddled with one corner of her hijab.

"Was your dad going to say 'yes' to a guy who's not settled or able to give time to his daughter?" he asked, having had this conversation with her many times before. "And you know how I feel about you. You're the only place that feels like home." When she didn't budge, he sighed and continued, "You're already the coolness of my eyes," knowing she loved hearing the expression. *The coolness of my eyes,* the famous loving expression used in the Qur'an, and a figure of speech in Arabic literature, which equates "eyes becoming cool" with "finding refuge from a storm" and "being a place of love and safety."

"I don't care, you should have asked before." Aliya turned her back to him. She loved giving Kashif grief, especially about that point.

"You'll never let this go, will you? Even when we're 97 years old, right?" He laughed. His height casted a shadow over Aliya's shadow.

"Even at 97," she replied, turning back around, pretending not to have noticed that their shadows had merged. She failed at keeping a straight face, and her giggles were the kind of sounds Kashif knew he could never get tired of for the rest of his life.

...

Aliya had just put on the final set of golden bangles on her wrist when the front doorbell rang. Her heart was already beating out of her chest, but by the time the bell rang, which in turn caused a commotion of people running around the house, she could hardly breathe out of nervousness and excitement. The day was finally here: after having both of their parents agree to meet for the engagement, called *baat pakki,* Kashif's parents and family had officially arrived to ask for Aliya's hand in marriage from her parents. It was custom that the man's father would officially ask the woman's father for her hand in marriage.

The doorbell caused a snowball effect of chaos in her house. From her room, Aliya could hear the hustle and bustle downstairs and her *ami* anxiously screaming directions at everyone. "Is everyone ready?! Zainab, I told you to put the chair over there! Ohhooo check the *naans* in the oven!" Her mother's panicky loud voice brought a smile to Aliya's face, yet at the same time, it made her even more nervous. Having waited for this day for so long, she couldn't help having a hundred or so thoughts running through her mind.

What if it doesn't go right? What if her parents say 'no'? What if Kashif changes his mind? With that, she took a deep breath, recited her *du'as,* or prayers, and tried to stop all the negative thoughts from creeping into her mind. She looked in the mirror and steadied her hand to put on the final *tikka,* the traditional piece of forehead jewelry. She stared at herself in the mirror, beautifully dressed in a traditional Pakistani light green flowing *shalwar kameez* with a golden *dupatta* hanging from her shoulder to her waist, and a green hijab. Staring at herself, she tried to put on the final piece. *You're not fully dressed until you put on a smile,* her abu would always say before dropping her off at school as a little girl. Standing up, she took another deep breath, whispered *"Bismillahi Rahmani Raheem* (In the name of Allah, the Most Compassionate and the Most

Merciful)," and walked toward her bedroom door, staring at it for some time before slowly opening it. It was time.

As Kashif and his family entered, they were greeted happily by Aliya's family. Aliya's abu, ami, and *nani*, her maternal grandmother, greeted each entering guest, as the fathers hugged, and the men and women gave each other courteous bows with their hands over their hearts. Aliya's abu gave Kashif a handshake and a warm hug. At the same time, Nani pinched his cheeks and gave him a hug that lasted uncomfortably long, showering him with prayers and blessings as she was about to burst from joy, barely able to keep her excitement. "Please don't squeeze his cheeks, tell any embarrassing stories, or make him feel uncomfortable, Nani. Please," Aliya had prepped her grandmother, who she felt would still let her excitement and excessive emotions of love get out of hand. Her nani had forgotten all about the pep talk by that point.

They all proceeded to gather and sit in the living room while Aliya was still upstairs, not expected to come down until both parties had agreed to the engagement. Everyone wore their best clothing: traditional colorful Pakistani *shalwar kameez,* long flowing dresses with dupattas for the women. Kashif had dressed in a white *shalwar kameez* with a shiny green vest, matching the theme for the *baat pakki* as Aliya's family had decorated the house in the same colors. A set of two chairs were set against a green and white wall that was set as a stage, while the rest of the couches were in front of and surrounding the chairs. It was tradition for the bride-to-be not to be present in the beginning and be represented by her *walis,* the guardians, usually her father, brother, or uncle. Both Aliya's father and uncle Kamran were her *walis* that day. A visibly nervous Kashif sat on a couch next to his parents, while Aliya's parents sat adjacent to them. Her two aunts, uncles, and five cousins were all seated on chairs along with Kashif's older brother Shahid, and younger sister Yasmine, and their spouses on the other side of the family room. After some usual chatter and pleasant conversation, the room became quiet, awaiting the purpose of their gathering. As everyone quieted and turned their attention toward Kashif's abu, the only sound in the room was Nani's, trying to keep her happiness inside. Kashif's abu, Asghar, glanced at his wife Munir, who returned his look with a nod while smiling, signaling to proceed. Kashif's abu cleared his throat, sat forward in his seat on the sofa next, and addressed Aliya's father. As is the Islamic tradition, his father started with, "Bismillahi Rahmani Raheem, I start in the name of God, the Most Compassionate, the Most Merciful."

"My dear brother, Asif," he began, "We have known you and your family for a long time." He paused, trying to find the right words. "There are people who sometimes are so beloved to you that they start to become more like family, and you and *Bhabi*," he gestured toward Aliya's ami, "have become like my own brother and sister over the years." There was a slight tremble in his voice. "My brother, you know my son, Kashif, well. He has grown up in the same type of house and family as yours, and right under your own eyes, you can see he is a good boy. You are free to ask anyone in the community about him, and I'm sure you'll hear the best of things that you already know to be true. He is a good Muslim, a good son, and a good brother, and I know for a fact he'll make a great husband."

Kashif felt his face blush as he tried to listen to his father's words over the sound of his heart pounding faster than it ever had before.

His father continued, "And we have seen your daughter grow up right before our eyes too, what a beautiful angel she is, *Alhamdulillah*- praise and thanks be to Allah. We have reached a point in our lives, my brother, where they both are no longer just kids, hard as it is to believe. They are in their twenties and so…" He paused, catching himself as both the mothers had already started to cry out of sheer joy. "We have come here to ask for your daughter's hand in marriage to our son. Even though, as a father, I know you don't feel anyone is deserving of your daughter, but I assure you, she will be a daughter in our house just as she is in yours." He looked into his friend's eyes, which had become wet with tears.

Aliya's father took a deep breath and smiled; he looked at his wife and lovingly put his hand on hers. Asma, Aliya's ami, gave him a gentle nod of her approval for him to continue. But they burst into tears before he could. The whole room, by this point, had been sniffling and crying with tears of joy.

"My dear brother," Aliya's abu finally continued. "We are honored you are here today. What you are asking from us, though, is our most precious jewel. Nothing in this world is more valuable to me than my daughter, my firstborn..." He broke off and sniffled as his tears ran down his cheeks. Sitting at the top of the steps and listening to every word and her abu's words, Aliya began to cry, herself.

"But it is a dream to have a son like yours that we can call our own son. And so, of course, we accept," her father responded. The whole room exploded in joy as everyone rose and hugged each other over the good news. Nani, finally able to cry out loud out of happiness, shrieked the loudest. She went straight to Kashif to give him a big hug and kiss and squeezed his cheeks hard in both her hands.

"Mere sonna baita," she exclaimed a little too loudly, causing Aliya to laugh at her, calling him, "my handsome son." Afterward, Aliya's abu gave a warm hug to Kashif, and her ami hugged him and squeezed his cheeks, followed by her aunts and then, her cousins, as per tradition.

"Mubarak ho, baita," Aliya's aunts and uncles hugged and congratulated him.

"Congrats Kashif Bhai!" Aliya's little five-year-old sister, Zainab, came rushing to hug him. "Now you'll really be my brother!" She screamed, throwing her arms around his neck, forcing him to bend down a bit because of the height difference.

Aliya heard her loud words and melted on the inside. Kashif and Zainab had become good friends throughout her short life, all starting with him having her as a student in his Sunday School kindergarten class. Kashif loved teaching, and once he learned that Aliya's sister was in his class, he used it to his advantage. "Who wouldn't have?" he had joked about it to Aliya later. Kashif would give Zainab extra homework, telling her she would have to ask her older sister for help. By that time, Kashif and Aliya already knew they liked each other, so it was a way to get closer. He would leave little messages hidden in Zainab's book for her to find. And the cutest of all for Aliya, Kashif and

Zainab had developed their own secret code and handshakes. Zainab's favorite was the "I love you" in sign language they would give each other every time, before leaving.

"You point your thumb out, and raise your index and pinky fingers like this," he once said, showing her. "And close your middle and ring fingers. And then bring them over your heart. This means 'I love you.' Practice it tonight to perfect it. Work on it with your sister at home, she'll help you with it." He smirked telling her, smiling at the thought of little Zainab showing Aliya, and giving her the message of "I love you."

"Did I ever tell you why this sign means 'I love you,' Zainab?" Kashif asked as Zainab finished her hug.

"No, tell me!"

"Well, when you make the 'I love you' sign, you see the pinky is the letter 'I,' the thumb and index finger make the letter 'L,'" he said, tracing a capital L as she raised her index finger and thumb. "And from the extended pinky, all the way to the thumb, create a 'Y.'"

Now that Kashif was the groom, all guests present would have fun teasing and bothering him, again as per tradition. After the final cheek squeeze—or what Kashif hoped was the final one—the distribution of sweets began. It was Pakistani tradition to serve an assortment of sweet *mithai:* yellow round *ladoos, sugary brown balls of gulab jaman,* and white squared *burfis.* Everyone fed each other, and they all fed Kashif extra and as much as they could as again, the custom of officially and playfully bothering the groom had started. Aliya's little nine-year-old cousin, Arza, was satisfied that she had stuffed as many *gulab jamans* in Kashif's mouth as was possible, a feat Kashif worried would cause him to puke on his future bride. Then, Aliya's father asked, "Well, let's bring out the bride-to-be. What do you say, Kashif?" He looked at him, playfully laughing at the last part. Kashif blushed, and everyone laughed as Aliya's sister and mother went to the stairs. Aliya was already giggling uncontrollably and had to be told by her mother to stop laughing.

A bride should be shy and blushing, her mother had advised her earlier, again an old Pakistani tradition. As they walked beside Aliya, her mother's arm in her arm, symbolizing the mother giving her daughter away to her future son-in-law, the same tradition which would be followed at the *nikkah,* the official marriage and *shaadi* celebrations. As Aliya gracefully and slowly descended downstairs, everyone in the living room stood up to welcome her. Entering the room, she kept her head and gaze lowered. Kashif felt his heart beating even faster as she approached, and a sudden rush of contentment filled his mind and body. *The coolness of my eyes.* She looked beautiful. He felt he still had not told her just how beautiful he thought she was, how elegant and graceful she was! How could he tell her... show her that she lit up every room she entered? That even the sun would be jealous of her light, and the moon couldn't be as bright as her? The words escaped him when he saw her and tried to explain that she lit up his world more than the sun lit up the world.

As she entered, he felt overwhelmed with his love for her. He thought his heart would burst from how fast it was beating. But seeing her descend the stairs gracefully on their engagement day, he sensed a sudden calm and peace. At that moment, he knew that there would be no one else but her. Aliya stepped forward slowly to give Kashif's parents a hug, both of whom returned her embrace happily. She still kept her gaze down as she passed Kashif, not looking at him, keeping up with the Pakistani tradition of the bride to be being shy. The whole room was too busy gushing at the new couple to notice Aliya purposefully stepping on Kashif's foot while walking by. She continued looking down and he tried not to show his pain-ridden face after getting his foot squished. She stood next to him as everyone in the room cheered and applauded for them. Before sitting down, next to one another, Kashif turned to Aliya and handed her a bouquet of flowers. She took the bouquet and shyly looked into his eyes. Kashif crossed his eyes at her, and she tried with all her might not to laugh, but he so badly wanted to hear her laugh.

They were seated on separate chairs a few feet apart, the "halal gap" per Islamic tradition, as they were still not allowed to touch, for they were not yet officially married. Kashif and Aliya had not touched or stepped out of what was permitted in Islam, and the foot stepping was the first time they had touched. It was something Kashif made a mental note to bug her about in the future. The official marriage ceremony of *nikkah* was decided to be in the following month, and only then would they be recognized as a married couple. Sitting together, Aliya took a quick peek at Kashif, dashingly handsome as always, she thought. *My knight in shining shalwar kameez,* she mused, a joke she made a mental note to tell him later. She noticed that he had gotten a haircut, but didn't have his hair too short, something she had asked him to do.

"Your short hair makes your nose look too big," she had teased him, but he understood she liked his hair long. She noticed he had gelled his hair, which he never did, and his beard had been freshly trimmed. She loved that their clothes complimented each other perfectly. Her father's voice brought her out of her daze as he had started reciting a *du'a,* which was a prayer for the new couple.

"May they always be the coolness of each other's eyes, *ameen.*" Afterward, everyone was busy talking, celebrating, and planning for the upcoming wedding festivities. Kashif and Aliya used this moment to whisper to each other.

The engagement was official, and the celebrations were on the way for both families. The newly engaged couple were a month away from their wedding date. Basking in the moment, little did they realize that anything could happen between the engagement and the wedding date.

CHAPTER FIVE

ALIYA

I t was three weeks later, and Aliya was in full wedding preparation mode, slightly panicking as the wedding was only two weeks away. Sitting on her bed, she had only just finished the phone call with the wedding dress designer, finally able to customize the dress the way she wanted it to be. Usual Pakistani wedding dresses were long, flowing, and heavily embroidered with a great deal of intricate work and details on them, but Aliya wanted to make sure her hijab would fit comfortably and stay in place. The hijab was one of the hardest decisions she had ever made, but one of the most rewarding for her: the feeling of peace, contentment, and happiness that the hijab brought her was irreplaceable. It was also a condition for her to find a spouse, as some of the suitors had asked her to remove the hijab if they were to be married. "Uh, remove *yourself* from here," she responded once to a potential suitor, Fayzan, a medical student seven years older, someone her parents had tried setting her up with a few years back. She always had a witty response back to any sort of nonsense. Even though she had no interest in Fayzan from the beginning, she appeased her parents' wishes and agreed to at least meet him.

"His breath kind of stunk," Aliya complained to her ami in the kitchen the next day after having met and spoken to him, trying to make *any* excuse to get out of meeting and speaking to Fayzan a second time.

"We'll give him a *tic-tac,*" Ami responded sarcastically, raising one eyebrow unamused as she put away some of the bowls in the cabinets.

"His eyesight isn't great, you know," Aliya said quickly while thinking hard, trying not to look Ami in the eyes.

"We'll get him *contact lenses.*" Ami turned to her and folded her arms, not giving her another inch for excuses.

"He… will be in school for like *five* more years," she sighed loudly, dramatically waving her arms.

"And so will *you* while you finish your Ph.D.," Ami retorted back with her hand on her hips and looking at her straight in the eyes. *Ami and her dedication to making sure her children had the highest level of education,* Aliya thought. They had had many of these conversations over the years: Ami wanted Aliya to get her Ph.D., and Aliya wanted to open her own restaurant.

"Umm, I don't think I need a Ph.D. to run a restaurant," Aliya said with a nervous laugh as she realized this conversation was not going down the way she had been hoping it would.

"Aliya," Ami finally said in a serious tone, not allowing for any more excuses.

Aliya sighed, "He doesn't want me to wear the hijab," she revealed in a low voice, finally looking at Ami.

They both gazed at each other for a while, not uttering a single word, but their eyes agreed in mutual understanding. "I'll call his mom tomorrow to tell her, 'no thanks,' then," Ami responded with a finality.

Coincidently, the hijab was a deal-breaker in the other way for Kashif, for he only wanted a hijabi. She always liked Kashif and knew she always wanted to marry him from the moment she met him at the young age of fifteen. And when he made his feelings known to her two years ago and his intentions to marry her, Aliya knew there was no one else. The only hurdle was that Kashif was still working his way up in his structural engineering firm, which required working long hours while also taking classes at Al-Fihriya University. "Just let me finish and get promoted. I'm almost there," he had said. "Right now, I'm working and going to school full-time, and it's taking up my whole day, every day. But it's almost over," he explained while she remained unsatisfied with this answer. "I'm not going anywhere *insha'Allah* (God willing). I promise." It also helped that both Kashif and Aliya's families had been family friends for many years, and so when they decided to get married, they told their parents right away, as is the Islamic custom.

When Aliya told her parents, well, she did not exactly *tell* them. Finally mustering up the courage, she had walked toward her parents' room with her heart beating faster than a Ferrari and sweating out of nervousness, but her parents knew her better than she knew herself sometimes. Aliya walked up to their bedroom door and stood there, catching herself and taking deep breaths before knocking and asking to come inside. Ami and Abu were sitting on their bed and welcomed her in. She walked up to them, stood there, and froze. Her breathing became louder, and she suddenly forgot how to speak.

"Uh... I..." she started stammering. "I like, I mean... I like you," she stumbled between breaths.

Her parents gave each other a puzzled look, waiting for her to finish her sentence. "I like you too, Beti," her abu replied with a knowing smile.

"I mean... I like... I like you to... I like to... I..." She couldn't find the words or her breath.

"Uh *huhhh,*" Ami responded sarcastically with a playful smile, understanding where this was going.

"Yeah, he... um... I mean phone... okay?" Aliya jumbled up her words, her body frozen and without realizing what she had been saying.

With a twinkle in their eyes, her parents smiled at each other. Turning to her, "Do you want me to talk to his ami?" Ami asked slowly, letting the words linger in the air. They were enjoying their daughter's nerves bursting into puzzling words.

"No? I mean, yeah, cool," Aliya responded robotically, still unable to move and wondered if her parents knew who she meant.

"Do I know this aunty?"

Aliya nodded.

"Is it Kashif's ami that will call me?" she asked.

How her parents knew these things, she could never understand! *You'll know when you have kids yourself,* was always the famous answer Pakistani parents gave.

"You can tell him to tell his ami to call me," Ami continued.

Aliya took out her cell phone and texted "yes" to Kashif. Not a minute later, the phone rang and both mothers were laughing and talking wholeheartedly. And so, it had begun.

Her parents' blessings were always the most important factor for her, after, of course, doing things Islamically and making sure to keep God happy. Being the oldest child, she knew the hardships her parents had endured while raising her: both young while working long hours, trying to make ends meet while raising a daughter. The beginning years were extremely financially difficult for her parents in their marriage, and the news of a baby only added to their pressure. While they eventually worked enough to gain financial stability years later, raising Aliya in the early years was an immensely hard task, one that Aliya herself understood. She knew her mother had given up her dream of becoming a doctor to raise her. Her father worked two jobs and both put aside their desires for the sake of raising their daughter to become a good human being. The sacrifices they had made for her were not lost on Aliya and she vowed to take care of them as they grew older. And having their blessings in her marriage was a big part of that. On top of that, their wisdom and experiences were second to none for Aliya. She knew that if they said, "yes" and gave their blessings to a man, then that meant he must be worth it.

Two weeks before the wedding, Aliya's phone rang. She saw Kashif's name on the screen and answered with a sweet "hello," but Kashif's usual calm voice didn't answer. Instead, a worried and anxious voice delivered the news that made her shoot up and run immediately to her family:

"My dad had a heart attack this morning. We're in the ICU now," he said with a shaky voice.

Aliya's family made their way immediately to the hospital. Moments later, everyone nervously huddled in the ICU waiting room, waiting for an update from the doctors. When they finally arrived, the news wasn't good. "He's going to need a second procedure, I'm afraid," the doctor carefully informed the families. He explained that the first procedure, which was to place a stent in his left main coronary artery, did not work as effectively as expected, so Kashif's abu needed a second procedure. This time, a small device called an Impella was required to be placed in his heart to help it pump blood and give his heart some time to recover.

"We're hoping this will stabilize him," the doctor explained before returning to the operating room.

News quickly spread across the community and it was only a matter of time before over forty people were waiting with Kashif and his family, huddling around his mother in prayer. Kashif didn't look at or talk to anyone; rather, he quietly kept pacing back and forth.

"It's going to be okay, insha'Allah," Aliya said, trying to comfort him when he stopped pacing and simply stared out of the window. He seemed lost in thought. "Kashif, look at me," Aliya said, trying to break through his thoughts; she knew he was not thinking about anything positive. He finally looked at her and weakly nodded. "We're all praying for him, and he'll be fine. But, you have to take it easy, take care of yourself," she said softly. He looked at her and felt a warm sensation calming him, bringing him out of his negative thoughts. She always had a way of making him feel better.

"Yeah, insha'Allah. Thank you," he responded quietly.

But the news kept getting worse. After the second procedure, one of the doctors finally came out of the surgery room and informed the group huddled outside, led by Kashif, that Abu had been intubated and was unconscious. Aliya and her family stayed until night, when the hospital staff made everyone except one visitor leave.

"You go home, get some rest and come back in the morning," Kashif hugged his ami, "I'll be right next to him, all night." It ended up being the longest night of Kashif's life, one where he didn't sleep at all. Instead, he prayed the whole night on the prayer mat for his abu's recovery. He tried not to think about his wedding, which was coming up in less than two weeks. At that moment, he just wanted nothing more in life than for his father to wake up.

A few days later, the situation was still the same. They played the Noble Qur'an into his ears, hoping he could hear it, hoping it would help his abu find ease and a cure. Kashif still tried not to think of the wedding, but what's the use, he thought to himself. The issue was becoming larger by the day, right in front of him: less than ten days from the wedding and Abu was in the ICU. One week before the wedding, Kashif and his ami had to make the call: after all the planning, they had to postpone the whole wedding and all the events leading up to it. There was no way Kashif could get married without Abu present, without him being by his side. So, they had to postpone it, *for now,* Kashif thought as he was confident abu would recover soon. Over the next few days, he listened to and observed the doctors, hoping to get any form of positive news. Abu was a medical doctor himself, so Kashif always went to him for medical advice. This time, he had to try to piece things together the best that he could, all on his own without his abu. Kashif heard the nervousness and disappointment as they spoke and updated each other on his abu's medical status. He eventually learned to read the doctors' and nurses' facial expressions as they looked at the monitors and numbers. They were concerned, he knew it.

"You're going to be alright, Abu," Kashif whispered to his father as he lay intubated and unconscious in the ICU. He wasn't sure if he heard him, but he needed him to know.

It was four days later, at the time of the planned wedding, that he found himself sitting next to his abu in the ICU. After months of planning, excitement, and preparation, how could he have even begun to think that this was where he would be on his wedding day? *Allah is the best of Planners,* as is stated in the Qur'an. "But how can this be the best?" lamented Kashif.

CHAPTER SIX

AMI AND ABU

Three days after their planned wedding and about two weeks after Kashif's abu had entered the hospital, the situation had remained the same as Abu had not woken up. His ami was sitting in the corner of the room, reciting her prayers as usual. Kashif was leaning against the door frame, trying to listen to the nurse update the other nurses on Abu's status, when Kashif heard a low moan. His mother shrieked, running to the bed, as Abu finally opened his eyes.

"Alhamdulillah!" Ami screamed, "You've come back to me!" She cried. As he awoke slowly and gained recognition and consciousness, he looked up at Kashif and his wife. His eyes started to tear, realizing where he was. "Munir," he tried to speak to Kashif's ami, but was unable to.

"Shhh, it's okay, Abu," an emotional Kashif said, holding his hand. "You're going to be okay. We're here with you. The doctors say you're going to be okay and will recover," he said, forcing a smile, trying to be encouraging and keep his voice from shaking. The truth was the doctors were very concerned about his heart condition after the significant heart attack. The road to stabilization and recovery was going to be a long one. But Abu was awake and conscious now, which was more than a pleasant surprise to some doctors- and a miracle to others.

Over the next few days, the reports looked positive, and the doctors hoped that Abu would recover and return to good health. He was fully conscious and awake, but unable to regain his speech fully. Numerous people from the community and his work, friends, and family came to visit.

"Asghar Bhai, you really gave us a scare. But get better, for you and I still have to go to Chai House for some tea like we talked about," joked Uncle Hasnain, one of Abu's oldest friends. Abu smiled and scribbled something weakly on his pad which he used to communicate and turned it towards Uncle Hasnain so only he could read it. As he read, they both laughed.

"What's going on there?" Kashif's ami called from the corner of the room in her chair, reciting prayers with prayer beads in her hands, flipping each bead with each prayer.

"Oh nothing, Munir Sister, he just asked me to take him right now, but that he'll drive," Uncle Hasnain responded with a smile. Ami gave the two a frown while trying to hide her smile, watching the two laugh away, happy that her husband was feeling better.

Kashif's parents, Asghar and Munir, were well-known and liked in their community. Everyone knew they loved each other deeply, and knew of their sweetest love story, as Kashif would always recall. It had been thirty-seven years into their marriage, but they could pass as a new, young couple. The couple had met while Munir was a freshman in college, where she worked at the school library. It was there that Asghar first saw her and made sure it wasn't the last. He made excuses to go to the library as much as possible, trying to come up with different ways to talk to Munir: asking for directions, for this book, for that author, when his books were due. Only after two months of this Munir discovered that Asghar wasn't even enrolled in the college and that he only came to see her. When she complained and warned him that she was going to file a complaint against him, it was then that Asghar declared his feelings for her and asked her for her hand in marriage. "You're the most beautiful, gentle, and patient person I have ever met," he said in front of others in the library. Taken aback and embarrassed at this proclamation, Munir refused and told Asghar to leave. But Asghar was not one to strike out just once; he tried again a few weeks later, a few months later, and then a year later. On the fourth try, when Munir had gotten to know who he was and his family, she finally slipped him a note which read, "Come talk to my father," with his phone number written on it. The rest, as they said, was history.

Now in the hospital, he would slip her notes and make her come quickly to read them, feigning an emergency. *I love you,* a note read. *You make me feel alive,* another note read. Their love grew deeper and more genuine every day, and sometimes, it felt to both as though every day, their love was only beginning to grow.

A few days later, as Dr. Saunder gave the encouraging report that since Asghar was making progress toward recovery and they would be shifting him down from the ICU, the ground suddenly shook. Screams and yells were heard on the ICU floor as the hospital staff tried to keep themselves from falling while also ensuring their patients were okay. The earthquake only lasted a few seconds.

"What was that?" a nurse had asked.

"Was that an earthquake?" confused voices erupted on their floor.

Just as things seemed to settle and get back to normal, the lights for the whole floor went out. Screams and yells erupted on the floor as the entire floor went dark. Kashif heard Ami gasp in horror, and he made his way to where she was sitting by Abu's bed. Kashif felt for her hand in the dark.

"It's okay, Ami, I'm right here," he reassured her, holding her hand as she tightly gripped his hand back. A minute later, the generators kicked on and brought back only some lights on the floor.

But Kashif's abu's room remained dark. The floor was full of loud panic with the voices of shrieking patients, doctors screaming instructions, and nurses running back and forth. Kashif heard a girl scream from the next room, yelling for her grandmother. As he was about to turn to her, the sound of machines beeping loudly next to Abu caused him to turn around. The earthquake and power outage had caused all of Abu's IV tubes to stop working, and Kashif noticed Abu had stopped breathing. Before he could scream to get help, the doctors came rushing in, and a crowd of people started working on Abu, trying to resuscitate him. Ami's hand was crushing Kashif's, but neither of them noticed. He held Ami as they stood on the side, trying to control her in her hysterical crying, both wide-eyed in shock. The noises and panic of the people on their floor grew louder and louder. In their room, there were the sounds of tools clanking and instructions being shouted out. The noise ripped through the ICU room like a thunderous wave, or so it seemed to Kashif.

And then… there was silence.

As quickly as the room had become loud, it fell flat into silence. A few seconds later, all the lights on their floor came back on. The room was full of doctors and nurses, but they all had stopped working, stared at each other, and then, they solemnly looked down in silence. The silence in the room was deathly loud. As everyone in the room became quiet, Kashif, horrified, looked at each of them.

"Do something! Do something!" He kept yelling. But all the staff in the room could only mournfully bow their heads.

"I'm so sorry," Dr. Saunder said to Kashif, who, in turn, stood frozen in shock as his father's pulse had stopped. Dr. Saunder called the time "9:49 PM."

CHAPTER SEVEN

THE BEGINNING

T he sky had become overcast, bringing in a light drizzle as the imam led the congregation the following day for the *janaza*, the funeral. Over 100 people were present for Kashif's abu's *janaza*, each one hugging Kashif, offering him their condolences, and trying to find the right words to comfort him. Kashif, in turn, heard but remembered none of those words. Imam Dawood Murphy led the prayer at the masjid. He headed toward the cemetery, with the men following and carrying the casket behind him. The body was wrapped in two plain white cloths and placed inside the casket in a simple light wooden box as per Islamic burial. Everyone huddled together as Imam Dawood started reciting words from the Qur'an and prayers for his abu. Kashif just stood and stared at the casket, again not hearing any of the imam's words or prayers.

"Death is a painful reality," the imam said. "One that God Almighty reminds us again and again of in the Qur'an. 'Everyone of you shall taste death,' Allah said in Surah Aly-'Imran, and to Him, we will all return. So, our brother here, he's just one step ahead of us in his journey, and we should use this moment to remind ourselves that we will one day, and it could be any day, join him." The light rain started to pick up and become heavier. As Imam Dawood spoke, Kashif stared blankly at the casket.

"How are you?" Everyone kept asking him. But he wasn't sure how he was or what he was feeling. The truth was, he felt nothing. *Numb.* Up until that point, Kashif was completely numb.

"But that does not mean that for those of us still here, death isn't a painful experience," Imam Dawood continued. "It's okay and acceptable to mourn and grieve, and it's normal and human to cry. But, we must remember that this is Allah's will, and it is a sign of faith to accept the passing of our loved ones and bear their loss with patience." Imam Dawood looked out at the crowd as they nodded; he noticed Kashif in a daze with an unsettling look on his face. He continued, "Remember, dear brothers, death is only a temporary separation for family members going to *Jannah*, to Paradise. For people going to *Jannah*, and we pray our dear brother Asghar is one of those admitted to Allah's *Jannah*, we will be reunited there with our loved ones, and we will never suffer separation again."

As the rain slowly picked up, the numbness that engulfed Kashif was starting to wash away, and he felt something for the first time since yesterday: anger. It was boiling inside Kashif, beginning to rise and becoming apparent on his face. Within a few minutes, the rain had turned into a heavy downpour as Kashif's abu's body was lowered into the ground, each person present poured dirt on the casket, said a prayer, and stepped back. After the final person prayed and stepped back, they all turned to Kashif. He remained standing still, staring at the ground. *Boiling.* For Kashif, Abu had been his best friend, mentor, biggest believer, and most ardent supporter in life. Abu had taught him everything he knew and how to handle whatever life had thrown at him.

Kashif had given up opportunities to travel and work elsewhere so he could take care of his parents. *Wa bir walidayni ihsana* – be the best to your parents, God has repeated many times in the Qur'an. He had always taken this to heart. The rights of parents and the duty of children to take care of them is an essential part of Islam, and he had always had the intention to take care of his parents, especially as they became older. *Paradise lies under the feet of your mother,* as the hadith (confirmed saying) of the Prophet Muhammad (ﷺ). *The father is the middle of the gates of Paradise, so keep to this gate or lose it,* was one of the hadiths on fathers that he had always kept in his heart. His parents had always taken care of him when he was younger, causing a strong sense of gratitude and responsibility to take care of them in return, which was deep inside Kashif. But at that moment, he felt he had let his abu down.

How could I let this happen? Why didn't I see the signs of a heart attack approaching? His abu was still young, only 63, "...the age of the Prophet at his passing," he heard one of the community members tell him in an effort to comfort him. *I want nothing more than to see you married, Baita,* Abu's words kept playing in his head. What was supposed to be his greatest and happiest moment, his wedding, and his parents, arm-in-arm with him, leading him to the wedding stage, were all gone. His life's aim of caring for his father was gone. His best friend and biggest supporter was gone. *How? Why?* And then, he remembered the power outage. The hospital that had been left in darkness. He still felt he was in that same darkness, the panic as the lights came back on and his father's lifeless body. *Why?!* In that one moment, his life had completely changed. When the lights and power came back on, the old Kashif was gone. A new Kashif had been born and pushed out into the world. He was angry. And the boiling rage inside of him had reached the surface.

What seemed like a lifetime for Kashif after everyone had poured dirt on the casket and prayed, and as the rain had turned into a thunderstorm of heavy downpour, Kashif continued to stand motionless. As the sky had turned from overcast to thunder to pouring rain, Kashif's sadness had also transformed from sorrow to grief to anger. And the anger was still in full boil. Samir, having known Kashif all those years, noticed the look change on Kashif's face. Everyone in the crowd waited for Kashif to move or speak, but he could not. Drops of rain ran down his face. The rain felt warm, like blood. By this time, his hair had become soaked and hung over his face. All that was visible was a scowl.

Samir walked toward him, "Hey Kash, let's go. It's over," he said, gently putting his hand on his shoulder. Samir noticed, for the first time, a look of rage on his friend's otherwise calm face.

The scowl didn't leave Kashif's face as he turned to him, "No, it's just beginning."

CHAPTER EIGHT

SOMETHING GOING ON

T hey say that if the Earth stopped spinning for just a couple of seconds, the momentum would trigger the mountains to break apart and the oceans to cause earthquakes, giant tsunamis, and devastating winds. It would cause the whole world to crumble and fall apart. Watching a loved one die in a matter of seconds causes the same effect. It causes ripple effects that destroy any sort of life for that person who has witnessed a loved one die. Perhaps what's even crueler than this: only that living person suffers, only that living person's world falls apart and is destroyed, while the rest of the world continues moving on. This was a cruel reality Kashif and his ami were beginning to learn. Their old life was shattered.

In the following days, Kashif's house was flowing with people pouring in, to visit and offer condolences and support. Family, neighbors, and community members brought food daily and sat with Ami and Kashif throughout the day, to help them heal. Kashif's attention and mind, however, were only focused on one thing: trying to get updates on the power outage and supposed earthquake. It was reported in the following days that the ground shaking and power outage were not caused by an earthquake; rather, it was caused by an eruption from a building north of Ridgefield Park City in a laboratory known as the Paramus Lab, owned by someone very familiar to Kashif, a scientist by the name of Dr. Carson Daye.

Kashif had been childhood friends with Carson, but life had taken them on different paths after high school, and over the years, they had grown apart. As a child, Carson was a brilliant mind, spending most of his time on science projects and reading complex scientific books even adults had a hard time understanding. As an adult, he became a lead scientist and researcher for the city. However, Carson had developed an unusual reputation for holding extremely unorthodox and, as whispers around the city continued to grow, illegal scientific experiments. He hadn't seen Carson in many years, but he heard all the unsettling rumors. Regardless, investigators discovered that activity from Carson's lab caused an explosion that shook the entire city, causing a massive power outage in several areas, including the hospital where Kashif's abu was being treated.

This caused Kashif's father to die, along with 12 others in the ICU. Carson had not been seen in public, or it seemed by anyone in the city, in a long time. However, police investigators had found that Dr. Carson Daye had not been in the city at the time of the explosion.

Who had been in his lab? Kashif wondered.

After a week, to Kashif's dismay, it was reported that the police had given up the search and ended all investigation surrounding the explosion and power outage. Confused and enraged, Kashif knew he had to meet Police Chief Thomas Eames to discuss this. He called the police chief's office over and over again, and after three days of getting the runaround, the office finally gave him a time to meet. *I need answers, and I'm going to get them.*

9:49 AM, read the time on his watch. Kashif had already finished the coffee he was offered by the police receptionist, Gladys. He was anxious, shaking his legs while sitting. He didn't have restless leg syndrome, but might develop it while waiting, he thought to himself.

"Can I get you another coffee, Mr. Razvi?" Gladys, in a high and excited voice, asked Kashif. She had been stealing looks and trying to make eye contact with him the whole time while he waited at the police precinct to meet with Police Chief Thomas Eames.

"No thanks," he responded, forcing a smile and looking

away quickly. "Um, when is Chief Eames expected to be in?" asked Kashif, clearly annoyed.

"I'll see if I can reach him again. I'm so sorry that you had to wait so long already," exclaimed Gladys, quickly realizing she was probably speaking too fast and loudly. She blushed.

He was supposed to meet with Chief Eames at 9:00 AM. Kashif shook his head, looking at his watch again for the time. The watch reminded him of Abu, who had given it to him when he was younger. From a young age, Abu had always included Kashif in whatever activity he was doing. He recalled being 10 years old and working on a watch for the first time with him on their work desk at home.

How do watches work, Abu?

Well, Baita, do you see this mainspring? And this device here is called an escapement. It releases the watch's wheels to move forward just a small and exact amount. And with each swing of the balance wheel, this will move the watch's hands forward at a constant rate.

"He's coming up now, Mr. Razvi," stated Gladys proudly, not breaking eye contact with Kashif.

"Thank you," he replied, looking out the window, feeling the sadness and anger filling inside him. Grief was a strange thing, he thought. It was a mixture of emotions that Kashif felt at a very deep level and was learning to be almost impossible to speak about.

The door to the lounge opened, and a large white man with broad shoulders and a straight posture, walked in. His military experience still resonated in his walk and speech.

"Ah, Kashif!" said Chief Eames in his booming voice, putting out his hand for a shake. "Very sorry to hear about your father. This city owes a large amount to Dr. Razvi for his dedication to the medical field," he said, shaking Kashif's hand firmly and looking him in the eyes, still keeping a straight face. "I don't know if you were aware, but he operated on me once. He saved me." Before Kashif could respond, Chief Eames walked toward his office, "Come in," he said.

"Twelve years as Chief of Police, but they still expect me to go to them and answer all their questions!" complained Chief

Eames about news reporters as he sat behind his desk inside his room. "Hah! Well, they'll learn. I run the show around here," he said with a hardy laugh. The room was large, with windows on adjacent walls, stacks of cabinets, and a row of chairs lined up against the walls. The air in the room was heavy, filled with the strong smell of cigarettes and smoke. Boxes were scattered across the floor, and many opened with files all over the room. Folders and stacks of papers were scattered all over his desk. Chief didn't seem to mind the messy room as he offered Kashif a chair with a pile of papers. Kashif moved the papers onto the desk and took a seat. He briefly noticed the headlines on one of the articles, *"Terrorist Organization 'Smoke Squad' Claim Responsibility for Kidnapping."* He turned his attention back to Police Chief Eames.

"Thank you for your time, Chief. I wanted to get some information about the... incident at the lab. It caused a lot of damage, as you know," Kashif stated, looking around the room; the uncleanliness and mess of folders, files, and papers everywhere caused a distraction.

"Yes, we looked into it," Chief Eames responded absentmindedly, sifting through papers on his desk and side drawers. "Unfortunately, we didn't find anything," Chief said, looking up at him finally.

"Surely, there must have been a reason for the power outage caused by the lab," continued Kashif. "A big power surge which caused an outage throughout the city; I mean, there has to be some reason or cause?" he urged.

"Look, Kashif, we did a thorough search, Dr. Carson Daye wasn't available, but we can ask him some more questions when he returns. But we already spoke to him on the phone. He thinks, maybe, there was an issue with the generators, so he'll get some people over there to check those out. Otherwise, there's nothing," he said with finality. As he kept rummaging through folders, Kashif noticed one of the folders had slid out pictures of what looked to be children. Before he could look closer, Chief Eames quickly took the folders and put them in his drawers. "Look, uh, that's all I have for you, I'm afraid." He continued shuffling about nervously, seemingly occupied with other matters and avoiding eye contact with Kashif.

"I still have some more questions." Kashif turned his gaze back toward the Chief, whom he noticed had started to sweat from the forehead.

Chief stood up and started to lead Kashif by his arm out the door, "Sure thing, you can let Gladys know and she'll write down all your questions, and we can set up another time maybe," he said quickly while walking toward the door. "For now, sorry, I have another meeting." He pulled one of the files underneath his arm and locked the door behind him. He patted Kashif on the back. "I'm sorry again, kid, truly. Your father will be missed." He hurried out. Kashif was left standing in the tiny area between the Chief's office and the waiting room. As he walked out, he noticed a card had fallen from one of Chief Eames' folders. Picking up the card, he read *Jack's Bar & Ring*.

Frustrated by the meeting, he angrily stormed past a nervous and smiling Gladys, who yelled as he walked out, "Nice seeing you, Mr. Razvi!"

I can't believe this, he thought irritably, pressing the elevator button. In deep thought, as the doors opened and he stepped in, Kashif didn't notice a woman running towards the elevator from across the hall, yelling at him to hold it.

"Hold it, please!" she called out, but Kashif, lost in his thoughts, didn't hear her. She reached the doors right in time, just as the doors were about to close.

"Hey, thanks for nothing, pal! Almost spilled my coffee," she exclaimed, out of breath. Looking up, she noticed it was Kashif, and her tone changed. "Oh... I'm sorry, I... uh... I didn't know it was you."

Still, in deep thought, Kashif continued to stare away, not hearing a word. The woman noticed this, but nervously continued, "I'm so sorry about your father. May Allah have mercy on him and grant him *Jannah*."

"What? Oh... ameen." Kashif snapped back to reality after hearing the words, *your father.* Finally, looking at the woman, he noticed the familiar face of Zara Rehman.

"Thank you... I didn't realize you worked here," he said, looking at her badge hanging from a lanyard.

Zara and Kashif's family had been long-time family friends and growing up, the two had been in the same grades in their elementary and Sunday School classes, even though she was a year younger than he. They never spoke much, but they would always be in the same circle of family events and friends. Zara's parents were well known for cooking the best traditional Bengali food, which they served in the local food shelter each weekend. Her brother, Fares, and Kashif had met volunteering at the food shelter and became close friends growing up but had drifted apart as they grew older. Zara was wearing a long black dress with a blue hijab and a blue overcoat. Out of respect and following proper Islamic etiquette, Kashif kept his gaze on the door instead of directly on her.

"Yeah, I work with the Deputy Chief. Just got promoted, Alhamdulillah." She gave a little laugh at the last part, not directly looking at him either. She had worked hard for her promotion. As one of the only hijabi women on the force, it was not easy, but she had earned her stripes, and when the time for promotion came, no one objected.

"Nice," responded Kashif, genuinely impressed. "But, your police chief is something else. Completely useless and, if you don't mind my saying, shady. You guys are stopping the investigation of the power outage caused by the lab… The one that caused the hospital to lose power." He shot her an angry look.

"I'm sorry, I didn't know he called the investigation off." After a pause, she lowered her voice, "I agree with you, though, on the useless part."

Surprised, Kashif turned to look at her for the first time. The elevator came to a stop on the 4th floor, where Zara stepped out.

"Wait," Kashif said. "I just want to know what happened and who's responsible," pleaded Kashif, putting his hand on the elevator door, keeping it from closing. *"Please."*

Zara stopped and turned to look at him, thinking about it.

"If you know something and can help, please tell me. I know the Chief is hiding something."

"Shhh." Zara looked around to make sure no one was in the hallway. "Not here. The walls are always listening. Follow me," she whispered as she led him to her office.

"I came into this department three years ago, and from the first day, I felt what you're feeling," Zara said while taking a seat behind her desk. She motioned to Kashif to take a seat across from her. "Everyone's hiding something and sometimes, I feel like I'm the only one not in the game." She explained, worriedly.

"Hiding what?" Kashif leaned in and listened closely.

"I don't know. I'm still figuring it out." She paused. "But, I've already said too much." She quickly changed her tone, as if remembering where she was. "You asked about the lab explosion and power outage. We did investigate it. There was only one person there at the time, apparently."

"Who?" Kashif asked, not hiding his rage.

"There is usually a team of scientists there all the time so this must have been after hours, but Carson Daye, your old friend, wasn't there."

"I haven't spoken to him in years."

"I know, but Fares still does. They remain closer than I like them to be," Zara revealed.

"Really? I mean, Carson's changed so much. As a young kid, I knew he loved inventing and creating all different types of experiments. He had an infatuation with testing on animals, but then…" he paused, unsure of how to state the next part. "The rumors? Testing on humans?"

"You have no idea. I've heard Fares and him sometimes talking on the phone and I don't like what I hear."

"What kinds of things do you hear?"

"It all doesn't make sense to me and Fares doesn't talk about it. I know he's been working with him, but I don't know to what extent. Fares has changed too, I'm afraid."

They both looked at each other in silence, a sadness growing in the space between them.

"As for the lab," she said, folding her hands on her desk, "There was only an older scientist there, Ben Yurkovich. We asked him a bunch of questions, but honestly, he looked too old to be working there, and his health was not in good condition. Anyway, he didn't seem to know much at all. All he said was that the generators must have overheated, causing an explosion. That was his story." She raised her eyebrow.

"A story that you're not buying," Kashif responded, reading her facial expression.

"No," she said, looking straight at Kashif. "But, the Chief and his team did. It was all wrapped up too rapidly if you ask me. Almost as if they wanted to close it quickly. In my opinion, there was so much more on the scene that we didn't properly look at."

Zara noticed Kashif becoming silent and lost in thought again, and an odd look had come across his face, one of anger and determination, a look that wasn't sitting well with her.

"But I'll keep searching. I haven't closed the case, even if the department has. I just have to make sure they don't find out, but I'm going to keep investigating and see if I can find more," she said, standing up, hoping to break his train of thought.

"Thank you." Kashif rose up from his seat, the unsettling look not leaving his face.

"Of course." Zara opened the door and led him out. "Oh, and I know you haven't met or spoken to Fares in a while, but I wish you two were still friends. He could use a good friend these days."

"Yeah, it's been a while. How's he doing?"

"Honestly, I don't know what he's up to half the time. I just hope he's staying out of trouble." She sighed, looking slightly worried.

Kashif nodded.

"Thanks again. Please, do let me know if you find anything more," he said.

"I'll keep searching."

Me too, he thought to himself, walking out.

CHAPTER NINE

THE SUIT

T he events at the police precinct didn't sit well with Kashif. The police chief, the folders he had been going through, Zara's statements: the whole thing left a very unsettling feeling in Kashif. He felt dissatisfied. *I have to find out more. I have to find out the truth,* he told himself on his way back from the precinct. He couldn't help but keep thinking of what Zara had said. *There was only an older scientist there. Ben Yurkovich. Yurkovich. He must have more answers,* he thought. *But how can I get them, and how can I get to him?* By the time he reached his workspace lab, an idea was brewing in his mind.

The lab that Kashif and Samir shared and worked on their projects and experiments was opposite Kashif's apartment, on the top floor of the Al-Jazari building in the city's center. At their workspace, Kashif told Samir what he had learned from Zara.

"You saw her?!" was all Samir could respond with, seeming interested more in the girl than Kashif's dilemma. "So... how is she?" He asked hesitantly, hoping it didn't give him away.

"What? That's what you got out of everything I said... oh wait, do you *like her* or something?" Kashif asked, squinting his eyes.

"What, no... I mean, sure, maybe. Did you notice any ring on her finger?" Samir continued inquiring.

"Oh, brother." Kashif sighed. "I can ask her if she's interested if you like," Kashif said flatly.

"Really, would you?" Samir's eyes opened widely in

surprise. "I mean, yeah, if you could, that would be sweet. It would be good just knowing what she thinks, you know," he said in a hopeful tone and smiling.

"Sure, yeah, next time... but, *Yurkovich...*" Kashif tried to get back to his point.

"Yeah, Yurkovich. Let's look him up," Samir responded, turning his chair towards X-Bot, their supercomputer.

The supercomputer was a work of art; over the years, both had put their minds together and developed an extremely powerful computer and search engine not even the government could get their hands on. Samir had casually bragged, *"The most powerful computer you'll ever see. Illegal? Sure, but powerful enough and able to search and find anybody and any information on any site without leaving a trace? Yes."* Information that even the police could not get a hold of. Naturally, they kept X-Bot a secret, for a machine capable of this much information and power was not meant to be in anyone's hands, they concluded. Except their own. They had agreed to use X-Bot for their projects only, but on that day, they were in need of any and all details and information they could find on Ben Yurkovich.

"Let's see what we can find on him," Samir said, sitting in front of X-Bot's five-foot wide and tall screen. "Looks like he's about to drop dead any second. Dude's a living relic," Samir pointed out to Kashif, who stood behind him. "Seems like he has quite the experience with human biological experiments, countless years' worth." He continued looking at his profile from classified documents.

"I think we should pay him a visit," Kashif said, not blinking while looking at the profile on the screen.

"We?" turning around, a surprised Samir responded.

We have to find out what happened and who this Yurkovich is," Kashif firmly stated.

"Yes, but... how? That place is a crime scene, and..." Samir paused, looking at the screen, "It looks like his only listed address is that building, which is weird."

"I'm going," said Kashif with a serious face.

"Planning on just sneaking in?" Samir asked, intrigued.

"If you're not going to help me, I'll have to figure it out myself."

"No, I didn't say that... in fact, I can help," Samir replied, a half-smile forming on his face with a twinkle in his eyes. Kashif wasn't sure what that meant, but he liked the sound of it.

"Remember the US Army asking us for a 'special suit'? A suit that could deflect bullets, defy gravity, and give super strength?" Samir recalled walking backward slowly. "Sure, they took back their offer before we could say 'No.' It looks like they decided to go with some billionaire's design which looked like a bat," he said the last part mockingly. "But I didn't stop working on it," Samir said, having led Kashif to the corner wall of the lab. "Let's just say, I've been playing around with some ideas." A devilish smile formed across his face.

Samir took out his cell phone, pressed a few buttons, and a few seconds later, the back hall of the room opened up to what they called "The Playroom." As the wall opened up, it revealed a large secret hall with windows looking out to the Firdaus River, a room where they experimented on anything and everything that was of interest. Kashif and Samir would use this room to test new technologies and ideas, from robots to devices, to machines; all of it was created and tested here in "The Playroom." As Samir went ahead excitedly into the testing lab, Kashif paused. He remembered the only other person who had seen the room was Abu.

"What is going on with you, Baita? Constantly working and no time for us or anything else?

"I'm sorry, Abu, but let me show you what I've been working on. It's very exciting."

"What I want you to show me is your seriousness about life outside your work. I hope you haven't been missing any salah? Never your daily prayers."

"No, Abu, of course not."

"I want you to show me that you're serious about your future, getting married, and settling down. It's time now." He put his hands on his shoulder and patted his back, *"But okay, let's see what's been keeping you away from getting married."* Abu let out a gentle laugh.

"As soon as I'm done with this project, I'll focus on marriage, Abu, don't worry. Check this out," he said, handing him a pair of small lenses. "It's a prototype right now, but it's a mini telescope we can put on our eyes like a contact lens. You can choose how far to see with it."

"Come on!" His thoughts were broken by Samir excitedly waving him over to a table. Kashif found himself holding the lenses on the table, last placed there by Abu himself. Entering the room, a heavy sense of regret walked in with him and started to consume him—all the time spent there and away from his parents, away from Aliya. Walking into that room, anger started running through him again.

"I've been working extensively on this. You weren't interested, so I went ahead myself," Samir explained as Kashif walked over. On the table lay an armored bodysuit with a one-piece thobe covering from top to bottom. "Look what I added to it, and if you're actually serious, maybe this will help you go in and out of the lab discreetly. Put it on."

"I don't see any difference to what we originally had," stated Kashif, putting his arms and head through the black thobe. The thobe was thick like a coat that was tight from the top and loose, flowing from the bottom. Similar to standard thobes, it had a small collar and a patterned design around the buttons of the chest. Under the thobe was a light metallic material running inside and covering him as a body shield. They had designed the thobe and metal shield to be *fairly bulletproof. Fairly, meaning it would still cause damage to the material,* Samir had said.

"Okay, what's different with the thobe-suit?"

"Try these," Samir said, giving him long black gloves.

"Gloves?" Kashif questioned, putting them on, reaching up to his forearms. "Nice and warm, now what?"

"Let me get some bricks I saved for these," Samir ran excitedly to a cabinet.

"What?" a confused Kashif wondered out loud.

"Here," Samir took out a dozen bricks and stacked them up. "Punch these."

"Did you say *punch them?*"

"Just do it," Samir replied impatiently while full of energy.

"Um... okay, fine." Kashif looked at the bricks stacked up, then down at his gloves, and started to punch but stopped to ask, "How hard?"

"Oh, for God's sake, just punch them as hard as you can!"

"You're gonna pay for my hand surgery," mumbled Kashif, returning to the bricks. He looked at them and back at Samir, wide-eyed and waiting with excitement. Taking in a deep breath, he punched a stack of bricks.

"Ow!" Kashif screamed in pain, holding his hand.

"Yeah, that's what I figured," Samir calmly replied, raising his shoulders. "Now try this..." moving towards the gloves in Kashif's hands.

"What the heck, man?!" Kashif yelled, pulling his hand away, still feeling the tinge of excruciating pain.

"You're a strong guy, but a regular human punching a wall of bricks will hurt, obviously," Samir casually explained.

"Obviously!"

"But now, try this. *This* is what I've been working on. Squeeze and clench your fist twice and then punch."

"No, you do it!"

"Come on. It'll be worth it. Plus, you've already punched it once. Try it again. Squeeze your fist twice before punching again."

"What's going to happen?" Kashif asked apprehensively.

Samir sighed. "You'll break the bricks this time. Now, go for it!"

Kashif looked at the bricks again in a worrisome manner. Taking a deep breath, he started to punch the block of bricks again, but this time he clenched his fist twice. He heard the gloves generate a mechanical sound as if an engine had turned on, and as he punched this time, he didn't feel any pain as the bricks shattered against his fist.

"Yes!" exclaimed Samir. "Success!"

"Woah," Kashif said, looking at his hands as if they were unearthly beings. "How did you do that?"

"I added an extra boost to the gloves, so when you squeeze twice, it activates the boost and adds a layer of cushioning on the gloves. So, you don't feel it while your arm acts like a rocket.

And the thobe-suit is made from a different material from what we originally worked with. This material is slightly more bulletproof, but still not completely. I want to make it completely bulletproof, but the issue is it will be too heavy," he explained. "I'm still working on that, though."

Kashif was thoroughly impressed. Samir was the best mind he had ever met when it came to mechanical engineering; finding pet projects was always a hobby for him.

"Only downside is I don't have a working face mask yet, so you'll just have to wear a ski mask. But otherwise, the suit is good to go."

"I think this is exactly what I'll need going to the Paramus Lab," said Kashif confidently.

"You're really going to do this, aren't you?" Samir stopped, looking at him straightly.

Kashif felt a sense of thrill and excitement for the first time in weeks. "I'm really going to do this," he said determinedly. "Now, where is your suit?"

"Uh… there's only one. For you."

"You're not coming with me?"

"What part of me looks like someone who can sneak around?" He said, pointing up and down at his body, emphasizing his belly. Samir was a broad-shouldered and tall man, and Kashif noticed that he was currently a little bit on the heavier side.

"Yeah, you've put on a little bit of weight, but you still train in kickboxing," Kashif responded.

"I'll let the Brazilian Jiu-Jitsu black belt do the sneaking around," Samir said flatly. "Plus, I'll be more useful to you from here. I'll walk you through the whole area and be your eyes and ears through your earpiece. From here," he pointed to X-Bot.

"Fine," Kashif drew out, slightly disappointed, but he understood.

"Okay, and lastly, remember if you get caught…"

Kashif anticipated something useful and wise from Samir.

"I don't know you," Samir said, half-joking.

CHAPTER TEN

PARAMUS LAB

It was almost midnight when Kashif rode his motorcycle to the back of the giant chemical building, which housed a laboratory on the northeast corner of the city. The front of the building was closed off by police barricades and security tape, too risky to enter from. The back had an entrance but was blocked off by a small, forested area. The whole premise was fenced off.

Kashif parked his bike near the back and went through the forested area toward the fence. The night was quiet. Not a sign of life or any light was coming from the building. He crouched down in the grass in front of the fence, "I'm here. It looks pretty abandoned," he whispered into his earpiece, connected to Samir, who stayed behind in their lab.

"Okay, zoom in with your lens scope, and let me see the area and premise," Samir responded. In another one of their pet projects, he could map out the entire building using the view from the contact lens and have it displayed on his computer.

As Kashif crouched in the tall grass next to the fence, he felt his phone vibrate. He looked at it for a few seconds as it displayed "Aliya." His heart jumped; he had been wanting to talk to her badly as she was always good at giving him the right advice and guidance in his most difficult moments. But he knew he couldn't pick up right then and there. Silencing the phone, he put it back in his pocket, making the intention and a mental note to call her back.

"That's strange. It looks like the building is basically empty," said a surprised Samir.

"Basically?" whispered Kashif.

"I'm not getting any person's movement in the building, but there seems to be some activity in the basement; in that case, a few people should be there."

"Yurkovich." Kashif stood up. But instead of taking a step forward, he froze, rethinking everything as his heart had started beating into his throat, and he felt the sweat under his arms and neck. He had never done anything like this before. The only other time he had broken into a place was as a teenager, along with his friends, Michael Marmol and Carlos Walker. They had skipped school and snuck into the movie theater, where they spent most of the day watching three movies. But this was nothing on the same level. This held severe criminal charges: breaking and entering, and trespassing onto private property. All these thoughts were running through his head as he closed his eyes, took three deep breaths, and relaxed himself. *I'm doing this. I need to do this. For Abu.* "I'm going in," he said into the mic. "And by the way, these contacts are very uncomfortable."

He squeezed his way quietly through the opening of the fence and crept low while hugging the walls of the building. He crept up to a window, and after getting confirmation from Samir that no one was in the hallway, he opened it slowly and made his way in. Kashif's heart was beating as fast as it ever had and he felt a sweat continuing to pool on his back. Samir was sitting back and eating grapes in the lab, but his heart, too, was starting to pound harder and faster with every move Kashif made.

Kashif snuck down the empty and dimly-lit hallway as Samir gave him directions to the lab. He turned the corner and went down south to the end of the hallway to a door that read, "Basement." About to try the handle, another door adjacent with a red light on it, caught his attention. The door was almost hidden and had a few locks visible on it.

"Take the basement door," whispered Samir.

"I have a feeling it's that door."

"No, that's just a closet. I can see it," Samir responded.

"I have a feeling something's there," Kashif said, walking towards it. "It's locked," trying the handle. "But I got it." He squeezed his fist twice and broke the handle.

"Okay, this is not what I had in mind when I told you about the power gloves," Samir complained.

"You're in this with me now, buddy," whispered Kashif, slowly opening the door. Samir was right, it was just a janitor's closet, but Kashif still went inside to look.

"There's nothing there. Get out of there," warned Samir. In the dark, he could see a boring closet with cleaning utensils, supplies, and some coats hanging on the wall. As he turned around to leave, something caught his attention. The loose material of his thobe was moving as if a wind was blowing it. He took off his gloves to feel it.

"I feel something. It's a breeze." He started to feel the walls and made his way to an air duct at the back of the room behind the coats, and as he felt his way up, he felt a handle, to his surprise. There was no door but a handle inside the wall. "What's this?" He slid his hands into the handle and pushed, shifting half of the wall.

"There's something here," said Kashif. As he pulled back the large door, that's when it happened. His whole world went dark.

"Samir, what happened?! I can't see!"

"What do you mean you can't see?" Samir replied, concerned.

"I can't see. *I can't see!*" panicked Kashif.

The darkness swallowed him up.

CHAPTER ELEVEN

YURKOVICH

I can't see! *I can't see!"*

His world suddenly went completely dark. In a state of shock, he fell to the floor, rolled over, and lost sense of where the door and walls were. The claustrophobic thought of being stuck in a dark closet, in a dark hallway, of an abandoned building was mortifying. He felt his world closing in and his chest tightening; his lungs screamed for air. Kashif started hyperventilating. Reaching for anything and feeling his way, he finally felt the wall behind him and the coats hanging before him. He was breathing heavily, gasping for breath.

"What do you mean you can't see?!" Samir shouted.

Trying to speak, Kashif's voice was stuck in his throat along with any air. Samir could hear his breathing becoming heavier.

"You're having a panic attack. Stay calm and take deep breaths!" Samir yelled. "Your lens scope must have gone offline and turned off. I'm restarting them now."

Kashif was able to listen to Samir's words but did not respond. He felt his chest was about to crush due to the tightness; he was losing consciousness.

"I can't seem to get them turned back on. Take them out," Samir said.

Sinking into a dark abyss, Samir's voice propelled him back up, and he reached for his eyes; he tried to take out the contacts, but they were in deep. "They're... stuck," Kashif slowly cried out between breaths.

After a minute, but what seemed a lifetime, the lens turned on.

"Can you see? Talk to me," Samir pleaded.

Slowly, the black started to turn into a dim light. Eventually, he could see he had fallen into the corner of the walls and was underneath the coats. He sat up and crawled to the door, opening it with the little energy he had left. When he opened the door, he saw a pair of feet.

"Go back inside! Hide!" Samir yelled.

Not realizing there were two security guards doing rounds just outside, he was just inches away from the guard and the panic came back in full force. He took a quick breath before Samir could repeat, "Run back!" He quickly turned and closed the door quietly.

"Did you hear that?" Kashif heard one of the guards say outside the door.

"Hmm? Yeah, just the old man downstairs," the other one said nonchalantly as they kept walking away from the closet.

Kashif was fully awake by that time, his heart practically beating out of his chest. *This is insane. What am I doing?!* He thought. But the words, "man downstairs," jolted him back up again, reminding him why he was there. He sat still, and when he heard footsteps walking away from the door, he straightened up, cleared his mind, went toward the wall with the door in the closet, and opened it.

The entire wall was a door that opened up, revealing a massive hall: the underground lab. The door opened to a catwalk with stairs towering over the huge lab. Kashif ducked toward the edge of the stairs, peering down into the enormous room before him. Surveying the lab from above, he saw and heard no movement or sign of life inside the lab. Still, with his heart pounding, he quietly descended the stairs.

The lab was full of tables with strange bottles, with unusual fluids and materials. There was a bizarre and odd stench that Kashif had never smelled before. Most likely the different chemicals being mixed together, he thought. Clearly, someone had been working there recently. But at that moment, the lab seemed deserted. Kashif straightened up and walked quietly, trying to make sense of all the strange experiments and papers. Walking up to a table with flasks and shuffled papers, he picked up a paper on a desk. *Transformation,* it read in English across the top, but the rest was written in some kind of encrypted code. He lifted another paper that had been torn into a few pieces, in which the only legible part read, *The current mixing of flesh and metal produce convincing results...*

Intrigued, Kashif moved to pick up and analyze another paper when there was a noise behind him. He rushed to duck under the table, sitting motionless. The noise came again, this time more audible, a groan from the floor near him. Remaining hidden, he tried to look around for the sound as the moans became louder, sounding like a wounded animal. He crept closer to the sound, keeping himself out of view, and spotted a balding older man seated on the ground with his head down and back toward one of the counters.

"I know you're there." The man groaned in pain." I don't care anymore." He went quiet after that.

Yurkovich.

While still crouching, Kashif made his way toward the man. He noticed the man was in and out of consciousness. He patted his arm, and the man woke up with a jolt and yelled in a state of delirium, "Huh!? No! I'm done, I said, no more! I'm not going to do it anymore!"

"Shhh!" Kashif whispered, trying not to be heard and found.

"I'm done, you hear me! All of you. I've figured out how to escape, and I'm done!" He panicked, pausing between heavy breaths. "You can all go to hell." He managed to get out before he started coughing deeply and violently as he fell to his side.

Kashif helped him back up to a sitting position as the man tried to fight him, with his *yarmulke* falling to the side of his head.

"I'm not one of them," Kashif quietly whispered to him, gently fixing his *yarmulke*.

The man finally opened his eyes and looked up at Kashif, studying his mask and thobe. He tried to speak but could not as he winced in pain. Suddenly, a frightened look came across his face as he said, "You shouldn't be here," between heavy breaths.

"I need answers. Were you the one responsible for the power outage that happened here last week?" He asked Yurkovich.

"I was," coughed Yurkovich.

"You… you killed a lot of people," Kashif stated.

Yurkovich stared weakly at Kashif with pity, "But, I set myself free, finally."

"What are you talking about?"

Yurkovich weakly unbuttoned his shirt and showed a device stuck to his chest, with wires piercing his skin and running into his heart. "They can't control me anymore."

Kashif stared in shock. "What is this? Who did this to you?"

"They won't let me die. They kept this device on me to kickstart my heart so I couldn't die. Not until they wanted me to. But I figured it out. Finally, I've figured out how to turn this off. Now, I can die in peace."

"Who did this?"

Yurkovich coughed loudly and violently, "I don't have that much time. Tell them, tell everyone, for me. Give everyone a message from me. Will you do that?"

Kashif nodded.

"Run. Run from this city. They will destroy us all. He will release the monster."

"What monster?" demanded Kashif, "And who will release it?"

Yurkovich moaned in pain.

"I'm going to stop this once and for all. I'm going to destroy whatever they are doing," Kashif said, looking at the wires going into Yurkovich's chest.

Yurkovich's eyes opened widely. "You will? You will? Yes, you have to; you must. You must save everyone."

"Who is behind this?" asked Kashif.

Yurkovich fainted in and out of consciousness, muttering what seemed like names under his breath.

"What? Yurkovich, wake up," Kashif shook him.

"Stop, Hammerhead..." he quieted and went silent.

Kashif shook him, trying to wake him up again.

"Tell me, what are they doing here?"

"Iris Hill..."

"Iris Hill? What about him?"

"Get... Iris Hill." Yurkovich opened his eyes and looked, deathly scared, at Kashif. "They're building... a monster. To release on everyone. To destroy everyone." He then grabbed

Kashif's shoulders, bringing him closer to him. "Find Echo Mas. And stop them."

"What is Echo Mas?"

But that was the last bit of information Yurkovich shared before he dropped to the floor, eyes rising toward the ceiling before they closed. Kashif tried to shake him awake, but he was gone. Immediately, a deafening alarm and red emergency lights suddenly blared around the lab. Kashif heard loud noises and footsteps running toward the lab. He hid in the corner behind a desk near the door. As the security guards came rushing down, yelling into their headsets, and went to check up on the dead body of Yurkovich, Kashif quietly slipped up the stairs and out of the building.

CHAPTER TWELVE

AFTER THE LAB

We have to find out who Echo Mas is," Kashif proclaimed after walking through the events again with Samir.

"Way ahead of you, buddy; I've already begun searching. But there's nothing anywhere on this Echo Mas. It's like he doesn't exist," Samir responded. "Or she."

They exchanged perplexed looks. "This doesn't make any sense. Yurkovich mentioned Iris Hill. He said, 'Get Iris Hill.' Did he mean to get him or get him to help stop whatever monster is coming?"

"Iris Hill is no saint; he has a reputation for being involved with gangs in some way."

"Yeah, but if Iris Hill is involved, then this is bigger than we thought. And what about this Hammerhead?"

"Got info on him. Look at this guy; no wonder how he got his name," Kashif said, analyzing his profile. Isaac "Hammerhead" Nolan was a broad-faced man with strong features and a large forehead. "It says he's a shipping captain at the docks, and everything goes in and out through him."

"And Carson, where can he be?" Kashif sighed, sitting down.

"No sign or update on him."

Kashif kept staring at the screen, not blinking, in deep thought. "What do we do?"

"What can we do?" Samir asked.

They both sat quietly, contemplating.

"We have to go to the police," said Kashif finally.

"And tell them what? That you broke in and witnessed

Yurkovich dying? Plus, didn't you say you had a bad feeling about Police Chief Eames?" replied Samir.

"Yeah…" a dismayed Kashif said. "But so, then what, what can we do?"

"We go and find this Hammerhead, and we ask him a few questions," Samir calmly replied, looking at Kashif. Kashif raised his eyebrow in confusion and disbelief. "Forcefully, if we have to," he finished.

"No, no way. I'm not doing that or breaking into any place again." Kashif stood up and paced back and forth.

"It's our only way. You heard what Yurkovich said, they're doing something dangerous, and we need to find out what that is and stop it."

Kashif kept pacing, not responding.

"You don't have to hurt anyone. And you won't get hurt. Come on, you're a BJJ black belt at Rollstar Academy," Samir said.

"Oh yeah, easy for you to say. Why don't you come with me, huh?" responded Kashif.

"I'd just hold you down. I'm not in the… physical shape you are in," said Samir rubbing his belly with a smile. "And you won't be alone; I'll be with you from here," presenting the lab room and computer. "I'm more useful here, looking out for your six and helping you navigate. Plus, you're already more experienced than I am!"

Kashif kept pacing back and forth, trying to listen to Samir through his deep thoughts.

"We can't just ignore this, especially if we can stop something dangerous from happening. And we're in this together," Samir said, trying to be encouraging.

After a couple of minutes, Kashif stopped and looked at Samir. "You said I won't get hurt. How?"

"The suit," Samir responded, pointing to it on the table. "Let me make some more exclusive additions," Samir smiled with a twinkle in his eyes as Kashif winced.

CHAPTER THIRTEEN

LOSING BALANCE

The following day Samir and Kashif worked nonstop on the suit and planned how they would make their way into the docks. They had spent the entire day and worked into the late afternoon, with the suit having gone through a number of alterations, when Kashif's phone rang. He went to the side, stared out the window, cleared his throat, and answered, "Hey, asalaamu alaikum."

Aliya's voice on the other end was not as welcoming. "Where are you? Are you coming?!"

"What?...Oh, were we supposed to meet today?!" He slapped his forehead.

"I'm here at your mom's, and you're not here? Are you serious?" She was furious.

"Ah, I'm so sorry, I forgot; I was so caught up in work. I'm truly sorry."

"Typical."

She had a right to be furious, he thought. Aliya had been nothing but supportive and a calming force in Kashif's life. Still, in return, Kashif had become consumed with the outage, the suit, and finding out what happened that caused Abu's death. He had subconsciously pushed Aliya to the background in his life. But he knew he had messed up big time at that point. Kashif apologized profusely before he got cut off.

"Listen, I know you're not well mentally and emotionally; I get it. But completely becoming consumed in your work and disregarding and ignoring everything is not the right way to grieve.

You need to talk about it, and you know that you can talk to me. You know I'm here for you. How long are you going to keep ignoring me?"

It had been two months since his abu had passed, and it was apparent to everyone that Kashif wasn't doing too well. Since Abu's passing, *his murder,* Kashif kept himself secluded from the people who cared about him the most. In return, this downward spiral had become steeper. He had cut himself off from everyone, he was short with people, and his appearance was disheveled. But, the most apparent change was his anger: Kashif always seemed to be angry. And he knew that the person he had been hurting the most was Aliya, his one true love. Still, she stayed by his side, comforted and talked to him. But he didn't know how to open up to her or really address his feelings: the anger, the pain, and the loss. There was an emptiness in his heart and life from where his father had been. How to communicate all of this was lost on him. Aliya knew this, and she was understanding. But lately, he had become so lost in his work, so consumed by something which she could not understand, that for the first time since getting to know him, she felt distant… almost too far away to ever reach out to him. And that was an unsettling feeling… to feel ignored, set aside, of no significance in Kashif's life.

"I'm not ignoring you, Alz."

"You haven't talked to me in two days. How many times can I keep calling and texting you before you respond?"

"I love your calls and texts, and you're right; I'm sorry. I'll wrap everything up in a bit."

"Can we meet later tonight?" she asked.

"I… have plans tonight," he said hesitantly.

"Oh, really? You want to tell me about them?" she questioned, clearly offended.

"Listen, it's complicated. Not, I mean, not with you. But, like you said, I need to let myself heal, and that's what I'm doing. Trust me. I'm getting answers and closure."

"What are you talking about? How are you getting answers?"

"I'll explain when we meet, okay? And you're right; I'll open up more to you, but right now, I can't. I'll explain everything later. I promise."

"I… don't even know what to say to that."

"You're still the only place that feels like home," he said.

"Okay," she said, not sounding too convinced. "Sure. See you later."

That night, the plan was finally going to be set in motion. They needed to find Hammerhead, and he was to be found by the docks. "You're going to sneak into the docks and find out who Echo Mas is and what Yurkovich was talking about," prepped Samir. "It'll be simple," he said casually.

"Yeah, as you sit here behind the desk." Kashif rolled his eyes.

The docks were located on the north side of the city next to Firdaus River, a closed-off area to the public as small ships came and went, mainly carrying business cargo. At 10:00 PM, it was show time. Kashif rode his motorcycle to the docks and made his way to the fence of the shipping yard, his suit looking different than the night in the lab.

"You're going to like these," Samir said earlier, excited as he sat exhausted in his chair. "Improvement number 1: not have you look like a burglar with that black ski mask on and black thobe. So, allow me to introduce something I've been working on for some time now: your new face. Press the button on your belt."

As Kashif pressed the button, his whole world went dark and claustrophobic as a metal shield was extracted from his suit and covered his face and head. After a couple of seconds, Samir turned on the lens, and Kashif was able to see through the eyes of the face shield.

"Woah!" Kashif shrieked in amazement, walking towards a mirror. The face shield had blueish slits for eyes, and as he pressed the button again, it retracted back into his suit. As he extracted it again, the face shield contained smaller pieces extracted out and met at the nose as a center point. "Very cool."

"I've connected an earpiece inside the face shield so we can communicate. And speaking of communicating, since there's no mouthpiece, I've added a speaker system so you can talk. But we wouldn't want your voice to be detected, so I've adjusted the voice settings. Go ahead and talk."

"Testing, bismillah, testing," a squeaky high-pitched voice came out of the face mask. "Hey! What did you do to my voice!?"

His voice squeaked, "I sound like a chipmunk!"

"This level is for if you're ever being annoying, I'll just set it to this level." Samir laughed. "Let me get to the right voice level. How about I make it a little bit deeper than your normal voice? Speak now."

The voice that came out now was deep and intimidating, "Testing, bismillah, testing. Woah, I sound kind of scary. I like it."

"Me too. We'll keep it to this level. Now, improvement number 2: changed the thobe color to blue, and added a hood to fully cover your head, with added protection in case... well, hopefully, nothing hits you on the head," he said with a faint laugh. He then picked up a brick and threw it at Kashif.

"Hey man, watch it!" shouted Kashif ducking away from the brick.

"You're supposed to let it hit you; otherwise, how will we know it works?" questioned Samir, raising his arms.

"You mean you didn't actually test this before I put this on?"

"Yeah, well, I didn't have all that much time. Can we try, please?"

"Are you serious? Ugh, fine, but gently toss it, I guess."

"Yeah, sure, just stand right there," Samir quickly replied, already holding another brick. "In fact, turn around. Let's see how much you feel it."

"This is a bad idea. I don't even know where you keep finding bricks," a nervous Kashif remarked, turning around slowly.

"Okay, tell me what you feel."

After a few moments, a tense Kashif became impatient, "Will you hurry up already?"

"Uh, turn around and look," replied Samir.

"What?" Kashif turned around and noticed Samir pointing to the ground next to Kashif's feet, where three bricks lay.

"Bro, I threw three of them right at the back of your head! You didn't feel the impact?" He said excitedly.

"Uh, no, actually, I didn't," said Kashif, feeling the back of his head.

"Time for test number two: a bat," said Samir, getting up.

A confused Kashif looked on as Samir retrieved a metal baseball bat and got into a swinging pose. "Come on, turn around," said Samir, ready for a full swing.

"Okay, take it easy, will you?" Kashif said, turning around.

Samir swung as hard as he could at the back of Kashif's head, and the hit knocked Kashif forward. Kashif fell face-first to the ground, unmoving.

"Oh my God, are you okay?!" Samir ran to him.

He shook Kashif on the ground, but Kashif lay still. "Kash, get up!" He retracted his shield and noticed Kashif was unconscious and unresponsive. "Hey, bro, get up. I'm sorry!" Samir kept shaking him. When Kashif didn't move, Samir jumped up, panicking. "Oh my God, what did I do!? I'm… I'm going to go to jail. This is all over; I've killed Kashif. I'm not going to do well in jail, I…" Samir started panting, talking out loud. "This is all my fault!… I'm going to go to jail…"

"Hey, genius. I'm fine," Samir heard a voice behind him. Turning around in a flash, Kashif stood smiling ear to ear. "That's what you get for making me punch those bricks. Now we're even," beamed a satisfied Kashif.

"You're alive! Alhamdulillah!" Samir screamed. "And you're an idiot! Don't ever do that again!"

"Well, it worked," Kashif replied.

"You really didn't feel anything?"

"I felt it, but it didn't hurt.".

"It worked!" Samir said triumphantly. "Now, for the third improvement: a jet pack."

"A WHAT?" asked Kashif.

"Just kidding… sort of, well, I've thought about it. The third trick is actually on your hands and feet. Look at them."

"What am I looking at?" Kashif said with his hands out.

"Go near the wall and try to… *climb* the wall."

Kashif gave a side-eyed look, not believing him again. "You've done something crazy cool, haven't you?"

"Well, let's see if it works."

Kashif went to the wall, touching it with the palms of both his hands; he raised himself up. To his surprise, he felt relative ease in picking up his weight as his hands stuck to the wall.

"Good, now your feet too."

A moment later, he was hanging entirely from the wall,

clinging from his hands and feet.

"Woah!" a surprised Kashif exclaimed.

"Go ahead, try climbing the whole wall. You should be able to walk it."

As Kashif carefully stood up straight against the wall, he walked all the way horizontally on the wall until he reached the roof. "This is amazing! How did you do this!?"

"Van Der Waals interaction. Everything we touch has electrical interactions between two or more atoms and molecules that rub against each other. This suit takes those molecules and atoms and keeps them in contact with each other." Kashif turned to the ceiling and hung upside down, walking on the ceiling towards Samir. "The intermolecular forces between the two objects keep the charge intact, causing the two surfaces to remain together. But the key is to keep them together."

"Maybe I'm just so excited about this," Kashif said, walking right toward Samir, face to his upside-down face, "or it's the rush of blood to my head, but I have no idea what you just said, dude."

"It makes things stick together. Okay, you can come down now," Samir chuckled.

"This is so awesome!"

"Yeah, I think you're ready to go all the way tonight… you're sure you want to do this, right?" He asked as Kashif jumped down from the ceiling, landing in a crouching position on the ground. He didn't respond; something was holding him back.

After a moment, he stood up straight, "I think so," he finally said.

"There's no turning back from this if you do," Samir said slowly, with a finality in his tone. He could not shake off the feeling that something momentous was going to happen that night, something that would drastically change both his and Kashif's lives.

Kashif felt it too, so the two best friends stared at each other and, without speaking, gave each other a firm nod.

CHAPTER FOURTEEN

BISMILLAH

T*here's no turning back from this.* The words kept repeating in Kashif's head as he arrived at the docks later that night. It was a warm night, but Kashif felt a chill when he reached the fence of the docks. *Maybe it's just the breeze from the river,* he thought to himself. Or maybe, it was his nerves making his blood run cold. He did not want to break through the fence to leave a trace or climb it as the fence housed spiraled spikes on the top. The only way over was to jump from the roof of the building outside the fence.

Okay, Van Der Waals, do your thing. He looked at his hands and feet as he started to climb the side of the building. He climbed to the roof outside the fence of the docks and looked out. The city had begun to become unusually foggy at night lately, but that night was a clear one. Kashif was able to look out at the premises of the main shipping buildings, the ships, and the administration building. Samir had tracked Hammerhead's movements, and discovered he was usually at the docks at this time. Kashif knew what he had to do: sneak into the admin building and hopefully find Hammerhead. They had to find out who Echo Mas was. *Or what.* At that hour in the night, most of the premises would have been deserted, he thought, so he was not expecting to run into anyone, yet he stood frozen.

From what?

Fear? Anxiety? Nerves? More like all of the above. If he went ahead and started, *there would be no turning back from this.* Kashif knew he had already come too far to turn back now. But deep down, what was holding him down like an anchor tied to a ship, was fear. *This was terrifying.* His heart was pounding, sweat accumulating under his arms and back. "Kashif," Samir spoke into his earpiece from back in the lab.

When Kashif did not respond, he asked, "I can hear you breathing heavily already. Are you okay?"

No response.

The silence between the two passed by like two ships that had just missed each other at sea.

"Maybe we can think about this and try again another day," Samir finally spoke. Kashif had felt fear in his life plenty of times, but this was different. This was life-changing. A point of no return. This was being thrown into a new future, one he had not prepared for and had no way of knowing where it would lead or what would be the outcome. The fear of something unknown creeping up, tapping on a shoulder and asking to follow it along toward a dark path… that fear crawled through every inch of his skin, practically consuming him. The fear was slipping under his skin and into his bloodstream. Kashif was frozen.

At that point, his mind went to a place of finding comfort: he remembered the Prophet Muhammad (ﷺ). A source of solace and comfort, the Prophet's life and events are not just mere stories that people learn while growing up; instead, they are guiding principles in life. The Prophet (ﷺ) was human; after all, he felt love, pain, happiness, sadness, and disappointment. And Kashif, a believer, was supposed to learn how he could handle those moments, feelings, and experiences and follow and act similarly. Still, Kashif remained paralyzed, remembering when the Prophet (ﷺ) had felt afraid.

The narration of the story of revelation is fascinating. It was a dark, quiet night when it all happened. The Prophet Muhammad (ﷺ) liked to get away from the hustle and busy life of Makkah and retrieve in the Cave of Hira in the mountain called Jabal Al-Noor (Mountain of Light) just outside the city. There, he (ﷺ) found some solace and time for meditation. Jabal Al-Noor, about seven miles outside Makkah central, is still a large mountain housing a few small crevices and caves today. This particular cave is more so a tiny crevice as it can only fit one person at a time. Not only that, but it is also a forty-minute trek up the mountain.

A small, quiet, dark place is the perfect place to get away from society and meditate. It is also a terrifying thought for many to be in. Being far from any person or sign of life alone, high up in a small dark cave, was scary enough. Not many people would be able to survive in an environment such as that, where any sort of help could never arrive in time and especially where any wild mountain animal could attack. But as the narration went, the Prophet Muhammad (ﷺ) was alone, meditating in the cave one night when he unexpectedly heard a noise: someone or something had entered. Looking up, to his fright, he saw a lone white figure appear unexpectedly inside the cave, a being the likes he had never seen before. As the space was tight, when he stood up, he was right in front of this strange figure. Instead of freaking out or running away, he asked the stranger who he was. The figure did not respond, instead hugged him tightly in an embrace to the point where he felt his chest might explode. After letting go, the being made a strange request, "Recite."

"I don't know how to recite," he responded in shock. Even in that frightening moment, he didn't run away. Instead, the Prophet (ﷺ) replied honestly, "I don't know how to recite," meaning he was not a poet and did not know how to read or write. This being, he learned later, was Angel Jibril, who hugged him tightly again and told him to recite.

"I don't know how to recite," the Prophet (ﷺ) replied again. The third time that the angel hugged him and commanded him to recite, the Prophet (ﷺ) asked in return, "What should I recite?" At this, Angel Jibril recited to him what became the very first Ayat-verses of the Noble Qur'an.

Kashif remembered this incident and how frightening this experience must have been for the Prophet (ﷺ) yet instead of running away, lying, and reciting anything he could think of at the moment, the Prophet (ﷺ) showed extreme courage and immense honesty: he bravely stood his ground and faced what was in front of him with the truth.

Calmer, Kashif stood up, said, "Bismillah," and jumped down toward the docks.

CHAPTER FIFTEEN

AFTER THE DOCKS

Two hours later, the wind flapped loudly against his thobe as Kashif whipped down the road on his motorcycle.

"Overall, that went pretty smoothly. I would say even easy," Samir spoke through the earpiece.

"Speak for yourself," Kashif replied, unmasked under his bike helmet, as he slowed down to a red light. "My heart was beating out of my chest. I still can't believe I did that."

"But hey, we got answers."

Rupert Everton, the shipping manager who was the only person in the admin building, gave them answers but raised even more questions.

"You saw how scared he was and not of me. He was almost... relieved to see me, an intruder looking for Echo Mas and to 'fix things' as he said."

"Echo Mas is not a person," Everton had explained after Kashif broke into the admin building and questioned him. "It's the main ship that comes to the port. I've had no problems here, but recently they made an agreement with Carson Daye to carry some of his cargo. I dunno what's in his containers, but it comes with high security," Rupert, a small middle-aged man, explained, shaking in distress. "I can't even stop 'em from bringing in and shipping out deliveries. But they've made me keep quiet."

"Made you? How?" Kashif inquired.

He didn't respond but gave Kashif a nervous look before lowering his head.

"Who are they?"

"There are two main guys who run it. I only know the name of one of them. They call him Hammerhead. The other one is outside right now," he pointed out the window.

Kashif's heart dropped as he peeked out the window and saw Fares talking on the phone while instructing others around him.

No! His breathing started getting heavy, and a sadness gloomed over him. He saw Fares get into a car and drive off. Kashif could barely think.

"This other man, when's he coming here next?"

"I dunno, there's no schedule that they even give me," Rupert replied, almost in tears.

"Do you know where I can find them?"

He shook his head, but looked Kashif right in the eyes of his mask. "Look, Mister, I don't know who you are, but you have to stop them. I don't know what they're doing, but I know it ain't right, and I don't like it."

"Last question, the explosion at the Paramus lab, do you know anything about it?" Kashif asked hopefully.

"The Paramus lab explosion? No, I have no idea."

"Well, besides the lab explosion, I think I got my answers. I'm going back," he said to Samir as he hopped onto his bike and started to ride toward their lab. Unmasked under his helmet, he rode off in his thobe as Kashif and Samir were still trying to make sense of it all.

"How could Fares be involved in this?" Samir wondered, sounding hurt.

Fares, Samir, and Kashif had been childhood friends who had grown apart in the last few years. To see Fares involved with the wrong crowd and in the wrong business hurt both of them.

Kashif broke the silence by saying, "What can we do? We're not exactly kids where I can go tell his parents. It'll hurt them too much. Plus, the way Zara turned out, it's too surprising. I don't think she has any idea how bad it is."

He rode onto Broad Street, one of the busiest and liveliest streets in the city. Broad Street was where all the action happened: the fanciest restaurants, priciest stores, performance theater, and enough street performers that always kept the street bustling with life, even late at night. He pulled up at a red light, still in mid-conversation, when he heard the commotion. Loud screams and yells were heard a block up ahead as people ran frantically away. Kashif slowly made his way toward the end of the block to see. "What's going on?"

"Run!" yelled a woman that ran past him. "There are gunmen in Koenig's Restaurant!" People were scattering to safety. Gunshots and screams were heard inside the restaurant.

Kashif parked his bike behind the block, and while getting off the bike, he pressed the button to release his face mask but suddenly stopped. The mask did not retract. He pressed the button again and again, but nothing happened. More gunshots and screaming erupted from Koenig's as Kashif pressed the button even harder.

"Samir, the facemask isn't working!" He shouted in panic under his helmet.

"I'm not sure why. Let me try from here," Samir replied quickly. "Try now."

"It's still not working! Hurry, man!"

"I don't know what's wrong, but you can't go in there without your mask, obviously, so just come back to the lab and let the police handle it."

Kashif turned to the restaurant as louder screams and gunshots broke out. "I can't do that!" With that, he ran toward the restaurant.

"Kashif, turn back! It's too dangerous! And the face shield!"

But Kashif had already made up his mind as he ran to the front of the restaurant with his helmet covering his head and face.

Bending down to look inside the front window through the glass into the restaurant, Kashif saw men in black suits holding guns in the air. "They're about 50 people in there," Samir noted, scanning the restaurant.

"Fifty hostages," Kashif growled.

"Kash, listen to me. This is way too dangerous. You're going to get caught or worse…"

"I can't just sit around and not do anything…"

Peering through the window glass, one of the gunmen held a man in a chokehold while pointing the barrel of his gun at his head. He could make out only a few words as he heard someone counting down. Without thinking, he stood up, took a few steps back, and ran at the glass.

"I won't!"

An elderly man screamed at the gunman wearing a ski mask, black suit, and black tie, holding out his hand and demanding his phone.

"Let's go, Grandpa. Everyone, hand over your phones *now!*" He repeated more sternly. When the defiant older man refused a second time, the gunman hit him in the head with the bottom of his gun, knocking him out cold. Screams of anguish from the other hostages filled the restaurant. Three other gunmen went around to the others, grabbing their phones.

"I don't think you all understand what's happening here," the leader of the men screamed at the hostages, strolling past them. *"Jauveria Rashid,* you tell us where she is, and we leave you all alone to enjoy your fine dinner. But the longer you make us wait, people are going to get hurt. Now, *where is she?!"* he shouted.

When none of the scared people responded, he looked around and grabbed a frightened man, putting him into a rear-naked chokehold. "Maybe this will help you all remember." With his other arm, he pointed his gun at the man's head.

"No, please!" people shouted.

"Someone start talking! We don't have all day; I'm giving you all three seconds! Someone better start talking! Three... two... one..."

CRASH.

The large front glass window shattered into pieces as a person in a thobe and motorcycle helmet burst through the front of the restaurant and landed on the thug holding the hostage. Kashif knocked him unconscious. The rest of the gunmen started shooting at the intruder as he ducked behind a table for safety. Bullets tore through the table and hit the man in his thobe and metal suit underneath, causing a metallic sound as they ricocheted off. The guests continued to scream in disbelief and horror as the shooting continued nonstop for a full minute. Glasses broke, and plates shattered. The gunmen finally stopped shooting as the restaurant went quiet. The only sound was that of glass crunching under one gunman's boots as he slowly and carefully went behind the table to look at the outcome of their target, only to find no one was there.

"He's gone!" the man shouted as he looked back, suddenly noticing the helmeted man jump from behind another table, clenching his fist and then punching two men across the restaurant. They crumpled to the ground, out cold. The masked man walked toward the last gunman, who panicked and started firing away. Kashif ran to his side and jumped into the air as his helmet flew off. He clenched his fists twice and landed with his fist first into the man's jaw, knocking him out.

"Your helmet!" Samir shouted as Kashif turned around. He faced the crowd, who stared at him in shock and awe. Breathing heavily, he felt his face as the face shield had enclosed, covering his face. Kashif heard Samir sigh in relief. Nobody in the restaurant moved as they continued to stare at this masked man, who took out five armed thugs in a matter of minutes. There was a moment of quiet as the crowd continued to stare in shock; some had their phones out, recording the whole thing.

"It's okay," Kashif said, raising both his hands, "you're all safe." The silence was broken by police sirens as police officers came running into the restaurant with guns drawn.

"Freeze! Hands up!" they shouted at Kashif, who casually put his hands up and responded, "It's okay; everyone's safe."

"On the ground! I won't ask again!" Another officer shouted with his gun out, pointed directly at Kashif.

"Woah, Woah! I'm not the bad guy!" Kashif pleaded with raised hands, retreating toward an exit.

"Stop moving! On the ground!" Another shouted as Kashif continued to move back. Then, one officer shot at Kashif, causing the bullet to ricochet off.

"Hey, Officer, *I'm not* the bad guy!" Before he knew it, he found himself surrounded by officers with guns drawn. "On the ground!"

"He saved us!" a woman in the restaurant spoke up.

"Yeah, I have it all on video," another man said.

But the police continued circling closer. Kashif stood frozen in shock as only a loud "Get out of there!" rang through his earpiece, causing him to move, push three officers back and punch another one before he ran to the back of the restaurant and into the kitchen.

He heard officers chasing him as he kicked open the back door, hopped onto his bike, and rode off. He heard shouts and screams behind him, but he knew they wouldn't catch up to him.

"Why didn't they listen to me?" Kashif asked, back at the lab, a clear hurt in his voice. Samir tended to the wounds on Kashif's arms as some of the bullets had penetrated through the suit and bruised Kashif's arm.

"Not every day, a man in a full-body metal suit is seen, especially at a crime scene," Samir said, applying bandages to his wounds. "They didn't know," he answered. The TV was on as the news reported the incident.

"Shocking news coming from one of the busiest restaurants in RP City as gunmen stormed into Koenig's Restraurant and held the patrons hostage," the TV anchor reported. "But what followed next was even *more shocking.* Let's go down to Saimah Arshad, who's at the scene for the live report." The screen went live outside the restaurant as news reporter Saimah interviewed the witnesses at the scene.

"We were inside, and they came in, shooting, talking about looking for a woman named Jauveria Rashid," one man said quickly, wide-eyed. "Then this…this… *man* in a black thobe just burst through the glass and started fighting them."

"I don't think the bullets affected him," another woman said into the mic. "But he hid behind a table and then just appeared out from behind another one, and he punched two of them, and they went flying back. It was unbelievable, I couldn't believe my eyes!" She said, still in shock.

"I was so scared. Who was he?! What did he want?! Who dresses like that and does that?!" the next woman shouted in horror.

"The police didn't give him a chance to talk," another man said. "They just came running up and fired at him. But he saved us, this… *metal man!* He moved so quickly, and he just… like, disappeared afterward, like… a ghost!" he screamed into the mic.

"Well, there you have it," said Reporter Saimah Arshad, looking directly into the camera. "Unbelievable accounts of a masked man in some form of metal suit crashed in and, according to these witnesses, saved them and disappeared like a ghost. Police have commented that there is a lookout for this man. They are warning everyone that he is *armed and dangerous* and asking anyone in the city to contact them if they have any information about him. They are speculating he could be an ally of the known criminal, Laser. Right now, we're waiting for the police chief to arrive and tell us more, and I'm going to be right here to find out. For now, back to you," Saimah finished.

"I can't believe it," Kashif sighed, annoyed at the news report.

"I know, they called the thobe *black*," Samir responded. "Did it look black in the light?" he quipped.

Kashif gave him a serious look. "Armed and dangerous," he repeated after the news anchor.

"Well, at least you had some witnesses," Samir responded with a sigh of relief. "Let's lay low for a while. In the meantime, this suit needs a lot of work, starting with the face shield," he said, putting on his lab goggles and getting to work on it.

"Yeah, right now, my arm is in danger of falling off," he winced in pain. "But who's Laser?" Kashif asked, turning to X-Bot.

CHAPTER SIXTEEN

THIS IS GOING TO CONSUME YOU

What happened to your arm?" a concerned Aliya asked the next day, touching the bandages around his forearm in the lab.

"Ah, this? It's nothing, really. You know, it happens during rounds… in Brazilian ju jitsu," Kashif responded casually, trying not to lie. "How was Hiba's graduation speech? I bet she did great," he asked excitedly, trying to change the topic.

But Aliya knew him better than he knew himself sometimes. She stared deep into his light brown eyes like she did when she knew his thoughts. There are some people who can look you in your eyes but see through to your soul. She knew. She had a way of knowing him so well, which sometimes surprised Kashif. She continued to stare at him, with her face and eyes full of worry, waiting for him to speak, to answer her. Turning away and not meeting her eyes, Kashif walked toward his desk in the lab where she had come to see him.

The silence between them now was palpable and loud.

"I know it was you," she finally stated in a low, upset voice. "At the restaurant. In the thobe and that suit. *The one they're talking about, the one the police are looking for,*" she emphasized the last part. "I've seen that suit here. What are you doing, Kash?"

He finally turned to her with a defeated face. There was no point in hiding anything, he thought. "Finding answers," he said finally. "I have to get to the bottom of this, Alz." Then finally, meeting her eyes, he said seriously, "Whatever it takes."

"By putting on a mask and beating up people?!" She almost

screamed. "What are you doing? Look at yourself. I knew you were up to something. That's why you've been missing my calls and have been so tired and just so… absent-minded. Look at me," she said as he turned away, resting his weight on the table. "You're going to get hurt! Is that what you want? Look at yourself," she pleaded.

"Alz, I'm fine. And I'm making progress. I want to, no, I *need* to find out who did this, who's behind the lab explosion. There's something more going on, and I'm going to find out who is responsible. And I feel like I'm close. Once I do, I'm done. I promise."

She continued to stare at him in disbelief, her eyes becoming watery. "I know you, Kashif Razvi," she said calmly after composing herself. "And I know where this is going. This is going to *consume* you. You're going to get in so deep that you won't be able to get out. Even if you want to, I fear you won't be able to." She was almost crying. "You know if you don't stop now, you will only spiral down deeper and deeper. This metal suit which I know you have here, is not an answer. It is not a way out of your grief. This is the door to more pain, to trouble." Kashif continued to look down, digesting each of her words as if it were a bitter pill that needed to be taken. She was right; he knew that.

"And what about us?" she pleaded, stepping closer. "How are we supposed to go on while you're into this?"

"Is that what you're worried about? I'm not going anywhere, Alz." His voice sounded angrier than he wanted to show. "I'm not married to this," he tried to soften, "I'm going to marry you. But I need time, okay?"

"You're going to get hurt."

"I'm fine, and I *will be* fine. Bullets can't even harm this suit," he said. She folded her arms while studying his arm, a look that pierced him harder than any words she could have said.

"Look, I need to do this. And afterward… it'll be fine. Now, please, let me get to my work," he said with finality, still tired and unsure if he found the right words. Aliya was disappointed, he knew. She gave him a look of disapproval as she shook her head and started for the door with her arms crossed.

"Wait for me," he said finally to her as she reached the door. "Please."

She turned around to look at him with sadness in her eyes. After a moment, she gave a slight nod and left.

"Robbery, stabbing, *arson,*" Samir emphatically read the last part a few days later after researching everything he could on Laser. "Even arson. Our guy has been busy."

"So, every violent crime you can think of, this guy is capable of," Kashif responded, sitting in front of X-bot.

"And he's connected to almost every gang in the city," Samir added, showing him clippings of articles connecting him to different crimes. The numerous articles on him did not leave room for error: Laser was a known felon, a dangerous man, and, even more unnerving, currently a free man. He was broad-shouldered, had a face with sharp features and a broad smile, with red wavy hair which was almost shaped like a lightning bolt, Kashif thought.

"And look at this, who he has plenty of photos and links with." Samir pointed to the screen. "None other than Iris Hill."

"We all know it's not just rumors. Under the table, Iris Hill funds these gangs, who do the dirty work for him. I feel Iris Hill is definitely involved with the lab explosion. But getting to Iris Hill seems impossible; he's rarely ever seen in public, and getting to him would make a lot of noise. But Laser, now maybe that's more plausible," Kashif said, staring at his picture on the screen. "And Carson, he's not innocent, obviously. I know he's involved too."

"Involved maybe, but a mystery man for sure," Samir said, rubbing his chin and beard. "There doesn't seem to be any record of him anywhere." He turned to Kashif. "It's like he doesn't exist."

"We'll find him," Kashif responded. "It was his lab; he knows what happened and what's been going on there."

"In the meantime, there's something I wanted to ask you," Samir turned to Kashif. He cleared his throat and paused. "I've added some major enhancements to the suit that I want to show you, but I can't help but feel we can really take this suit to another level."

"Oh? How?"

Samir looked up at Kashif nervously, already anticipating his answer, "adding a team member: Nathan. He..."

"No, no way," Kashif interjected, shaking his head at the

thought of bringing in their colleague and close friend from Al-Fihriya University.

Samir let out a sigh. "I knew you would say that but hear me out. Nathan is a genius. He's quite possibly the best mind in engineering and robotics that I have ever met. Both him and me putting our heads together, we could create something that would make you unstoppable."

"Samir, we cannot bring Nathan into this. It's too dangerous." He looked Samir in the eyes, "I do not want to get more people involved in this and endanger their lives," he added with finality.

"Fine, fine," Samir raised his hands in defeat. "It's just, I'm already using some of his ideas and work already, I thought he could help. But you're right."

"How are you using his work?" Kashif inquired.

Samir smiled, getting up from his chair, "I've worked out how you can stay safe while getting shot at."

"I wasn't planning on getting shot again," Kashif nervously responded. "But of course, if there's anyone who's going to shoot me next, it would be you." Samir gave him a satisfied smile, leading him to his work table where the suit lay. After putting it on, Samir took more bricks out of his drawers.

"Not bricks again," Kashif moaned. "You know you can start your own construction company with all those."

Dismissing his comment, "I actually never told you what I've been working on. Stand over there, away from the table. I'm going to throw this brick at you," Samir said.

"Of course," Kashif muttered under his breath as he stood on the spot Samir asked him to stand on.

"This suit is nanotechnology. It will adapt and learn your movements and instincts. I've updated it so that if it senses any sort of object shooting toward the suit, you can block it. All you have to do is raise your left forearm. So, get ready."

Before Kashif could ask any questions, he found a brick heading directly at him. His reflexes kicked in; he raised his left forearm and closed his eyes while turning away, anticipating the brick would hit him. To his surprise, no brick hit him. When he opened his eyes, in front of him was a blue gel-like material protruding out of the suit, covering his front body as a shield. The brick had hit the shield and dropped to the ground.

"Woah!" Kashif touched the gel shield with his other arm. It felt soft, absorbing his hand as he pressed into it. He moved his left forearm, and the shield moved with it.

"It's a highly eccentric material," Samir said, walking toward him. Kashif put all his fingers through the gel material before pulling it out. "But that's not all it can do. This material absorbs friction and heat, so if an object hits it at high speed, the gel will essentially catch it and absorb it. After that, it can fire back any object with the same speed it came in with. So, any bullet would get caught in this gel, and at your command..."

"I could fire it back?" Kashif wondered, finishing his sentence.

"Exactly," a proud Samir said, walking back. "Now, let me go get my gun and shoot at you," he called back, exiting the room.

A moment later, Kashif's head sprang up, "Wait, what?!" He yelled after him, not sure if he was joking or not.

CHAPTER SEVENTEEN

CHANGES

O h, I can't even see," an annoyed Ms. Johnson peered closer, struggling to put the key in the door to lock it but not finding the keyhole in the dark of the night. "We need to fix that dang light over this front door, boys," she called out to her two 10-year-old twin boys, Isiah and Joseph, who had already gone out. "Boys! Wait for me, don't go running off, you hear me?!"

"We're right here, Ma," Joseph called out from the front steps.

"There's so much fog I can't even see you," she said, turning to them, finally locking the door. "Where's Isiah?"

"He just went a little ahead, but I see him right there," Joseph pointed down the street.

"Isiah! I don't see you. What did we talk about?!" Ms. Johnson yelled out into the fog, unable to see her son.

"I'm right here. I can see you, don't worry," Isiah called back. She could hear his footsteps skipping around the sidewalk.

Shuffling to put her keys in her bag while walking out onto the street, in an instant, she stopped hearing his skipping and heard other footsteps quickly approaching.

"Hey, get off of me! Ma!" Isiah yelled in sheer fear.

"Isiah!" she screamed in panic as she and Joseph ran to his voice.

"Hold him good, get him here," a man's harsh voice called to another as Isiah continued screaming. "Quick, quick, go go go!" The voices whispered to each other.

"Get off of him!" Joseph pushed one of the men who Ms. Johnson could barely make out in the dark and through the fog. She heard a loud smack as Joseph landed backward on the ground to her feet.

"Isiah! Isiah!" she shrieked, running toward the voices. She swung her bag blindly into the fog, hitting something. She heard a gunshot but kept swinging in panic. Her frightening dread grew as she did not hear the sound of her son any longer. She only heard tires screeching away and her own voice screaming at the top of her lungs.

"Isiah! Isiah!" She continued to shriek as she felt herself fall to the ground, and her world went even hazier and darker. Soon after, the only thing she remembered was Joseph and some of the neighbors trying to wake her up as she lay on the ground.

Ridgefield Park City was a bubbling metropolis established a century ago on the banks of the Firdaus River as a fishing and shipping dock. Over the decades, what started as a small town grew into a heavily populated city full of life and business. And crime. Crime, especially in the past few years, had started to skyrocket in Ridgefield Park City. Small gangs had begun to form, eventually turning into bigger organizations. The biggest crime mob, known as Manderlay, had all but entangled with every aspect of the city. They had gained a presence in hospitals, businesses, banks, the only bar in the city, and even the police force. Worst of all, the rise and success of the Manderlay gang caused offshoots of other gangs. It was all but known that Manderlay and their associates had infiltrated the police force, so their run of the city was all but unchecked for the past few years. From unreported crimes to overlooking criminal activity, intimidating judges, and light sentences if there was even a conviction, RP City residents were fed up with the police force and the gangs. And the recent kidnapping of elderly neighborhood resident Ms. Ruby Johnson's son a couple of months ago, right in front of her home, seemed to be the final straw for many of the residents, who had had enough.

But in the past six months, there was finally a response, an unexpected one, but something that seemed to be an answer to the crime. The mobs were having their plans broken apart, criminals attacked, and crimes stopped. The city had started to get turned upside down, all due to one man.

Kashif walked to his building on a cool afternoon after *Dhuhr* prayer in the masjid, six months after the restaurant incident. This was Kashif's favorite weather: dark, cloudy, and slightly windy. What started as a slow walk turned into a brisk jog as he could feel the clouds rumbling and a downpour approaching. Hurrying around the corner on the sidewalk, he noticed a sign posted outside on the pole, making him stop.

Wanted: For disruption and disorderly behavior, altercation with law officials, impeding crime scenes, and vigilantism. A large reward is offered for any information on the vigilante.

The picture attached was one that a bystander had taken soon after the restaurant incident when Kashif, in his suit, stopped a grocery store robbery.

Hmm, he looked at the wanted poster, unsure how to feel. As he stared at the poster for a moment before heading upstairs, a sense of sadness and guilt started to bubble up inside him. In the past few months, he had tried to but had not kept his promise to Aliya, that of stopping from suiting up and finding reasons to fight. "I don't want to continue," he had told Samir. "But what am I supposed to do if a robbery or burglary is happening? Just wait for someone to get hurt before the cops show up? And even then, what justice have we seen the cops do?"

"If you can help, then yeah, I guess you should. But every single time?" Samir had asked.

"Wouldn't that be the right thing to do?"

Unsure of what to say, Samir found himself aiding Kashif again and again as he continued to suit up. X-bot helped them hack the police radio, allowing them to hear all the police chatter and calls for help. Before the police could show up, Kashif, in full suit, had started arriving at the crime scenes. Instead of relying on the police to try to apprehend and put criminals in jail, Kashif was leaving them tied up in front of the police station for everyone to see. It became a show for the whole city, as photographers, journalists, and TV reporters were always there to report the criminals on the front steps of the police precinct. But this was a problem for RP City's police force: not only was someone doing their job, but they could also no longer have any excuse to let these criminals walk. And so it had begun, as Aliya had warned Kashif about how he would descend deeper and deeper. What had started as stopping crime soon became suiting up and *waiting* for something to happen. And, of course, this was causing frequent run-ins with the police, reporters, and civilians. The city was ablaze by his vigilantism. In return, the media could not get enough of him. News segments and newspaper and magazine articles were dedicated to him. The city, however, was divided on his vigilante behavior, with some in the news and media praising him while others condemned him.

"What we're seeing with this masked man is what happens when people distrust the police and when they see justice not being served. The government and police forget that their service is to the people," a social commentator debated on the most popular talk show in the city, *Jasmine Live in the City,* hosted by popular young journalist Jasmine Amjad.

"The law cannot be taken by any civilian," the other panelist counter-argued. "What he is doing is giving rise to lawlessness, which will be the fall of this entire society. Why do we give him a pass? Let him work *with* the police!"

Despite catching criminals, deep inside, however, Kashif was starting to feel guilty for breaking the law himself, but more than anything, he had grown distant and farther from Aliya. She had been right, he thought; he was starting to sink in too deep. He missed her company, their conversations, the life they had planned together before the suit. On the other hand, he also felt a sense of motivation every time he thought of Abu. The longer he continued, the more this internal battle inside him raged.

As he continued his way upstairs, he stopped at the door, knowing Samir was there and working on his suit. Some new enhancement awaited him, but the idea of a new gadget or feature didn't excite him this time. For the first time, he felt dread opening the door. *I don't want to do this anymore.* He hadn't seen or talked to Aliya in almost a week and knew his heart was missing her. *How can I go so long without even talking to her?* he thought. He turned around, pulled up his hoodie as the rain had started to pour, and decided that he needed to see her.

When he reached her house, her abu opened the door.

"Asalaamu alaikum, Baita," he said, opening the door. The

usual wide smile and warm look he was used to was no longer there. Instead, there was a look of apprehension.

"Waalaikum asalaam, Uncle. I'm here to see Aliya. I know it's been a little while, but I wanted to surprise her."

"Oh, she went out… to go see you actually, at your place," her abu spoke hesitantly. "But you're here… I guess she didn't tell you?"

"Oh, no. She didn't tell me anything." He felt almost embarrassed.

Aliya's abu gently placed his hand on Kashif's shoulder, "Baita, I know you have been through a lot having lost your abu, and I care for you because you are like a son to me." His eyes began tearing up. "I know you have been feeling a lot of anger, but don't let the anger consume you. There is a Pakistani proverb that goes, 'People who fight fire with fire end up with ashes.'"

"Thank you, Uncle," Kashif replied, looking down. Kashif could not get out of there fast enough, but something about that Pakistani proverb stuck with him, and he began to wonder if there were any ashes to come.

"Kashif's not here," Samir said, opening the door back at the lab to Aliya. "But come on in if you'd like to wait; I'm not sure where he is actually."

"Yeah, I don't either," she replied, clearly upset under her umbrella. "It's fine. I guess I should have called. Just tell him… um, I have a lot to talk to him about."

As she turned around to walk away, her phone rang; her screen read *Kashif*.

"Hello?" She quickly picked up but couldn't hear or understand what Kashif was saying. "I can't hear you, the connection isn't clear enough… What?" she said, trying to understand his voice amongst all the static. "Your voice isn't clear; there's too much static."

"I'm saying I miss you," Kashif spoke loudly, realizing the heavy rain was causing a disruption in the service.

You was all Aliya had heard before she hung up, frustrated. Kashif quickly jumped on his bike and raced to his apartment, only to find she had been there, but had left after the phone call. The heaviness in his heart was becoming overbearing. There was one other person he could talk to in times like these, so he decided to see his ami.

Ami was never the same after Abu's passing, Kashif knew. Once a funny, energetic, and positive person, she had become a shell of herself. She stopped going out, turned off her phone, and spent most of her days quietly at home, reciting Qur'an and du'as.

"Asalaamu alaikum, Ami," he called loudly, as was his habit when entering the house. Closing the front door, he took off his shoes and sensed the quiet in the house; it seemed no one was home. Heading upstairs, something caught his eye about the house that made him pause, a feature he had never noticed before. Ami was a caretaker to her core: her parents, children, family, husband, house, plants, and her community; she dedicated her every waking hour to caring for those around her. "You care for everyone except yourself." Kashif had to remind her to eat, sleep, and rest properly. With the passing of Abu, however, her whole life turned upside down, and she had lost that sense of care. Climbing up the stairs, Kashif noticed the plants were not their usual lively selves and hadn't been watered in some time. He sighed, upset at the turn of events, and continued walking upstairs.

Ami was home alone, sitting in her bed reading the Qur'an. "Waalaikum asalaam, Baita, where have you been?" She smiled, patting the back of his head as he sat down. Even though she didn't mean them maliciously, the words felt like a crushing blow, taking the air out of his lungs. *Where had he been?*

"I know; I'm sorry, Ami," he looked down. "Where's Yasmine, is she not home?"

"Your sister just went out for a while," his mother's eyes were on him with a warm smile, studying his tired and nervous appearance.

Ami had stopped wearing makeup and dyeing her hair since Abu passed, and a patch of white hair had grown on her head. It was the first time Kashif noticed her whites.

"Ami, you haven't watered the plants in some time. What's going on?"

She sighed, looking away. "I know, I've been absent-minded of late. But they were dying anyway. Just like we all are, we all have to go one day."

"Don't talk like that, Ami," he said, upset. He had never heard his mother speak in such a defeated manner before.

"Baita, when you lose someone at this age, it changes you in a way you can never imagine: you lose a big part of your *own* self." She gently put her hand on his face, and he could feel the tears welling up behind his eyes. "You get used to a way of life and a routine. I would wake with your father and pray the morning prayer with him. We'd sit and read Qur'an together. Have breakfast, go for a walk, work on our garden, go out, and spend the days together. That was the life that your father and I took years to build together. That was not just my routine but my happiness. Now... it's hard to find a new routine. I can never replicate that happiness in this life. It makes you lose balance as you try to find a new routine. It's the hardest thing, but I guess it will take time. And the plants will find time in the new routine. I hope so anyway." She gave him a wounded smile.

Kashif's heart was breaking into pieces listening to her, watching what she was turning into. And how he hadn't been with her, taking care of her. He felt the guilt drowning him. Sitting next to her as she lay in her bed, holding her hands, he noticed how frail and old her hands and she, herself, were starting to look. This was a new hurt.

"I'm sorry I haven't been here much, Ami," he lamented sorrowfully, the tears starting to blur his vision. His heart was already crying. "I should be *here,* I know." He couldn't help holding back the tears as they slowly rolled down his cheek.

"Where have you been?" she asked softly, wiping his cheek dry.

Taking a deep breath, he hadn't planned anything to say, but at that moment, he just let the words come: "I have to tell you something." His voice broke, looking down. "I've been selfish, doing selfish things. I don't even know how to explain it," he stammered.

"You don't have to. It's okay."

"No, you don't know, you... can't even imagine."

"I know where you've been and what you've been doing. I hear about it whenever the TV is on. And whenever someone comes to visit, it's all the other aunties talk about," she said with a warm, knowing smile.

"What?!" How parents know these things, he'll never understand. *You'll know when you have kids,* as goes the famous Pakistani parents' answers.

"How... do you know?"

She clicked her tongue, "You don't think I know *my boy* when I see him on TV?" She waved her hand. "A mask isn't going to hide you from me."

He stared at her, speechless.

"Don't worry, I haven't told anyone." She winked.

"I... I don't know what to say. You've known, but you didn't say anything?"

"Why do you do it?" She asked, genuinely curious.

His voice and face hardened. "I had to find out about the lab and who was behind it. Who caused the outage? I needed to know who was responsible for what happened to Abu. But then... it started to take a turn and take a life of its own. It began to become almost... an obsession. It feels good going out, fighting. It began as an outlet for my anger. Then, it just became all about me. I've forgotten about others. And I don't want that; I'm losing control."

"You might think it's about you, but you seem to be helping people," she responded after a moment.

"It's not about them, though."

"When you save a person, whether you want to or not, despite your intentions when you help them, it becomes about them, too."

Kashif stared into space, absorbing the words.

"Sometimes I wish I could just... take out my anger, hurt, sadness like you do. If I were you, I might also do the same thing," she said, turning his face toward hers.

"Ami, no," he said, his voice wavering. "You don't want to do this. This... is not the right way; I know that now."

"I know. Qur'an helps, and so does du'a. Something you need to do more of. Pray more, Baita."

"You're right."

"But I am secretly proud," she continued. "I worry about your safety, of course, but I think you are helping people." Kashif was speechless. He wasn't prepared for this conversation, nor did he expect this reaction.

"And you should hear what the other aunties say," she laughed.

"What?" He asked worriedly.

"They are so intrigued; it's all they talk about. *They think you're a jinn,*" she laughed. "But I know when I see my boy. Flesh and bones. Mask or no mask."

When she noticed Kashif's worried face, she changed her tone. "How long will you do this for, Baita? I can't lose you too."

"You won't, Ami. I... I have to find out who did this to Abu. Who did this to us."

"And? Have you?" She inquired.

"I'm close, I know it. And when I do, I'll get answers. *We* will, and we'll get some closure, I promise."

Ami didn't answer with words; her eyes spoke in a way only a mother could. *I'm worried, be careful,* they said.

"But it's getting out of hand. It's... consuming me," he said, remembering Aliya's words.

"I know, Baita. But you don't want to do this for too long," she said weakly. "Because what's the point if you're losing yourself and your future wife over it?" She said, surprising him as he looked up. "We will all go through tests in life, but we have to decide if those moments of pain and hardships will break us or define us. Elevate us or cause us to sink. Is this elevating you, making you better?"

He felt paralyzed, sitting still while listening.

"Maybe you're right, I won't lose you, but you're losing Aliya. You have to ask yourself: are you gaining more than what you're losing?"

"I haven't lost her," he said, feeling a chill run through his body.

"Aliya's been talking to me, and she's very worried. How much longer are you going to keep her waiting, keep her guessing? Do you think it's fair to her?"

"She knows how I feel and what I'm doing. I told her to wait for me," he tried explaining, not believing his own words now.

"She loves you, but she can't wait forever. Neither can her family. Talk to her," Ami said reasonably.

"What do I do, Ami? How do I make the right choice?"

"Pray, ask Allah. Pray *Salatul Istikhara;* it's the best form of prayer when we need guidance and answers. That's what it's there for, after all. Go, pray it right now." Kashif nodded and went to pray.

The belief is that Salatul Istikhara is the prayer for guidance, to be shown the right path. It is meant to be prayed when a person is in between two choices, unsure of which choice to make, so they ask God for clarity on what to do and which path to take. The answer can come in different ways, sometimes in a dream, sometimes in a calm and comforting feeling in the heart, along with clearing the way toward one answer.

He left Ami more unsure, carrying a heavier heart than he entered with. "Trust Allah and pray. He'll guide you, you'll see." Those were Ami's final words before he left.

For the next couple of days, he felt ashamed to call Aliya after not speaking to her in some time. And with each day passing, he grew more and more remorseful. But he wanted a clear answer from his istikhara. The following few days also fully indulged Kashif with new information on local gangs. It seemed that Samir dug up new information on the gangs' movements and activities each day, causing Kashif to focus on them. His personal life weighing heavy on his mind and heart, Kashif felt he was going out at night begrudgingly. His heart wasn't in it. His heart yearned for his old life, for his partner. He returned back to the lab two nights later, having made up his mind: the answer to his istikhara was Aliya. "I'm done, Samir," he proclaimed, throwing the suit on the table and walking away. "I choose her. And I'm going to tell her."

"But what about all our work? And the suit?"

"You can burn the suit for all I care," he called back, closing the door behind him, vowing never to return.

CHAPTER EIGHTEEN

ASHES

The weight was lifted, he sighed in relief the following morning. He called Aliya, but it went straight to voicemail, and his messages were not responded to. *She's angry with me, which is understandable. But I'm going to make it right.* And he knew how.

"This is exactly the one she wants," he said happily to the jeweler, having picked out the wedding band and ring he had promised her.

His heart felt light for the first time in months, and for the first time since his father had passed, he had a sense of peace and happiness. He tried calling Aliya again, but after another set of no responses, he decided to go to her house and tell her the good news with the ring: that he had chosen her. Vigilantism was in the past. Her love was their future.

Riding up to her block, there were a noticeable amount of cars than usual, parked on the street. He slowly rode toward her house, and at the corner of the block, he noticed her family had gathered in their front yard and porch. Everyone from her family was present, dressed in their best clothes, along with people he did not recognize. *Wedding clothes?* Kashif sat on his bike at the end of the block, out of their sight. But he had a complete view. The crowd of people was moving about, some hugging, some lining up next to a car. As people cleared his view, he noticed a car with "Just Married" written on the back. With his heart starting to beat faster, he got off the bike and moved closer, standing behind a tree a street away, watching in confusion. Every inch of his body froze when the front door opened, and Aliya exited the house. She was wearing a wedding dress, with another man walking beside her. The man was smiling and shaking others' hands, but Aliya had no smile on her face. She was staring downward, looking somber. Her parents came forward, and she hugged them and started crying. He could see her father holding her tightly while talking into her ear. After a moment, she began to smile and nod, although still emotional and crying. Kashif felt as if his heart had stopped beating. After her parents, Aliya stepped forward to meet her siblings, who had all lined up. Hugging each, one by one, she finally came to her last sibling as she bent down to hug Zainab. Little Zainab was crying and fighting off Aliya's attempt to hug her.

Kashif couldn't make out what Zainab was saying, but she made the sign for "I love you" with her fingers in sign language that he had taught her, and both sisters burst out crying as they hugged each other. After a long hug, Aliya stood up, and her parents opened the car's back door for her and the other man. When they were both inside, her father closed the door. Slowly, the car took off. The family waved goodbye as the car turned a corner to the next street. Kashif ran the opposite way towards the adjacent street where he would be able to intercept the car. He needed to stop this. He needed to talk to Aliya. But by the time he reached the other street, the car had already passed him.

He ran behind the car in the middle of the street. He screamed her name at the top of his lungs.

"Aliya!" He cried out loud. "Aliya, stop!"

The car kept driving down the road, and he kept running desperately after it, calling her name. But the car did not stop. He ran, and ran, and ran...

A block later, he began running out of breath as the car continued.

"Aliya!" he yelled while running. He realized he was crying, but the tears were drying up on his face as he ran.

"Aliya! NO!" He sobbed while yelling.

She didn't hear him.

"Ya, Allah! Oh, God!" He cried out loud.

As the car started to pull away, his crying turned into wheezing and severe shortness of breath. His chest tightened painfully. Each breath he took burned his throat and lungs. He stopped running and bent down, panting heavily. His world started to spin and go black. He felt he couldn't breathe anymore, and the lack of air blurred his sight. Everything around him was going dark as he fell to his knees in the middle of the street. He felt himself hit the ground, knocking the little wind left in him. His chest continued to tighten, each breath becoming more and more painful than the next. He didn't realize he was having a panic attack.

"Ya, Allah! Ya, Allah! No! Ya, Allah, no!" was all he could say.

As he lay collapsed in the middle of the street, the world around him began to go dark. The last thing he remembered seeing was the ring in the box that had fallen right in front of him, and the only words he could utter were, "Ya Allah, ya Allah."

CHAPTER NINETEEN

THE HIT

Everyone in the family had huddled together in the family room in front of the TV, with Kashif's brother, sister, their spouses, and kids all present, quietly and nervously chatting away. Kashif was the sole person standing, with no one talking to, looking at, or paying him any attention. As the TV turned on, the room quieted down, and everyone raised their cupped hands together and lowered their heads in prayer. The imam came on the screen and somberly started reciting du'a, a prayer, for the recently deceased. "We pray for the forgiveness of our beloved brother, who was always troubled but never showed it. We ask Allah for his forgiveness, grant him an easy life in the grave, and grant him Jannahtul Firdous- the highest level of Heaven."

Kashif didn't know who the deceased was, but he prayed along. He closed his eyes as the imam continued the prayer but suddenly stopped. Opening his eyes, Kashif looked up at his family; strangely, everyone stared at him.

"What are you doing here?" his sister, Yasmine, demanded.

"You shouldn't be here," his brother Shahid said coldly.

"You killed them," said his young nieces together, staring blankly at him.

"What?" was all Kashif could utter, shooting up to his feet in shock.

The imam continued on-screen, "We pray for him, even though he killed his father and his wife, Aliya. May Allah forgive him for what he did." This time, the imam on the screen looked directly at him with clear anger on his face.

"No!" Kashif yelled, rushing out of the room to the front door. As he opened the door, Abu and Aliya were standing on the steps staring at him, shaking their heads in disappointment.

Kashif woke up with a scream, soaked in sweat. His nightmares had gotten worse. He couldn't take it anymore. As he sat there in bed, he broke down and cried helplessly.

Why is this happening? He thought. *I can't do this anymore.*

The following week was a blur.

Blood pressure through the roof... you need to take care of yourself... take these medications...

Kashif, are you even listening? You've disappointed us... missed deadlines... pack your stuff... Fired! He's not there... Pray for him.

Different voices from random conversations, parts of events, and nightmares that felt more real than reality, Kashif couldn't explain anything or remember most things concretely about his surroundings.

It had been a week since Aliya had gotten married and moved out, during which Kashif had not only lost her, but the crushing sorrow left him paralyzed mentally, emotionally, and physically. As a result, he was fired from his work for missing days and deadlines. With his life suddenly falling apart, he fell into a deep depression. Not eating, sleeping, and being unable and unwilling to leave his house, the downward spiral seemed to have no end.

"You have to eat Baita," Ami pleaded. She had been staying with him since Aliya left, and he fell apart. "Kashif, your sister has been bringing you food, but you haven't touched any of it. Are you listening?" He barely heard while curled up in bed, facing the wall.

"Hey Buddy, you okay?" He remembered Samir whispering to him one day. When Kashif didn't move or respond, Samir gave Ami a defeated look but assured her, "It's okay, Aunty, he just needs time." She looked on remorsefully, watching her son's heart break before her own eyes.

A loneliness that was crushing. How could reality feel like a nightmare? How is it that the clock is ticking, but time stands still? How can I have everyone around me yet still feel so alone? Why does breathing take energy and hurt with each breath? The loneliness, the depression, the confusion, and the guilt was all taking a toll on Kashif. He found himself unable to think straight or sleep. When he did, his nightmares woke him up, and he did so, screaming, only with the sinking realization that reality was worse than the nightmares. To say he loved Aliya was an understatement. What was his life like without her? She was the only one who understood him, the only one who really saw who he was and still loved him despite his flaws—the only one who could lighten up his life just by being there.

But how could she just leave like that?

Without saying anything?

Without telling me, without even talking to me, without an explanation that there was someone else?

I had asked her to wait.

She knew I loved her.

Maybe her family pressured her into the marriage?

Maybe she didn't really love the other guy. Maybe she still loved me more.

Maybe she'll come back. Or maybe I'll never see her again.

The growing amount of thoughts, doubts, and questions in Kashif's head and heart caused a black cloud over him. That was all he could think about. He chose her, but she didn't even bother telling him she chose someone else?

To add this, on top of losing Abu was a crushing weight. Already grieved by the passing of Abu, suiting up and finding the people responsible had given him a sense of hope and purpose in getting some form of justice. Though, in his heart, he wasn't content or happy with breaking the law, being a vigilante, or fighting, but primarily for having spent so much time away from his family and Aliya. He ruined the one good thing that he had. Both were gone forever.

The following days were all a blur and the same: Kashif lying in bed, too paralyzed to move, heartbroken by his own actions, which pushed Aliya away. As he lay there in bed, soaked in sweat and tears, all he could think about was her. *Where was she? Who was she with? Why did she just leave him?* He felt he had reached his breaking point. Without much thought, he slowly rose from bed and made his way to the balcony. The light rain that had started earlier in the night had turned into a downpour, and Kashif was soaked by the time he reached the edge of the balcony. He looked out into the night, and then down to the street. The night felt cold and windy, the rain bringing a chill. A small voice in the back of his head told him to stand on the ledge. Kashif continued staring blankly at the street below him. He didn't care about the rain or being soaked; he didn't care about anyone seeing him. He didn't care about anything. *I just don't want to feel this anymore.* This pain, this anger, this hurt, it was all too much. The voice came back, but this time he felt a jolt. In a moment of shock, he fully woke up and realized where he was as he could see cars passing by twenty stories below him. Surprising even himself, he didn't panic or take a step back from the edge of the balcony.

As he stood in the pouring rain, he looked out at Ridgefield Park City. The city that had consumed him and kept him away. The city he tried to protect. The city that had taken his most beloved. He'd lost. He let out a primal scream into the night, yelling at the city. When he couldn't yell anymore, his screaming turned into crying. He opened his eyes, the downpour had increased so intensely, it blocked the city from his view. The little voice came back again. *This was the only way to make it all stop. Ya Allah, I can't do this anymore.*

This time, he listened to the voice as it grew louder, telling him to step onto the ledge. Before he could lift his foot, is when he heard it. About half a mile away, a voice chanted, "Allahu akbar, Allahu akbar!" The muadhin called the adhan for prayer from the Masjid into the night in a melodious voice.

"Allahu akbar, Allahu akbar!" *Allah is the Greatest.* Listening to the words, they hit him like a bolt of lightning. The words caused him to remember the meaning of what was being recited: Allahu akbar, Allah is greater than everything. Greater than his problems, his worries, and his life.

"Allahu akbar, Allahu akbar!" The muadhin repeated beautifully, causing a shock down Kashif's entire body. As the adhan continued, Kashif had frozen in place. With his head down, he continued listening.

"Hayalas Salah!" The muadhin continued the adhan into the

night. "Hayalas Salah!" *Come to prayer.*

"Hayalal Falah!*" Come to success.*

"Allahu akbar, Allahu akbar!" *Allah is the Greatest.*

By the time the adhan was over, the night had become quiet again. Kashif remained standing on the ledge, feeling himself breathe heavily, yet a calmness had come over him; it was almost as if he had been sleepwalking and had just woken up. Was this his answer from God? He had always kept up with his daily prayers, but in the last week, he hadn't done much praying or remembering Allah. He hadn't done much of anything except weep and mourn. But for the first time in a week, Kashif was starting to feel something besides pain and anger. For the first time in a week, he felt awake. He *felt.* He felt he needed to go to the masjid to pray and talk to his Creator. Sometimes, God sends us reminders and guidance in our daily moments. He had heard the adhan thousands of times, but it felt like he truly listened now for the first time. As he looked up toward the sky, an ayah from the Qur'an came to his mind: *"Verily, in the remembrance of Allah do hearts find rest."* Was this his answer from Allah? Right as he was sure he was going to jump? Taking a deep breath, finally feeling the rain and cold of the night, he stepped away from the ledge. Without much thought or effort, he dressed and made his way down to make it to the masjid for the early morning Fajr prayer.

CHAPTER TWENTY

IMAM DAWOOD MURPHY

Masjid Mariam, located in the heart of the city, is a beautiful structure reminiscent of the buildings of Cordoba, Spain, with its lush gardens, elegant architecture, beautiful colors, and walls decorated with Qur'anic inscriptions. Anyone viewing the masjid, even from outside, would stop and marvel at the designs, colors, and architecture. It was also one of the most peaceful places for deep thought, meditation, prayer, and simply getting away from the business and hassles of life for Kashif.

5:20 AM, Kashif looked at his watch when he entered, first taking off his shoes and putting them on the shoe rack before entering the men's *musallah,* the prayer area. About ten minutes remained before the start of the morning Fajr prayer, and there were already a handful of people sitting on the green and white carpets, waiting quietly, some praying while others silently recited the Qur'an, all waiting for the time for prayer and Imam Dawood Murphy to come out of his office. Kashif sat down in the first row behind the mihrab, the niche in the wall indicating the direction of the Qibla. Staring at the wall, something caught his attention. For the first time, Kashif noticed an ayah from the Qur'an outlining the borders of the mihrab. As Kashif read the verse, a chill went down his spine. "...Verily, in the remembrance of Allah do hearts find rest."

Above everything, he was already feeling, at that moment, sitting in the masjid, a sense of guilt rose from within: guilt for neglecting the masjid for the past week due to anger and sadness. Having a close connection with his Creator was something he held dear to his heart, but at that time, he felt it was starting to fall apart, along with everything else in his life.

The muaddhin gave the *iqamah,* call to stand and start the prayer, on the microphone as Imam Dawood entered. All the men stood and lined up next to each other, shoulder to shoulder and feet to feet, as is in the *Sunnah,* prophetic teaching. Taking his spot in front of the other congregants, Imam Dawood waited for everyone to continue lining up for *Salah*, prayer. He caught Kashif's eye and gave him a warm smile. Imam Dawood was a middle-aged man in his early forties, tall and light-skinned. His face always seemed to shine brightly especially contrasted with his green eyes and light brownish-red beard. Kashif had always had a good relationship with him. Once the prayers finished, Kashif walked to the imam's office and knocked on the door.

"Come in!" He heard the Imam's friendly voice from inside.

"Asalaamu alaikum, I was wondering if I could speak to you if you have some time?" Kashif asked hesitantly, in a low voice.

"Ah, Kashif! Waalaikum asalaam! Of course, come in."

"JazakAllahu khair," he responded with the Islamic greeting, meaning may God reward you with goodness.

"*Wa iyyak*, and to you," Imam Dawood responded.

Kashif took a seat and sat across the desk from the imam, and he tried to find the words to say, but his mind clouded his speech. The last time they met was six months ago after Kashif's and Aliya's baath paki when Imam Dawood had sat down with the couple to prepare them for their upcoming marriage. As was customary, the imam met them privately to prepare them and cover all areas of marriage, including expectations, rights, and responsibilities for both husband and wife.

"Tell him not to joke about having more than one wife," Aliya directed to the imam when he finished, teasing Kashif.

"My dear sister, I think he can barely handle one." He winked at them as they all laughed.

Kashif woke from his daydream and noticed Imam Dawood waiting patiently for him to open up. He had that same warm smile he shot Kashif earlier. Kashif felt embarrassed and finally tried to find words to speak, but the only thing he could communicate was his tears. The dam behind his eyes broke as the tears started flowing uncontrollably. Imam Dawood gave him a box of tissues. "Take your time, Kashif. These tears need to come out."

Kashif nodded while patting his eyes.

"I've actually been wondering when you would come. You've been through a lot, and I haven't seen you in the masjid in a while."

"I'm trying, Imam," was all he could reply in between the sobs.

"I know, and that's all God wants. In this world, we only get judged on the final result, but with God, He judges us on the journey itself. He judges you on your effort, your resilience, your patience."

With teary eyes, all Kashif could do was shake his head weakly. "Why is He letting this happen to me? I can't take it anymore."

"Do you believe God? Not believe *in,* but believe Him?

"Yeah," Kashif sniffled.

"Well, doesn't he say *La yukulli nafsu illa wusaha,* Allah will not put a burden on you more than you can handle? So, even though you feel like this is the breaking point and it's too much, He is telling you that you can handle this and get through it. As hard and tough as this is, you're tougher."

"I don't feel it."

"Your father was a great man and a good friend. Losing him is something we both can never replace. But with what happened afterward, with your marriage, it's truly heartbreaking; however, I do have some good news for you. But before we talk about that, let's do some introspection?

"Your father's death, yes, that was not in your hands or your fault. It was Allah's will and plan. But your heartbreak...well, I ask you, could you have prevented that? I always advise the youngsters not to give their heart to someone before marriage."

Kashif felt the words strike him like an arrow.

"All the times you two met alone and getting so attached to one another before marriage, was it the right thing to do?" He tried to meet Kashif's eyes.

"I like to say, love is built, not fallen into. It takes time to build it in marriage," he sighed.

Kashif recalled all the times he met Aliya on her roof, and he knew Imam Dawood was right.

"But don't beat yourself over it, let this heartache be a reminder. And now to the good news. Always remember, Kashif, that Allah never takes anything away from the believer without replacing it with something better." Kashif kept his gaze down but nodded while listening.

"I know you're struggling and going through a tremendous amount right now. You've lost a great deal, and it's clear you're in immense pain. But life… is strange; there is a balance in everything. When you lose, you also gain some things. We don't tend to focus on the things we do gain. I truly believe that when we're suffering, going through hardship, and have hit rock bottom, that's when we find something there at the bottom.

"What you're going through now, you might not understand through all the pain and suffering, but you're gaining patience, you're gaining strength, and gaining your reliance on Allah. And those things you'll use and need in the future, in some other part of your life. And so, when you're experiencing hardship in the future, what you've gained today will be useful. This pain will be useful to you."

Imam leaned forward, lowering his voice, and stared into Kashif's eyes. "Right now, you're in the storm, but you'll have more skills when you come out. A smooth ship never made a skilled sailor, as they say. I've heard you've kept away from everyone, and I understand, and that's fine, but it's better to speak with someone than not; if you don't, you may lose your mind. Talk to Allah; He created you and knows what you're going through better than anyone else. And you can talk to me; I promise I will try to be a good listener too. Don't hold it all in; it'll come out in ways you won't like."

Kashif nodded slowly, feeling slightly better.

"What are you feeling right now?" asked Imam Dawood.

After a pause, Kashif looked up and said, "Anger."

"And what can you do to get that anger out in a positive way?"

"I think… I have a way."

"Okay, just promise me you won't hurt yourself… or anyone else."

"I can't promise that, but I will take it out in a positive way," he said.

With that, he got up, thanked the imam for his time, and left. While going back home, he thought of what the imam said: *don't hold it all in; it'll come out in ways you won't like.* He knew how to take his anger out. And yes, people will get hurt, he thought.

CHAPTER TWENTY ONE

I THINK THE CITY NEEDS US

After a week, slowly and steadily, Kashif picked up the pieces of his life and tried to take a step forward. "Hey!" He heard an enthusiastic yell as he entered through the door to the lab. "It's great to see you, Buddy. Alhamdulillah." Samir looked relieved.

"I think it's time to pick up where we left off," Kashif stated seriously.

Samir walked him to the Playroom, and Kashif paused when he saw the suit hanging up on the wall. He walked up to it, face to face, and took a long hard look. *This* was what kept him away, and *this* was the reason he lost so much. Now, *this will be why I regain control and how I take out this anger.*

"Take a look at this," Samir said, throwing the day's newspaper at him. "Crime has gotten out of hand in the last couple of months. It had been trajecting upward for the past year, but the City's gone insane. I don't know what has happened to this city, it was once a safe place, but now, people can't even walk in front of their own homes without being afraid of getting robbed or abducted?" He complained as Kashif read the headline of a woman getting shot and having her son kidnapped right in front of her own home.

"It's been over two weeks since you've suited up. I'm not the only one who missed you," Samir said, tossing him another newspaper. "I think this city needs you." He read out loud as Kashif read the headline, "Masked Vigilante Disappears as Crime Rises. Who Will Save the City?"

Kashif returned his look in agreement, "I think this city needs us."

Samir smiled. "I like how you think, and that's why I've been working on some things."

"I knew you had been," joked Kashif. "Show me what you've got?"

"I've been thinking about what's the most efficient yet fastest way for you to get around. Behold... a jet pack," he exclaimed, removing a sheet from the suit like a magician. "Tada!"

The suit, though, looked exactly the same, which confused Kashif. "Um... I guess I'm supposed to wait for the prestige of this magic trick?"

An excited Samir got the hint, losing the excitement, "Fine, okay, so it looks the same, but it's not. In fact, the trick is it's supposed to look the same, not to give anything away. But if you notice the sides of the thobe, there's a slit across to your back, and on the metal, I've attached a small but powerful jetpack." He pointed to a small pouch on the metal part of the suit. "It's more to help you glide. The jetpack will automatically turn on when it senses you've been in the air, or you could push this button here," he pointed to a button on his new belt. "This will propel you upwards and should help you get from rooftop to rooftop."

"Wow, you've been busy," Kashif responded, rather impressed.

"You know I'm so fascinated by flight. Everyone knows about the Wright brothers, but perhaps the first person to make a real attempt at flying was a 9th-century Cordoban named Abbas ibn Firnas. He dedicated his life to constructing a flying machine and was the first to develop and test a flying construct. So many of the attempts at flying and flight designs came from the works of Ibn Firnas. Still, unfortunately, modern aviation and historians have yet to really honor him. Well, until now. This suit is a dedication to him. The jetpack essentially recycles the air causing you to take flight. "Go ahead, try it on."

"Thank you, Ibn Firnas," an amazed Kashif said, suiting up. As he did, he noticed a misty air faintly vaporizing out of the sides of the eyes of the mask.

"Oh yeah, the trick is to keep the jetpack lightweight enough so it doesn't bog you down. The misty, foggy air from the eyes is just the suit extinguishing air. And I've upped the power on the gloves, so they punch harder."

"Let's go test it out."

"Now we're talking. But first, I've also been looking into what our friend, Rupert from the docks, told us on Hammerhead. We might not be able to figure out where he is, but I think we know someone who does." He pulled up a picture of a man on X-Bot, "Henry Millstone. He's a known criminal, but after digging deeper, I found it seems like he handles the meetings and transactions between the different mobs like a broker. He's the link between all of them."

Kashif stared at the screen and picture of Millstone and thought out loud, "Why does he look familiar? Have we seen him somewhere?"

Samir looked at Kashif in surprise, then turned to X-Bot, typing away on the computer, "I thought the exact same thing. He pulled up news clippings showing Kashif. "Look, in all of these pictures of Iris Hill, notice who's in the back?"

Surely enough, Henry Millstone, a slim, petite little man, was in the background of all the press release events that Iris Hill had organized. "Looks like he's exactly who we should be talking to," said Kashif. "And I know where I've seen him; he's been on our campus a few times. Why would he be there?" Kashif said, confused and looking at Samir.

"Definitely who we should be talking to," agreed Samir. "However," he said, turning back to the computer and typing away, "I can't seem to find out where he is currently, kind of like Hammerhead, but I'll keep searching. We'll find something, I know it. In the meantime, let's try out these new goodies on the suit. And I think I know exactly where we can test these out." There was that mischievous smile again.

"Are you ready for the jump?" Samir asked into the earpiece back at the lab.

"Ugh, I guess. Are you sure about this?"

"Yes, we have to test the jetpack out before you use it for real."

"...from *this* far up?" Kashif felt the cool wind of the night as he looked downward to the ground.

"Yes, get ready. I'm counting down. 3... 2..."

"Wait, wait. Let me get ready," Kashif took a deep breath and sighed. He looked up into the sky. "Okay."

"You're going to jump forward and feel the glide under your thobe. Just go with it and land slowly. 3... 2... 1..."

Kashif jumped and fell right down. He felt himself hit the ground immediately. "Ouch."

The playground where they were testing his suit was empty at night.

"Let's try again," Samir said as Kashif once more climbed the children's swing set and stood on top of the bars. "I guess you're right that I shouldn't have climbed a building, but I feel silly jumping off a kid's swing set."

"Better to feel silly than dead jumping off a building," reasoned Samir.

"Fair enough." Kashif was ready for the second try and, after jumping, landed face-first right into the ground again. "Ouch. This is reminding me of when you hit me with bricks," he commented. After a few more tries of not lifting off nor gliding, he asked, "Are you sure you installed a functioning jetpack?"

"Oh, I see the issue. I didn't turn it on from my side." Samir gave a nervous laugh.

"Samir!"

"Sorry, but hey, it's all part of the experiment. Now we know it needs to be turned on from my side, too," he tried keeping a straight face.

"I'm going to throw you off a swing set, and then we'll see who's laughing. While throwing bricks at you. "

"Well, I'll just glide away because it's turned on now. So go ahead, climb up."

"Are you sure it's on?"

"Positive. 3... 2... 1..."

Spreading his arms, Kashif jumped and, this time, felt himself float in the air for a few seconds and thrust forward as he slowly descended, landing on his feet. "Woah! I felt it!" After a few more tries, he was gliding in the air effortlessly as the jetpack worked as expected.

"Now, let's try a higher altitude," Kashif said, looking around for a building in the neighborhood. "That house seems like a good bet," he pointed across the street. The house looked abandoned but had a high roof.

"3… 2… 1… Liftoff," as Kashif was flying in the air from that roof to the roof of the house next door.

"Woohoo!" he exclaimed, feeling alive again. Within no time, he was jumping from one rooftop to another in the neighborhood. "I'm flying!" he screamed, feeling like a kid.

"Awesome. But hey, I'm picking up some of the police chatter. Give me a minute," Samir said back at the lab. In the meantime, Kashif continued to jump from one house to another, testing how far he could float in the air. He stood in the middle of the street and looked around at the quiet neighborhood. Not a car or person in sight this late at night. He ran down the middle of the street and jumped, floating in the air a few feet above the ground. As he continued to rise higher in the air, he felt free. The higher he went, the smaller and lighter his issues weighed. He twisted himself around in the air, performing a somersault, flying upside down and downside up. When he could see the city lights in the distance and the moonlight shining on him, he laid down in the middle of the air while floating, relaxed as he drifted in the air, spinning gently in a circle. He had never felt that level of serenity and calmness before. He slowly rose higher and higher, going through clouds until the moon was entirely in his sight. He felt he could reach out and touch the moon. He had never felt this exhilarated yet calm and peaceful at the same time. He continued to float tranquilly. "Kash, the police seem to be onto something," Samir spoke, breaking his moment of zen. "The meeting we've kept hearing about. It's tonight."

Exhaling a deep breath and enjoying the peace and quiet, he took a moment before responding. "Let's go," Kashif finally responded, coming back to his senses. As he glided back down, something went wrong over a block of houses. He felt the jetpack give out and felt himself airborne and falling down.

"Oh no, no, *no!*" He screamed, crashing downward fast, as he noticed a backyard with clothing draped on line wire below him. He crashed right into the wire and clothes with a loud *thud*.

Disoriented after hitting the ground, he found himself entangled between different articles of clothing. Removing a red pair of underwear from his face, he heard a woman's voice yelling.

"Hey! You! You ruined my laundry!" A woman in a shalwar kameez came running out of the house. "You, whatever your name is, you *MutterGhosht*, you get out of here!" She yelled as she took off her slippers and ran toward Kashif.

"Aaahh!" Kashif tried to get a hold of his surroundings while retreating toward the front of the house with a pair of socks hanging off of him and the woman chasing him with her slipper.

Kashif ran down the street and tried the jetpack until he lifted in the air. The only voices he could hear were the woman yelling at him, "I'll get you MutterGhohst! You ruined my clothes!" and Samir laughing in his earpiece.

CHAPTER TWENTY TWO

THE MOBS

L ater that night, Kashif made his way to the edge of RP City near the docks, which housed abandoned buildings fenced off from the public.

"I picked up police chatter on their radios, and it seems like they're moving in on a meeting between gangs tonight near the docks," Samir had said earlier. "Why don't we check it out and give them a hand?"

The night was dark, and the abandoned warehouses didn't provide much light. Yet Kashif and Samir picked up an extensive amount of movement happening in the area. Having positioned himself on the rooftop of one of the warehouse buildings, Kashif could catch all that was happening in the main building right across from him. Despite the abandoned and closed-off feel of the area, the night and warehouses were anything but dormant. Having zoomed into the old building with his eye-scope, Kashif could see three black limos approaching the main building with binocular-level precision. Slowing down at the entrance to the side door of the warehouse, men in suits were escorted out of the limos by bodyguards with guns. "Looks like the red carpet for all the shady people in the City," he said to Samir through his earpiece. Kashif zoomed in and caught the face of each of the men, while back at the lab, Samir was able to identify them.

"These are all pretty bad men," Samir said after some time. "All part of different mobs. Almost all the people you are looking at have a rap sheet. I'm surprised some of them were even let out. Theft, breaking and entering… murder and trafficking," he said with shock and worry. The two guys that just got out of the back of the car are Malcolm Penn, better known as the Dealer, and Lucas Hugo, who goes by the Slicer. Slicer is the head of the gang RP Psychos, and I'm guessing those are the guys surrounding him."

Disturbed upon hearing this, Kashif continued watching as another man came out of the building and gave instructions to a group of gunmen. Looking at the man, both Kashif and Samir froze in disbelief. *"Fares...!"* Kashif gasped.

"I can't believe Fares is one of them," Samir said, clearly distressed. "Kashif... hold on, I'm doing facial recognition on some of those guys; Fares is talking to... and I can't believe this, they're... *cops!"*

"What?!"

"Three of them. I'm taking a screenshot of what you're looking at. We can use this later," Samir said.

"I'm going to take all these guys out right now," growled Kashif.

"Slow down, let's see what they're even up to. We don't know what's going down tonight."

A van pulled up near the entrance of the warehouse building. A few men and women exited the car and greeted the guards at the door as they entered the building.

"I'm turning on the infrared," Samir said as the van pulled into the building. Capable of now having a visual inside the building using heat sensors, what Kashif and Samir saw inside the building made the hair on their necks stand up. Inside, one of the gunmen ripped open the van door, and three women, who were gagged and tied up, were pushed out of the vehicle. As they were led toward a room with a long rectangular table with people sitting around, Kashif's blood started to rise. With each passing second, he became more and more enraged.

"Oh my God. Looks like we know what they're up to. Those girls are going to be sold and trafficked."

"I can't believe this! I have to go in," whispered Kashif angrily.

"Wait! Wait!" Shouted Samir. "I'm using the sensors on your suit, and the police are coming up from around the building. But... hold on..." Kashif! They're going to enter a trap! The mobs' guards are waiting for them down that alley where the police are entering.

They're going to get ambushed by these gunmen."

"I don't have time. Either I go to them or save these three women," responded Kashif.

"Kashif, those girls aren't going anywhere yet. We can track them down. But that's our police force, and there are more of them than the three girls. They're going to get massacred in a matter of moments."

Kashif hesitated for a second, but when he looked back at the building, the girls were beaten and taken further away, trying to fight out of their shackles. "They should have planned better," he stated, closing his face shield.

"Kashif, go save those men!"

The girls were taken into the room with the long table. After a moment of pause and thinking, he said, "I know what to do. I'm going to get the girls," standing up. "Bismillah."

The warehouse with the hostages had three floors. The meeting was held on the second floor, where the three girls were kept as well.

"Make sure we have the back alley secured," Police Detective Fahim commanded into his walkie-talkie.

Detective Fahim and his team had been monitoring and working on finding out the day and location of the meeting for weeks. They finally discovered the information from one of their own who had infiltrated one of the gangs and had given information about the trafficking ring. The police had surrounded the warehouses from all sides. Still, their intel informed them to sneak toward the main building from behind the warehouses. Their goal was to reach the main building, where the meeting was taking place.

"Roger that, Sir," a reply returned a few seconds later.

Over the past few months, the RP Police Force, led by Det. Fahim had gained enough information to finally move in and take down the human trafficking movements of the gangs. They had discovered that the main gang involved in the kidnappings and selling off of victims was known as the Vipers. Everything went through them, and they were hosting the meeting today. Waiting for and finally discovering the big meeting day, it was showtime to take them down.

Today's the day, Detective Fahim thought as his men had positioned themselves in the alleyway, ready to rush into the building. Neither the Detective nor any of his men noticed a figure gliding from the rooftop of the adjacent warehouse to the main building.

Landing on the rooftop, Kashif noticed armed guards on the roof. Using his opportunity to surprise them as they were faced the other way, he quickly ran toward them before they could fire any shots at him. Hearing footsteps behind them, the guards only heard a mechanical noise charging up and a flying fist before their world went dark.

CRASH.

Kashif kicked open the door on the roof to head downstairs.

"What was that sound?! Hey! Up there!" He heard gunmen call from downstairs. Having the element of surprise gone, Kashif clenched his fists and sprung toward the gunmen first.

"What's that sound?" Mr. Hex questioned nervously, shifting in his seat on the round table in the meeting room.

"Boss, we got company," one of his men informed him. "It's that ghost guy."

"Take him out! I'm tired of this clown," demanded Mr. Hex.

Hearing gunshots and screaming growing louder and louder as it approached right outside the meeting room door, a frightened Mr. Hex called out on his radio, "Everyone, give up your positions and come here! Take the Ghost out! Now!"

"But Boss, we have the police surrounded," questioned one of the men back.

After hearing screams and shouts, suddenly, it grew eerily quiet outside the meeting room. All the members ducked, hiding underneath the table. The silence outside caused panic inside.

"I don't care about them. Everyone get here now!" Mr. Hex shouted, fearing for his own safety.

The snipers and gunmen, positioned and ready to ambush the police, made their way back into the main building instead. Noticing their movement, the police force moved in and gave chase. Little did the police force realize that this saved their own men.

"Head into the building! Now!" Detective Fahim shouted. Leading the charge, he and his men stormed into the main building's first floor, but his whole team froze at what they saw.

With a line of unconscious men lying around, the officers saw the vigilante man fighting the Viper's men.

"Surround them!" Detective Fahim yelled. "Take out the Vipers, don't let any of the gang members leave!"

Instead, the police force surrounded MetalGhost, as he threw the last standing gunmen to the ground, all the others having run away at the sight of the police.

"Hands up!" They yelled at him with their guns drawn.

"Are you serious?!" MetalGhost, shouted at them. "They're all going to get away!" He pointed at the retreating criminals.

"Yeah, but you're not!" one of the officers yelled back as his team neared MetalGhost, backing him up to a wall.

"Detective, most of them have gotten away," one of the officers reported on their radio.

"You're wasting your time on me. They've gotten away! Mr. Hex is here!" MetalGhost yelled back. "Where are the girls? Are they safe?"

"Yeah, they're fine," said Detective Fahim, coming toward his team. "Lower your weapons, men."

The officers nervously and slowly lowered their weapons as they continued to surround him. "You and I need to talk," said Detective Fahim.

"You have the mob and the gangs here, and you want to talk?" asked MetalGhost, trying to figure out his next move.

"We've got some of the men, and they'll talk. And the girls are safe," Det. Fahim informed him.

"You're welcome," Kashif responded sarcastically.

"Yeah, thanks, but we don't know you or why you're here. Why don't you take off your mask and come with us?"

"Why don't you go chase those guys who are getting away while you still have the chance?"

"We'll find them. But you, you're a hard one to find. Are you a cop?"

"No."

"Maybe you should be," Det. Fahim responded honestly.

"I think I'll be going now."

The officers raised their weapons again as Det. Fahim responded, "I don't think so. We can't reward vigilantism. Not a good precedent."

"There is no precedent. And if I were you, I'd tell your men to lower their weapons. Or they're going to get hurt."

The officers tensed up, their fingers ready on the triggers. They stood prepared in the firing position as Det. Fahim and MetalGhost stared at one another. Neither moving nor blinking, waiting for the other to make a move.

After a long moment, there was a sudden loud commotion behind them. Some of the gang members who were being arrested had broken loose and were running away, causing the officers to turn around quickly. But the gang members were immediately apprehended by the nearby policemen. When the officers surrounding MetalGhost looked back around toward where he had been, they noticed he was gone.

"Find him! Surround the warehouse, don't let him escape!" The commands came in. But within a few minutes, just as MetalGhost had used the split second to jetpack up and scale the walls to the windows and out to the roof, he had jumped from one building to another and was gone into the night.

The following day, the news was ablaze with the night's events. For the first time, the police force took a positive step in cracking down on the gangs, and the news of the human trafficking ring came to the forefront. No longer could anyone ignore the fact that this had been happening in their city. And no one could ignore that the police had successfully stopped the trafficking meeting and had actually arrested some of those involved. However, the police force had become secondary news.

"He barged in and took out those men! He saved us! If it wasn't for him, we..." one of the three girls held hostage broke down crying while giving an interview.

"What did he look like? Did you speak to him?" reporters asked.

"He wore a blue thobe, but underneath, he had a metal-like suit covering his body," the second girl recalled. "And he moved so fast. He was like a ghost, as people say."

"He really is what they call him, a *metal ghost*," the third girl chimed in.

"Yeah, the MetalGhost saved us," the other girls agreed.

They continued giving news reporters testimony that it was Kashif who had saved them rather than the police. The news called him a "hero," but the police quickly took over the story and called him a vigilante and, in turn, made sure to spread the news that *they* had saved the day.

"My team had to fight him, try to stop him from... doing whatever he was doing," an angry Police Chief Eames shouted, giving a statement. "We don't know why he was there or if he was working with the gangs or not, but he fled instead of staying and working with us. What does that tell you?"

"I guess you were right," Samir said, turning off the news.

"It was a tough call that had to be made within a second," Kashif responded. "Maybe, in theory, you were right. I should have gone to help more people than the girls. But I just couldn't get myself to. I figured if I went in, the mobs would bring all their men to stop me, distracting them from their ambush on the police. It worked, Alhamdulillah." He knew Samir was still feeling conflicted, having told him to save the officers, the same ones who wanted to take him in and were painting him as a criminal.

"Alhamdulillah," Samir responded. "So, *MetalGhost,* you like that name?"

"Is that what they're calling me? I guess it has a good ring to it."

"Well then MetalGhost, with everything that happened, how do you feel?"

"It felt... good. I was angry and took it all out on those thugs."

"Good, but I've been working on something.

"Like what? The jetpack worked great," Kashif responded.

"Yeah, but I was thinking of another way of getting you out of danger. This is my biggest masterpiece," he said, holding out his hand.

Kashif looked at his hand with confusion, "Uh, what is it?"

He opened his palm, presenting a bulky black watch inside. He put it on Kashif and stood back with great anticipation.

"You got me a watch?" Kashif wondered out loud, checking it out on his wrist.

Samir just smiled, put his hands on his hips, and emphatically stated, "Ladies and gentlemen, I introduce the next wonder of the world."

The watch started to beep and vibrate, causing Kashif to look up in a panic. "Stand still and trust me," Samir replied as he pressed a button on one of his computer pads. What happened next truly shocked Kashif.

The watch opened up, and metal from the suit started mechanically shooting out, wrapping around his arm, covering his chest, legs, and entirely all-around Kashif's body. Within five seconds, Kashif was fully covered head to toe in his metal suit with the thobe around it. "Wow!" screamed Kashif, observing the armor all around him.

"Now, press the button on the side of your belt."

Kashif noticed the newly placed button around his waist and pressed it. Within another five seconds, the metal retracted back into the watch as if it had never shot out in the first place.

I was thinking what is the best way to suit up, but also suit down when you're out. This way, you can blend in with people outside when needed, and you can also easily suit up when needed. You can also press the same button on the watch for the same effect."

"Good thinking," Kashif responded, shaking his head impressed. He pressed the button on the side of his watch, and the armor shot out again, wrapping itself around him.

"And maybe the best part," Samir pointed out the new blue thobe. "I know your favorite thobe is the one your dad gave you, the one you two had worn to match. So I stitched this one by copying it." Kashif walked over to a mirror and was overwhelmed by the reflection. The thobe resembled exactly the blue thobe given by Abu. It was indeed his favorite piece of clothing, as it reminded him of Abu. And now it was a part of the suit, and it would be with him whenever he went out. Kashif looked at himself up and down in the mirror.

"Samir Khan, you've outdone yourself this time. This is perfect."

CHAPTER TWENTY THREE

WE MESSED UP

T hank you all for attending." Police Chief Thomas Eames' voice echoed loudly from the podium microphone in front of the Court House for an official statement a few days later. The much-awaited press conference was finally underway, with the whole city watching. Surrounded by cameras, microphones, and news reporters in front of him and the police force standing behind him on the steps of the Court House, he continued, "The Police Force of the great City of Ridgefield Park, take this time to address the recent incidents with this menace vigilante."

"MetalGhost," the news reporters corrected him.

"Fine, *MetalGhost*." Chief Eames sighed, annoyed, finally saying his name after avoiding it publicly up to that point. "There seem to be some in the city, undoubtedly a minority, who actually applaud this criminal. But within the last few weeks, his disruption of police work has gone too far when taking the law into his own hands."

"Disruption?" Samir stated, watching the news back in the lab with Kashif. "More like doing your jobs." He took a bite of popcorn.

"Did you really bring popcorn?" Kashif asked.

"Oh, this is going to be quite a show." Samir smiled, eating another bite. They returned their attention to the screen. Kashif noticed Police Detectives Fahim Kazmi and Zara Rehman standing behind Chief Eames.

"The City of Ridgefield Park, at this time, officially announces to this MetalGhost vigilante to turn himself in immediately, right here, right now. He has hidden for too long. This is your moment, MetalGhost, to stop hiding and come out in front of the city. Show yourself," Police Chief Eames continued.

"Nah," Samir responded to the screen.

Kashif stood behind Samir, his brows together, watching in deep thought as he folded his arms.

"We promise not to harm MetalGhost..."

"Because you can't." Samir laughed.

"We would like a civil dialogue. The city deserves to know who this person is and his true intentions," Chief Eames finished.

"Chief, what do you have to say about MetalGhost bringing in a few of your own officers found to be working with local gangs?" A reporter asked. After the incident at the warehouses with the mobs, Kashif and Samir focused their attention on the three police officers who they witnessed working with the mobs. Waiting for them until they were alone, Kashif apprehended each one, tied them up, and left them in front of the police precinct. Attached to them were photos of them from the night of the meeting, proving their involvement with the gangs.

"I'm glad you asked, as I was about to mention just that. This is the problem with this criminal. This is the problem with vigilantism. He kidnapped those men and left them out in the cold. But what he *doesn't know* is that those were our informants. They had infiltrated the gangs and were giving us all the info and intel we needed to reach the gangs and their meeting. Because of those officers, we knew about the trafficking ring."

Samir sat up straight and turned to Kashif, both with shock on their faces. They stared at the screen and listened in confusion.

"This is what happens when you're not involved with doing things the right way. He has jeopardized those officers, their safety, and all the work and information they have spent months gathering; getting close to the heads of these gangs is now over. We have lost the one leverage we had. He has jeopardized not only the safety of the officers but the safety of the city as well. And you call him a hero? It's only fair that he pays for this."

"Kashif... I messed up," Samir responded, upset.

"We're asking this MetalGhost to come here today so he can face the consequences of his vigilantism. If he's truly a hero, he will stop hiding. If he really wants to help the city, then it's high time he worked with us, not against us."

Kashif and Samir were left stunned by Chief Eames' revelations. Samir slouched in his chair, looking at Kashif in dismay.

"Maybe I should go," Kashif said, surprising Samir.

"What? You can't be serious. Why would you do that?"

"Because we messed up. I'm no hero. He's right, we've been breaking the law, and clearly, we were wrong. And look, it's just a matter of time before they catch me. Maybe I should talk to them. Maybe I do need to pay for my mistake."

"It was my mistake, Kash. And let's go back for a second. Do you really think they'll catch us?" Samir turned around, surprised. "Never."

"Maybe we can start working with the police, though. I can go and just talk to them."

"Going there is turning yourself in. Do you think they just want to talk? Do you want them raiding our lab? And what about your mom? They'll question her for knowing about you."

Kashif thought to himself quietly before responding, "I think a talk could be a step in the right direction. But not like this." Kashif assured Samir that he wouldn't show up at the courthouse.

Kashif took his coat and walked out.

"Where are you going?" Samir asked.

"I need to think."

"Asalaamu Alaikum Ami." He entered, taking off his shoes. The sound of multiple loud voices and laughter was a pleasant welcome to Kashif as he walked in on a group of Ami's friends who had come to visit.

"Kashif, Baita! So good to see you! Come here!" He felt mauled by the overly affectionate aunties.

"Have you lost weight? Have you been going to the gym? Is that a new hairstyle?" They all asked simultaneously and loudly.

Overwhelmed by the attention, he did not even know where to start as he began backpedaling toward the kitchen.

"Kashif Baita, in here." He heard Ami calling out. He pointed to the kitchen while retreating away from the chatty aunties, feeling lucky to avoid answering any questions.

"Whew, you saved me, Ami, I..." Kashif started as he turned around but paused when seeing who was in the kitchen. "Oh," was all he could say, staring at Zara and Fares, standing with Ami.

"Zara and Fares came to see me," Ami told Kashif, smiling at them.

"Asalaamu alaikum, we've been meaning to come by for some time to see Aunty. But we were just leaving now," Zara said. Kashif's eyes, however, were glued on Fares.

"Hey, old buddy, it's been a while. Really sorry about your dad. He was always one of my favorite uncles. We all miss him," Fares said with a sad face.

"Waalaikum Asalaam. Yeah... thanks," Kashif replied quietly. He took a step closer, standing face-to-face with Fares.

"And um, heard about your engagement too. That sucks, man. Rough go for you lately, yeah?" Fares continued, also taking a step forward and staring back at Kashif. Standing in front of him, Kashif was surprised at how much taller and bigger Fares had become. Growing up, they were the same height and build, but Fares was now at least five inches taller, with big broad shoulders, chest, and arms. He wore a white T-shirt with a black leather jacket, but it was clear he had a muscular build underneath.

"Yeah," Kashif whispered coldly. There was clear tension in both of their voices and stares. Zara and Ami, sensing the awkward silence between the two, spoke up together.

"If there's anything you need, please let us know," Zara quickly said.

"Thank you, my lovely daughter," Ami responded, hugging her.

"Yeah, let me know, Kash. It's been a while, and it would be nice to catch up sometime," Fares said.

"Sure, I would love to hear what you're up to these days," Kashif responded to the insincerity with his own.

"I've actually been involved with some cool projects that I think you'd love since you're into technology and engineering." Fares was not breaking eye contact with Kashif.

"Yeah? I would love to hear about it." Kashif kept his gaze on him. "I've been working on some gadgets myself, with the help of

Samir."

Finally blinking and remembering Samir, he turned to Zara, "Samir, our friend, who's single, by the way," he blurted out. "Uh, I mean. Maybe since both of you guys are single, I've been thinking that you might be interested? In each other, I mean," he stuttered. He was ruining Samir's moment, he knew it.

Zara smiled politely and looked over to her brother, who responded, "Yeah, that's an interesting idea, Kash," almost dismissively. "Looks like we do have a lot to talk about. You, me, and Samir." He laughed while giving him a pat on the back. "Catch you around. Take care, Aunty. Really nice seeing you."

As they exited, Ami gave Kashif a disapproving look. "What was that? Everything okay between you two?" She asked as Kashif was still processing the fact that Fares had been in his house after everything he knew Fares was involved in.

"And you know, I was actually hoping *you* would consider Zara. You know I've always just adored her. She's wonderful," Ami looked at him, almost pleading.

"Ami, please," Kashif responded, hurt. "Plus, she'd be better for Samir."

Ami sighed, "You're both my sons, so of course, I'd be happy to see that too." She was clearly a little sad about his response.

Their conversation was interrupted by the loud uproar in the family room, the aunties exploding into chatter as the news came on. They were watching Police Chief Eames' press conference from earlier in the day.

"That's *him!*" One of the aunties stood up, pointing to the screen as the news put up a picture of MetalGhost. Finally, looking at the aunty who spoke, Kashif felt a nervous sweat drip down his forehead. "That's him!" She yelled again angrily, pointing at the screen. "This *pagal,* Mutterghosht, he ruined the clothes I had put out for my son's big event! He just crashed right into it, like a *ghadda."*

"Did you just call our City's hero a donkey?" The other aunties asked, laughing hysterically.

"Hero?! Ha!" She waved off the comment. "He's a ghadda who doesn't know where he's going. I'll get him, and then you'll all see."

"Yes, I would love to. We'd love to see you hit him with your shoe." They all laughed harder.

Ami slowly walked over behind Kashif, intertwined her fingers into his hands, and rested her head on his arm. She looked at Kashif and tried not to laugh as he put his arm around her. "Did she really call me *mutterghosht, a Pakistani meal made of peas and goat?*" He sighed, whispering. Ami couldn't help but giggle at this. Giving in, Kashif joined her, as they both laughed.

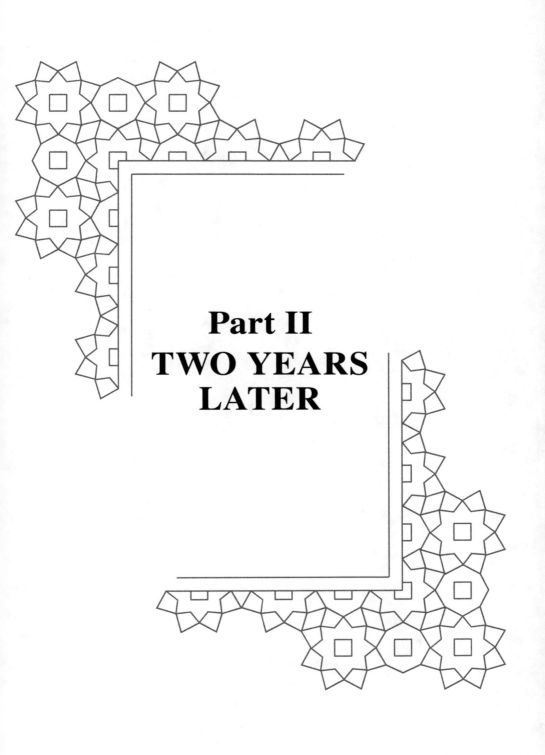

Part II
TWO YEARS
LATER

CHAPTER TWENTY FOUR

THE GHOST KILLER

My dear *friends,"* said the man who had called the meeting, quietly but emphatically. His voice was calm, yet it sent an unnerving cold chill down the spines of everyone who heard it. Addressing his distinguished guests seated around the long table, the man stood tall, wearing a full-length white buttoned-up lab coat. The top two buttons of his coat were unbuttoned, revealing a strong protruding chest, and the sleeves of his coat were folded up around his muscular forearms. The coat had small stains of red blood splatter covering it. Still, otherwise, his appearance was clean, with a clean-shaven face revealing his strong jaw and slick gelled-back hair with a reddish dye. He had a calm demeanor and voice, yet his eyes displayed anything but.

"We're far from friends, Dr. Daye," Malcolm Penn, a tall, lean man known as the Dealer, responded. "And I don't know everyone in this room." He glanced suspiciously around the table. "I don't like that," he said, looking back at the man everyone secretly called the Mad Scientist.

"Oh, where are my manners?" The Mad Scientist smiled widely, revealing perfectly white and straight teeth. "I'm sure some of you are familiar with each other. But a formal introduction is needed, of course." He looked to his left.

"Allow me to introduce the ever so handsome Mr. Hugo, better known amongst you all as *Slicer.* As most of you may know, he is the man to go to if you need any weapons in this city. He leads a brave group of men who have been given a rather unfortunate name by the public," the Mad Scientist added a sad, dramatic effect to his tone.

"No, we like the name," a tall, buff, bald man standing guard behind Slicer stated. "It's who we are. We're The RP Psychos," he boasted with a mischievous half-smile looking around at all the seated men.

"Thank you, Sal," the Mad Scientist gave him a slight bow. "Next, we have Mr. Winston Hex, the most important financial manager in the city. Let's just say he has an incredible amount of influence with the banks. If anyone requires any *financial assistance,* they may call on Mr. Hex and his Manderlay associates." The small round man twirled his mustache as he suspiciously looked at all the men in the room with his small beady eyes behind his round glasses.

"To his left, we have Mr. Seth Waters, who… um, what was that name they call you, Mr. Waters?" Mad Scientist asked.

"Bone Collector," a man standing behind the seated Mr. Waters spoke up in a harsh voice. He wore all black and smiled menacingly at everyone.

"Let's just say, when you do business with Boss, you better keep your end of the deals. For those who don't, they get to see personally why he has been given that name."

"Something none of us here would like to witness," Mad Scientist assured. Bone Collector sat quietly with his legs crossed and his left hand covering his mouth and holding his chin. A humorless and grim man, he stared directly at Mad Scientist unblinking, clearly not entertained at the idea of being present. "Bone Collector is the head of the Vipers, any sort of narcotics that come and go from the city, go through the Vipers." Moving along, I introduce…"

"We all know who this is," Slicer burst out. "Everyone knows the most powerful man in the city, if it isn't the secretive Iris Hill." The room went quiet, looking at a tall, bald, dark man, impeccably dressed in an expensive black suit and red tie.

"Let me make this very clear," Iris Hill spoke, after a moment, in a deep voice. "You all don't know any Iris Hill; you only know me as Black Dread. And you should all pray you never have to see Black Dread in full form," he introduced himself, looking around suspiciously. "If you need anything shipped in and out of the city, we can talk. Otherwise, I don't need to be seen around with any of you, and keep my real name out of your mouths."

"What do you have to hide, hmm?" Mr. Hex confronted him. "And was that a threat? I came here under the pretense of an alliance. How can I trust someone who threatens me openly?" He gave a cold look directly at Black Dread in the eyes.

"Maybe you'll see my full form and be an example for the rest," Black Dread fired back, with his eyes on fire.

"Gentlemen, please," the Mad Scientist pleaded calmly with his hands out. "This *is* an alliance, I assure you. One that will greatly benefit everyone here. I'm sure we all can agree that having powerful friends is advantageous, especially if we share similar goals," he reasoned. The two men gave each other a final stare as they shifted their attention back to the Mad Scientist. "Moving along, we have come full circle to you, Mr. Penn, who we all know, and we appreciate you hosting us in your fine establishment of Jack's Bar & Ring. Our friend, Mr. Penn is better known as the Dealer." The Dealer gave a courteous nod. "And I thank Mr. Henry Millstone, who helped me gather all of you great gentlemen here today, as I'm aware he works closely with you all."

The Mad Scientist patted the back of a short, petite man sitting next to the Dealer. The awkward slim man looked frightened but peered around proudly.

"Area's clear, Boss. I'm coming in," a voice radioed into the Mad Scientist's phone. The door to the room opened as a large man with a steel plate across his chest, black tights and shirt, and jet red hair standing on his head looking like a lightning bolt walked in. He came in with an air of importance, smiling as he looked around, finally standing behind the Mad Scientist. There were large metallic bands across both of his wrists, which became more visible as he crossed his arms in an X, having the bands rest in front of his chest.

"Did you get struck by a lightning bolt?" asked Slicer with a laugh.

"No, with a laser bolt," the man shot back.

"This is my trusted colleague, Laser," the Mad Scientist introduced.

"You talk about trust, but still had your men check the area?

Check *my* area." The Dealer raised his eyebrows curiously.

"And now, I trust you," the Mad Scientist reasoned.

"And why should we trust you, Doctor? As far as we know, you're just a lab worker for the Black Dread," the Dealer sneered. Laser took a step forward, anger in his eyes directed at the Dealer. The Mad Scientist put his hand on Laser's chest to stop him from proceeding. "I'd be careful, Mister," an incensed Laser called out. "Our men, you won't even see coming. We work in the dark, in the shadows. We're here right now. And we will kill you without you even seeing us." Laser threatened.

"Laser, it's okay," the Mad Scientist cooled him down. "It seems you have been mistaken, I'm afraid." He remained polite, turning to the rest. "Mr. Hill and I share common interests and vision," he moved his hand toward Iris Hill. "And he has taken great interest in my work and believes in the promise of that vision. One that I hope to share with you all.

"Gentlemen, you are the most feared and successful men in this entire city. And not just this city, but neighboring cities as well. For the past decade, no one has been able to touch you, let alone question you. You've built empires, the likes of which this whole country has never seen. For that, I applaud you. But..." The Mad Scientist's quiet calm voice changed, turning into a deep, dark one. "All of that has changed in the last two years. Before, you used to work *with* the police, now they are after you, on to your plans. And worst of all, this... it's all because of *one man*. Or should I say *Ghost?* This one man, a fascinating marvel of a man, no doubt, has turned your lives upside down. He's been breaking up your meetings, dealings, and movements." He glared at each seated man. "Time after time, I've sat back and watched him turn your operations upside down. One man has forced all of you to go underground. And you can't seem to stop him or get to him? *One man*. Or is he *really* a ghost? How long do you think you can sustain this? How long can you remain in the shadows? Certainly, I didn't think just one man would beat all of you again, and again, and *again*. It's pathetic." He raised his voice in disgust. Laser laughed mockingly. "Well, as it turns out. We can fix this problem, this *Ghostman* problem. I happen to know how to kill ghosts." He looked at his hand while rubbing his fingers together.

All the men sat up straight, listening intently.

"See, we can all work together and take out our shared nuisance. And *we* can turn him over to the authorities and go back to business as usual," he finished.

The men at the table sat quietly. "And how do you propose we do that?" the Bone Collector finally spoke in a harsh and menacing voice.

"You all know I'm a man of science. And my science experiments are proving incredible, life-altering results. I know how to kill the Ghost. What I need from you all are... *volunteers*. Subjects for my experiments."

"Your crazy experiments caused the major outage in this city. That set us all back. What the hell were you doing?" the Dealer questioned.

"Progressing the human race," the Mad Scientist responded slowly with a chill in his voice.

Everyone in the room felt uncomfortable again. No one spoke, quietly sharing disturbed and unsettling looks.

"Do you care to explain what you're talking about?" the Slicer finally asked.

"Explain? No, I'll show you. In a matter of time, I will show all of you. I will lure in this MetalGhost, and I will kill him. I am creating something that even he can't defeat. What I need from you is for your people to provide me with more subjects so I can improve my designs. That will be your contribution. Along with staying the hell out of my way. And when I kill MetalGhost, we will meet again and discuss compensation."

"Compensation?" A chorus of confused voices called out.

"Compensation. For taking out the man who is destroying your businesses as we speak." The Mad Scientist truly looked mad as he stared at each of the criminal leaders. The veins under his right eye began to protrude under his skin, eerily in the shape of a spider, as if it was about to crawl out from behind his eye.

The quiet in the room was palpable. "First, kill him, and show me his head. Then, we will talk," Slicer said.

The Mad Scientist smiled widely, content while standing above the rest.

- - -

"I love what MetalGhost has been doing," the commentator on TV news discussed with his panelists. "He's stopped muggings, shoplifters, robberies, carjackings; I mean, he's done it all," opined the commentator to his colleagues. "When you look at the effects of his actions, we're seeing, for the first time in recent memory, a *decrease* in violent crimes, and the drug lords have been put on notice that they cannot continue ruining this city."

"You seem to paint a very happy picture, but it's not all rainbows and butterflies with this guy," a panelist retorted. "Crime hasn't just stopped as you are stating; rather, it's now gone underground. Do you think these mobsters and gangbangers have just closed up shop because of this one guy? No, MetalGhost surprised them and has given them a blow, but they will counter. They always do. And who even knows what's behind MetalGhost's actions? It's not like we've heard from him."

"You seem to be wary of the intentions of MetalGhost."

"What do you suggest he do?"

"Last week, he arrived at the scene of a holdup at a local store; well, instead of working with the police, he fought with them. And the criminal got away."

"By all accounts, the police started the altercation with him first."

"They are the authority. If they are present, then why not listen to them and work with them? We have seen in the past year, MetalGhost fighting with civilians and the authorities. You call that being a good citizen?"

"In all fairness, the bounty of half a million dollars that the Police Chief has placed on his head hasn't helped. Unfortunately, it has had a negative effect, and civilians are now trying to apprehend him and fight with him. What is he supposed to do when people are attacking him?"

"I will reiterate what I have been saying since day one, it is time for MetalGhost to work *with* the police. It's not a good look when we have videos and pictures of him fighting the police and civilians. Let's remember: *we didn't ask for him. He* has decided to suit up and supposedly help the city. Well, help by not harming innocent people. He has turned this city upside down."

"He *has* turned this city upside down, and we're not liking all the dark things we're finding on the other side. But those are things we have to come to terms with, confront, and deal with as a city. We can't blame him for those dark things we have allowed and created."

Kashif listened with his heart sinking upon hearing each word. He sighed, putting his hands in his face, a crushing depression sinking him into a seemingly downward spiral with no bottom. MetalGhost was as much of a labyrinth for him as it was for the city.

"Don't watch that stuff," Samir said as he walked in behind him. "They'll say anything to get more viewers."

"They're not wrong," Kashif muttered, still hunched over. "What am I doing here, Samir?" He turned to him. "I'm losing control of this situation. And I'm not motivated anymore. Remember the reason why we started? Have we gotten any closer to finding out who killed Abu?"

Samir felt the jab was personal. He had been searching, trying his best to find out more about the explosion and Carson Daye and any sort of lead that could lead to him, to no avail. *So far,* Samir thought.

"Not yet, but that doesn't mean we should give up."

"It's been three years, and we're not getting any closer." Kashif felt a wave of anger rising.

"I know you're frustrated, but you can't give up."

"What's the point?" Kashif stood up. "It's not like any of this will bring him back. It's not like it will bring her back." He leaned on a table with his head down.

Samir had no words to respond. It had been three years, but as each day passed by, he knew his friend missed his father and Aliya even more. He knew it was eating away at him. After Kashif lost his job, Samir helped him get back on his feet by getting him hired at Al-Fihriya University as a professor. This was a step in the right direction as it helped anchor Kashif. But Samir knew Kashif needed closure for a new and fresh start, and the only way was to find those responsible for that night. At first, MetalGhost was a good escape. It was almost like a drug. A pet project for Samir. For Kashif, a gateway to letting his emotions out. But all of that turned upside down. The authorities and media had turned on Kashif over the past year. His face was plastered on every wanted poster, and the reward had caused many run-ins with local civilians. Of course, there were always cameras that recorded situations that MetalGhost encountered, misconstrued like throwing down cops, fighting with bystanders who had attacked him, then running away - the negative images were becoming a norm.

"Have faith. We'll get them," was all Samir could say.

"I'm going to bed early today, man," Kashif responded in a somber tone.

"It's only 6:00 PM."

"Good night."

CHAPTER TWENTY FIVE

MAGNETIZE

K ashif, are you there?" Samir called him. "Dude, get up.
There's a holdup at Jaylem Bank."
"Let me sleep," Kashif grumbled, half awake.

"There are hostages," Samir confirmed.

Kashif let out a loud sigh, turned over, and tried falling back to sleep. "Let the police handle it."

"The police are *also* the hostages."

Kashif opened his eyes begrudgingly.

"There's a guy who's gone through armed bank security and officers. I don't think this is a typical case."

Kashif didn't respond as he lay in bed. "Hostages," Samir reiterated again. "Including members of the Police Force!"

"Ugh, fine man." He unwittingly and slowly rose and put on the watch. "Be ready in the lab."

The scene outside Jaylem Bank was chaotic, as the roads leading to and surrounding the bank were all blocked off by authorities. Located at the heart of the city, the traffic and commotion were paralyzing the financial district. The police had barricaded the nearby blocks as reporters, camera crews, and civilians gathered in an attempt to get a view of the action. Kashif, fully suited, landed on the rooftop of the Shafi Tower near the bank. "Look at that scene," Kashif said slowly, sighing at all the commotion.

"This may be a good time to go down and work with the police," Samir suggested.

"That will make this whole mayhem worse," Kashif responded

unenthusiastically. "I'll have to listen to their procedures and protocols. That's going to be too much of a headache. And I'm not in the mood to deal with them, nor do I trust them. I'm just going in, and hopefully, out quickly and quietly." Kashif glided toward the bank roof and tried peering through the windows down below. The bank was a tall building with high ceilings, with the roof standing about fifty feet above the ground. Kashif looked below, and with a limited view, he was able to see a line of people sitting against a wall. He noticed a police officer standing up and running toward the other side of the bank with his baton in hand, out of Kashif's view. A few seconds later, the same officer was violently thrown against the wall, knocking them out.

"What on Earth is that?" Samir gasped.

"As you said, this doesn't seem to be a typical case. I'm going in. Bismillah." Kashif responded sluggishly as he stood up and broke through the window into the bank.

The crowd shrieked as the thunderous sound of glass breaking was followed by MetalGhost landing on his feet on the bank floor. After he landed, a few seconds later, glass from the ceiling came crashing down around him. The screams were followed by sighs of relief as some of the hostages shrieked in happiness. Kashif clenched his fists, ready to strike the approaching henchmen. He turned around and around again with his fists up. No one approached.

"Oh my God, yes!" Cried a few seated hostages against a wall. They were civilian men and women, bank workers, security guards, and police officers. Each of them looked terrified, and Kashif couldn't discern whether or not it was because of the sight of him. Lowering his fists and standing straight up, he peered in closer. He noticed each of the hostages had a flat black object the size of a basketball seemingly stuck to their chests. Looking around, to his surprise, there was no one else in the quiet lobby. Kashif walked up to an officer wincing in pain, and propped up against the wall, "Are you okay? Where are they?" He asked, putting his arm on his shoulder to help him sit up.

The officer, clearly in pain, gazed up, and suddenly a look of terror appeared on his face as he pointed weakly behind Kashif.

Turning around, and before Kashif could blink, a flying object struck him on the chest, causing him to fall to the ground. Sitting up, he inspected the black, round, metallic object now stuck to him. Before he could make sense of what was happening, a loud greeting caused him to stand up.

"Hey! You came! Wow, awesome!" A friendly-sounding voice spoke from across the hall. Searching for the voice, an oddly dressed figure came forward from the vault. The vault doors had been blasted open, and bags of money were placed on the floor. The man was dressed unusually in full-body black spandex, a light blue jacket, a black ski cap covering his face, and red and white lace-up shoes. Over the spandex was what seemed like a steel-like material covering his entire body, and he had grey steel-looking gloves on. As Kashif, again, checked the object stuck to his chest, the man walked toward the center of the lobby. "Sorry about that, man. Everybody's gotta have that on, you know?" He said sympathetically.

"What on Earth is this?" Kashif pointed to the object attached to him and all the others.

"Magnets!" the man exclaimed excitedly with his arms out. He sounded like a teenager, Kashif noticed.

"Magnets," Kashif repeated, trying to make sense of it. He walked closer to the man standing in the middle of the lobby. Immediately, all the hostages started to shriek. As he continued walking, he was met with a sudden force that stopped him from proceeding. It felt like he had hit an invisible wall.

"What the…!" Kashif called out.

"Yeah, sorry, dude, that's as close as we'll be able to get, unfortunately," the kid yelled out, shrugging his shoulders.

"Magnets," Kashif called to him, standing about twenty feet away, unable to get any closer.

"Magnets! What you have on you is a magnet, and look at this…" he displayed his metallic suit. "It's all magnetic as well. Cool, right!? What I have on is a giant magnet, and you all have the same poles, so you all will repel off of me. No one will be able to get close because of the same poles," he explained in one breath quickly. "Are you… uh, are you impressed, Mr. MetalGhost?"

"Very," Samir whispered to Kashif back at the lab.

"Of course you would be," Kashif muttered to Samir in the earpiece.

"What?" the kid asked.

"Nothing. How do I take this off?" Kashif demanded.

"Oh, you can't, Mr. MetalGhost. I mean, *I can,* but that would defeat the purpose of why I'm here." He laughed shyly. "But don't worry, Sir, I'll take them off in a short while."

"He sounds like a kid," Samir commented. "But I can't seem to find anything on this kind of thing."

"He's definitely a kid," Kashif responded.

"Hey, who are you talking to?" The young man asked, confused.

"Myself," Kashif spoke up, directed at the magnetic kid.

"That's weird… but okay, I guess." He scratched his head.

"What's your name?" Kashif asked.

The kid stood up straight. "I thought you'd never ask!" He exclaimed with excitement. He cleared his throat, "My name is… Magnetize!" He boasted proudly.

Kashif could only stare back, unsure of what to make of all of this. "You're just a kid."

"Young man, yeah." He tried standing taller and sticking his chest out. "But hey, it's awesome that you're here. I wish you could come closer. I'd love for us to check out each other's suits."

Kashif's head was starting to hurt. "Yeah, *sure…"* he replied, still unsure if this was really happening. "Let's go outside and have some coffee?" Kashif asked sarcastically, causing Magnetize to laugh. "Let's take these magnets off so I can come closer, yeah?"

"Ugh, no, sorry, I'm not supposed to," Magnetize apologized.

"Supposed to? Why? Who sent you? Who are you working for?"

"No one, I'm by myself. But actually, I got this idea, kind of from you; I really look up to you." He took a few steps closer, causing Kashif to be pushed back a few steps.

"Um, I'm not a criminal."

"Hey, I'm not a criminal either, man."

"You're *literally in the middle of a bank heist!"* Kashif pointed out. "And you have hostages." He moved his arms, presenting them.

"Oh, don't worry about that." Magnetize lowered his voice. "I'm not going to hurt them. They'll be fine," he assured.

"Then why don't you let them go?"

"I can't do that, plus I'm almost done here."

"You know I can't let you go, Kid." Kashif tried taking a step closer to no avail as Magnetize stood still.

"My suit has stronger magnets, so you can't move me. But don't worry, no one is going to get hurt. And I'm just wrapping up."

"Keep him talking, Kash," Samir whispered in his ear. "He's just a kid. I'm sure he'll reveal something."

"How did you get involved in this?" Kashif asked. "You're probably still in school. What school do you go to?"

"I… can't tell you," he answered, a little confused.

"You look like you go to Central High School, don't you?"

"Ew, gross dude, they wish."

"He has to be from Bergen High, I bet," Samir said. "They have an excellent science program. Let me look there."

"Okay, I'm talking too much again, and I know I shouldn't. I gotta go, Mr. MetalGhost," he said nervously before turning around and heading back into the vault. Kashif could hear him stashing money into a bag. Looking over at the hostages, they all stared at MetalGhost, unsure of what they were witnessing. Kashif stood, thinking. *Magnet,* he thought. Suddenly, an idea came to Kashif. Darting from one desk to another, he tore out the phone cords and began tying them together. *If I can't get close, it doesn't mean nothing else can.* He strung together the cables into a tightly knit rope. Magnetize reappeared with full bags in each hand and one behind his back.

"Well, it was awesome talking to you, Sir. I really wish we could talk some more, maybe... *HEY.*" Kashif threw the cords toward Magnetize, wrapping them around him. He held it together with all his strength as Magnetize shifted and twisted around, trying to escape. Kashif ran to the other side of the hall, wrapping the cords around him tighter.

"I told you, I'm not a bad guy!" Magnetize called out in desperation, squirming and trying to wiggle out of the hold.

"You're robbing a bank. You know I can't let you!" Kashif yelled as he reached back to the desk, tightening the cords more.

But when he looked back, he could not avoid the flying object that hit him directly in the head. Falling back, he felt more magnets hit him as they stuck to his body. Magnetize broke loose and walked towards him, picking up the bags.

"Those bankers won't miss a few dollars. They're all corrupt anyway. It'll go to better use this way," he explained shakily, his voice cracking.

As Kashif sat up, everyone in the hall could only watch as Magnetize took out a small magnet from his back, opened it up to enlarge it to half his size, and then threw it into the air toward the ceiling. The magnet stuck to the roof. Magnetize then raised his hand and flew into the air toward the magnet on the roof, attaching himself to it. "I hope we meet again, Dude. How can I find you?" He asked from the ceiling.

"Don't worry. I'll find you," Kashif replied.

Magnetize pressed a button on his belt, and all of the magnets attached to the hostages and Kashif instantly fell to the floor, releasing them of Magnetize's wrath. The magnets then flew back to Magnetize, who collected them before jumping through the ceiling window.

CHAPTER TWENTY SIX

I'M NOT A HERO

Bank Robber Escapes as MetalGhost is Unable to Stop Him.
Strange Robbery at Jaylem Bank with MetalGhost.
Was MetalGhost Working with the Bank Robber?
After Bank Robbery, Iris Hill to Increase Police Reward on MetalGhost's Capture.
MetalGhost Couldn't Save the Day.

Kashif sighed, turning off his phone as the news headlines upset him even more. The previous day's events at the bank had weighed heavily on his mind and heart. *I look up to you,* the kid who called himself Magnetize had said. Kashif felt even more depressed at the thought. With his hands on his head, he sat on the kitchen counter, feeling paralyzed in every way.

"Ya Allah, help me," he moaned desperately.

He didn't know how long he sat there crumpled on the counter until a sudden urge erupted inside him: an idea sparked up. He sat up with an impulse to do something he never thought he would or could do. Kashif hopped up, took his keys, and jumped on his bike. He was off to the masjid to do what he had never done before.

"Asalaamu alaikum. Can I talk to you, Imam Dawood?" He gently asked.

Imam Dawood Murphy was just finishing up his Qur'an studies class with his students. "Waalaikum asalaam, my brother." Imam Dawood gave him a broad smile and a pat on the back. Noticing Kashif's serious demeanor, he said, "Walk with me." He led him to his office.

Kashif sat across from the imam as he did the last time he had opened up to him about his personal struggles.

"Imam, I... need your help." Kashif tried to find the right words. "I don't know where to begin. I just... I tried, I did." He broke down. "But I couldn't avenge his death. And it's my fault she left. It's all my fault..." He realized that he wasn't making sense, which frustrated him even more.

"Tried what, Kashif?"

"Tried... everything. And look at what it has cost me," he said furiously.

Imam Dawood shifted in his seat with a sinking realization of what Kashif was alluding to.

"I'm not a hero, Imam." He looked up with anger raging in his eyes. "I never wanted this. I don't see myself like how some see me. I'm not a savior or a protector. I started because of anger, because of revenge, because I needed to get to whoever killed my father. I continued to release my anger for Aliya, having left me. I... wanted to cause so much pain to those who caused me so much pain. I wanted them to lose like I had lost." Kashif was breathing heavily and shaking. "Saving people and helping them, that's not why I do this. The truth is, I don't really care about people. In these last three years, I've learned that people don't really change. You get rid of one thug on the street, and then another one just takes his place. You out one corrupt politician, another one is waiting in line behind him. Sometimes I wonder if people are even worth saving. I'm doing this for me; yes, I'm selfish. And the fact is, it feels good hurting certain people. But if they happen to be the 'bad guys,' then it's all right, isn't it? I just look at it as they're in my way. My way of getting to whoever did this to Abu. I'm not a hero. I'm not in it for anyone else, but for me. I'm not the city's savior. How do I get the world to see that? That I'm not their hero?"

Imam Dawood sat stone-faced, the warm smile having escaped his face. He listened as the biggest secret in RP City had come to his door, revealing himself right in front of him: *after all these years, Kashif Razvi was the vigilante, MetalGhost, the man who some hailed as a hero and others, as a criminal.*

Imam Dawood glared alarmingly at Kashif, unsure of what to make of what he had just heard. The man responsible for fighting crime in the city and saving so many people had just revealed himself to him. He was, in Imam Dawood's eyes, a figure of hope and good, who had saved so many, and that man had just confessed that he had no intention of being a hero. Imam Murphy sighed as he leaned forward, putting his hands together.

"Well… that explains a lot. About where you've been," he responded in a low voice. "I knew you were having internal struggles but this… I couldn't even have imagined." His eyes widened.

"What do I do? I don't want to do this anymore. I can't do this."

"Kashif…"

"Being a vigilante, is that even acceptable in Islam? I know it's not. We can't just take the law into our own hands."

"True…"

"And what's the point? I'm on every wanted poster in the city. They paint me how they want to." He finally felt he could get that off his chest.

"Are you surprised, though?" Imam Dawood asked.

"All I know is I can't do this anymore. Am I disappointing Allah? Is this all a punishment for what I've been doing?"

Imam Dawood sat back, stroking his short reddish beard in deep thought. After a moment, he asked, "Do you know the story of Waleed ibn Waleed, the Sahabi of the Prophet Muhammad (ﷺ)?"

"No, I don't think so."

"I've been thinking quite a bit about your circumstances since you came into the limelight. About your vigilantism and actions, and it really reminds me of Waleed ibn Waleed. His story takes place during the time of the early migration of the Muslims from Makkah to Madinah. As we know, the Muslims in Makkah had started to become persecuted, and it was only getting worse as each day went by. It started with a boycott of all the Muslims in the city but then grew to be much more vicious. So much so that the Quraish stopped fearing repercussions and publicly started hurting and even killing the Muslims. It was at this point the order came from Allah for the Hijra. The Muslims had to pack up, take whatever they could carry with them, and set on the journey to settle in Madinah.

"However, the Quraish saw this as unacceptable. They decided that they could not let the Muslims just leave. So as the Muslims started to migrate, they captured two Sahabi, Ayyash ibn Abi Rabbiah and Hisham ibn Al-Aas, and put them in a makeshift prison. Keep in mind that they didn't even have prisons in their society but created one just for these two. As if that wasn't bad enough, the leaders of Quraish would cruelly put the two of them in shackles and parade them around the city to show everyone what would happen to them if anyone else tried to emigrate and upset their establishment. And there was nothing the Muslims could do about it; they had not been given permission by God to fight, but also they were too weak to fight.

"So the Muslims in Madinah felt paralyzed, unable to do anything for their two brothers who were being held as prisoners until one man, by the name of Waleed ibn Waleed, the famous Khalid ibn Waleed's older brother, said, 'I will go and save them.' So he rode by himself to Makkah secretly, and in the middle of the night, he snuck around and found where they were being held. He avoided the guards, jumped over the wall without anyone seeing, cut them loose, and rescued the two as they rode back to Madinah to safety."

Kashif listened intently.

"It was Makkan law at that point that no one could help or aid these two prisoners," the imam continued. "But, what were the Muslims to do? Leave two of their innocent brothers to be tortured unjustly?" He paused.

When Kashif didn't respond, Imam Dawood continued slowly, emphasizing, "You're right, vigilantism is not encouraged, but sometimes the law needs to be broken when it is unjust. When the society and system are corrupt, in that case, you do the right thing to help the people."

Kashif listened with an open mind, taking in everything being said.

"But, Kashif…" The imam's voice grew heavier. "I fear the hardest part is knowing when to stop. You can't do this forever. I'm not sure how long you should do this, but maybe that will be a discussion in the future. After you've found your answers, what I would advise, Kashif, is trying to work *within* the law. Maybe work with the Police Force."

"I'm not sure how I can do that," Kashif confessed.

"I know you will figure it out in time."

They both stared at each other quietly. Still taking in the words, Kashif suddenly felt, for the first time, a sense of relief and some clarity.

"So you are helping people, but what is this talk about not wanting to help others? I don't believe it. I've seen you out there; when you see someone in distress, you help them. You save them. Even if it means putting yourself in harm's way. That's courage, that's bravery, that's strength. It was Abu Bakr as-Sadeeq who said, 'Taking pains to remove the pain of others is the true essence of generosity.' Maybe you don't feel like you're making a difference, but I assure you, you are. Most of the city sees you very differently from how you see yourself."

"What's the point of saving others if I'm losing a part of myself? I couldn't save myself and what I had. I lost Aliya… Why can't I forget her?"

"Love can be cruel like that. What has happened to you is a calamity, no doubt. I was shocked, myself, for I was looking forward to your nikkah. And especially after your abu passed, the loss for you was infinitely harder. A heartbreak like yours is truly one of the heaviest loads to bear, especially when you keep it all inside as you have. I'm sorry you couldn't be with her, but it's not your fault. However, when that door closed, the door to MetalGhost opened, and look how many people you have helped since then!"

"I'd trade MetalGhost and everything I've done if it meant I could have her as my wife. I was ready to do it too, but… I was too late."

"What you're going through is one of the tragedies of life, for us to stumble upon another, who lights a fire in our heart that cannot die, but then realizing they are not always who we spend our lives with."

"How do I put out this fire in my heart? It's burning me every day. Everything reminds me of her. How do I forget her?" He mourned, the tears running freely.

"I know you've rejected proposals. Maybe you should give

others a chance?"

"How can I when I'm still stuck here like this? I don't want anyone else. It won't be fair for anyone to be with me when I have someone else in my heart."

Imam Dawood sighed. "Kashif, greatness requires sacrifice," he spoke slowly.

Kashif sighed loudly, dropping his head.

"I'll pray for you, brother—more than ever. Never underestimate the power of prayers. Don't stop being patient now. Keep going, keep having hope. But you need to help yourself, allow yourself to heal. And believe me, once you start looking at other proposals, it will help you move forward."

Kashif sat for some time, taking in everything the imam had said. He sighed as the realization that the Imam was right started settling in.

"And one last thing, Kashif, if you allow me to mention something I've noticed."

Kashif nodded.

"Your anger. I can see that's a problem. Your lenses are all fogged up, and what's fogging it is your anger. Your anger is driving you and not allowing you to see all the good that you're doing. Kashif, listen to me, you're helping people. You're doing good. And once you let go of your anger, you'll not only see things more clearly, but you'll feel better. And isn't that what you want, and why you're here?"

"How do I let go?"

"Allah warns us that anger is a very dangerous emotion, one that, if it's not controlled, it can destroy our whole faith. Now, that's a very serious statement," he sat forward. "And on the other hand, we're taught in hadith that whoever withholds their anger, Allah will withhold His punishment from that person. Look at that! That goes to show us what anger is and the difficulty that must exist with holding it in, because look at the tremendous reward associated with being able to control it. You already know there are many ways in which Islam teaches us to control our anger, and maybe we'll go over that in detail at a later time. But for now, how about this: next time you get angry, think of your father."

"My father? That's what makes me angry, thinking about him

and how evil people were responsible for his death."

"I know, but try this: I knew your father for over 20 years, and yet, I never once saw him angry... well, just once actually."

"Really? When?"

"In many ways, your father's character embodied the Prophet (ﷺ). See, the Prophet (ﷺ) used anger as a tool to teach and fix people, as a form of medicine, really. Just as we give medicine to cure someone, he would drop a little bit of anger when he saw someone doing something wrong in order to fix their behavior. It was used as a medicine, given in small amounts and only when needed. And I remember your father only got mad once, when his younger rowdy son, one time at the age of 10, was playing around during Salah at the masjid." He winked at Kashif.

"Oh yeah..." Kashif couldn't help but smile, remembering the moment. He ran his hand through his hair, remembering as the Imam continued.

"Instead of focusing on your prayers, you decided to make all the other kids laugh and disturbed everyone else's prayers too. Your father was disappointed, and he brought you to me."

"I never messed around in Salah again after that," Kashif nodded.

"See, like medicine."

"Next time you get angry, remember your father. He truly was a great man, and I do miss him dearly."

"Yeah..." Kashif sighed.

"I hope that helps, and it helps you see things a little differently. Because the way I see it, your anger is going to destroy you. And we don't want that. Plus, we'd have to change your name to Angry Man, and I don't know if you want that either," his eyes twinkled.

Not able to hold a straight face, Kashif smiled, shaking his head.

"Always remember the hadith, 'the strong man is not the one who wrestles others; rather, the strong man is the one who controls himself at times of anger.'"

"Thank you, Imam Dawood. You are right, and I will try," he sighed.

"You're welcome. Come talk to me anytime, please. I worry

about you. You have a lot of anger in you; you're a loaded gun. I just want to make sure you don't have the barrel pointed at yourself."

Kashif nodded, but before exiting, he turned back. "You might not hear from me for a while," he quietly said. "But don't worry about me. We'll talk again, insha'Allah."

"Insha'Allah," Imam Dawood replied, concerned.

When he returned home, Kashif walked up to the MetalGhost suit hanging in the Playroom. Standing face to face with the suit, he stared at it, peering straight into its eyes. Sighing, he put away the matches and lighter he had left earlier next to the suit. He walked out of the room and closed the door, with the suit hanging behind him.

CHAPTER TWENTY SEVEN

MONSTER

I t was a perfectly tranquil and quiet night in Ridgefield Park City. On a relatively warm and pleasant night for November, the city was active and alive. And since Eid two weeks ago, there had been no crimes, no major news to report, and no MetalGhost sightings. The city was as calm and peaceful as it had been in a very long time. Little did the city know that it would be a very long time after tonight when it would be this peaceful again.

"Asalaamu alaikum, so nice to see you!" Ami welcomed the guests to her house. Her friend, Mahnoor Aslam, entered and hugged Ami warmly, followed by her husband, Faisal, who gave her a courteous slight bow while putting his hand on his heart. They both took off their shoes as they entered, while Ami held the door open for the final guest and the real reason why everyone was gathering—their daughter, Amira.

"I'm not listening to any more excuses from you," Ami had sternly said the previous day to Kashif. "I can't just sit back and watch you mourn yourself to death. You've been rejecting proposals and declining even to meet people for too long now. You're not going to die alone, not under my watch."

"Ugh, are you really going to force me?" Kashif lamented.

"Yes, force you out of love," she responded firmly.

Kashif knew this day would come when Ami would "force him out of love" to meet other women with the intention of marriage. And so the day had come when she invited her friends over with their daughter for dinner, with the hope that Kashif would talk to the daughter and they could get to know one another, despite

Kashif's protests.

"Wear this," his younger sister, Yasmine, said a few hours before the dinner, showing him a nice T-shirt and pants.

"I was just going to wear a black shalwar kameez," Kashif shrugged, eyeing the shirt and pants combo.

"And that's why you're single," she replied, shaking her head. "No style. That is also why you need me there tonight, to help you," she pointed out. "It's like you've forgotten how to talk to girls." So they practiced how to show interest, how to ask questions, and how to be charming. "Good luck, brother," Yasmine loudly sighed an hour later, rolling her eyes, clearly not happy with the outcome of her lessons.

"Amira! So good to see you! You look beautiful," Ami exclaimed as Amira walked gracefully and shyly through the door. Kashif had to admit that Ami was right. Stealing a look, he noticed Amira was indeed beautiful, and suddenly he felt himself breathing a little bit faster. Everyone sat in the family room as the parents chatted casually while the children sat nervously and quietly, Kashif and Amira avoiding each other's eyes. Yasmine struck up a conversation with Amira, and the two were chatting and laughing in no time. After a short while, dinner was served, followed by tea and desserts.

"Why don't we let the two kids talk while we go back to the living room?" Aunty Mahnoor proclaimed a little too excitedly. Everyone nodded happily and headed over to the adjacent room, leaving Amira and Kashif to themselves in the dining room. Ami was the last to exit the room; standing behind Amira, she gave Kashif a stare that said, *take this seriously, and do not mess it up!*

Noted. Kashif raised his eyebrows in response.

When they were alone, the two looked at each other and smiled. Amira was beautiful, especially today. Her light brown eyes shined brightly in her elegant long white shalwar kameez and green hijab.

"Well, good thing this isn't awkward," Amira joked sarcastically. They both laughed nervously as it broke the ice.

"Can I pour you some chai?" Kashif asked, finding he needed to do something with his hands.

"Sure, thanks. So, what are you looking for?" Amira asked.

Someone who is totally cool with me going out each night and beating people up.

"Um, someone down to earth, fun, and a good Muslim, I guess," Kashif stumbled on his words. "How about you?"

"Yeah, same." She nodded.

"So, what do you usually do for fun?" Kashif tried to remember his sister's list of questions to ask. *Show you're interested in her,* she had said.

"Between getting my Ph.D. in Communications, teaching, memorizing the Qur'an part-time, and taking care of my parents, I wouldn't say I have time for too much fun at the moment."

Kashif nodded, clearly impressed while playing with a napkin to keep his hands busy and to have something to look at.

"But I guess you could say swimming; I do enjoy a good swim. How about you?"

Oh, I don't know. I dress up in a highly sophisticated metallic suit and fight crime around the city.

"I… um, well, I like to build things… I'm into engineering and robotics. I teach that myself," he stumbled.

Robotics, nerd! He could hear Aliya responding to him in his mind.

"That's… interesting," Amira tried to say genuinely, with a smile.

Trying to focus, Kashif attempted to continue confidently, "Yeah, I enjoy designing and building. For example, I designed and built those tiny rickshaws." He pointed to the shelves in the corner.

"Oh," Amira responded, surprised. "I've been noticing those. They are very nice."

"I built a small engine in them so they can actually run. Here, let me show you," he said, getting up and walking toward the shelves. "I made them for Ami," he said, holding one and turning around. When he looked back, Aliya was sitting in the seat, with her face in her hand, looking wide-eyed and impressed at Kashif.

Wow, Kash, they're beautiful, Aliya said slowly.

"What?" Kashif's heart dropped, along with the rickshaw in his hands, before he caught it.

"I said they're beautiful. The intricate details are quite exquisite," Amira responded. "Are you okay?" She stared at

Kashif, who stood still with wide eyes.

"Yeah…" he spoke under his breath.

Before Amira could respond, the house shook as the lights flickered and the sound of clinking dishes filled the house. The shaking stopped after a few seconds, followed by loud shrieking from the family room. Kashif and Amira hurried to the other room, where everyone sat.

"Is everyone okay?" Yasmine asked nervously. Before they could respond, the ground shook again.

Kashif and Ami stared into each other's eyes knowingly and shared a look of horror. *It can't be. Not again.*

Everyone huddled together around the family room, looking around in worry and confusion. "Let's see what's going on," Yasmine turned on the TV. All the channels were reporting the earthquakes, but something much more sinister was happening.

"We are LIVE at Judge Square near the docks as one of the buildings is on fire. We are being told it is a chemical plant belonging to Iris Hill…" The news reporter was cut off by a loud roar and shaking behind her. As the reporter ducked for safety, she looked back in shock as the camera zoomed in on what seemed like a silhouette of a giant figure coming out of the fire. "Are you getting this?!" She screamed.

The colossal figure appeared, standing about fifty feet tall with an enormous muscular build that ripped its shirt and shorts. The face of the giant was burnt and scarred with giant angry red eyes. Its figure resembled a human, with a bald head, oversized arms, and legs. Its skin was charred and rocklike, and towering out of the side of the building, it was anything but human. The giant roared again, a loud, deep yell full of anger. Onlookers nearby scattered and ran in fear and panic. As it took a giant step forward, it turned its attention to the screaming people. With a sudden burst of anger, it flipped a nearby car over entirely with a mighty blow with one hand. Noticing the news reporters, cameras, and flashes, it ran toward them with loud, powerful booming steps. The bystanders dispersed frantically as the monster flipped a news van.

"Oh my God!" the people yelled. "What is that!?"

Back at the house, everyone was in disbelief at what they were witnessing. It took Kashif a few moments before he realized he was frozen in shock. He stared at the ground, unable to decide what to do. When the news reporter screamed, "help!" as the monster threw another vehicle toward people running away, Kashif snapped out of his paralysis. He slowly started backing away toward the kitchen. Everyone turned to him.

"Where are you going?" Ami asked.

"I... ugh... I have to go," he said slowly, staring at the screen. "I'll be back, don't worry," he continued, backing away into the kitchen. Ami followed him, and in a low but fearful voice, whispered, "Where do you think you're going?!"

"Ami, I have to," he replied as he gently held her.

"Are you crazy? It's too dangerous!" She clutched onto him hard.

"I have to try. I'll be fine. Make du'a for me," he said, still holding her.

He kissed her head, and as he backed away, turning to leave from the kitchen door, Ami called, "And what about them? What about Amira?"

Kashif paused, slowly turned around, and whispered, "She's not Aliya, I'm sorry," as he exited the door.

"Samir, come in. Are you watching this?" Kashif radioed in. "Samir, are you there?" to no response. The call to his cell phone went unanswered. Kashif couldn't help but begin to worry. He jumped on his bike and followed the countless police sirens; it seemed the entire city's police force was headed towards the monster, as they should. When he arrived near a blocked-off area downtown, Kashif couldn't believe his eyes. An enormous monster, standing taller than some of the five-story buildings, had made its way and stood angrily in the middle of the city. The monster tore through the streets, smashing cars, buses, and whatever came in its path as it stormed into the city's busiest area. The noise from all the commotion of the sirens, people screaming and running, and officers directing people to safety only added to the chaos. A police officer yelled, "Move, move, move!" He waved his arms frantically to everyone in the area to take shelter in the stores. Kashif was pulled into the moving crowd but stopped dead in his tracks at what he saw in the direction of the monster.

An army of tanks, helicopters, and snipers had arrived and surrounded the monster, and they were unloading a heavy arsenal of gunfire on it. Giant floodlights from the helicopters were on the large beast, lighting up the dark night. Kashif was pushed in with a crowd of people into a deli for shelter; the last thing he saw was the giant monster roaring and flipping over a tank with its brute strength. The screaming crowd of people entered the deli, and an officer ordered them all to move to the back, turn off the lights, and lay low. Kashif felt as if he were sleepwalking, being pushed here and there without control. Everyone in the dark deli was panicking as worried whispers and cries spread across the store. The group of people stood as quietly as possible, trying not to make any noise or movement in the dark. It was only a moment later, when a police car came crashing right in front of the deli, that Kashif snapped out of it, as the sheer terror of screams filled the space. He had to make his choice. Slowly retreating, he moved behind everyone, slipping toward the back. When he reached the back, he felt the cold wall behind him as he pressed himself against it. The coolness of the wall felt refreshing against his neck and back. He rested there for a moment, but the cold wall also gave him a jolt, waking him up from his trance. Hesitating for a moment, he closed his eyes and whispered, "Bismillah." Reaching for his watch, he pressed the side button, and it was a matter of seconds before he was fully suited. No one noticed as MetalGhost stood behind them all. As the crowd huddled together and continued to scream with each loud bang and gunfire outside, Kashif stepped forward, and a different kind of screaming occurred.

"It's MetalGhost!"

"Thank God you're here!"

"It's MetalGhost, everybody!"

The crowd sighed with relief as a genuine sense of calmness came upon them. Everyone was starting to gather around him, staring at MetalGhost with hopeful eyes. As MetalGhost took a step forward, they cleared the way for him. Kashif could feel people touching his suit, feeling it with their hands gently as he walked towards the front. "Stay here," he turned around slowly, "It'll be okay," he tried reassuring them.

Walking out to the street, people were still running

helter-skelter in all directions as the giant was fighting against the armed forces on the ground and air. Kashif saw a gut-wrenching moment when the giant picked up some of the soldiers and tossed them away over buildings as if they were nothing. The monster roared as the gunfire continued assaulting it, but it did not seem harmed by it.

"MetalGhost!" The screams started coming from the people on the street. "Save us!"

People began gathering around MetalGhost, gazing at him in awe. This was the first time MetalGhost was on the ground amongst the people. The crowd circled around him with hopeful and frightened gazes. MetalGhost looked down as a little boy walked toward him with wide eyes. "You can do it. You can save us," he quietly said. MetalGhost gave him a nod before noticing the line of police cars and officers behind the monster, shouting orders. Taking a step toward them, the crowd that had circled him, started clearing the way for him as they all tried to get a good look at and feel of his suit.

"I thought you'd never show up!" Det. Fahim Kazmi looked relieved, calling to MetalGhost as he approached them.

"Is anything working?" MetalGhost asked, looking at the monster.

"Nothing seems to be harming it. All the bullets, grenades, and whatever heavy artillery we're throwing at it, it's not affecting it, except making it angrier."

"Let me try. Tell your men to clear the way."

Det. Fahim radioed in, "Stay clear. MetalGhost is going in! I repeat, stay clear!"

"And tell your men not to shoot at me, for once," MetalGhost added with an edge.

Det. Fahim glanced at MetalGhost, taking the insult in stride. He picked up his radio again while still staring straight at MetalGhost. "And don't shoot him for God's sake."

The night became eerily quiet and still as all the firing at the monster suddenly halted. All eyes shifted towards MetalGhost, as he walked down the middle of the road towards the monster. The officers on the ground, the soldiers in the tanks, snipers on the roof, everyone paused and stared at MetalGhost. The whole city watched as the monster looked at the approaching figure and roared at it as if it recognized MetalGhost. It took a step forward, and MetalGhost broke into a run and took flight toward its head. Clenching his fists twice, he flew closer to the monster's face as it tried swatting him away. Avoiding its hand, when he reached its head in the air, he punched as hard as he could, first with a right hand in between its eyes and then with a left jab. The monster screamed in pain as it stumbled backward, turning to its side. For a moment, the monster seemed stunned. But only a moment later, it turned around and swung at MetalGhost. Ducking the punch, MetalGhost, again, super punched it twice, causing it to fall back against a building. MetalGhost could hear people's gasps as the monster slammed backward into a building, shattering the windows. Landing on the rooftop, the sniper looked amazed as MetalGhost planned his next attack. Thinking about his next move, MetalGhost knew what he had to do as he flew down and tried punching again. This time, the monster swatted with a backhand and struck MetalGhost with a mighty blow.

"Aaahh!" He crashed through a building window. MetalGhost felt as if he had just been hit by a truck as he lay on the ground wincing in pain. Slowly getting to his feet, he took a few moments to catch his breath. He could hear the monster step closer to the window, peering in, searching for him. When the monster peeked through the window, it was met with another set of blows to the face, causing it to trip backward, almost losing balance. This time, MetalGhost had a better plan. *I have to close the distance. I need to stay as close to him as possible.* He flew behind the monster and landed on its shoulders. The monster swatted at him as he flew onto his head, this time striking itself. Screaming in anger, it took a few steps back, but MetalGhost kept close. He continued moving from one side to another like a fly as the monster continued to try swatting him away. Angering the monster more, MetalGhost kept floating and flying behind the monster, causing it to spin and become dizzy.

It's working! He thought to himself in an effort to confuse the beast. He didn't see it coming as the monster caught MetalGhost off guard, and with a mighty leap, grabbed him in the palm of its hand. The beast had him. It brought MetalGhost close to its face and eyes and snarled loudly at him.

"AAAHH!" MetalGhost screamed in agony as the monster squeezed him harder. MetalGhost could feel his ribs breaking. The monster continued to crush him. Starting to lose focus, the world began fading into blackness as he felt his lungs were about to burst. He could barely hear the onslaught of bombs and explosives being fired at the monster. The monster focused its attention on the soldiers and officers firing away and threw MetalGhost into the side of a building two blocks away. He fell twenty feet to the ground with a crushing slam right onto the sidewalk. Recoiling in pain, his view was upside down as he saw the monster continue fighting the gunfire and Police Force. Trying to sit up, he knew he had broken some bones in his sides. His suit was also damaged with cracks and fractures to the chest piece and his helmet. With all his might, MetalGhost stood up, took a few painful breaths, and ran toward the monster again. This time, he knew what he had to do.

Taking the monster by surprise, he landed on its head, moved toward its eyes, and super-punched hard downward. The entire city froze in shock at what they saw, as the monster let out a loud piercing shriek, heard miles away. MetalGhost held his fists in position inside the eye socket of the beast. Screaming in agony, the monster reached for its damaged eye. MetalGhost flew to the other eye and punched into the other eye socket. The beast screamed and roared into the night. MetalGhost felt his suit giving out and his jetpack starting to falter. He made his way to the rooftop and fell in pain, his sides and ribs throbbing in agony. A few of the officers in the building hesitantly stepped closer and tried to help him stand. They backed off as MetalGhost screamed in pain, realizing his arm was probably fractured.

"Give me your grenades," he winced and struggled to speak, for talking only made the pain worse. The officer handed over three grenades and backed away. Taking quick breaths and holding his side, MetalGhost got to his feet, turned, and looked back at the monster, who was stumbling around blind. *Time to finish this.*

He fluttered in the air out of control toward the monster's head, unpinned the grenades, and threw them into its mouth. As he tried flying away, the monster grabbed him again in its palm and squeezed hard. In a few seconds that felt like a lifetime for

MetalGhost, he could only see bright lights as his world went black.

"Hey," a voice called him. "Hey, get up." He felt someone shaking him. MetalGhost woke up on the rooftop of a building. The explosion threw him to the next block, knocking him out. Gaining consciousness slowly, he noticed the row of officers looking down at him. MetalGhost felt utterly broken, with his suit still attached to him but shattered in different places.

"You did it," the voice spoke to him.

He looked up, remembering the monster. Stumbling to the ledge, he looked down and saw the dead carcass of the beast. Kashif exhaled in relief. But before he could sit back down, the monster caught his attention again. The dead giant lay in the middle of the street, but it seemed as if it was moving. *It is moving!* He looked closer. Noticing the body squirm, it started shrinking smaller and smaller, as if it was deflating. Lost in disbelief, he saw the body contract inward as it slimmed and shrunk, and within an instant, the skin and insides burst into liquid. The monster was gone, leaving behind a slimy pool of liquid.

MetalGhost stepped onto the ledge, holding his side with his arm. A helicopter circled around, shining its giant searchlight on him. Protecting his eyes from its blinding light, he looked down and noticed people starting to gather, all staring up at him. The look of awe and amazement filled their eyes as people began piling into the streets. The crowd gathered around the building.

"You did it!" Someone shouted from below.

"You're our hero," Another followed.

MetalGhost slouched, every inch of his body in immense pain. He looked back, noticing the officers staring at him hesitantly, still with their weapons in hand.

"Talk to us! Who are you under the mask?!" Shouts came from below.

"What do you want?!" There were more shouts.

The officers nervously took steps closer to him, raising their weapons. *Is this really happening?* was all Kashif could think. Another officer stepped forward in front of him, putting his hands up, signaling his team to remain calm as he stood between

MetalGhost and them.

"You should talk." The officer turned back, handing him his megaphone. He pointed downward at the large crowd.

Taking deep breaths, MetalGhost stood up, took the megaphone, and analyzed the officer. He was a young man, MetalGhost noticed. The officer nodded at him. Turning around, he saw that the size of the crowd had grown substantially, filling up back out a couple of blocks.

Behind him, he heard the officers loading their weapons, ready to fire at any moment. Finally, he felt something other than pain: anger.

Raising the megaphone, he spoke. "This city has seen too much pain, too much suffering, and too many have gotten away. No more. To all the gangs, criminals, and corrupt officials out there: I'm coming for you. So all of you in this city, get ready. If you want peace, prepare for war!" He turned to look behind him, "And to all the corrupt police in this city," he growled, *"I'm coming for you."*

MetalGhost heard the radios of each of the officers, and a familiar voice shouted angrily, "Fire, you idiots! You have him! FIRE!"

In a split second, before the officers could pull the trigger, MetalGhost ran and jumped off the rooftop to the next building. The pain caused him to scream in anguish. He heard the officers chasing him and the helicopter following him as he continued running and jumped to the next rooftop.

"Follow him!" He heard Police Chief Eames' voice on the radios.

MetalGhost knew his jetpack was damaged, and he couldn't outrun the police on the rooftops. From the rooftop of one of the buildings, he looked down at his location. Recognizing where he was, he ran toward the adjacent building's rooftop and jumped off, knowing what was below. He landed on the restaurant Kebab Heaven's large and soft patio umbrellas and rolled off to his feet. A crowd of people shrieked in fear. He ran down the alley, still in extreme pain, until his body gave out and he collapsed. He fell to the ground, out of breath and unable to move. Laying on the ground, people started walking toward him. He could hear their murmuring but also the shouts and screams of the police officers.

"Don't let him get away!" He heard officers running towards him.

Crumpled on the street, MetalGhost looked up and whistled with all the energy he had left in him. One block away, the crowd heard an engine turn on and rev; within a few seconds, his bike appeared, parking itself next to him. With all his might, he picked himself up, jumped onto the bike, and rode out of the crowd, leaving them in a state of amazement.

Having initiated the automatic self-ride feature, the bike took Kashif to the apartment and lab as he swerved in and out of consciousness. Whirling in and around the streets, Kashif tried his hardest to keep a hold on the bike's handles as it made its way safely to the building. Having tracked the bike, Samir was waiting by the door, "Come on, you gotta help me help you, Bro," he shouted, trying to carry the badly beaten Kashif upstairs. "You're getting fat, I'm telling you," Samir complained, huffing and puffing as he carried Kashif. Instead of heading toward the lab, Samir opened Kashif's apartment and laid him down on the sofa. "My God, you're bleeding, and I can already feel broken bones." He gasped in shock as Kashif screamed in pain. Samir quickly found bandages to stop the bleeding and a wet cloth to wipe away the blood from his face.

"You'll be alright, man, but we gotta get you to a hospital and fast," Samir said, worried.

"Where were you tonight?" Kashif asked.

"What? I was…" Samir paused, a worried look coming across his face.

"I called you, so many times," Kashif, breathing heavily between each word. Noticing the apprehensive look on Samir's face, he asked again, "Are you okay? Where were you?"

A nervous Samir stood up, not looking at Kashif. "I..." he started but stopped himself, clearly thinking. Taking a deep sigh he continued, "I have something I need to share with you..." A sudden loud knocking and pounding on the door shook both of them. "Police! Open up!"

Samir's face went pale in shock, looking back at Kashif, who was too beaten and bruised to show any expression. They locked eyes, Samir's eyes were full of worry, while Kashif's were full of pain.

"Open up right now, or we'll break this door in!" The shouts came from outside. Samir stood up, placed a blanket gently over Kashif, and pulled a small table out, in front of him.

"I have to do this," he confessed apologetically, walking out of the room and toward the door. "I'm coming, Officers," he called out, slowly opening the door. An entire SWAT team rushed through, pushing Samir out of the way. With guns pointed, they searched each room.

"Clear!" one shouted from the other room. "I've got one here!" another called from Kashif's room. Samir felt himself shaking in fear.

"What is going on here?!" Samir shouted in confusion. Det. Fahim walked in and put his hand on Samir's shoulders, turning him around. He led him to the room where Kashif was lying injured and bleeding. As they entered the room, they walked into five SWAT team members with their guns pointed at Kashif, sitting up on the couch, facing the TV with the news on. *Unbelievable!* Samir thought. To his immense surprise, the bruises and blood had been wiped away, his face flawlessly clean, looking fresh. His hair was parted perfectly and neatly to the side, and he wore new pajamas under a blanket.

"Can we help you, Detective?" Kashif spoke weakly from the sofa.

Det. Fahim's face showed confusion and embarrassment. "I'm sorry, gentlemen, we received reports that MetalGhost came this way. Maybe… uh…" Det. Fahim looked around. "Even into this building." He gave a slight shrug.

"MetalGhost? Here?" Samir gasped in surprise. "We just saw him on TV." He pointed towards the news. "They just reported he was heading toward the docks area, I think."

"Why would he be here?" Kashif asked weakly.

"False report, I guess," Det. Fahim responded, scratching his head as he looked around the room, inspecting it.

Samir noticed a few drops of blood on the floor leading towards Kashif. He slowly stepped forward, covering the view of the drops before Det. Fahim caught sight of them.

Det. Fahim turned his attention to Kashif, examining him. "Are you feeling okay?" He asked, surveying the blanket and weak response.

"I'm not feeling too well since earlier today. Just trying to rest up and feel better," Kashif stated. *At least I'm not lying.*

"Hmm," Det. Fahim responded.

"Sir, we got Laser," a voice chirped on the Detective's radio.

"Roger that, I'm on my way," Det. Fahim responded. "You do look a little sick." He turned back to Kashif and nodded. "I'm sorry for troubling you both. We'll be getting out of here. I hope you feel better, Mr. Razvi."

As the SWAT team and Det. Fahim took their leave, Samir closed the door and rushed back to the room. Kashif pressed a button on the device under his blanket, and a giant screen projecting out of a small round object in front of him on the floor, turned off. The projector screen in front of Kashif disappeared, revealing the actual image behind the screen of Kashif sitting crumpled as before. By the time Samir ran up to him, Kashif was spitting up blood.

"That smoke screen projector really came in handy for once," Samir remarked in amazement. "I take back calling it your stupidest invention ever. I guess sometimes you do need a full life-sized filter." Samir shrugged, tending to Kashif.

CHAPTER TWENTY EIGHT

LASER

The aftermath of the monster left the entire city shaken to its core. Witnesses spotted a man secretly exiting the building from which the monster broke loose, causing a chase and eventual capture by the police. The man was one of the most wanted criminals in the city: Laser. Detective Fahim Kazmi brought him in for questioning, but Laser revealed nothing. His court case was only a few days long, short, and decisive: guilty on all accounts of illegal experimenting and creating the monster that caused so much destruction and havoc, including five deaths. Laser admitted he hadn't intended to let the beast loose at that point; instead, he was still experimenting when the monster broke out.

"Still, I enjoyed watching our beautiful work take life," he proudly boasted in court.

Our. Everyone knew he wasn't working alone, and Det. Fahim made sure he stayed behind bars until he was willing to talk. Or until they handed down the eventual death penalty.

Laser laughed all the way back to his cell after the verdict.

"You think these cell walls can hold me?! I'll see you all soon!" He howled and laughed while being led out in chains after the verdict. "Especially *you,* Detective," he taunted. His menacing stare and smile brought an uncomfortable chill down Det. Fahim's spine. Laser's maniacal laugh could be heard from afar as he was led out of the building.

Detective Fahim slowly opened the front door to his house, entering the dark hallway. Stepping inside, he carefully and as quietly as possible, closed the door behind him, realizing it was late night and his wife, Aisha, and two children, eleven-year-old Yasir and six-year-old Alayna, would be asleep. It had been a long day, finally putting to end the case of crazed criminal Brett Owens, infamously known as Laser. Even though Laser was locked up in the highest level security jail, Det. Fahim still felt unsatisfied and far from entirely content. He knew this was just the tip of the iceberg in the fight against the biggest criminals in RP City, as now the mobs had been put on alert, and he knew they would respond back. *The war is just starting.* But this was what he had been asking for and working towards his entire career. After having been on the force for twelve years, he had finally gained enough evidence and rank to start going after them all. But the toll was beginning to weigh heavily on him. He felt tired and aged, but his determination to clean up the city had not wavered.

Quietly taking off his shoes and putting away the keys in the hall, the thought of his bed relaxed him. *Finally,* he thought, heading toward the stairs and up to his room, *I can get some rest.*

Beep beep, his phone buzzed. Checking the phone, the screen displayed a video message marked "urgent!" in his police department group. *Strange to get a message with a video at this time,* he thought, as the group was strictly for law enforcement officials to send top priority updates and important reminders. *What could this be?* Wearily, he stopped at the stairs and instead, turned to enter the dark living room. Sitting on the armchair, he opened the message.

The video opened to a man sitting in the corner of a dark room that looked like a jail cell, his face hidden in the shadows. The man started to laugh. Louder, louder, and louder. After a minute, the man in the video stopped to clear his throat as if to make a speech to an audience.

"Good evening, *Detective Fahim!"* he stated, and started clapping slowly.

Det. Fahim felt his heart completely drop and his stomach turn.

"You did it. You *finally* did it. You've put me away!" The man in the video exclaimed, still in the shadows. "But what did I tell you? These walls cannot hold me," he remarked mockingly.

A chill went down Det. Fahim's neck, his heart racing, and an alarming fear was creeping in.

"If you're seeing this, then know it's already too late," the man in the video proclaimed, laughing. "I'm already out of this hell hole of a prison." The man slowly moved out of the shadows to reveal his face. *Laser!* "If you're seeing this..." He continued while laughing maniacally. Laser crouched down to his knees and started crawling slowly toward the camera. "Then I'm already long gone from this joke of a prison you had for me." He continued laughing. "I told you, I would get out."

Gasping in complete disbelief, fear struck through Det. Fahim like a lightning bolt as he sat in the dark room, frozen.

In the video, Laser continued crawling forward menacingly and brought his face right in front of the camera, his face and voice now turning sinister. "If you're watching this, then I'm already far from the prison. In fact..." He paused to smile, "I'm probably *in your house... I'm probably... already... behind you.*"

The detective slowly let out a whimper as a hand appeared from the dark behind him and landed gently on his shoulder.

"Hello, Detective." Laser's deep and slow voice came from behind him in the shadows. Meanwhile, the video recording of Laser continued showing him laughing hysterically.

Shaking and breathing heavily, Det. Fahim slowly turned to his side, looking up at the frightening smiling face of Laser. Hearing his own voice laughing at the detective from the video, Laser began howling in laughter even louder.

"You... but... *how?*" Det. Fahim's words barely came out, shaking from disbelief and shock.

"Shhh." Laser brought his finger to his lips. "You wouldn't want to wake up your family. They were sleeping when I last checked."

"No!" Det. Fahim rushed out of the chair, but Laser grabbed his shoulders and slammed him back into it.

"Don't worry, they're fine... for now. They'll enjoy the show of watching me tear you to pieces." There was a chilling edge in his voice, as he brought his face right in front of Det. Fahim's.

Moving in front of the detective, Laser reached into his pocket and retrieved a knife.

"How did you escape?"

Laser laughed again and sighed loudly, in satisfaction.

"Did you really think I wouldn't have another... what did you call it, ah yes, *monster,* ready to get me out? I have many pets. I was always going to break out, but I enjoyed the whole show you had put on. And I got to meet some of my lovely old friends back in the cell. Thank you for that opportunity." He smiled.

Det. Fahim couldn't believe what he was hearing. "Are you telling me they escaped too?"

"Your problems just got much bigger, Detective."

"Mad Scientist. You work for him; we know it. And we'll find him and get to him too."

Laser brought the knife to his face as if pretending to think. "Hmm, maybe, but you know who won't find him? You. After tonight, no one will be able to find you or your family." He brought the knife to his hostage's face. "I've been waiting for this moment," he said menacingly, digging the tip of the blade into Det. Fahim's cheek. As he started to cut the skin, the window behind him shattered loudly as MetalGhost crashed into the living room.

"Not you again!" A stunned Laser shouted angrily.

"Your little visit is over. Time to go back to your home in jail," MetalGhost casually remarked.

Laser quickly pointed his arms at MetalGhost, shooting red laser beams out from the metallic bands around his wrists. Kashif raised his forearm, releasing his blue shield that deflected the laser beams. Laser screamed, rushing toward MetalGhost and throwing a right hand. Blocking it easily, MetalGhost held Laser's fist in his hand in the air, not noticing Laser reach with his other hand into his pocket and retrieve small burning, sand-like particles. Before he could react, Laser threw the flaming sand into MetalGhost's face, lighting his mask on fire, burning and melting it. He fell to the ground, rolling in pain and trying to put out the fire, as the metal of his mask started burning Kashif's face and blinding his sight.

By this time, Aisha and the two kids came rushing down and into the room.

"Stay back! Don't come here!" Det. Fahim yelled to his family.

"Ah, welcome, welcome! Today, I have quite the show for you, kids. You get front row seats to watch this vigilante and your father die!"

Regaining some vision, MetalGhost looked up just in time to

see Laser rushing toward him with another handful of burning sand. He clenched his right fist twice just as Laser reached him and swung. The thunderous sound of Laser flying across the room, crashing through a wall, and landing with a crushing fall in the hallway, shook the entire house. Slowly getting to his feet, MetalGhost turned to face the family. They gasped in shock and shifted to the other corner of the room in fear of the terrifying sight of MetalGhost standing with a burned mask and black smoke rising from his head. MetalGhost winced in pain as he hobbled to where Laser fell, hands up, ready to punch again. But after seeing the damage on the other side of the wall, he put his arms down and rested his body against the wall. Laser was knocked out.

Still grimacing in pain and dizzy from not fully seeing because of Laser's burning sand, MetalGhost sat against the wall.

"How did you know he was here?" Det. Fahim called out to MetalGhost, while hugging his family.

"Your little police group, *let's just say* I get any notification before you guys do," he revealed.

"You've hacked into our system?!"

"Hey, you said it, not me," quipped MetalGhost raising his hands up.

"Well, I guess it's a good thing you did." He looked down, then up at MetalGhost, "You saved my life. And my family."

"Yeah, don't mention it," MetalGhost replied as the family cat, Prince, nonchalantly entered the room, smelled him, and cuddled up with him as he sat on the ground.

"I can see you're wincing; you took quite a beating at the attack. How're you holding up?" He asked, walking closer to him.

"Still in pain. It would be better if your men didn't chase and shoot at me."

"That was not my call. I'm sorry," Det. Fahim sympathized. After a moment, he pleaded, "I should know who saved me. You can tell me your name."

"You know my name. You all gave it to me," he said as Prince purred loudly on his lap.

"How about Cat Man?" Det. Fahim said with a slight grin.

"Don't push your luck," MetalGhost replied, getting up. "Your police friends are here." Before Det. Fahim could speak, the police sirens started to become audible in the distance.

MetalGhost looked down at Laser and his metallic bands which shot out lasers. He took them off and put them on himself, and studied them. "So I'll see you around," MetalGhost remarked, bending down to scratch Prince behind the ears.

"You can't just go. You can help us. You know, you can be part of our force," petitioned Det. Fahim.

"I'm not a cop. I do things my own way."

"Your way is crashing through my entire window?" He commented, pointing to the broken window and glass behind him.

"Did you prefer I rang the doorbell instead and waited for someone to open it?"

"Fair enough," Det. Fahim sighed.

"Plus, you all have been making my life miserable." It felt good to get that off his chest.

"Let's talk about it."

"Let me guess, at the precinct? Maybe after an arrest? That would look good on your record."

Det. Fahim stared back in silence. After a moment, he took out the handcuffs from his back pocket, held them in front of MetalGhost, and threw them out of the room.

"Would I like to arrest you? Yeah... I would have before. Do you think we've made your life miserable? You've made our lives and doing our jobs impossible, especially the last two weeks after the attack. The city has turned against *us* now. Now, we're the bad guys for trying to take you in. But at the same time, I can't deny you've helped the city. If only we could work together," he confessed.

"You're not all good guys, you know," MetalGhost responded.

"You don't think I know that? But you know what, *I'm* trying. I know the bigger fight for me is inside my own police force than outside of it, but I'm trying. I'm trying to clean this all up, *within the law!*" He fired back. "And you're not helping. Especially now, with all your friends joining in."

"Friends?"

"Yeah, your copycat buddies."

Kashif felt as if the ground beneath him had shifted. "What are you talking about?"

Det. Fahim examined MetalGhost, surprised, "Oh, so you haven't met them yet, huh? Well, we've been getting reports. We've been tracking them. We've basically begged the news and papers not to publish anything about these other... freaks—the lunatics who are trying to copy *you*. You've got fans, you know, and they want to be like you. See, you've opened a dangerous door. A door to lawlessness, to vigilantism. And soon, all the crazies are going to barge in, and there won't be a way to close it."

"Copycats?" MetalGhost whispered in shock to himself.

"Yeah. So come, let's talk about this. It's about time. Listen to me; enough of the vigilantism. It's not a good thing for the city in the long run."

MetalGhost didn't respond, as he lowered his head in thought.

"Work with us, we could do so much good for this city, together. Leave this vigilantism behind. Why keep working in the shadows?"

"The shadows keep me safe; I don't need any more attention. And our talk will have to be another time. Maybe when half of your police force isn't about to break into here, followed by all the reporters."

Det. Fahim sighed. "Fine, but how can I find you?"

MetalGhost walked towards the back door, "You won't. I'll find you."

A moment later, Det. Fahim's house was stormed by the police. As Kashif rested unnoticed on the roof, all he could think about was one thing: *copycats*.

CHAPTER TWENTY NINE

MEMORIAL

T he morning light slipped through the curtains and hit Kashif directly in the eyes. His every attempt at darkening the room as much as possible seemed to fail each morning, for the sunlight always found a slither to peek through. Awake now, he sighed, knowing the light wouldn't allow him to fall back to sleep. Rolling over, the sudden realization of the day struck him hard, sinking his heart. It had been four years since the passing of Kashif's abu, four years since it all changed, and since it all started. Four years of torture, pain, suffering, and anger. This year, Kashif and his ami had finally agreed to hold a du'a – prayer, at the cemetery and then to recite the Qur'an for his father at the masjid. For four years, Kashif had not spoken about his father's passing, nor had he opened up about his feelings or everything he had gone through. Instead, he had closed himself off. But today, at the cemetery, he had agreed to say a few words. Words that he had not prepared or planned to say.

He headed for the door but stopped when he noticed himself in the mirror. Wearing a black shalwar kameez, he stared at his reflection and remembered what people have been telling him more and more recently: *you're starting to look so much more like your abu*. It was the best compliment he could get. And staring at his reflection now, he realized it was true; he resembled his father more and more. Except Abu was always smiling, and Kashif's face was permanently fixating on a scowl for the past four years. *I wonder what Abu would have done in my place?* That was a thought that had started creeping into his mind lately.

Imam Dawood Murphy stood in front of the crowd that had gathered at the cemetery, reciting the Qur'an and *du'as* for Kashif's abu and all the deceased. Finishing the prayers, he looked up at Kashif and nodded to him to proceed to the front and say a few words. Walking to the front and turning to face the gathering of people, Kashif was surprised at how many people had shown up. He realized and marveled at how many people had loved and respected Abu. As he scanned the crowd, he noticed those who his abu had called friends, who had known him longer than Kashif had been alive. He knew they missed him too, for they told him whenever they met him. Starting to feel overwhelmed at the sight of so many loved ones, Kashif could feel the tears about to rush out, and his breathing became heavier. He even noticed several of his own friends, many of whom, out of grief, he had blocked and shut out. Clearing his throat, he noticed one face in the crowd, which changed everything. The sadness, the guilt, and grief changed the moment he connected eyes with a figure he had not expected to see. He locked eyes with Aliya's father. Suddenly, the anger returned, starting to rise. Aliya's abu looked at him with sadness. Kashif looked down and thought for a while, trying to regain his composure. A moment passed in silence as he thought. Looking back up and out at Abu's friends again, he spoke.

"'There's nothing we can do. Your father is dead,' the nurse had said pointedly without much emotion," Kashif began. "I'd learned by then that the 'care' from 'patient care' was mostly missing in healthcare professionals. Instead, they're pretty cold. That's what I felt right then, too, after the earthquake and after Abu passed; I started to shiver, but after that, I felt nothing for a long time." Kashif paused. "We all handled this news differently. My brother talked to the nurse, trying to make sense of the bombshell news she just casually broke to us. Ami didn't accept it. She laid down her prayer mat and started praying right there in the hallway of the ICU, spending a long time in *sujood,* in prostration. I just stared at Abu, lying on his hospital bed, and I felt nothing. I only stared away. After months of planning, as many of you know, we canceled my wedding three days before it was supposed to take place because he was in the ICU. But at that moment, I would give up the whole world just to have the nurse's words taken back. My

parents were my biggest supporters, best friends, teachers, sense of comfort, and anchors. They did everything in their lives for me, and Abu was passing away right in front of me. And there was nothing I could do for him." Kashif felt the tears starting to come as he relived the moment. But he held them back.

"Life can be cruel like that. Helplessly watching your own father slip away. *'I want nothing more in my life than to see you married,'* he had told me, to lead me down the aisle on my wedding day. Yeah, life can be cruel like that. One day, we're planning my wedding, the next, Abu's janazah. I can only imagine what he would have thought of what happened afterward. In a way, I'm glad he didn't see or witness what happened. The heartbreak, the hurt, the pain, the suffering we went through on top of losing him; sometimes it still feels too much to bear," Kashif locked eyes, again, with Aliya's dad. His eyes showed pain.

"It took him only a few moments to pass. Besides the usual *'I'm sorry'* and *'I love you,'* we would whisper to him, we played *Surah Rahman* in his ear, hoping that would be the last thing he heard."

Stopping again and looking out, the crowd listened intently to his every word. "What we don't realize is losing one parent really means losing both in a way. My ami, my rock, has never been the same since. I haven't been the same either, for losing a loved one is you losing a big part of yourself. Pain changes you. Grief is a strange thing. It comes at you in different ways, angles, and times, and it changes how you view the world: it's hard to love a world that's taken a beloved from you. We're taught from a young age to have sabr, to have patience, and trust in God's plans, but these are the times we have to put that into action. Even though it's so hard, and even though there are a million *why's*, this is the test. So, we're still trying to be content. We thank Allah for the years He gave us with Abu. We've read many times that Prophet Muhammad (ﷺ) reminds us that we're travelers in this world. Reading that is one thing, but I really feel that now."

Kashif paused and lowered his head again, waiting for a moment. With his head still down, he closed his eyes and continued, "I can't believe it's been four years. It feels like just yesterday, but it also feels like I haven't seen or spoken to him in so long. I think for the rest of our lives, it will always feel like just yesterday, yet so long ago. I know I haven't fully recovered and maybe never will, and I know I haven't spoken about all this either. And I'm sorry to all of you. To my friends, I know I haven't been there for you or been present, and I'm sorry. Please keep him in your du'as. Inna lillahi wa inna ilaihi rajioon, to Allah we belong, and to Him we will return." *I know I haven't found who did this. But I will, I promise.*

He opened his eyes and lifted his head, noticing even more people than before. To his surprise, he felt lighter after speaking, almost as if he needed to get these thoughts off of his chest. Taking a breath, a weight seemed to be lifted from his shoulders. The anger seemingly leaving. Scanning the crowd, to his surprise, he spotted Det. Fahim and Det. Zara present. As he walked, the crowd of people shook his hand and hugged him. He noticed Aliya's father had left by then. As he finished meeting everyone and walked back to the masjid, a new sense of motivation kindled inside him. But this time, it wasn't anger leading the way. It was the realization that his father had touched so many lives, and everyone here loved him dearly too. His heart and mind burnt with the desire to find out who was responsible for his death. It was justice not just for himself, but all those here who loved him also. For the first time since the monster attack three weeks ago, he couldn't wait to suit up.

CHAPTER THIRTY

HOW THEY FALL

Jose Rodriguez took a deep breath, inhaling the city's familiar scent, and smiled. "Oh, how I missed this place," he said to himself, continuing his stroll down the sidewalk. Jose was born and raised in Ridgefield Park City, but had spent the last few years away. Finally returning, he took in the smell, air, and noise of the city that he loved and that made him who he was. Dressed casually in blue jeans, a black windbreaker, and a ski cap, he had been walking for an hour, enjoying the sight and sounds, and reminiscing about his childhood in the city.

This city has changed so much in the past six years, he thought. Noticing the fog the past few days, he had never seen the city so foggy while growing up. Reaching the crosswalk, the light across the street blinked and counted down to turning green at the busy intersection. Hurrying to cross the road, he noticed an elderly woman next to him drop a grocery bag with vegetables and fruits falling out.

"Oh!" She cried out, bending down slowly to pick them up.

Jose turned around, and noticing the traffic light about to turn green any second, he rushed back to the middle of the street, bent down, and helped the elderly woman put all her groceries back into the bag. He picked up the bag, held her arm, and helped her cross the road.

"Thank you so much! You're an angel," the elderly woman gushed.

"You're welcome, Ma'am. Can I help you carry your groceries?" Jose asked, returning the bag.

"Bless you, young man, I'll be okay. I'm almost home." She smiled brightly.

"Have a good night." Jose waved to her as she walked ahead. Jose smiled and turned, looking up to see his destination. Taqi's Grocery & Meat Store, the sign read. Growing up, it was every other weekend that Jose visited Boxcar Bagels across the street and then shopped at Taqi's Grocery & Meat store with his mother. The good memories kept flashing before him as he took in another deep breath, retrieved a gun from his pants pocket, and entered the store.

"Everybody on the ground! Do it, now!" He screamed, slamming the door shut behind him.

The store was crowded with customers when the gunman entered, shouting loudly at everyone to drop to the ground as he slammed the door shut behind him, locking it. The store erupted in panic as shoppers began running helplessly behind racks for shelter, but a single gunshot into the air caused everyone to stop and drop flat to the ground.

"Everyone, line up here against the wall!" Jose shouted, pointing to the wall across the register. The people hesitated, frozen in fear. Jose jumped over the register counter and pointed the gun straight at the elderly man's head, behind the counter, while bringing him around. "Do it, now!" he screamed, standing behind the frightened cashier with one hand aiming the gun at his head, while the other hand held him in a headlock.

The crowd slowly walked toward the wall with their hands up.

"You…" Jose pointed toward a middle-aged husky man in the corner. "Close all the shades of the store." The man trembled in fear, getting to his feet slowly with his hands up. He closed the blinds to the front of the store, shutting out the view from outside. The man kept shaking as he sat back down against the wall with the other hostages.

"You…" the gunman pointed at a teenage girl. "Take your phone out and post on all your social media sites that you're being held hostage here and that I'm calling for MetalGhost to come. Not the police! Do it now!"

The girl took out her phone and started typing away.

A few minutes later, the lights in the entire store started to flicker. The gunman circled around with the cashier still in his grip, pointing his gun out. After a minute of quiet, the lights of the entire store went out, leaving the hostages frightened and screaming in the dark with the gunman.

"MetalGhost!" Jose shouted. "I'm here for you. I'm looking for you." He called out in the dark. The whole store erupted in screams as floating blue eyes with steam transmitting out of their ends, appeared in the middle of the store. MetalGhost took hold of the gun and threw Jose against the register. As the lights flashed back on, MetalGhost stood with the cashier safely by his side. Jose stood up after being thrown and picked up his gun. MetalGhost took a step toward Jose but raised his hands and called out, "I surrender. I'm not here to hurt anyone." He tossed his gun away to the ground, showing his empty hands. "I just needed to get to you. I need to talk to you. To show you something important."

"You can talk from behind bars," MetalGhost responded, reaching for him.

Jose ducked and ran in front of his hostages.

"This is not what you think. I'm not a criminal," he pleaded.

"You know, this is the second time someone has said that to me *as they're committing a crime*," MetalGhost confessed.

"Look, I didn't know how else to reach out to you. I have something you need to see." He moved toward the front door, opening it. "Everyone, you're free to go," he said, with the door open. The confused crowd looked around at one another, then up at MetalGhost before running out of the store.

"This is the only way I knew I could get your attention," Jose called back to MetalGhost as he closed the store door again, leaving just the two of them inside.

"You're insane," MetalGhost responded.

"You won't think that after you see what I have to show you."

"Go ahead. You have two minutes before I turn you in."

Hearing police sirens outside, Jose looked at MetalGhost, "Not here. They'll come barging in any minute."

"Then you better start talking fast, right here, before they come," MetalGhost countered, not budging.

Jose reached into his windbreaker slowly, raising his other arm in the air and taking out an envelope. He opened the envelope, took out a few pictures and showed him.

Staring at the pictures before him, MetalGhost gasped in shock, "What the hell is this?!"

"Proof," Jose responded calmly. "Like I said, I need to talk to you. And there's a lot more you need to hear and see." Both men stared at one another as MetalGhost thought of what to do. Hearing footsteps of the police outside. "Roof," he said, running to the back of the store.

The store's roof was a closed-off spot between two taller buildings, the perfect location for a private meeting. Jose stood face to face with MetalGhost, still holding the pictures in his hand.

"What is this?! Who are you?!" MetalGhost grabbed Jose's shirt by the chest.

"My name is Jose Rodriguez. I'm a journalist here in RP," he responded without fear. "Like you, I'm also tired of all the corruption and crime in this city. What you said after you took out that monster, I'm with you. 'If you want peace, prepare for war,' that's what you said, right? Well, these pictures…" He reached into his envelope, taking out more to show MetalGhost, "This is war."

"I… I can't believe this. Ya Allah!" MetalGhost cried out.

"Is it really surprising, though?" Jose asked. "What did you think was happening? I knew it, but I needed proof. And just last week, I got my proof." He pointed to the pictures.

"This was last week?" MetalGhost could not believe what he was hearing and seeing.

"It's been going on for years, right under our eyes."

"Why didn't you take this to the police or report this?"

"Police? You're joking, right?"

Staring at the pictures, he knew Jose was right.

"And the news media, who will want to take this story? Whoever reports this, will die." He stared at MetalGhost. "It isn't safe for anyone. And I know how they work; I don't trust any reporter, journalist, or any person in this city with this…" He took a step forward, holding out the envelope for MetalGhost to take "Except you. I only trust you."

Kashif stood stunned, looking at the pictures before him, again and again. It was all starting to click, all beginning to make sense. "If this goes public…" He paused, staring at Jose.

"It will turn this whole city upside down," Jose finished. "It will change everything."

Kashif paced back and forth, trying to think straight, contemplating his next move. Things just took a drastic change for the worse, he thought. After a moment of pacing, he stopped and came towards Jose again. "What do you want me to do with this?"

"The city needs to know the truth. But it needs to come from a reliable source: *you*," said Jose.

"Half the city hates me and wants to see me dead."

"And the other half will follow you. They already do."

MetalGhost started pacing again, trying to figure out what to do. The only solution to this new problem was horrifying him.

"You know what you have to do," Jose pleaded.

"No… there has to be another way," Kashif said, still pacing.

"It's the *only* way. The only way is to battle this head-on. Frankly, I'm surprised you didn't figure this out yourself, with your high-tech suit and gadgets and all."

"I was busy fighting other fights."

"This is the only fight that matters, man. We fix this, and we fix so many problems for so many people. This is what's wrong with our city," he said, pointing to the pictures. "Fix this, and you fix the city. I'm coming to you, not as a journalist or a reporter. I'm coming to you as a citizen of this city. And I know what's at stake for me. I'm putting my neck on the line. I know I'll get killed if I get caught with this," Jose said passionately.

Kashif was frozen, unsure of what to say or think. Jose was right. He knew there was only one thing to do, but he tried thinking of an alternative solution.

"You have to do what's right. Only you can fix this. The only way is through…" Jose said as Kashif focused on his words. It was the last thing he heard before his world was blinded by light, followed by darkness. The thundering and crashing noise of the explosion came afterward. With his ears ringing, Kashif found himself on the ground, Jose lying unconscious next to him. Looking up, he noticed that the roof was on fire after the explosion. With his vision blurred through the fire, he saw a group of figures standing on the other side of the roof, all dressed seemingly in black. Before he could react, one of the figures threw a ball toward him. A second before it exploded, Kashif grabbed Jose and jumped off the roof. Landing on the street, his ears still ringing, and his vision was blurry. Kashif ran down the road and took a turn into an alley. Catching his breath and trying to regain vision, he sat against the wall. Hearing noises above him, the black figures followed and looked down from the roof. *Who are they?!*

But he didn't wait to find out. Picking up Jose, he ran the other way, towards the street, and jumped into the air, taking flight. In a matter of seconds, he was far away from the store roof.

"Head to my place," Jose whimpered slowly, not fully awake. "16 Lakeshore Drive," he said before falling unconscious again. Kashif headed in that direction and landed in the backyard of a small house. Searching Jose's pockets, he found a house key and entered. The small living room was modest, with a single couch, coffee table, and TV. The rest of the room was full of papers and clippings scattered everywhere on the ground and plastered across the walls. Placing Jose down on the couch, Kashif moved toward the postings on the wall, noticing they were all reports of police activity. He turned around when he heard Jose moaning and waking up.

"Welcome to my humble abode," he winced in pain. "I would offer you something, but I don't think I can move."

"Are you safe here?" Kashif asked.

"Until you make a move, I don't think I'm safe anywhere."

"Who knows about this? About you?"

Jose sighed, trying to sit up, but the pain caused him to lie back down. "When I took those pictures, I didn't exactly go unnoticed. I was spotted, but I was able to get away. I don't think anyone saw my face, though."

Kashif thought for a second. "I hope they didn't see it tonight either." He turned back towards the news clippings. "What are these?"

"You asked me why I didn't just report all this? Well, I tried. Those are my stories, but the newspapers and media didn't want my findings."

Kashif stared at the stories, anger and rage burned inside him. Moving from one story to the next, he felt himself about to burst.

"I can't believe this," he confessed angrily, punching the wall.

"You see the pictures with them; it's all true. I've been tracking this for over a year now, MetalGhost. It's time now to stop it. That's why I came to you."

"Why did you wait so long? Why now?" Kashif turned around. Jose looked up at him, tears forming in his eyes. "Because there's one more thing you should know," he cried. He pointed to a picture on the wall, and Kashif turned to it. "That little girl, she's six years old. And she's my niece, Diana. They took her. I guess... I guess we don't take things seriously until it happens to us." Jose then lowered his head.

"She's being held captive right now. Tonight. I think tonight, they will do what they do to all the others." Pain filled his eyes. "You have to save her," he said.

This was more than Kashif could handle. He could not stand around any longer.

"Where?" He growled, turning to Jose.

"I don't know where she is. But you can find him at the Jamison Court buildings. I know the office is on the top floor of the main building, room 949." Jose looked up but found he was the only one remaining in the room.

"I cannot believe this! How could I let this happen for so long?" Kashif screamed on his way to Jamison Court, relating to Samir everything that had happened, about the pictures that he had seen. Samir was speechless.

"Everything was a lie!" Kashif screamed. "All of them... Detective Fahim! ...Zara!" Kashif fumed in frustration.

"Calm down, Kash," Samir said, trying to pacify him as he could hear the rage in Kashif's voice.

"I'm going to kill these people."

"Listen, man, don't do anything out of anger. Don't do anything you'll regret."

"Samir, how could we have missed this?! They will pay."

"Kashif, you need to calm down first and think straight. Recite your dua's, they'll calm you down. Let's talk this out, but before that, recite *La hawla wala quwata illa billah*. Keep reciting this until you reach the location."

La hawla wala quwata illa billah, la hawla wala quwata illa billah, Kashif kept repeating to himself. *There is no power or strength besides God. There is no power or strength besides God.* The du'a, meant to be recited in times of extreme distress or weakness, reminds us that even strong people feel weak in front of God and His might. And in those moments of weakness and distress, only God gives strength. At that moment, as Kashif looked below at the city while flying, he felt weak and powerless. How could he not have seen the signs? How could he let this go on for so long? The thought made him feel sick and weak. *La hawla wala quwata illa billah, la hawla wala quwata illa billah.*

Jamison Court's financial district, located in the wealthier and affluent part of the city, is home to many financial institutions of well-to-do families. Various amounts of the biggest businesses and companies all housed their headquarters there.

"Okay, Kash, you're here. Let's make sure the area is clear," Samir started the plan as Kashif landed.

But Kashif said, "Plan's simple, Samir. I will go in and stop this."

Samir sighed. He knew this needed to happen, but he couldn't shake the feeling of fear and anxiety in his stomach. Before he could respond, Kashif was already in front of the main building. "Room 949," he heard Kashif repeat.

Flying up to the ninth floor, Kashif remained out of view and peeked through the windows of the room. The lights were on, and only one man sat behind a large wooden desk. The man was heavy-set and tall, wearing a fancy beige suit. He was facing away from the windows and was turned toward the wall. Spinning around in his black leather chair, he stood up to leave but turned pale when he looked towards the windows. What he saw made him freeze. Outside his ninth-story window, in the night, a person floated in the air. And not just any person, his worst nightmare: *MetalGhost.*

"Aaahh!" The man ran for the door. He heard the window shatter behind him and felt a hand violently grab the back of his neck. Before he knew it, he was airborne, having been thrown toward the wall. Crashing against the wall, he landed upside down with a loud thud. His vision was blurry as he saw a pair of feet slowly walking toward him. MetalGhost grabbed the man by his coat and brought him face to face.

"Hello, Chief Eames," he growled. "You piece of garbage," he yelled, throwing the police chief across the room. MetalGhost walked toward him as he cried out in pain.

"What do you think you're doing?! You're making a big mistake!" Chief Eames screamed out angrily.

"My mistake was not figuring it out earlier," MetalGhost snapped.

"What the heck are you talking about, you vigilante criminal? You think you can just come in here and do what? What's your plan, huh?!"

'I want to kill you. But no, the city deserves to have you stand before them in shame; they deserve to see you go down."

"I haven't done anything. You're a lunatic!" He cried out, crawling backward on the ground.

MetalGhost reached into his thobe, pulled out the pictures Jose had given him, and brought them in front of the Chief. Staring at the images, his eyes turned wide, his face twisted from fear to shock. "How did you…?" He stuttered. He looked from one picture to another of him laughing and shaking hands with Slicer, Bone Collector, and the Dealer. Another image showed him sitting in front of a line of girls chained together on their knees on the ground. And a third revealed the Chief was handing the criminal leader, Black Dread, an open briefcase of weapons.

MetalGhost picked him up and threw him against the window, shattering it. Chief Eames screamed in pain on the ground; slowly getting to his arms and knees, he crawled toward his desk in an attempt to hide behind it.

"You were supposed to protect this city. Instead, you've been behind kidnappings, working with the drug cartels, letting these mobs off the hook, and committing human trafficking. You monster!" He yelled, walking toward the desk.

Chief Eames suddenly jumped up from behind the desk with a gun drawn and fired a round of bullets at MetalGhost, who drew out his blue shield. Chief Eames continued firing until his gun was empty, but not one shot hit his target. He stared in disbelief at the bullets floating in the air inside the blue shield. MetalGhost held the bullets in the air momentarily, then flung them back. The shots fired back at the Chief, who ducked under his table, avoiding the bullets that tore through the wall behind him.

"Where are they, the victims? Where are you hiding them?" MetalGhost walked over to the whimpering Chief on the ground. "Tell me!" He screamed, standing tall above him. When he didn't respond, MetalGhost pulled him up again by his coat.

Staring face to face, the Police Chief let out a slight laugh as he winced in pain. "You're too late," he said, breathing heavily. "You're always too late. It took you how many years, huh? You're pathetic. If you only knew the truth. All the criminals in this city, *they used you.* They knew they could distract you easily with a small burglary or petty crime here and there so that you would look away. Meanwhile, these mobs were able to operate on a larger scale. It's all on you."

Kashif stared deep into the Police Chief's eyes, enraged, but he tried not to get distracted from his goal.

"Tell me," he roared. "Where are the girls you're trafficking? I'm not going to ask again," he threatened.

Chief Eames laughed again. Kashif had reached his limit. He flung the Chief over his shoulder with extreme intensity and force that he crashed straight through the window and fell out of it. Kashif could hear him screaming while free-falling out of the window into the night. Kashif ran to the window and flew out, diving toward the falling Chief. He came face to face with the Chief again as he was falling and picked him up in the air right as the Chief was about to hit the ground. Kashif threw him down on the ground outside the building on the chilly night. The Chief cried in fear and disbelief.

"Let's try this again! You tell me, or you're going for another ride," Kashif yelled.

The Chief cried out in fear, "Okay, okay! But it wasn't my fault! They made me do it!" He wept.

"Shut up! I don't want to hear it. *Tell me!*" He grabbed his throat and began squeezing.

The Chief gasped for air, mumbling something inaudible. Kashif loosened his grip around the Chief's neck to allow him to speak more clearly.

Still gasping for air, he blurted out, "Echo Mas."

Stunned, Kashif let go of the chief. "My God..." he gasped. It was all starting to make sense to him. "Echo Mas is the ship at the docks..."

"It's where they take them. And once they're on the ships, I don't know where they get taken. I swear!"

Kashif felt his heart drop. *Echo Mas,* he thought. He knew he had to get there right away.

"Oh, my God!" He heard shocked voices behind him as people from the buildings started coming out to witness the scene. Kashif turned around to the frightened onlookers. He walked toward a woman and looked at her scarf wrapped around her neck. "Can I take this?" he asked. The woman stood still, frightened and confused, before handing the scarf over to MetalGhost. Kashif took the scarf and tied up Chief Eames's arms and legs together. Flinging him over his shoulders, he took off into the night.

Just as they landed in front of the police precinct, the word of MetalGhost's action had gotten out. As soon as he landed with the Police Chief, he was swarmed by cops with their guns drawn.

"What is going on here?!" Detectives Zara and Fahim rushed out of the precinct.

MetalGhost turned to them. "Did you know? Did you know what he was doing?"

"What are you talking about?" Det. Zara called out, confused.

He threw down the Chief and took out the pictures, handing them to the detectives. They looked through them in disbelief. "Chief...?" Det. Zara couldn't find the words. She turned from the pictures and stared in shock at the Police Chief tied up, lying on the ground.

"I know where they are keeping the hostages in all of the kidnappings. I'm going to get them," MetalGhost told the two before flying off.

Both detectives stood in shock as their police chief lay bound on the ground before them, evidence of his wrongdoings in their hands. News reporters swarmed them as the other officers tried to form a wall and keep them away. The detectives looked at each other in disbelief. They knew their lives had just turned upside down for good.

Arriving at the docks, Kashif made his way straight to the main building. Crashing through the door, Rupert Everton jumped with his hands up, "I'm innocent!"

"I know. Where is Echo Mas?"

"They're all there right now. I don't know what's going on, but they're in a rush to sail," he cried out, pointing to the south end of the docks.

"They're not going anywhere!"

"Do you have any guns?!" Rupert questioned.

"No," Kashif responded while walking out.

"But they have so many, why don't you?"

"Because I don't kill people," he said as he took off toward Echo Mas. *Although tonight might be different,* he thought.

"Please take them all out, all of them!" He heard Rupert shouting from behind him.

Echo Mas was a mid-sized ship that blended in with all the others entering and exiting the docks and port, as if the criminals were careful not to have it stand out in any way. Kashif heard the chatter of people giving orders as he rushed up to the docking ports.

"He's here! It's MetalGhost!" He heard shouts as the gunfire started showering upon him. Pulling out his shield in front of him, he continued walking toward the shipping containers, ready to be ported onto the back of the ship. Once the gunfire stopped, the men started running toward him one after another. Super punching as many of them as possible, he continued walking ahead. A group jumped from behind on top of him, trying to take him down. Throwing off the men while walking, one of the men tasered him, causing MetalGhost to scream out in pain. His shield retracted, and five men kicked him down as they all took out their tasers. Tasering him at high voltage, MetalGhost fell to the ground. With more men rushing in, kicking and beating him with bats, along with the tasers, Kashif screamed out in agony at each hit. Not letting up, the men continued their attack until Kashif felt himself losing control of his senses. His suit began to heat up due to the tasering, and Kashif felt it burning him inside. Unable to move on the ground, the men continued pounding and beating him until he eventually stopped feeling the bats and kicks.

The sounds started to fade. His world slipped into blackness. Disappearing into a quiet, dark world, he saw an image of a girl forcefully taken away by faceless figures. The girl reached out to him, begging him to save her. *That's my niece. Save her, Jose's words rang in his ears. That's my niece... Save her.*

The words jolted him into action.

With every bit of energy he could find, he lifted his hand slowly and pushed through the pain to raise his left forearm, retracting his shield. With his world still dark, his hearing was the first to return. The sound of the clanking of bats and fists on his shield was followed by the heavy breathing of the men as they halted their attack, unable to strike MetalGhost. The group backed up while looking down at the immobile, beaten, bruised man. After a moment of stillness and quiet, Kashif jolted his eyes open and ferociously super-punched the closest assailant with all his strength, causing him to furiously fly back into a group of men, crashing into and knocking them all out. He turned around and ducked as one of the men rushed toward him with a flying fist. He punched the man unconscious, then flung his body into another group charging at him, knocking them all to the ground. Catching his breath, Kashif looked around to find a large red shipping container. He broke the lock and chains and opened the container. A door loudly creaked open, revealing a dark space. From the cold darkness inside, quiet whimpers and shrieks reached his ears. As his eyesight adjusted to the darkness, what his eyes settled on knocked his breath out more than the men had.

Three rows of young girls, gagged and chained together, stared out and returned his gaze with shock and tears.

Kashif fell to his knees, "My God! I found you all... you're all safe," he exclaimed between breaths. Breaking their chains and untying them, the girls broke down crying and huddled around Kashif. Hearing the police sirens approaching, "You're safe now," he whispered weakly to them as he collapsed to the floor. Each of the girls helped him to sit up slowly. "Diana... are you here?" He asked, still dazed.

A frightened young girl stepped forward. "Your uncle, he saved you. He saved all of you," he said weakly. Diana broke down in tears, hugging MetalGhost.

With the sounds of police officers approaching, the authorities found the girls huddled around MetalGhost. The police took them all to safety, while MetalGhost refused medical attention. He knew where he had to be. After ensuring the girls were in good hands and safe, he flew out into the night, heading towards Lakeshore Drive.

Arriving at Jose's house, he noticed the door had been broken in. His heart dropped as he ran into the living room. "Jose!" He yelled. Looking out at the scene in the living room, Kashif fell to his knees. "No!" He screamed in anguish. Jose lay on his couch as he had left him, but he had bullets in his head and body. They had found him. "Noooo!" Kashif continued to yell in anguish while bursting into tears.

CHAPTER THIRTY ONE

AFTERMATH

Three months after the groundbreaking, horrifying, and shocking events, RP City was set ablaze and turned upside down. Angry protests outside the police precinct were a daily occurrence. The city had witnessed its chief of police responsible and involved in many horrific criminal activities. To make matters worse, an internal investigation inside the police force revealed a handful of other complicit officers. In a turn of events, the officers Kashif had apprehended and brought in before from the ambush at the warehouses were, in fact, involved and guilty of plotting against their own police force and working with gangs. After all those terrifying discoveries and especially of the corruption inside the Police Force, the city had had enough. *End the Corruption! The Police are the Problem! We Deserve Better!* The headlines roared. In other parts of the city, riots erupted against the police as citizens felt they could no longer trust them.

On the other hand, the mobs and gangs of the underground world were not quiet either. With their primary resource inside the police force eliminated, the chief himself, and their layer of protection uncovered, they now felt exposed. They did not take the actions of MetalGhost lightly, and they let him know in the most brutal of ways. The gangs began reaching new heights of brutality, sending him messages by killing civilians at will. A nurse walking home after work. A construction worker during his shift. A retired school teacher. And each of the victims had notes posted onto them for MetalGhost:

MetalGhost is to pay.
Death to MetalGhost.
The Vigilante is Next.

No one in the city felt safe anymore. The war had escalated to another level. The biggest and most painful message MetalGhost received was through the murder of Jose, the real hero, in his opinion.

"The protests continue outside the Police Force for the tenth straight day as the RP Police have yet to name the new police chief," the news anchor reported. Kashif sat on his couch, unsure of how long he had been sitting there, having blocked out the TV blaring the news. He sat forward with his head lowered, staring at the piece of paper in front of him.

The result of selfishness.
The blood is on your hands.
The day MetalGhost turns himself in is the day this city will be safe.

-S.S.

For the hundredth time, Kashif re-read the note he found on Jose. They had found him. They had killed him for exposing the chief and ensured he never spoke again. He felt crushed. If only he had protected Jose better. He left him in his house, knowing he was in danger. The guilt was ripping him apart.

The note was signed *S.S.,* as were many of the death notes on the recent victims.

Who could that be? Kashif thought.

He and Samir had searched as much as they could, but nothing came up for who could be leaving these messages. But Kashif had a feeling he would find out soon enough. Whoever this was, was fearlessly intent on taking out MetalGhost, and Kashif would be ready for it.

His thoughts were broken by hearing something on the news which caught his attention. He turned to the TV and turned up the volume: "Just breaking that the Ridgefield Park Police Force will officially announce that Detective Fahim Kazmi has been voted in and given the Chief of Police position. The detective is a thirteen-year veteran known to be tough on crime. Kashif stared at the screen, finding himself both surprised and slightly optimistic at the same time. Maybe this would be a good time to speak to the new police chief as MetalGhost; perhaps they could work together, he thought. But he knew security was at an all-time high around him. He decided to let things cool off before talking to the Chief. Or at least, that was what he thought until Samir walked in with two pieces of paper in his hands.

CHAPTER THIRTY TWO

POLICE CHIEF FAHIM KAZMI

It was a cloudy and rainy night in Ridgefield Park City, but the pulse of the city was anything but overcast, for it was full of lights, life, and excitement as it was the day of the swearing-in ceremony for new Police Chief, Fahim Kazmi. There's one thing to have the swearing-in ceremony in the police station or court, but this was no ordinary event. After the public fall of disgraced former Police Chief, Thomas Eames, the city was on edge. Would another corrupt person come into the role who could easily be persuaded by money and fame? Or would they get a headstrong leader who would fight crime and work toward rooting out corruption at all levels and areas? The city needed a strong leader, and there was uncertainty and skepticism surrounding Fahim Kazmi, despite having a reputation as an honest, quiet, and thoughtful man. News media outlets had painted him as a good cop and detective, but feared he was "too nice and soft" to make any real change. The truth, as almost always, was somewhere in the middle. Fahim Kazmi had made his way up the ranks not by being a high-profile figure, but just the opposite: someone who did his job while laying low and out of the spotlight.

The inauguration was a public affair, with news media outlets broadcasting the event live. The ceremony was held in the massive Ridgefield Park City Performing Arts Center, with a large attendance expected. It was a list of who's who as every prominent figure in the city and neighboring cities, from the mayor, lawmakers, representatives, and the entire police force.

"I still can't believe we got invited!" Samir gushed with joy as he parked his car. In the passenger seat, Kashif was less enthusiastic about the invitation that Samir had brought to him a week ago. Not only was he not thrilled to be Samir's plus one at the event while representing Al-Fihriya University, but he was also wary and nervous about the event from a safety aspect.

"With everything going on, this is the ideal time and place for the lunatics in this city to try to crash the event," Kashif said, clearly uneasy.

"I hear you. I hope they have their security airtight," agreed Samir.

"It's not just the mobs. It's the people in the police force, too; we still don't know who can be trusted."

"What can we do? You got your suit, right?" said Samir.

"But there will be too many people. No way I can save everyone if something happens," retorted Kashif.

"Relax, nothing will happen insha'Allah, plus I have a plan B, so don't worry about it. Try to remember this is a happy occasion. And you're not attending as MetalGhost. You're attending as Professor Kashif Razvi."

"Your plus one date, you mean."

"Precisely."

"Well then, you want to go in by holding hands, Honey?" Kashif joked as Samir elbowed him.

Inauguration Day was full of excitement around the city, almost like a holiday celebration. As the event approached, streets were closed off, and security was extremely tight as guests started arriving at the hall. The rest of the city, those not present in the hall, were glued to their TV sets. The feel in the air was similar to that of a national presidential swearing-in, and for Ridgefield Park City, it might as well have been for the city that had endured so much and was looking forward to turning a new page. One could sense hope and excitement about what the future would bring. With a sense of optimism in the air, there was hope for the first time that things were changing, and it was the first day of a new and better time.

A red carpet was rolled out for each important VIP who arrived, posing for pictures and taking interviews. All the major news networks lined up to get the perfect shot and story. Kashif and

Samir, however, made a quiet entrance through the side entrance. This worked fine for Kashif as he hated public gatherings, and both were not VIPs anyway. But Samir loved public affairs and social gatherings. He was soaking it all in, even his entrance via the side doors. He felt like royalty.

"Will you stop posing and walking like that?" Kashif rolled his eyes once they got through the security checkpoint and received their wrist tags.

"Like what?" Samir asked as they took the stairs up.

"Like you're the Queen of England," he replied, entering the beautiful and massive hall of the PAC. "Ugh, so it begins," Kashif sighed, entering. "You know, I still think it's a better idea that I stay back and mask up, just in case."

"Relax, this is great!" exclaimed Samir, smiling and waving at people across the hall with an air of importance, taking in each moment. "Plus, have you seen the security around here? There are officers lined up for blocks, so I'm feeling pretty good about tonight. Think about it, how often do you get to relax and take it easy? Plus, again, I feel confident with plan B."

"Which is...?"

"Which is not your job to worry about. Your job is to worry about Plan A, which is to loosen up, enjoy, and have fun! Again, I feel good about tonight."

"I never feel good when you do," Kashif grumbled.

"You try, just try, for once in your life, to enjoy something. Forget about everything for a moment and enjoy this moment for the city. This should be a good distraction for whatever is going on in your head."

They walked toward a round table near the corner of the giant reception hall, just outside the doors to the main hall, which had yet to open.

Normally, Samir would have been right. But this was not a distraction from Kashif's inner demons. This was not an escape from the fire in his heart and mind; rather, they were walking right toward it.

"Whoever's behind all the kidnappings and killings, they're here. I can feel it. And..." Kashif scanned the room, lowered his voice, and looked remorseful. "Aliya's father is probably here too.

He's the head of his IT company, after all. I'm not looking forward to any of this."

"Cocktail, Sirs?" A waiter approached them.

"Does this contain alcohol?" asked Samir.

"Yes, Sir," replied the young man courteously.

"No thanks, then," replied Samir with a forgiving smile as the waiter made an apologetic bow and walked away.

"Ah shoot, you're probably right," Samir replied to Kashif. "Why do you keep touching that?" He pointed to Kashif, who hadn't stopped scratching his wrist.

"It's this darn wrist tag. It's so itchy," Kashif complained.

"Of course, you'd complain about my contribution to the event," Samir responded.

"Of course, you'd be behind these wrist tags." Kashif eyed Samir.

"My students and I volunteered to provide these wrist tags for this event, and it's how we got an invite." Samir winked. A moment later, he noticed a man at another table, smiled, and waved at him. "Well, if I see you with Aliya's father, I'll come and give you a hand," he assured, patting him on the back. "But for now, I see Hiro over there. Gotta make sure we have a budget, you know." He winked as he walked away, leaving Kashif alone.

Hiro Tanaka was the Treasurer for the city, and Kashif had come to know he was very generous, giving the University and their own department funds that they had been using to advance the suit with new technology. Samir and Hiro were good friends, and Samir had always been able to convince him of the importance of their research. *Research,* Kashif thought. *More like putting together a suit and testing it to make it as indestructible as possible.*

As Kashif watched Samir and Hiro hug and greet, he, on the other hand, had no intention of meeting anyone. He turned around in an attempt to face the wall, but his eyes connected with a familiar face. That's when his heart dropped. Asif Ali, his once father-in-law-to-be, had seen him and was walking toward him. Kashif could feel his heartbeat quicken as Uncle Asif approached.

"Asalaamu alaikum, Baita. I thought I saw you when you entered. How are you?" Uncle Asif said in a gentle voice.

Kashif and Uncle Asif had always been on good terms; he had accepted his marriage proposal to his daughter, after all. But after Aliya had gotten married and moved out of Ridgefield Park City, things had become awkward between them. What was once a loving and budding father-son relationship had halted and changed rapidly due to the quick marriage of Aliya. But the old feelings still existed. Uncle Asif had always liked Kashif the best for his daughter. But after his father's passing, not only was Kashif not the same as before, but Uncle Asif was also no longer clear about Kashif's intentions. Kashif wouldn't give him a proper timeline for the marriage to continue.

"Take as much time as you need, Baita," he had said to Kashif, knowing he was grieving. "We're with you, always." But he felt guilty for not keeping up with that promise. He knew that Kashif still loved his daughter, but it had been two months, and he wasn't sure when Kashif would be ready for marriage. After three months, he had gotten a proposal from his best friend, whom he had known his whole life, Ahsan Latif.

Ahsan had asked Asif many times for his son, Sufiyaan, for marriage to Aliya. However, he had refused because Aliya had rejected the idea. But after three months and more insistence from Ahsan, he hesitantly agreed, for he wanted Aliya to move on and start her life anew. He and his wife had persuaded Aliya to agree to the marriage, but she wouldn't agree. It became a family affair, as everyone in the family, from Aliya's aunts to her uncles, had come to persuade her until she finally agreed, but unbeknownst to others, halfheartedly. Her heart was still with Kashif, and her father, knowing that fact, still gave her hand to another. And now, he always felt guilty for what he had done. He knew his daughter wasn't happy and knew Kashif hadn't married since because of the heartbreak. And he knew the two still missed each other. He held great remorse about how it all went, about not telling Kashif what was happening. *How could I?* he had thought. Kashif had been mourning. Asif wanted to still be there for him, if not as a father-in-law, then as an uncle. However, Kashif grew more and more distant following Aliya's marriage.

"Waalaikum asalaam Uncle, Alhamdulillah, I'm uh, I'm well. How are you?" Kashif replied in a weak voice.

"Alhamdulillah, it's truly good to see you. I was actually at your abu's grave to pay my respects the other day. I really do miss him. Such a great man," he said and then turned to him. "And so are you."

Taken by surprise, Kashif wasn't sure what to feel about that comment; it was a mixture of confusion, anger, and heartbreak. How could he stand there and say these things when he married Aliya off without even telling him? A part of him was still angry at Aliya for not answering his phone calls, for not telling him about another proposal, for marrying another man.

Kashif didn't respond while looking at the crowd of people, all mixing and gathering while they stood at their table. Uncle Asif also looked at the crowd and sighed. "I'm sorry for what happened, Kashif," he confessed. He paused while still staring out, "And how it all happened. It must have made things so much worse for you. Grief on top of grief. And for my part, I'm sorry." He looked down, touching his wrist tag nervously.

Kashif continued to stare out, but he felt frozen and unable to move. He could tell he was breathing harder and faster. He continued looking out, all the memories and feelings of losing Aliya flooding back in. Watching her get into the car in her wedding dress, driving off, of her not looking back... his heart felt like exploding. He had recurring nightmares of that scene many times before and still did. In his dream, Aliya turned around from the back of the car to look at him. They made eye contact as she was driven off. Fighting back the tears, he closed his eyes and just nodded, not knowing what to say—not expecting to have that conversation at that time or ever.

"If there's anything I can do to help you, please let me know." He put his hand on Kashif's shoulders, which felt heavy with grief. "And be strong, especially now that... you might see her..." He trailed off. Kashif stared at Uncle Asif and turned pale. His heartbeat suddenly stopped, and he felt like someone had squeezed his lungs, not allowing him to breathe. Seeing his shocked and confused face, Uncle Asif continued, "Now that she is planning on moving back to the city with her family.

"Be well, Baita. I'm always praying for your family." He patted him on the back again while giving a wounded smile before slowly walking away.

Kashif was still frozen in shock, reminiscing about the last time he saw Aliya driving away. And she was back, his recurring nightmares becoming a reality.

After a few moments, Samir waltzed back in a very elated and energetic mood. "It's done! We're going to get whatever we need concerning funds!" He laughed and gave Kashif a big pat on the back. The jolt brought Kashif back to reality and into the moment.

"What? Oh, yeah, that's good," he said, not showing the slightest bit of excitement.

"What's wrong with you? You look like you saw a ghost."

"Not yet," responded Kashif quietly.

"What?"

"She's coming back."

"What, who?"

"Aliya." He turned to face Samir. "She's moving back to the city."

"Oh… yeah, I know, that's kind of crazy."

"What?! You knew, and you didn't tell me?" demanded Kashif.

"Yeah… well, I thought you did too. I noticed on X-Bot that you had pulled up her profile, and it said her new address in the city. It looks like you got around the lock I put around her name." He eyed him.

Embarrassed that Samir found that he had searched her up, Kashif had no response.

"I know it sucks, man, but don't let her distract you. Look, they're opening the doors to the hall. It's showtime."

Guests slowly started entering the grand amphitheater, taking their seats as a few hundred people filled the hall. The amphitheater hall was magnificent and glowing, highlighted by a brightly lit stage set with multiple chairs and a single podium. Kashif and Samir took their seats in the middle row with a few other Al-Fihriya University staff members. Samir moved toward the center of the row with his students as Kashif decided to take the end seat. The event started with a beautiful rendition of the United States national anthem by Katherine Briggs, a student at the university, and then a speech by the oldest serving police chief of the city, Summer Wali, the first female police chief, over 50 years ago.

Following this, the swearing-in of Fahim Kazmi was officially set to begin. "And at this moment, I ask Fahim Kazmi to come up to the stage, accompanied by his family," announced the Honorable Judge Adam Kennedy, the highest-ranking and oldest serving judge in the city, a tall, dark man, showing signs of age as he hunched over slightly. Fahim Kazmi, dressed in his police uniform, was accompanied on stage by his wife, Aisha, son, Yasir, and daughter, Alayna. Judge Kennedy greeted the new police chief and shook his and Yasir's hands, while Aisha placed her hand on her heart to greet the judge, who returned the same.

"And now the moment we have been waiting for," Judge Kennedy called out to the audience, his voice shaking from old age. Before Judge Kennedy could finish his statement, he was distracted by loud voices and noises coming from outside the hall. What sounded like loud chatter at first turned into screams. And then gunshots. The crowd inside the hall began slowly and nervously chattering as the voices outside began roaring louder and closer. A few seconds later, smoke started appearing from the other side of the doors before the doors flew open, and a dozen men ran into the room with rifles, wearing black shirts with bulletproof vests, green army pants, green trench coats with sleeves ripped off, and gas masks covering their faces. The way they all synchronized and moved swiftly in unison, it was clear these were not just civilians but trained fighters.

Smoke started filling the stage, and those onstage began coughing. "Ah yes, the moment we *surely* have been waiting for," a slow, loud booming voice from backstage spoke. Appearing from the smoke, a tall man slowly walked forward, with his heavy footsteps echoing loudly as he approached the front of the stage. The man was large and dressed the same as others, but his trench coat contained patches of different symbols. His voice was menacingly loud from behind a gas mask and amplified with an echo throughout the hall. Only his eyes were visible, and they were screaming with rage. The men with guns surrounded the hall and locked the doors, stationing themselves at each entrance. The crowd roared and shouted in fear and panic, realizing they were locked inside.

"Settle down, everyone," the large masked man on stage spoke slowly and carefully. "The less you panic, the better it will be for you all," his voice sounding sinister behind the mask. Reaching the front of the stage, he looked out quietly but with menacing eyes at the shrieking crowd. He seemed to be scanning each face in the audience before turning to Judge Kennedy, Police Chief Fahim, and his family huddled together in fear surrounded at gunpoint.

"We come here in front of you today as your fellow citizens. We come here in the name of justice," the man on the stage announced to the crowd emphatically. *"Real justice..."* He suddenly grabbed Judge Kennedy by the back of his neck as the crowd gasped in fear. "Because justice has not been granted by the likes of these people before you today," he said with his voice rising.

The army of men loaded their guns loudly as they stood in the aisles.

"This city is tired of watching so much injustice occur again and again. It's men like these that have made our city weak!" The large man, clearly the leader, continued to squeeze Judge Kennedy's neck, who let out a cry. "Weak men are the cause of hard times. And so hard times need strong men. I'm sorry, your honor, but it's time you were put on trial for being weak!" The man roared. "For letting Ridgefield Park City fall to injustice and vigilantism. I ask you all here today, what has this man done to stop criminals from taking the law into their own hands? Men like the MetalGhost, a coward hiding behind a mask who has been allowed to cause fear and chaos. And what has that led to? More vigilantism, more cowards, more lawlessness who follow his wicked path. What did men like this do when MetalGhost continued to take the law into his own hands and failed this city over and over again? I know this all too well; I was there when he let the bank robber go free. He's no hero. He's a criminal. And what did this man do? This man who is supposed to serve justice?" He squeezed the back of Judge Kennedy's neck harder, causing him to scream out in pain. The crowd gasped again, yelling and shouting rising from the audience.

"Everyone sit down," the leader said before calmly continuing, "Or you will be put down." He nodded toward his armed soldiers.

A few masked men started patrolling the aisles as the rest stood guard at the doors, all with their rifles in hand. Two of the masked men made their way to the camera crews, struck the reporters with the back of their rifles, and grabbed hold of the cameras of the news crew members. They focused the cameras on the stage, broadcasting live to the whole city.

Kashif glared at Samir with wide eyes, who shook his head in disagreement. Kashif realized he was right: he could not suit up in front of everyone.

"The answer, my dear friends, is nothing. Men like this one are part of the cancer that has been spreading throughout our city! And before cancer ruins the whole body, you must remove it. And that's why the Smoke Squad is here today," he said the last line slowly, with a finality. He pointed his gun at Judge Kennedy, shot him in the stomach, and threw him with one hand into the front row among the shrieking crowd.

Without looking back at Judge Kennedy, the leader strolled toward Fahim and his family, huddled together. "Ah yes, our new shining bright light," he loudly proclaimed. "Except, all I see when I look at you is cowardice. I've seen this all before." He viscously snatched Yasir away from the rest of them.

"No!" Fahim stood up and tried to attack the leader, but he was met with a blow to the face from the back of his gun, causing him to fall back. The crowd screamed again as Kashif looked around but saw no opportunity to sneak away as the crowd was trapped inside, and the men with guns stalked the aisles closely.

"Today is a day for *real* justice!" the leader screamed on stage. "And we only have a simple request. This city has seen enough vigilantism, and it is time now for the return of law and order. We now call to trial... *MetalGhost.*"

Kashif froze and felt the hair on his arms and neck rise upon hearing his name, and he turned slowly back toward the stage.

"MetalGhost, we know you're watching this," the leader scowled straight into the cameras that his men were now controlling. As the crowd waited in confusion and panic, Kashif sat down in his seat, thinking about what he could do.

"Come, save this boy. Come and *reveal yourself!* It's time for you to have your justice, too. We will let this boy go, and no one here will get hurt *if* MetalGhost comes here and shows us his face. We know you're watching, MetalGhost. We know... you're *here.*"

The crowd roared again in confusion and shock. Kashif stared in a rage at the leader on stage, then looked out at the worried faces of the hostages in the crowd. *This is because of me.*

"Come! Your city, which never asked to have you, is calling you now. Come in front of them now." He gazed around at the people's shrieking and screaming. "Come save them now."

I'm causing this. I can't just sit here. Only I can stop it.

"You love this city, but it holds no loyalty to you. This city is bleeding because of you! You've poisoned us, and nobody can save this city except us. It's time for you to unmask."

The crowd looked around in desperation, some yelling for mercy, some in anger at their captives.

I have to face this. I can't let anyone else get hurt.

"Maybe I don't have the MetalGhost's attention yet," the leader continued slowly on stage. He took his gun and pointed it at Yasir's head as the crowd screamed again.

"No! Stop!" yelled Fahim, being held back by one of the Smoke Squad members.

"I'm afraid the time has come," the leader proclaimed, looking at the crowd, not blinking with a crazed look in his eyes.

Kashif looked back at Samir amongst the chaos. They stared at each other, determined looks on their faces. Kashif returned him a look as if to say *I have to,* but Samir, with fear-filled eyes, shook his head in protest to say *don't.*

"It's too bad, another casualty so MetalGhost can hide," the leader cried out, unlocking the safety of his gun.

Kashif closed his eyes and took a deep breath.

"Three..." the leader started counting. "Two..."

"Stop!" Kashif spoke out, standing up.

The crowd rose in an uproar of shock and amazement, staring with dropped jaws at the only one in the crowd standing: Kashif. The entire hall murmured quietly, staring at him.

"I am MetalGhost," Kashif revealed, looking straight at the leader as the room went drop-dead quiet.

CHAPTER THIRTY THREE

I AM METALGHOST

T he entire city stopped for a beat. Every set of eyes in the city was glued to whatever TV or screen was available, from gyms to the shipping dock, each house, every cell phone, and the big screen on Broad Street. The city had stopped to look at what was happening, taking in what Kashif Razvi had just said.

The atmosphere inside the PAC hall was the same, and the tension was palpable. Everyone was staring at Kashif, who stood alone. With fierce eyes, the leader quietly focused on Kashif, studying him. After what felt like a moment that lasted a hundred years, the Smoke Squad leader finally turned the gun to Kashif.

"No, stop. He's lying. *I'm* the real MetalGhost," said a voice from the back of the hall.

Everyone gasped and shifted their sight to the back. It belonged to Won Chang, Kashif's brightest student at Al-Fihriya University.

"Enough," another voice spoke up, "I'm the real MetalGhost," said a man near the front while standing up: Samir.

The leader, clearly enraged, gawked from one standing man to the other. He raised his gun at Samir but stopped as he heard another voice, "Stop, I'm MetalGhost." Another person stood up, and then another; one by one, more and more people began standing up.

It was at that moment that it happened.

A mechanical noise started humming louder and louder, and before anyone could move, each person's entry wrist tag started to vibrate. After a few seconds, the full metallic body armor of

MetalGhost slithered out and over each person wearing the bracelet. The crowd screamed in shock and confusion as the MetalGhost body armor wrapped itself around each audience member. The leader shouted in anger on stage as the gunmen looked around, confused.

One man seated near the door watched his hands and body as the suit overtook his whole body, and within seconds, he looked like MetalGhost. In shock, the man looked up and couldn't believe his sight: a hall full of other MetalGhosts. Before the man could fully comprehend what was happening, a gunman ran up to him and fired a shot at him. The man screamed in fear, but the bullet struck his head and hit the floor with a metal *clink*. The man paused and looked back at the gunman in surprise as everyone around him also froze. Each of the MetalGhosts stared at each other, and after a moment of realization, the man turned to the gunman and ran up to him, tackling and punching him. Everyone in the crowd followed suit, realizing they had the advantage now.

Amid all the chaos, Kashif suited up himself in the actual MetalGhost suit. He rushed up to the nearest gunmen and took out two of them before they could fire any shots. Kashif looked up, and all around him, he heard the sound of metal clinking and people shouting. MetalGhosts had outnumbered the gunmen, and they were attacking the armed men. The leader on stage had begun to panic. He turned around to run with Yasir still in his arms but stopped in his tracks. Fahim was standing right behind him in his MetalGhost suit. The leader froze, and they stared at each other.

"Here I am," Fahim growled as he took a gun and shot the leader in the head. The shot echoed throughout the hall, and the sound of the leader falling to the ground off stage. Fahim's shot stopped everyone. The entire hall gasped, staring at the stage as Fahim stood there with Yasir in his arms. Fahim's suit retracted back into his wrist tag, and he looked back at the crowd with a determined look on his face. As he stood, he appeared like a changed man.

Another mechanical sound broke the silence and the crowd's attention. People stared at each other as their suits now started to retract and go back inside their wrist tags again. One by one, the audience members' suits began retracting and coming off, with each person coming back into view again of each other. The tags then started to fizzle and bubble as each one burned to a liquid state, almost as if self-destructing.

Everyone then turned their attention back to Fahim on stage, as he had just shot the leader of the Smoke Squad. He looked back at the crowd and shouted in a firm voice, "This is a new day in Ridgefield Park City. No, no more vigilantism. No more allowing criminals and mobs to run free. This is the first day of a new city."

The doors to the halls burst open as members of the police force, having finally made it through battling the henchmen outside, barged their way in and began escorting each person out to safety. Kashif and Samir followed the crowd, laid low, and left the building without anyone noticing.

CHAPTER THIRTY FOUR

COPYCATS

I t was around 3:00 PM the following day when Kashif opened the heavy wooden door into Samir's office at Al-Fihriya University. Samir took great pleasure in knowing he had the nicest office on campus, especially considering this was one of the most prestigious universities in the country. Having earned the enviable position as Head of the Scientific Technology Department and a renowned genius in the field of robotics and engineering, his own office was one of the finer perks that came with the position.

"Ah, I was wondering where you were," Samir called without even glancing up. When he did look up from his tablet, he stopped and stared carefully. "What happened to you?"

Kashif walked in wearing a white dress coat, white dress pants, and a blue dress shirt, but his right arm was in a sling under the coat. "Took a nasty fall yesterday, just had it checked out." Kashif feigned sadly. "But makes for a good alibi too." He followed up with a knowing half-smile.

"Sure," Samir nodded with sarcasm. "Or maybe you just missed seeing Dr. Sarah," he said with a playful smile. "She still is single, isn't she?" he asked teasingly.

"Yeah, single and ready for you, Buddy," Kashif fired back, sitting down in the nice plush chair, exhausted.

"Have you seen the news?" Kashif asked.

"It's all everyone's been talking about," Samir showed him the tablet screen.

"Inauguration Under Attack: Who Saved the Day?" Kashif read out loud the headline. "Madness at New Police Chief Fahim

Kazmi's Inauguration."

"MetalGhost Saves the Day Again... But Did He?" read Samir. "Well, did he?" He asked quizzically, sitting back in his seat while folding his legs, looking out at Kashif with raised eyebrows.

"That was all you, man." Kashif sighed while raising his hands. "Honestly, I still don't know how you pulled that off."

"Plan B," he replied slowly with a smile. "Well, the hardest part actually was convincing the PAC to let our department provide them with volunteers for the event. Then, I was able to hand off the tags to one of our students without anyone thinking twice. It only took a week to put together the prototype suits in each wristtag," he said proudly.

"You're a crazy genius!" Kashif was genuinely impressed. "Smart that you thought that part ahead, but maybe next time, you can let me know beforehand?"

"Didn't have time," Samir retorted. "But you know what the crazy part is?" He paused, his tone becoming more serious and his face filling up with worry. "Not all of those suits were actually fully effective; those were only prototypes, after all. And some malfunctioned, meaning some of them were not going to have bullets bounce off them," he explained nervously.

They both sat silently but were thinking of the same horrifying scenario. *What if one of the non-functioning suits were fired on?* "Alhamdulillah, praise and thanks to God, that didn't happen." Kashif sighed in relief.

The phone on Samir's desk rang, and when he picked up and heard the news on the other end, he looked right at Kashif. "Oh, right. I'll be sure to pass him the information. Thank you."

"New Police Chief, Fahim Kazmi, is here downstairs to see you," he said, surprised after hanging up. "Well, it was nice knowing you. Remember, we don't really know each other, and I don't know anything about your nightlife," Samir joked.

"Hah, you're going down with me, brother." Kashif laughed as he exited the door.

Kashif made his way downstairs, and out in the hallway, he greeted the new Chief of Police.

"Professor Razvi, thank you for seeing me. I don't think we've properly been introduced." He reached his hand out.

"Oh, I think everyone knows you now, Sir," Kashif responded, smiling. "After everything that happened last night, I mean. And it seems like people know me too now. I've been getting curious looks and smiles all day." Kashif gushed.

"Ah, yes, that's actually why I wanted to see you. Do you want to take a walk?" Chief Fahim pointed forward. Kashif nodded, walking towards the stairs leading out to the courtyard.

"What happened there?" Fahim asked, pointing to Kashif's arm in a sling.

"Took a nasty fall yesterday, amongst all the craziness that happened," Kashif responded.

"May Allah grant you a quick *shifa*," Chief Fahim responded and then nodded. "'Craziness' is a good word. Things got pretty crazy quickly… until you spoke and stood up. That seemed to take the air out of the room." He side-eyed Kashif, trying to catch his response.

As they walked through the halls of the busy campus, students stared at them, pointing and whispering in their direction. Kashif was already well known as a popular professor, but now Chief Fahim had become a local hero overnight too.

"I want to thank you for your actions last night, Professor."

"I really didn't do anything," Kashif replied humbly.

"You stood up. You were the only standing one when no one else did, and that takes guts." He turned to him, looking directly into his eyes. "You bought my son time." Chief Fahim's tone was serious, but the last part was heartfelt.

Kashif remembered the look of anger and anguish on Chief Fahim's face the night before, especially when he fired the bullet. *Could I blame him?* He thought. Kashif nodded in understanding.

"Why did you do it?" asked Chief Fahim, returning to investigative mode.

Kashif looked out at the courtyard and pointed to a table where they could sit. "I guess, as you said, no one else was doing anything. I just didn't want to see what that guy was going to do," Kashif said, shrugging. "Who were they?" He asked, hoping to steer the conversation.

"They call themselves the Smoke Squad. We don't know too much, except that they're a bunch of mercenaries, but we're still looking into it. But going back, you stood up and announced you were MetalGhost. Tell me, Professor, what is it that you do at night?"

"Oh, you know, just running around on rooftops and gliding through the streets of Ridgefield Park City. Looking for people to beat up," Kashif said sarcastically, laughing.

Noticing Chief Fahim wasn't amused, he continued with a straight face, "Come on, Chief. Do you really think *I'm* this MetalGhost, running through the streets of RP? Look at me. I have a broken arm," showing his sling behind his coat. "Although, I do appreciate his willingness to take on the city's bad guys, helping your department out."

"He's not helping us. We don't need his help."

"Really? It seems like crime's dropped precipitously recently. I mean, you guys can even take a few weeks off, wouldn't you say?"

"The news only tells you what they want you to hear. He's made some real enemies, which is a problem for him and us. Crime hasn't gone down, Professor; the mobs are just waiting in the shadows, getting stronger by the moment. They know now not to be out in the open and risk being careless with the MetalGhost around. That is, until yesterday."

Kashif listened quietly, looking straight at the Chief, taking in the given information.

"Criminals just don't stop, Professor. They find new ways to do their business. And he's just pushed them to their new tactics."

"Which are?"

"Let's hope you never have to hear about them. Let's hope no civilian has to," he said, getting up.

Kashif, clearly in deep thought over what the Chief just said, finally looked up as the Chief was now standing.

"Well, um, I'm very confident that RP's best will be there to protect the people regardless of these new tactics. Especially with you at the head, leading the way. I'm confident in you, and you can always come to me if you need anything. And again, maybe your masked friend can help."

"He's part of the problem, him and his followers." Chief Fahim sighed.

"I'm sorry, *followers?*" Kashif asked, puzzled with a serious face.

"You think one guy becoming a vigilante isn't going to enthuse copycats, Professor? We've gotten multiple reports of copycats trying to be like him. Before, it was just one or two; now, there are so many. They dress similarly but differently enough that they stand out as another copycat. Each their own. Who knows who they really are or what they want? But now they're getting out of hand. We're going to have to start going after them now too. So you see the problem?"

"Really? Copycats?"

"We can't have people taking the law into their own hands, Professor. So, you see our conundrum with the masked vigilante."

"So, you want him to turn himself in? Or stop these copycats?"

"I... just want to talk. Others in our department, yes, they want to take him down. But then, others think he's a hero."

"And you?" He looked Chief Fahim Kazmi straight in the eyes. "What do you think of MetalGhost?"

Chief paused, thinking to himself before responding, "Again, I just want to talk to the guy. Not like he left his phone number for me to reach him or anything." He shrugged. "Anyway, thank you for your time, Professor. I'll be in touch if I need you."

"But I haven't proven to you that I'm not the masked vigilante yet," quipped Kashif, surprising himself for making the statement.

"I had my doubts, but you don't need to prove it," he said, taking out his tablet and showing him LIVE footage of the MetalGhost gliding from one building to the next.

"Would you look at that," awed Kashif. "He's good," Kashif said with a half-smile. As Chief Fahim departed, Kashif sat on the table in the courtyard, taking in the pleasant day. After a moment, he reached for his watch, "Okay, Samir, you can take off the suit now."

"Woohoo!" He heard Samir scream as he glided.

Kashif laughed.

"When you're done, we really have to talk about these copycats."

...

Since the memorial for Abu had passed, Kashif felt a large

emotional weight had been lifted from his shoulders. He could finally focus on the thought which had been running through his mind for days: *copycats.*

"What does he mean by 'copycats'?" A worried Kashif asked Samir.

"Looks like you're quite the role model now," answered Samir.

"This is not a joking matter, Samir. Why would others want to follow me?"

"Why not?"

"This is not a game. This is dangerous."

"Did you really think that a masked superhero would appear in the city, prove to be a success, and that others would just watch? Didn't you think there would be others who saw you and said, 'I can do that?' Or, 'I can do it better?' Frankly, you shouldn't be surprised."

Kashif listened to Samir intently.

"You've given people hope, even if you didn't intend to. Every day, people see you and think to themselves, 'There's the change we've been waiting for. And I want to be a part of it.' Of course, assuming that's their intention. You never know. But you've given people what they haven't had in a long, long time: hope. Hope for a better future."

"I've never wanted that," an upset Kashif replied. "I don't want to give them hope. Do you know what they've given me in return? More anger. People don't change, and the world isn't going to change. It's a cycle, and bad people will continue to come and go. I'm just here to find my answers."

"Maybe. But you can't say you aren't also trying to bring some good. Some semblance of sanity in this crazy world. And in that good, you've brought others. Whether you like it or not."

"I don't."

"Well then, why don't we find out who they are? Maybe you can meet them…"

"Not interested."

"And tell them to stop," Samir finished.

Kashif thought for a moment and sighed loudly, giving in. Samir nodded and turned to X-Bot. "Great, I'll dig around. Let's see what we find about these copycats. And *who* we find."

"I have no intention of knowing who they are. I just want to find them to stop them. They're going to get hurt because of me. And I can't live with that."

By that time, Samir was half-listening as he was completely indulged in his search.

CHAPTER THIRTY FIVE

THAT NIGHT

The following night was the terrible day of February 8th. It was a day Kashif begrudged each year, the day that Aliya walked out of his life and married another. It was the fifth anniversary of February 8th, and just as every one yet, he spent it alone. It had been five years, and he was still angry, still hurt, yet he missed her more than anything. On the cool, foggy night, the soft wind and the full moon shining brightly made for a pleasant rooftop night. Leaning back against the wall of a local building in his suit, looking out, he dangled his feet on the rooftop ledge, taking in the moonlight. *This is the kind of night she loved*, he remembered. Closing his eyes, he could hear the city bustling as usual, but all he could think about was her. *Where is she now? How is she doing?* Every day, he would be reminded of her, and the hurt and pain returned until he forced himself to try to forget. And every day, the thought of her returned to his heart. It was like losing her all over again each day… again and again. He would pick himself up to put himself back together each day, only to fall apart the next. He hated that she had become his weak point. Looking out into the city, he anguished, knowing she was back.

He looked at his gloves and pulled back a slip he had cut on his ring finger, revealing the wedding band he had bought for Aliya. He stared at the ring in pain for a few days after she had left. One day, he took the ring and welded it with a hot iron into his glove. Later, out of anger, he scratched into the ring a letter 'M.' MetalGhost was the reason he had lost her, so it was fitting that the ring should be with the suit. But he also felt close to her by having the ring on him.

He sighed, remembering how he loved and missed the little things, how he loved and missed her voice. He missed her low-pitched laugh, which she always covered with her left hand even though it was music to his ears. He yearned for her light brown eyes, which looked like the moon. A little scar on her forehead. He missed just how beautiful she was. And he missed how well they had gotten along, something he had never again been able to replicate. He was constantly reliving conversations and moments they had shared.

He moaned at the memories of her. Constantly, he relived their moments together. Just like water, if one tries holding onto it in the palm of one's hands, it will slip through the cracks; Kashif felt like he had tried holding onto Aliya, but she had slipped away from him. It made him angry and depressed at the same time. He felt stuck in this labyrinth of her memories, unable to escape. Unable to forget or move on. Sighing, he turned his face towards the darkened sky. "Why do I keep thinking of you? Why do I still miss you?" He called out into the night and addressed the moon.

He didn't have time to answer as he heard a noise behind him. Before he could turn to see what caused the noise, he felt two hands lift him into the air and fling him violently halfway across the rooftop to the other side. Landing in a loud and painful *thud,* he felt his sides burning in pain. Startled and confused, he tried to sit up to focus on what had happened but noticed another face looking down at him. The dark figure corked its arm back and swung down viciously with a fist aimed at Kashif's face. He ducked out of the fiercely incoming fist at the last second as the unknown hand brutally crushed the pavement where his head had just been. Kashif quickly rose to his feet and focused on the two figures standing before him. They were medium height but broad, dressed in shiny black full-body cloaks, with their heads and faces covered, revealing only their eyes. An unsettling feeling crept through Kashif as he noticed something very... *inhuman* about those eyes staring back at him. They were piercing red in color, unblinking, and raging in anger.

Without saying a word, one of them ran forward, jumped high into the air, and tried to land a kick on Kashif's head, which he averted. The second figure punched him in the chest, causing Kashif to fly back a few feet and hit the ground. Struggling to get to his feet and catch his breath, he heard the quick footsteps rushing toward him. As the figure came close, he clenched his fist twice and punched the cloaked attacker all the way across the rooftop. The figure landed with a crushing *splat,* but before Kashif could turn to see him, the second figure picked him up and flung him over the rooftop onto a lower rooftop below. Freefalling downward, Kashif's jetpack kicked in right as he reached the ground, landing on his feet. Looking back up, the figure that had thrown him stepped up to the building ledge and jumped off the roof, landing easily on its feet in pursuit. *What the heck are they? Are they even human?*

The second figure also jumped down, landing behind Kashif, now surrounded from the front and back. Taking out his shield, Kashif pushed both of them back as they charged, but as if one step ahead, one of them kicked his legs, causing him to land on his back. Both dark figures then jumped on top of him and started beating his head and body with crushing punches. Shots after shots, Kashif kept taking to the head. *Crrk,* his face shield began to crack after a moment, and he started to lose consciousness. Fighting to stay alert, he clenched his fist twice and used another super punch right into the chin of the one on top of him. He knew the force broke the figure's jaw as it sent him flying back. The other figure jumped on top of him, and Kashif super punched his chest. He heard its bones break as he also went flying. Kashif finally got to his feet, severely hurt and wincing in pain. But he was confident the two figures were down and done. To his shock, they were both standing up firmly when Kashif looked at them. Behind them stood a tall, dark man in a blue military-style jacket and pants, with golden pads on his shoulders and forearms and a red cape flowing from his back. He seemed to be floating in air. He wore a military-style hat that was lowered to cover his face as he stood with his arms folded and a mean scowl. The two figures moved behind the tall, dark man.

"You're as impressive as they say," the capped man spoke in a deep voice. "We would make a good team."

"I don't think so," Kashif replied angrily, unable to determine who the man was.

"Hm, very well. In that case, MetalGhost, you should be aware…" The tall man reached behind him and removed a round object, reddish in color. "That I run this city. Me, Black Dread." He threw the red object toward Kashif. It was a matter of a second before the red fireball reached him and burst into flames. Kashif jumped from the rooftop. The blast damaged his jetpack, as Kashif slammed into the ground hard and rolled over in pain. The explosion and flames burned his suit and body, and the fall had bruised his arms and legs.

Kashif tried to stand up and run with all his might, but as he turned the corner into an alley, the sight was worse than what he had left on the rooftop.

"Who's there?! What's all that noise?" He saw a group of three men in cargo pants and black tank tops walking over—*the Smoke Squad.*

"Aaahh, what do we have here?!" One of the members shouted out in surprise and with an evil smile. "Looks like it's the Metal Man." The noise above made them all stare at the rooftop as the two figures approached. They looked at each other, then ran, jumped to the next rooftop, and disappeared into the night as fast as they had come.

Kashif hunched over, realizing he was bleeding from his mouth as well as internally. He looked at the three men, overjoyed that he was stumbling and in pain. Turning to escape, the Smoke Squad members broke into a laugh as they chased after him. "What's the matter, Metal Man? Can't seem to fly?" They taunted, one of them taking out a knife from his pocket. Kashif broke into a run, but the world around him started spinning as he began seeing stars and losing consciousness. Breathing heavily, panic started creeping in. He turned the corner and continued running, unaware of where he was going. He heard the noises of the three men chasing him as they yelled, "Come back here! The real beating you're gonna get is from us!" They laughed maniacally. Kashif continued to run blindly, wincing in pain and out of breath. He turned a corner once again and was on the verge of collapsing before he heard a voice call out, "MetalGhost! In here!" Without looking to see who it was, he hurried to the voice and felt someone wrap their arms around him and take him indoors. He heard the man's voice whisper, "Stay down, stay here," as he laid him down on the floor behind a counter. The man then went back outside.

"Where did he go?!" He heard the Smoke Squad member yell.

"Uh, I think I just saw him go up that building over there; musta gone to the other street," Kashif heard the man reply. The three men hurried away to the other street. After a few moments, the man came back into the store.

"Hey, Brotha, you okay, man?" The man whispered in a high-speed voice. "Daaammn, you're bleeding all over the floor, Bro, gotta clean you up and my floor. You know I'm sort of a clean freak. I don't like no dirt around here... but I guess it's not every day you have *MetalGhost* laying on your store floor now, do ya?" the man said fast without taking a breath.

Kashif crumpled on the floor, winced in pain, took a few deep breaths, and finally regained consciousness as he looked up at the man who was still talking very fast. "I can't believe it. MetalGhost is in *my* store! Ooooh, Fatima is not gonna believe this!" He continued. Kashif focused on him, and he saw a plump, short, dark-skinned man with a beard and a big broad smile ear to ear staring down at him. And he was talking nonstop. His fast-talking was not helping the ringing in Kashif's ears and head, and as the man helped him sit upright, he was still saying something without taking a breath. When he finally stopped talking, he looked at Kashif in pain, "Oh, sorry! Sometimes I go on and on, and I don't realize what I'm saying." He laughed. "I'm Abdul Malik! And you are...? Well, of course, you're METALGHOST!" He screamed in excitement.

"Keep it down, will you," Kashif finally was able to say.

"Oh, right, sorry," Abdul Malik whispered. But then mouthed the words *MetalGhost!* in excitement. *In my store!*

He continued, "Let me, uh, get you some gauze; you're bleeding, man," and as quickly as he spoke, he went away and returned with some towels and gauze. Kashif felt his mask burning his skin, so he reached up and took off his mask. Abdul Malik gasped, retreating a few steps. The two men stared at each other in silence. Eventually, Kashif took the towels and wrapped them around his face and head. After a moment, Abdul Malik returned to his senses and helped clean Kashif up. Losing a lot of blood and wavering in and out of consciousness, Kashif could barely realize that he was sitting behind a counter in a convenience store. In an instant, the door to the store burst open as Samir rushed in, scooped Kashif up under his arm, and with Kashif's arm around his shoulder, helped him walk outside the store to where he had his car running.

"Hey! But wait!" Abdul Malik screamed, but before he could say anything else, the two men were out the door and had gotten into the car and driven off.

CHAPTER THIRTY SIX

THE GATEKEEPER

The following day, the front page of all the newspapers and the headline of every story surrounded what had happened the night before. The pictures of MetalGhost bruised and bleeding, getting chased by the Smoke Squad members, and of him going into Abdul Malik's convenience store, All Things Here. The biggest benefactor of all the reporting was none other than Abdul Malik. All day, Abdul Malik's store was full of reporters and a crowd of people listening to his story of what happened. And Abdul Malik couldn't have been happier telling and re-telling his story as many times and to as many people who would listen, talking his usual a-mile-a-minute.

"And then I said to him, 'Hey! Over here! I'll save you. I'll keep you safe!' He ran into my store right here… wait, no, no, he was limping y'all, and I don't think he really knew where he was because he was beaten up so badly, you know? So I took him inside, that's right. And then I hid him behind the counter. And then I told those fools following him, 'Wassup, you wanna mess with me?!' and I tell you, maaan, they ran outta here so fast." He stopped and laughed as the people in his audience stared at him admiringly. "And see, I used *my* superpowers. I tricked 'em! I told them he went over there, over the building, and they believed me." He continued laughing, clearly pleased. People continued to gather and listen intently as the next part was the part they were looking forward to hearing about the most.

"Did you see his face? Did you recognize him? Could you describe him to us?" Reporters that huddled around him questioned.

"What? Oh nah, like I didn't see his face, he uh, he still had his mask on, okay," he replied, looking away nervously. All day, he was giving the same answer. "But I tell you what, make sure to get something before you leave," he said, smiling. Business in his store had never before seen a better day.

The day after, he was still telling the story to whoever came in and would ask. *"Ahlan wa sahlan!* Welcome to All Things Here!" He greeted customers walking in. "Home of the MetalGhost savior!"

"Hi, do you have dishwashing detergent?" A customer asked from the door.

"Oh no, we don't have that here," he responded fast and loudly. Even customers who hadn't asked him any questions or for a story got to hear an earful of what had happened: "And then, I said, 'I'll nurse you back any day, bro.'"

At the end of the line, a man stood in a blue blazer, baseball cap, and dark sunglasses covering most of his face. By the time he reached the counter, the man had put a single can of soda on the counter and looked at Abdul Malik from under his hat and glasses. "Tell me that story again."

Abdul Malik saw the man's face and gasped. "It's you!" He whispered loudly. He motioned Kashif to the back of the store.

"Quite a lot of good stories you got there, brother," Kashif said, smiling.

Abdul Malik gave a shy smile, scratching his head, "Yeah, I think I remember some new details here and there. But hey, I didn't tell anyone about you, I mean you," he whispered.

"I've heard, and I appreciate that; thank you. I guess I don't need to tell you never to tell anyone."

"Naw man, your secret is safe with me, always," Abdul Malik said excitedly.

Kashif gave an appreciative nod and took a step back.

"It's just…" Abdul Malik continued, and Kashif turned to face him again. "It's just that, you know… now what? What's next for us?" Abdul Malik asked.

"Next? For us?" Kashif asked curiously.

"Yeah, you know, like I know who you are. We're basically a

team now, like that other dude who came and got you. We're all in this together now, brother!" He responded, moving his arms around excitedly as he spoke.

"Uh, no. Okay, listen to me…" Kashif started, but was cut off by Abdul Malik.

"Oh, come on, man, I can help you."

"Listen, bad things happen to people around me. You don't want to be a part of this."

"But I already am. And like I said, I can help you."

"How?" questioned Kashif.

"I don't know, like I can't fight crime or nothing, but um, OH! I know, I got information. People come and go from here all the time, and I hear things. *I know things.*"

"Like what?" asked Kashif.

"Whatever is going on in the streets, I know. I can get people to talk," Abdul Malik then pumped his chest proudly. "Like, for example…" He leaned in as if he was about to say something important but then moved back. "But nah, it's okay. You don't want my help, right? You want my knowledge? Then I gotta be part of the team."

"Listen, there is no team. I'm already trying to stop these other copycats. No more vigilantes, you hear me?"

"Oh, you mean like my guy that I talk to all the time? I know another one of these whatchu call 'em, copycats? Yeah, I know one." He paused, happy to see the look of surprise on Kashif's face. "Hey man, I can tell you, but if we're not on the same team, then…" he shrugged, raising his eyebrows and arms exaggeratedly.

Kashif knew he was trying to reel him in. And as crazy as he knew this was, it was working.

"Whatever information you need on what's going down around here, I got it," Abdul Malik said with finality.

"Okay, okay, fine," responded Kashif. "We can… work together." He sighed, failing to find better wording.

"Yesss!" Abdul Malik pumped his hand in the air. "Only one thing, though; I gotta have a cool nickname too. Like a superhero name, you know?"

"Ya Rabb, save me," Kashif muttered to himself, shaking his head as he knew he was going lower into the rabbit hole. "Fine,

what do you want to be called?" He started rubbing his head, feeling the pain from the day before returning to his head.

Abdul Malik thought for a moment and then snapped his fingers and exclaimed with a big smile, "The Gatekeeper! Like, I've been keeping your secret, right? I'm the keeper of that secret! And all the other secrets we have!"

Kashif strained really hard not to roll his eyes but agreed.

"Okay, yeah, fine. So, who is this guy?"

"Okay, what?" Abdul Malik pressed on with a huge grin.

"Okay... *Gatekeeper,*" he said, trying not to moan out of frustration.

Abdul Malik shook, "Ooooh, I love that. Gives me chills hearing you say that. Okay, so I know this guy; he's a doctor that works over at the hospital, Dr. Ahmed Karim. Tall, good-looking fella. He comes in here all the time and buys a few things. He's a real talker, too. Nice fella. Well, turns out Mr. Doctor has a different night job. He goes out and does what you do."

Kashif listened in silence. "He doesn't do what I do," he finally responded. "I want to talk to this guy. Can you tell me when he usually comes?"

"Every day, around noon, like clockwork."

"Tomorrow, I will need to talk to him, um, Gatekeeper."

"Say no more. I'll pull him into the back?"

"I'll be there, thanks."

Kashif walked out with a nervous feeling in his stomach about both adding a new "team member" and finally confronting one of the copycats.

Abdul Malik waited anxiously for Dr. Karim to enter the next day at the counter. The excitement had him in a jovial mood and chatting up his customers more than usual, as if that was even possible.

"Ahlan wa sahlan!" he shouted at a skinny teenage boy with glasses who approached the counter to pay. The boy jumped back and almost dropped his groceries at how loud Abdul Malik was. The door rang and opened at that moment, and Dr. Karim walked in, waving to Abdul Malik.

"Ahlan wa sahlan!" He turned to the boy at the counter while bagging his groceries. "The boring translation would be 'welcome!'

but the original meaning is, 'I welcome you as my own 'ahl,' meaning family and wish for things to be 'sahl,' easy, upon you," Abdul Malik over-explained with a big smile. The boy was so confused and nervous at the information thrown at him, the volume in Abdul Malik's tone, and how quickly it was said that he hurriedly paid, took his bag, and rushed out the door.

MetalGhost listened to everything from the storage room behind the counter, shaking his head.

"Hey Doc, how's it going, brother?"

"Asalaamu Alaikum, *akhi.* You're in a cheery mood today, even for you," Dr. Karim responded with a smile, approaching the counter. He was slender and tall, with a slight stubble of beard sprinkling his sharp jawline, a sharp nose, and dark, slicked-back hair. He always spoke with a twinkling grin.

"Waalaikum asalaam, yeah… no, I mean, I'm not, actually." His tone changed, becoming serious, "I, uh, listen, I've been having some leg pain right here," he said, accidentally pointing to his crotch instead of his leg. "And it's killing me, bro. I was wondering if you could look at it, you know?"

"Uh, your *leg,* right?" Dr. Karim responded, raising his eyebrow and scratching his chin.

"Yeah, right here," Abdul Malik continued, pointing to the same place.

"I can recommend an excellent specialist to help you with that. I'm a surgeon," he said apologetically.

"Oh… yeah, no, that's cool, you know," he muttered while ringing him up, thinking hard. "Oh, let me get you a bag for that over there." He took a step to his left and dramatically fell to the ground. "Aaahh, my leg! I think it's broken!" He wailed out in pain. "Help, Doc! I think I hit my funny bone right here," he said, pointing to his knee.

"Oh, my God!" Dr. Karim gasped, running behind the counter to help Abdul Malik on the ground. "Are you okay? Here, let me help you sit up," he said, kneeling next to him.

"My cane, I, uh, I think I have a cane in the back room. Can you get that for me?"

Dr. Karim nodded, standing up, and by the time he got to the door, MetalGhost walked up to the door, grabbed him with both hands around his shirt, and slammed him against the back room door.

Dr. Karim winced in pain and yelled in angry protest, "Hey!" before realizing who was before him, and his tune changed.

"Oh! MetalGhost! As I live and breathe." He stared up and down. "I was worried you got seriously hurt, but you look... uh, okay."

"Right now, I would worry about you getting seriously hurt," threatened Abdul Malik, standing beside MetalGhost with his arms crossed across his chest dramatically. He stared with a scowl as MetalGhost pinned Dr. Karim to the wall. "That's *right*. I'm with *him!* We're on the *same team*," he said emphatically.

Under his mask, Kashif rolled his eyes and sighed.

"Can you let me do the talking, please... *Gatekeeper?*" MetalGhost said, turning to Abdul Malik, who he realized was standing way too close to him.

"Yeah yeah, of course. I'll watch the door. And I'll watch your back, make sure he doesn't try to do nothing. Because otherwise, *POP POP!*" He shouted, pounding his fist into his hand.

Kashif sighed again, "Okay, no one is going to do anything, alright. Just watch the door," he turned back to Dr. Karim and let him go. "We're just here to talk," he said, looking straight at him.

"Okay, I don't know what's going on here," a confused Dr. Karim stated.

"I know who you are. You like to go out at night when your shift at the hospital is over. And you like to find trouble."

"Hey, hey..." Dr. Karim smiled with a twinkle in his eye. "I'm just following your lead, Captain," he said sarcastically.

"That's the thing. I don't want you following me: you and all the others. You're done. No more going out, no more vigilantism. You in your dark coat, you're all done."

"Dark Coat, I like that."

"No, you're done."

"I'm Gatekeeper, Dark Coat," yelled Abdul Malik proudly from the door.

"Well, Gatekeeper," Dr. Karim said, nodding to him, then turning to MetalGhost. "I think we three could make a good team. What do you say?"

"Yeah, yeah! I like that man!" Abdul Malik yelled excitedly, looking at MetalGhost.

"What? No! That's not the point I'm trying to make." He turned to Abdul Malik and said sternly, "That's the *opposite* of what I'm trying to say. There has to be an end to this vigilantism. It's not right. We all have to stop."

"You first," Dr. Karim said with a sly smile.

"I will; I'm not in this forever, I just want to find my answers, and that's it. But you all need to stop before you get too deep into it."

"Hmm, I think we're already pretty deep into it."

"I'm warning you. I'll stop you myself if I have to. I better not find you out again."

"Yeah, well, I have a little unfinished business to care of myself."

"Finish it. And that's it. And tell all of your other buddies it's over too."

"Oh, I don't know them. I never had the pleasure of meeting them. But fine, MetalGhost, I'll finish it, and that'll be it."

"Good. And the others, they're going to get the same message."

MetalGhost stepped back, and Abdul Malik turned to Dr. Karim apologetically and said, "Sorry about all that, but MetalGhost has his ways, ya' know." He laughed. As they both looked back, they realized they were the only two people left in the room. Abdul Malik shrugged. "Okay, Dr. Karim, that'll be five bucks."

"Here," Dr. Karim handed him the money for his shopping.

CHAPTER THIRTY SEVEN

THE OTHERS

A few days later, Kashif entered the lab and found Samir in front of X-Bot. "I've found more of our friends," Samir said, turning to him in his chair and smiling. "And boy, are they interesting."

"Tell me," Kashif responded seriously, walking up to the screen.

"Chief Fahim was right; there really are quite a few. I don't know how we've missed them. Look at all these." He popped up several different profiles on the big screen. "Where do you even want to begin?" Samir sighed.

Kashif stared at all the different pictures of men and women on the screen. Men and women who were known vigilantes who were following in his tracks, who were following *him.*

"Who's the most dangerous?" Kashif asked.

"Well, that's tough to say. But I think these two fellows here seem to be leaders of sorts. Let's start with the first, Mr. Dujana Awam." Samir pulled up a picture of a broad-shouldered, muscular dark-skinned man. "You might have heard of the group StreetHawks?" When Kashif shook his head, Samir continued, "Well, they're sort of a neighborhood peace group. Anti-war, anti-killing, anti-violence. In theory, anyway."

"Like pacifists?"

"Not quite," Samir responded, showing him the following few pictures. "Looks like these ended up being on the back pages of the papers, but these guys will do whatever they need to keep the peace." Kashif read the headline, "Local 'Peace' Gang Fight off

Store Intruders, Killing Three." He looked up at Kashif as he continued, "By any means necessary."

"Peace gang?" Kashif questioned.

"Oxymoron, isn't it? It looks like the media can't even help call a peace group a 'gang' if it involves black people," Kashif shook his head. "This man, Dujana, leads them. He's become a local hero of sorts, leading StreetHawks in making sure they root out any sort of violence from the Heights. The area has always seen the highest crime rates in this city, and it looks like he has had enough of that. So, it appears he took matters into his own hands. This seems to be rubbing the crime mobs the wrong way. Look at this video." He clicked a button, and a video of a street view from a store camera showed three dark-skinned men walking along the sidewalk. They're dressed in casual street clothes, each having a red bandana wrapped around their arms. As the men walked, a car approached, and three men jumped out and started to load their guns to shoot. The three men on the sidewalk hurried into a nearby shop right before gunshots from the men in the car blew out the windows and broke the door. They continued firing until they paused to reload, and then suddenly, from inside the store came shooting out three swinging pieces of metal that wrapped around each gunman, immobilizing them as they fell to the ground. The men tried to fight and claw their way out of the metal pieces wrapped around them, but all their struggles were to no avail. Dujana walked out slowly from the store as the car pulled away, leaving their guys on the ground. Dujana took a few slow steps towards the men on the ground, who, by this time, had given up struggling to get loose. Dujana said something to them with an angry face, then smiled down at them. The men who had accompanied him came out and dragged the three men into the store as Dujana followed.

Kashif glanced at Samir. "What did they do to them?" He asked, concerned.

Samir gave a firm look back and repeated, "By any means necessary."

Kashif exhaled a deep breath and sat down, clearly already overwhelmed.

"And that's just the first one," Samir said, noticing his worry. "We have another guy in the same area but opposite Dujana. Meet

Michael David McKenna," he said, pulling up a mugshot of a grizzled elder-looking white man with a five o'clock shadow, sharp nose, and jawline. "Now, this fella is not on the peace train. He doesn't just find bad guys. He hunts them down."

Kashif raised his eyebrows. "He what?"

"He's a military veteran, discharged from service. And not an honorary discharge either. He was kicked out. Well, he's using his military training to take out some bad men. He's taken out half of the Vipers himself. He even tried to take out Police Chief Eames himself before you did. It looks like he knew something before we did. But then, surprise, surprise, he was let go by the police. Seems like he's been laying low since."

Kashif had gone pale, looking stunned.

"That's a lot of information, I know, but let me show you just one more. This one is the most interesting. Check out this footage," he clicked on a button and CCTV footage appeared of a hotel hallway with a group of people gathered around with guns and smoking. The henchmen appeared to be shifting around nervously, some speaking on walkie talkies, while others gave orders. A door at the end of the hall opened up and a lady in a black leather top and pants walked in slowly. She wore a purple hijab and had a black cloth covering her face and eyes. As she confidently strolled toward the men, they blocked her off, with their guns out. The woman seemed to ask them to move, which they all laughed at. When one pulled out a gun and moved in front of her, she took out a small stick from her side, expanding it to reveal a bo staff, she expertly spun the staff and struck each of the men in a lightning pace, disarming them of their guns. With the men grabbing their wrists in pain, they charged toward her as she struck each of them while spinning her staff. After a few seconds, she stood tall over all the men. She then walked past them and opened a door and walked in.

"Wow," Kashif awed. He looked over at Samir, who was smiling, "Oh, wait for the next part."

Returning their sight back to X-Bot screen, a few minutes later, the woman was seen walking out with an unconscious woman tied up on her shoulders.

"Who is that!?" Kashif asked.

"Detective Amber Manson."

"Detective? As in, for the city?" Kashif was aghast.

"Looks like."

"What happened next?" Kashif asked after the lady on the screen walked out with the woman.

"Well, I guess we'll find out. This was only an hour ago, tonight," Samir said.

"No way!"

"I've been tracking this woman down, or more truthfully, have been trying to, but man, she's like a ghost. No trace of her anywhere, not even any clue as to who or where she could be."

"Hmm..."

"Absolutely no information on her, except for a few other incidents of her. She beat up what seems to be a police officer once too. I don't know how she's kept herself so hidden, not even I can find anything. And the way she fights, she's a hijabi ninja. A *ninjabi*," he laughed.

"We have to find out more and who she is. I'm sure you'll find out."

"I don't know man, there's been nothing so far. She keeps her tracks clean. I think we should call her the ghost," Samir turned in his chair facing Kashif. "I propose we call her Ninjabi Ghost," he said almost as if announcing. "And strip the word 'ghost' from MetalGhost."

"Oh, yeah? Really?" Kashif raised his eyebrows. "What will you call me then?"

"I don't know, Metal-Guy? Yeah, sounds about right."

Kashif gave him a light push. "Focus man, you said there are more out there."

"This is a lot of information at one time, I can tell. Let's hold off on the rest of these... characters."

"If those are just three of the copycats, then man, we have a big problem on our hands," Kashif responded, clearly perturbed.

CHAPTER THIRTY EIGHT

DARK COAT

t was a quiet, foggy night on 9th Avenue in the suburb of the city. By midnight, most neighborhood residents had gone to sleep, and there was scarce movement on the streets except for the flurry of activity in one seemingly abandoned house near the end of the road. It was the last house on the block before the river. The lights were turned on in the old house, now used mainly as a tile company warehouse. The innocuous-appearing house on a dead-end would not garner much attention or traffic except in this house. Behind the tile company was a clandestine, drug-dealing operation that had slowly started to make a name for itself. Few would have believed a drug business came out of that house.

The house and tile company were owned by Osama Hossein, an older man whose business was passed on to him by his father. Mr. Hossein, who did not spend much time in the warehouse, was a good, honest man but had slowly grown to realize that the manager he had hired to handle his business, Mason Pierce, started a little business of his own. Mr. Hossein never confronted or spoke about the drug deals Mason was operating out of his warehouse as long as everything was quiet, and he would get his share from the deals. Everything had been working out just fine for a few years, until that night when that quiet would be broken.

Four men, the usual henchmen who handled the bidding and selling of the drugs for Mason, were sitting around, playing cards in the house's garage late that night. They had made quite a great deal of money over the years from their drug dealings, and particularly that night, they were all sitting around in a good mood.

They had no idea that that mood was about to change.

The four men, Ricky, Salman, Bruce, and Stan, were in the garage with the garage door open. Boxes on top of boxes filled the garage, as they had just received a shipment and were expecting more to come. The smell of cigarettes filled the air as the four men played cards on a table at the garage door. The atmosphere was light, business as usual, but the mood changed when they heard someone approaching the driveway from the street. Their attention shifted from their game of cards on a little table to the driveway, waiting for the person to approach. But no one did.

The men looked at each other and shrugged. *Maybe it was just the wind and leaves,* they thought, as their attention returned to their game.

A few moments later, they heard footsteps again outside. Ricky, the shift leader, looked out into the night again while shining his flashlight into the driveway. *No sign of anyone.* He took another drag of his cigarette as the men returned to their game.

Thud, thud, bang. They heard noises on the roof. Someone was there. The men shot up from the table and drew their guns.

"Who's there?" yelled Salman, taking a few steps out to the driveway.

Ricky made a motion with his head to Salman to move to the other side of the garage. As the men spread out, they heard footsteps walking slowly and heavily on the roof, approaching the center of the garage.

Thud. Thud. Thud.

And then, quiet.

The only sound the men could hear were their own heartbeats, beating louder and louder with each passing moment.

The silence was broken by a row of boxes crashing down and one of the lights turning off as the men fired shots at the wall where the boxes had just fallen. But there was no one there.

"Come out!" Ricky yelled.

"See, I would, but did you know that second-hand smoke can cause nasal irritation and an ear infection?" A man's voice mysteriously spoke from the darkness as two metal objects came flying from the opposite side of the wall where the boxes fell, striking two of the men in their heads, knocking them unconscious.

"Not to mention respiratory infections such as bronchitis and even pneumonia? So, I think I'm good here," said the voice, now coming from the other side of the room.

Just as Ricky and Bruce turned around, two more metal objects shot out from the darkness like a bullet, knocking them both out. The assailant appeared as the men lay on the ground, grumbling and groaning. Dressed in a black doctor's coat and a surgical mask covering his mouth and nose, the man known as Dark Coat stepped forward, nonchalantly swinging his stethoscope around.

"Plus, what does a pack of cigarettes cost anyway these days, seven bucks a pack? That's what...?" He paused, scratching his chin while doing the mental math. "$200 a month? Over $2,300 a year?" He slowly descended into deep thought as he continued talking aloud, a usual flaw of Dark Coat's, "Man, that's a lot of wasted money." Distracted by his own thoughts and monologue, he failed to realize that Salman had risen up. Rubbing the back of his bruised head, Salman felt he was hallucinating seeing a doctor talking to himself in the middle of the garage. He leaned on a chair, picked it up, and slammed it on Dark Coat's back.

Crrraackkk, the chair crushed him as he fell to the ground.

The other men slowly rose as well as Dark Coat, on the ground in pain, reached into his coat, took out another scalpel, and nailed a charging Ricky, splintering him in the head and knocking him out for good. He then reached for two retractors from inside his coat, knocking out two of the others. Searching for the fourth, Bruce grabbed him from behind in a rear-naked choke attempting to squeeze his neck as hard as possible. Dark Coat elbowed Bruce in the stomach, bent down, and flipped him violently over his back, splattering him on the ground. Standing over Bruce, Dark Coat needed to give him just two punches to knock him out cold. Hearing noises behind him, he quickly turned and averted a flying table where the men had been playing cards and swung his stethoscope at a charging Stan, sending him flying toward the other side of the garage. Dark Coat expanded his stethoscope from both ends, revealing a nunchuck, and he swung again, knocking the men out until he was left standing on top of a stack of criminals.

"Another round, gentlemen?" A wearied and breathless Dark

Coat asked in a playful tone. "I guess that's game, then. Well, that was fun," he replied to his own question as the other men lay knocked out cold.

He grabbed a cell phone on the ground and dialed 9-1-1.

"Hello, hi! Yes, I'd like to report a crime, and please call an ambulance. There are men that are hurt." He hung up after giving the address.

A semi-conscious Ricky's world was blurry and spinning as he lay on the ground. He saw the frightening face of his attacker bend down over him. "I'll take this," Dark Coat said, showing him the forceps he threw at him. "You don't look so good. I think you need to make a doctor's appointment." He lowered his mask and revealed a big smile with perfect white teeth, ear-to-ear, as his world went black again.

The ambulance arrived, taking the injured men to the hospital. Ricky winced in pain, and his vision was still blurry as he came in and out of consciousness. His head was increasingly hurting from the ceiling lights that kept whizzing by, realizing he lay on a hospital bed getting rolled into the operating room. The doctors wheeling his bed were speaking, but he couldn't understand what was said. He tried lifting his head to understand the doctors' words but pain shot across his head and neck. Before being knocked out again with sleeping gas, the last thing he remembered seeing was one of the doctors by his side taking him into the OR. With slick black hair gelled back, the doctor was looking down at him, and he lowered his mask and gave a big familiar smile while speaking to the nurses, "Get me the scalpel." Ricky panicked and tried to scream as his world went dark again. The last thing he saw was that same smile, with bright white teeth from ear to ear, of Dark Coat.

After the surgery, Dr. Karim headed into his office, tired and wincing in pain but in an upbeat mood. *A chair to the back, what a night. That's going to take a few days.* He laughed to himself. Opening his office door at the end of the hall, he was taken aback by an unexpected figure sitting on a chair across his desk. A man he'd met once before: MetalGhost.

"Hello, Doc."

"How did you even get in here?" asked Dr. Karim, surprised

but amused.

"There's a door, a window, an air vent, and a drop ceiling," chided MetalGhost amusingly, pointing at each. "The same way I'll go out."

"You are something. You know that?" Dr. Karim responded, clearly entertained. "What can I help you with?"

"Oh, you know, just checking up on how your *business* is doing."

"Ahh." Dr. Karim smiled widely. He shut the office door behind him and sat in his chair behind his desk. "Business is as good as ever." He laughed hardily. "No shortage of scum in this city. Just making sure they see their doctor more regularly. Criminals need doctors, too, after all. Even if you have to tussle with them sometimes." There was that broad smile and a twinkle in his eye.

"Clearly," MetalGhost replied, unamused. "Beating up criminals and then performing surgery on them. Clever. But the men you… tussled with tonight, I need to know more about them."

"Sorry, akhi, doctor-patient confidentiality," Dr. Karim said emphatically, knowing he had something MetalGhost needed.

"I don't have time for this."

"You could have known if you took up my previous offer."

"You can't join me. I work alone."

"But you do need me now."

"Just information."

"Come on, man, you know I can help you out there," Dr. Karim said, sitting back.

"If I had a dime for every time I heard that. You, copycats, are something else."

"Copycats? Hey, man, I'm not dressed like you out there, like the others. I got my own thing."

"Original, too, I'll give you that. But the men you brought in and that garage, what can you tell me about them?"

Dr. Karim took a deep breath, folded his arms, pretended to think hard, and sighed.

"Come on… Dark Coat," MetalGhost persuaded, knowing he loved that name, a name MetalGhost had unintentionally given him earlier.

With a satisfactory smile at hearing MetalGhost call him Dark Coat, Dr. Karim recounted the story of what happened that night. "So, you see, just a bunch of nobodies. The small guys were doing the dealing for the bigger guys."

"Who are they working for?"

"I didn't ask."

"How could you not have asked?"

"I wanted to make sure we got him here in time for his surgery… and before my shift ended," he said with a wink. "But," he continued, noticing MetalGhost clearly losing patience, "I did find this in his pocket." He took out a business card. MetalGhost took the card, which read Jack's Bar & Ring. Turning the card over, on the back were written numbers. "Maybe a code or entry pass," said Dr. Karim. "This has become a recurring theme, as it's not the first time I've seen this same card on one of these thugs. Found the same thing last week. I suspect I'll find the same next time, too."

MetalGhost looked straight at Dr. Karim, "You're thinking of going out again? What did we say about fighting and suiting up?"

"I know, but I told you there was just that one thing I needed to do. Anyway, you don't hold a monopoly on fighting bad guys, brother," Dr. Karim responded straightforwardly to MetalGhost. "Besides, sometimes business at the hospital gets slow." He smiled, sitting back comfortably.

"I don't, but I do hold all the guilt when one of you copycats gets hurt. Just stay out of trouble," remarked MetalGhost, having had this discussion before with him.

Dr. Karim stared at MetalGhost as if trying to read his mind, not responding. After a while, he nodded. "Okay, fine."

"I'll look into this," MetalGhost said, holding the card to Jack's Bar & Ring.

"I've heard the name Hammerhead quite a few times. I was going to investigate myself, but it looks like you got this covered."

"Thanks." MetalGhost stood up to leave. He opened the door slightly and peeked out to ensure no one was in the hallway.

"Just going to walk out like that?" quipped Dr. Karim, pointing at the suit.

"Like I said, the same way I came in."

MetalGhost walked out and took the exit to the stairs. As he descended the stairs, he pressed on his watch, and within a few seconds, his suit had retracted back into his watch, leaving him in his everyday civilian clothing.

Mort Davis, the security guard in the first-floor security room, was almost half asleep on the job with the coffee cup in his hands, about to fall. This was his usual routine, as the security room was the best place for a nap, for he's left alone on the shift, and he never gets bothered.

He let out a loud shriek as the door burst open, and Dr. Karim walked in.

"Hey, can I see your security footage?" He asked Mort, trying to act busy and as if he wasn't just sleeping.

"Uh yeah… let me just… get this stuff out of the way, Doc… um, what can I help you with?" Mort sprang up and tried to clear the desk with papers, snacks, and empty snack packets and cartons.

"All the entrances and exits, please."

Mort pressed a few buttons on his board, zooming the security cameras while presenting the security footage on the screen. Dr. Karim studied the camera footage by scanning all the cameras and peering in closely at everyone entering and exiting.

"Uh, looking for something in particular, Doc?"

"Any unusual-looking man coming in or going out today?"

"No," lied Mort, as he hadn't looked at the security footage all day.

"Hmm."

As Dr. Karim scanned the front entrance video of people coming and going, he could not find MetalGhost nor anyone who could be close to his confident strut. He sighed and resigned at the thought that whoever MetalGhost was, he had just left the building.

"All right, thanks, Mort," he said as he watched the screen at the front entrance and people coming and going. Kashif Razvi was seen on the security footage about to exit the building, but as he was about to exit, he looked up at the security camera and gave a half-smile.

CHAPTER THIRTY NINE

MILLSTONE

S amir looked into the information Dark Coat gave them and found the man they had been looking for.

"I've finally found him, Kash. Dark Coat gave us some valuable information about Jack's Bar & Grill. I've been scoping out the place, and guess who I found goes there?" Samir asked with a broad smile and a level of excitement when he was about to reveal something big. "Meet Andrew Millstone." He pulled up a profile on X-Bot, revealing a picture of a large, heavy-set, short man. "This is the key to getting to Hammerhead. And Hammerhead is running the show on the ground for these mobs."

Kashif sat straight up. He hadn't forgotten what he heard at the docks, that a man named Hammerhead was the one that got away that night, the one in charge of the Echo Mas trafficking.

"Tell me more," he said sternly, analyzing the screen.

"Mr. Millstone here, if he looks familiar because he is, for we saw him at the warehouses. He is essentially a broker for all the crime mobs. I've tracked his movements, and he works with all of them. He's their middleman and the link that connects them all. Get to him...."

"Get to all of them," Kashif finished.

Samir nodded. "And he must know where Hammerhead is. He has that access as well as to all the other big-name crime bosses."

Kashif stared at the screen for a few seconds in deep thought. "Tell me, where can I find him tonight?"

"To get someone in Andrew Millstone's position to talk, you'll need to be very… persuasive."

"Don't worry. He won't be able to say 'no' to me," Kashif responded confidently. He knew what he had to do.

"Woah, woah! You're making a big mistake!" Millstone cried out loud later that night after Kashif found him. In his MetalGhost suit, Kashif took him to the top of the second tallest building in Ridgefield Park City, Islah Tower.

"You're not going to kill me! That's not what you do, *MetalGhost,*" Millstone nervously laughed as MetalGhost held him over the ledge of Islah Tower.

"No? You don't know me then," raged MetalGhost.

"Well, you better decide quickly. My guys are rushing up this building right now. You won't last long, pal," Millstone gave him a cold stare and smile.

MetalGhost smiled back, pulling Millstone's face close to his. "I went through all your boys before coming to you. We have *all the time* in the world. But I'm giving you one last chance. Let's start with the explosion in the Paramus lab. *Who did it!?"*

"The lab..." Millstone wondered out loud and started laughing. "That's what this is about? Hahaha, why do you care about *that? It happened four years ago! It's old news!"*

"Do you really think you're in any position to ask questions right now?" MetalGhost screamed. He tightened his grip on Millstone's shirt, starting to push him down further, almost entirely off the building.

"Okay, okay! Look, I don't know what happened that night. But that lab actually belongs to Iris Hill. If you want to get to Iris Hill, you'll have to get to Hammerhead first; he's the one who knows Mr. Hill's locations."

"Where is Hammerhead? And what's his real name?"

Millstone screamed, feeling his feet lift off the ground and completely in the air.

"Listen! I'm telling you, I don't know. No one knows his real name!" He yelled, more seriously than before.

"Where is he? You better be quick!" roared MetalGhost.

"Jack's Bar & Ring! Hammerhead, he's down at Jack's Bar & Ring. There's a secret side door he comes and goes from. He runs his business from the side rooms."

"When will he be there, and how will I know it's him?"

Millstone let out a faint laugh, "He ain't called Hammerhead for no reason. You'll know when you see him. He'll be on the long couches at the back of the hall. And he'll be there tonight because some big deal is supposed to go down."

"See, that wasn't so bad, was it?"

"Now get me outta here!" Millstone demanded.

Kashif felt the anger rise up inside him like a demon emerging. "No. Trash like you don't deserve to live. And what was that you said, what don't I do?"

The fear in Millstone's eyes deadened as MetalGhost released him into the air, and Millstone started falling from the building.

You can't just let him die.

But he deserves it.

It's about you. That's not you. Kashif paced anxiously back and forth, thinking to himself and deciding what to do, as Millstone continued to scream as he fell.

The Imam's voice rang in his head, *the Prophet Muhammad (ﷺ) said "The strong man is not the one who wrestles others; rather, the strong man is the one who controls himself at times of anger.'* And in an instant, he felt calm. Kashif released his grappling gun and fired it down toward the falling Millstone. The grappling hook bolted down in a fury and reached Millstone right before he was about to hit the ground, wrapped around his leg, and he was pulled and jolted all the way back up, ascending to the roof again.

"You're insane!" a terrified Millstone said, thrown back onto the roof, breathing heavily and in shock.

"Not completely," MetalGhost replied. "You get to live this time, but you better hope I don't meet you again. And as for your little escapades doing dirty laundry for the mobs, you're done. And I'll let them know you're done too. Here's your resignation letter," MetalGhost removed the cloth from his left ring finger, revealing the ring with a letter M carved into it. He punched Millstone in the forehead right above the eyes and pressed his fist into his skin, branding his symbol on his head. "Now, everyone will know you met me, and you've talked." Millstone screamed in pain, and when he looked up, he found himself alone on the roof.

"Well, the grappling gun works," Kashif casually stated, entering back into the lab where Samir was working.

At his desk, Samir took off his goggles and nodded proudly that his device worked, but then his face shifted in concern. This was not how he intended to have his newest invention used. "Not exactly what I had in mind for it," he responded, concerned.

Kashif looked down, "I know, I shouldn't have thrown him..."

Samir waited, and then finished the sentence "... off of one of the *tallest buildings.*"

"I realized that, and I was able to focus, and calm down. I was able to think clearly, look past the anger," Kashif remembered his conversation with Imam Dawood. He took off his shirt and shoes and started changing his clothes.

Samir continued to stare at Kashif, unwavering.

"I think I'm getting better, okay?" Kashif tried to sound convincing.

"You are, I admit. You're not as angry as you were. And I'm glad to see that, your anger scared even me."

"Alhamdulillah. But hey, we finally got to Millstone, and we got answers. He gave us when and where we can find Hammerhead—at Jack's Bar & Ring tonight."

"I'll look into it," replied Samir, still not breaking his gaze at Kashif.

As Kashif finished buttoning up his shirt, he turned his back and started to walk out after changing. Samir called out to him, "But the branding?" Samir kept his gaze on Kashif.

Kashif stopped at the door, turned, and gave a satisfied smile, "I think it compliments his face."

"Kashif, you cannot do that. You cannot *brand* people," Samir cautioned.

"Again, I know. I needed to send all the mobs a message, I didn't know what else to do," responded Kashif, about to exit the room.

"And where are you going now?"

"It's time for Maghrib prayer. I'm going to the masjid. You coming?"

Samir nodded, taking off his lab coat, and followed Kashif to the door.

"And after that, I'm going to the bar," he gave a side smile and patted Samir on the back as they exited.

CHAPTER FORTY

WAR DRUMS ARE GROWING LOUDER

Jack's Bar & Ring was a notorious spot in the corner of the city near the Firdaus River. The building was massive and divided into two large halls, one consisting of a bar, and next door was a full-out boxing ring and gym. Because of the city's strict alcohol laws, it was the only bar in the city, and it was well-known for all the wrong reasons. A usual spot for many of the underground criminal leaders, and as Kashif and Samir uncovered from Millstone, also a meetup spot for business deals. That specific night was the night for a meetup of a few gang leaders, including Hammerhead.

"I see a camera on the side door where the guard is positioned," noted Kashif from on top of the building across from the bar. "I can take it out," he said, zooming back to his normal vision from his lens scope, "along with the guard."

"I suggest you go in with as little noise as possible," Samir remarked.

"You want me to ask the guard nicely to let me in?" quipped Kashif.

"No, but you don't know what you'll find in there. Be smart; stay hidden as long as possible."

"Yeah, let's see how..." Kashif froze mid-sentence as the camera exploded into tiny pieces by a bullet from another rooftop. Kashif quickly shifted his sight to the rooftop and saw a man in a brown trench coat with a white cloth covering his face except his eyes, and a brown fedora hat, kneeling with a rifle gun. The man was looking through the rifle's scope, ready to fire again, this time at the guard. "No!" Kashif shouted, jumping off the building. He ran toward the guard, who panicked and froze at the sight of MetalGhost rushing up to him. Kashif quickly double-clenched his fist and super-punched him unconscious; simultaneously, he felt a bullet graze off his back. He carried the unconscious guard around the corner and laid him down behind the dumpster across the street. With the guard hidden out of view, he turned furiously, looking back at the rooftop building. The sniper was standing up now, taking aim at him. He pointed the rifle at Kashif, then lowered it.

Angry, MetalGhost walked to the building and scaled the side of the building wall toward him. The man took a step back as MetalGhost arrived on the rooftop. "MetalGhost," he calmly stated, "We finally meet. Now, why did you go and do that for?" He pointed to the unconscious guard.

Kashif stared at the man, finally getting a good look at him. Unwrapping the white cloth with checkered red diamonds from his head and face, Kashif got a good look at the infamous sniper. He was middle-aged with a long face and nose, a strong jawline, a scar running down across his left cheek to his chin, and a scruffy brown beard covering his white skin. Under his trench coat were magazine rounds holstered around his shoulders, crossing his chest. Not replying, MetalGhost walked up to him, grabbed him by the chest, lifted and threw him to the ground. The man winced in pain but did not fight. He only stared up as MetalGhost bent over him, still clutching his chest. "Who the hell are you?!"

It was Samir from back in the lab who answered, "McKenna. But they call him War Drum."

"Relax, MetalGhost. I'm not your enemy," McKenna calmly replied. His long golden hair blew in his face as his hat had fallen off.

"McKenna," snared Kashif. "You've been causing a lot of problems. But now, you're done."

McKenna pushed away Kashif's hand and stood up, "I'm just getting started. Why did you let that piece of trash live?"

"Because we don't just kill people," Kashif replied angrily.

"Those are animals, and I'm going to get rid of each of them in this city. I thought that's what you were doing here, too?"

"Yeah, not like you, though."

"You expect them to what, change?"

"No, but it's not about them. You don't know what killing another does to you."

"Oh, I know, MetalGhost," responded McKenna in a tone that made the hair on Kashif's neck stand. "I've killed more than I've liked, and there's no going back. It's time we take out the scum of this city once and for all."

"There is no we, and I'll take them out myself. My own way."

"Good, I will help."

"No, you're done. All of you. I'm sick of you copycats."

"Don't get a big head; I'm not copying you. Sure, you were the push I needed, but you don't know me, MetalGhost, or what's in me. I was born to do this." He eyed his sniper rifle.

Kashif remembered everything Samir had told him about McKenna. "You've killed too many people and caused too much chaos. Everywhere you've gone, you've caused destruction. That's not what this city needs. You're an anarchist. And now you're done."

"You think you have me all figured out, don't you?" McKenna laughed. "Well, you're not totally wrong. But I will do what you can't. I will clean this city from each and every filthy gang member and corrupt official, down to the last one. See, they don't fear you because they know you won't kill them. And that's the problem. *I'm that fear.* The fear that will stop another criminal from even taking a step into this city. And you can't stop me," McKenna said as he turned around and raised his gun again towards the building. In one motion, Kashif pulled him back, took hold of McKenna's sniper rifle, and snapped it in two with his knee. McKenna tried to swing at Kashif, but Kashif ducked, clenched his fist twice, and super punched McKenna in the stomach, causing him to fly a few feet back. He was about to go where he lay until he heard a woman's voice from behind him.

"You know, he could help you. We all could."

Kashif turned around to a woman dressed in a loose yellow and grey body suit, a flowing cape mainly covering her left arm and side, and a silver plate covering her face with a yellow glass shield from which she could see. She had a metallic band around her left wrist, and Kashif noticed a bow hidden behind her arm.

"Another one?" Kashif asked in disbelief.

"Asalaamu alaikum, brother," she greeted. "He's not the most... orthodox or even sane..." the woman said, pointing to McKenna on the ground wincing in pain. "But he means well and can be useful. He just needs a little fine-tuning."

"You must be the one they call NightStrike. WaAlaikum asalaam," he responded, putting his hand over his heart.

"I've been trying to meet you. I can help you," NightStrike responded, stepping closer.

Kashif sighed. "Listen to me, all of you. You all need to stop this. This needs to end here."

"You don't hold an ownership on vigilantism," quipped McKenna, wincing in pain.

"No, but I hold the guilt. This is not what I intended when I started this. I don't want you all following me," he said, turning to NightStrike. "I don't want to give you any illusions of this being grandeur. Breaking the law is not noble."

"It may not be what you intended, but what you gave us is so valuable," replied NightStrike. "Hope. You gave us hope that if we want to take back our city and if we want to clean it up, we can make that change ourselves."

"This was not what I intended," Kashif responded, taken aback by this. "I don't want to be the one starting this. You all take the law into your own hands. Where does it end? How many more people can we allow to do this? Why even have laws, then?"

Standing up, McKenna and NightStrike looked at each other, not knowing what to reply.

"How many more people will this lead to getting hurt? And that's on me. I can't live with that. Vigilantism cannot be the norm, and I do not want to set that precedent."

Listening to all this back at the lab, Samir had looked up all the information he could find about NightStrike, and spoke into Kashif's earpiece, "Her name is Eva Austin... yes, the same one who goes to your Rollstar Jiu-Jitsu academy. She's been robbed a couple of times by the gangs. Maybe that's why she started training and started taking on the local thugs."

Kashif's heart skipped a beat, and his eyes shot open in shock.

Eva Austin! No! Eva was a student in his gym, someone he saw every week. His heart sank at the sight of her taking on the suit, and the thought of anything happening to her caused Kashif to step back.

"Are you okay, MetalGhost?" NightStrike asked.

Taking a moment to get a hold of himself, he brought himself to look at the two again.

"From now on, you all are going to stop. You, McKenna, and Eva Austin," he said, turning to NightStrike. Kashif could tell she was taken aback by hearing her name.

"How... how do you know who I am?" she asked, shocked.

"I do my homework thoroughly. I know you all, and you all need to stop. This is not what the city needs. I won't repeat it. No more vigilantism."

"I tell you what, Chief. You tell us who you are, and then I'll think about it," McKenna replied sarcastically yet seriously. Kashif growled in anger and stepped toward him with his fist clenched. "Okay, okay," McKenna replied, taking a step back and raising his hands. "I'll think about it. I'll leave for tonight and let you do... whatever you're up to. Although, I have a feeling we are here for the same reason. Hammerhead?" McKenna asked.

Kashif paused, not responding.

"Yeah, see, we're not too different after all. But you should know you've woken up this city. And this city isn't just going to sit back and watch itself burn." He closed his trench coat, walked to the roof door, opened it, and stopped. He turned around, looking at MetalGhost, "The war drums are growing louder," he said slowly before leaving. Taken aback, Kashif tried to make sense of what McKenna had said.

"What did he mean by that?" MetalGhost asked NightStrike hesitantly.

"I'm not sure, but he is starting to gain some fans for his ways. He's dangerous; I won't lie. I do worry about him and his methods, but I also know he means well," Eva replied.

MetalGhost felt frozen in his silence.

"But you can't just tell us all to stop," Eva turned to MetalGhost, pleading.

"Listen to me. You all have to. You all have made my life so hard. Every time people see one of you, it's my face they put on another wanted poster. It's me they're after. I'm not your hero. I'm just here to find out who is behind all this."

"Me too."

"Then let me find out, and when I do, I'm done. We cannot have people taking the law into their own hands."

"I won't be doing this for too long myself," Eva sighed, turning around and looking out into the city. "I won't *be able* to," she said mournfully.

"Why not?"

She pulled down on her mask, releasing it upwards and behind her head. Simultaneously, a hijab that was draped around her chest moved up onto her head, covering her hair.

"I love this city. Looking out into it, like tonight, brings me so much calm. My favorite thing to do is bring a Qur'an to a rooftop on a night like this and recite it. I feel like I'm reciting to the city," she gave a small laugh. She paused, looking downward, her voice changed, "But I'm going blind. I'm almost there already. My right eye is almost completely gone. Just a matter of time before the other one goes." She turned and looked at Kashif. "I know what you must be thinking: an archer going blind?" She pointed to her bow and a metal band around her forearm. "But I can still shoot with my left eye."

MetalGhost was left speechless, a deep sadness rising like a shadow. "I'm sorry. Where are your arrows?" he asked, not seeing a quiver.

She pointed to her forearm band. "It creates arrows one after another and places them in a perfect position for me to shoot. This way, I can never run out of arrows. And this bow, I can easily latch it to the back of my arm." She retracted the bow to hide behind her left arm, behind her cape.

"Cool," MetalGhost marveled.

They both stared out at the city, silent for some time before an idea came to him.

"Here," he said, causing her to turn around.

She saw MetalGhost turn his back to her and reach for his face. When he turned around, he held a lens in his hand. "Put this on," he said.

"What? What is that?"

"The solution to your problem"

"That's a lens; it's not going to work."

"These aren't just any lens. Put it on," he insisted.

She hesitantly took the lens and inspected it before inserting it into her eye. She let a moment pass before she looked up at MetalGhost.

"It's just a contact lens? Yeah, I can see better, but it's not going to reverse my blindness."

"I want you to focus on that building over there," MetalGhost pointed far in the distance. "And then squint and focus real hard."

Confused, she hesitantly looked out toward the building across the neighborhood and focused. "Ya, Allah! What is this? How is it doing that!" she cried.

"It allows you to zoom in as far as you would like. This should help you see, for some time longer anyway. It's meant for people like you to slow the process of blindness."

Eva broke into a cry, which turned into a nervous laugh. "I... I can't believe this." She cried.

"Take it. Keep it."

"Really?" She gasped in disbelief.

"Yes. And I'll give you the other one, too," he said as she turned to him in surprise. "Only if you stop going out and suiting up."

She paused for a moment and looked down. MetalGhost could tell she was thinking.

After a moment, she raised her head. "Okay, fine."

"And not just you, all of you. You all need to stop."

"You'll have to tell all the others, yourself," she replied earnestly. "They won't just listen to me."

"Gather all of them, and I'll address them."

"Okay, but where?"

"Gather everyone next Tuesday night on top of the warehouses at the docks," he said, walking towards the edge of the building.

"And for tonight, you'll go back and let me do what I have to," he said, turning back to the bar door. She nodded as she looked at MetalGhost standing at the ledge, recited "Bismillah," took a step off the ledge, and glided towards the building.

Eva stood there with her new vision as MetalGhost landed on the ground in front of the building and entered the back door into the bar.

CHAPTER FORTY ONE

JACK'S BAR AND RING

I t was a fine evening for the local cartel, drug dealers, and gangbangers to meet, have a good time and make their dealings. The bar was dimly lit, smoke-filled, loud with music, and full of chatter, with waiters hustling and running back and forth from tables full of activities. Some tables had card games in action, and some had poker games. Other tables were lined up around the bar, and large TV sets. At the end of the hall were long l-shaped couches and tables where the VIPs were seated. It was a full house that night, and the noise and action were signs that something big was going down.

The jubilant and festive mood inside the bar quickly shifted as the noises yelling from the hallway turned louder. Before anyone could understand the shouting and screaming, the doors to the bar burst open, and a guard flew before crashing through it. Landing with a loud thud on the ground, he lay crumpled and motionless as the bar went silent.

I'm not wasting any time, Kashif thought when entering the building. He knew he had to get to Hammerhead and knew the only way forward was through each and every person in the building.

The guard moaned loudly on the ground as shouts were heard, roaring instructions to load up and whip out guns. The room quieted to pin-drop silence, all eyes on the door.

As MetalGhost walked through the door, the shouts and screams grew in the bar.

"Run!"

"Hide!"

"Get him!"

"Cover the boss!"

MetalGhost ran toward the back of the hall as henchmen and guards rushed toward him. Each was met with a super punch and kick, throwing them backward. As the henchmen fell and were knocked out, Kashif could see heavy guns getting loaded from the corner of his eye. He backed himself up against one of the walls and faced everyone. Within seconds, he was surrounded by dozens of gunmen, all pointing their pistols, assault rifles, and shotguns at him.

"You think you could just break in here and do what?!" One of the men holding an assault rifle yelled. "I've been waiting to get my hands on you!" he laughed maniacally. "What are you going to do now?"

MetalGhost looked around, noticing he was completely surrounded.

"Go ahead, shoot me," he growled in response.

The henchmen gave each other a confused look as one yelled, "Fire!" the room lit up with bright lights as rounds and rounds of bullets sprayed toward their target. But what they thought would be a bloody mess turned into a moment of utter surprise and confusion. The bullets they fired didn't strike their target, but they did hit *a* target. A big blue target. MetalGhost had brought his forearm in front, and a giant blue see-through shield was extracted and raised in front of him. The bullets flew into the shield, immersed in it as if they were stuck in the air in a gel-like material. Hundreds of bullets were embedded into the shield. Some made their way through and hit MetalGhost in the chest, causing him to wince. But most of the bullets were in the shield, floating in the air.

The room stopped in awe, and nervous murmurs started to arise, and all eyes were on MetalGhost and his shield of bullets.

"All done?" MetalGhost asked. "I don't have a need for these. You guys can have *them back!*" He screamed as he flung his forearm and the shield back with all his might as all the bullets that had been fired went firing back at full speed at their assailants. This time, the bullets hit their target. The explosion of bullets rammed through flesh, and screams of men flying back and falling filled the hall, blood splattering everywhere. A few moments later, only MetalGhost was left standing in the room.

Falling to his knee, he caught his breath from the shield throw, having taken the wind out of him. He looked up and saw over the pile of dead bodies in the center of the hall, people scurrying and moving around near the end of the hall where the l-shaped sofas were placed. He immediately made his way towards the back and pushed a few people out of the way, punching out more mob members who tried to stop him. He noticed a man in a nice fancy pinstripe black suit, red tie, and perfectly combed hair. This man was peculiar looking, for his forehead was more prominent and wider than most, and his eyes were farther apart than the average person. And this man was looking right at MetalGhost with fear in his eyes. *Hammerhead.* As MetalGhost ran toward him, he tried to get up from hiding between the couches and make his way toward the end of the hall. But before he could look back, MetalGhost was already standing on top of him, holding his suit from his chest.

"Hammerhead," he growled.

Hammerhead looked dead straight into MetalGhost's mask and gained the confidence to ask, "What do you want!?"

"Iris Hill. Was he behind the Paramus lab explosion? Is he Echo Mas? Is he the one kidnapping women?"

"Woah woah, that's a lot of accusations, Buddy."

"You better talk." MetalGhost squeezed Hammerhead's throat.

"Okay, okay." He winced in pain. "Yeah, he hired a guy to run some experiments there. He was working with someone on something big. But what does that have to do with anything?"

"It has to do with everything. Where is he?"

Hammerhead laughed. "You don't want to know. Bad things happen to people who go looking for him."

"I won't ask again," MetalGhost responded angrily.

Hammerhead laughed under his breath. "See, you think you can just punch your way through everything. That's not how it works, pal."

"Where is he?!" MetalGhost demanded, punching the ground next to his face.

"He's not here. I don't know where he is. But I can get the word out that you're looking for him. He'll find you," Hammerhead responded coolly and unfazed.

"Yeah? In that case, I can send your body with that message," he said, raising his fist and clinching twice.

Before MetalGhost could punch downward, he felt a strong force hold his wrist from behind him. Quickly turning around, he found himself staring back into the red eyes of a dark-skinned, shirtless man wearing blue jeans and no shoes. He was strong and exceptionally well-built, with muscles protruding from his chest, arms, and shoulders. There was something about this man that seemed... off, Kashif thought. His face was set in a serious and robotic expression. Before MetalGhost could move, the man quickly picked him up easily and threw him halfway across the room. As MetalGhost got up, he saw the man walking at a slow robotic pace toward him without saying a word or showing any emotion. Jumping up to his feet, he raised his fists, ready for a fight. The man quickened his pace as he approached closer, jumped high in the air, almost touching the ceiling, and tried to kick MetalGhost on his way down, but he averted the kick. As the man landed hard, the floor beneath him cracked. The man stood up and looked straight at him, and Kashif could see his eyes were angry red, almost as if they were inhuman. *Is this the same person who attacked me on the roof?*

MetalGhost clenched his fists, and as they were about to move closer, both men were interrupted by small flashes of light coming from the corner of the room. *Click, click* went a sound, and the flashes continued. Two young local reporters, Ben and Mikaeel, were standing behind a turned-over table, taking pictures of everything. The flashes from their camera seemed to affect the man as he looked confused and dazed by the light. Shielding himself from the camera lights, he retreated back and ran out of the room to the ring but not before giving MetalGhost one last deathly look. As Kashif looked back, Ben and Mikaeel had also fled. Kashif ran into the ring behind the man, but arriving in the hall, he stared into an empty room. Turning back to the bar, he noticed it was empty as well. Hammerhead was gone too. As Kashif gazed around the room, a sudden fear crawled up his spine and hovered over him like a dark cloud, making his stomach feel sick. He looked out into the bar at the bloodbath and bodies left in the wake. He was only now seeing the massacre.

I did this... He cried to himself in disbelief.

CHAPTER FORTY TWO

DUJANA

T he days following the night at Jack's Bar & Ring brought much chatter and noise in the city. News reports talked about nothing else: the scene at the bar, the amount of injured and dead gang members, the number of arrests made, and how the gangs have retreated underground again. In the underground criminal world, as if they needed more reason to hate their biggest nemesis, it was official that they needed to stop one man: MetalGhost.

For Kashif, things were just as chaotic inside him as out in the crime world. The sight of the strange dark man and the two reporters took a backseat in his mind, for all he could think about was the death toll at the bar. He had not killed anyone before, and it weighed heavy on his conscience.

"What other choice did you have?" reasoned Samir, trying to provide him some solace.

"I went in there. I went to them," Kashif cried out.

"They fired first. Unfortunately, it was kill or be killed."

Kashif shrugged, knowing he was right, but it didn't change the outcome of what had happened. He never intended to kill anyone, and it weighed him down heavily. He kept thinking back to the scene and knew he had no other choice, but taking a life wasn't sitting easy or right with him. Deeply upset, disturbed, and unsure of how to continue, Kashif was starting to feel lost again.

"You've been really good about not actually killing anyone up to this point, but again, you had no choice. And remember the overall good that you're doing. That we're doing," Samir said. "But some good news: I think I see an alternative." Samir rose and walked to X-Bot. "We don't want to kill anyone, but how do we stop someone who's trying to kill you? How do we... apprehend them?" He asked out loud. "I think we may have an answer." He looked at Kashif while pointing to the screen. "Remember I told you about Dujana?"

"The 'by any means necessary' guy?"

"That's him. The 'sort of pacifist.' He and his crew, StreetHawks, don't use guns. They're against them. And they don't go to the lengths of killing anyone. I've been tracking them, and what they use is very impressive. Have a look at this security footage."

Kashif saw on the screen a video of Dujana and his men fighting in the street against a group of men Kashif recognized.

"Smoke Gang," Kashif whispered with his eyes on the screen. The Smoke Gang members took out their guns, but suddenly, each of their guns flew out of their hands and into the hands of two StreetHawk members. Kashif looked at Samir in amazement, who nodded. Then on the screen, Dujana and the other members of his group threw what looked like handcuffs at the Smoke Squad members, but by the time the handcuffs reached each of the assailants, a rope-like material emerged and wrapped itself around each of the men. What followed seemed to be some kind of electric shock as each of the men winced in pain and fell to the ground, remaining unmoving.

"They call them rope cuffs," Samir said once the video stopped. "Created by two of their guys, the Burn Brothers. They're... like me. I guess you can say."

Kashif looked and listened in amazement. "That's amazing and exactly what I could use," he said.

"Yeah, I would work on creating a prototype of my own, but I'd love to see what they have already. What they have looks... almost perfect."

"Not all of these copycats are the same, I see," wondered Kashif out loud. "And how did those guns fly out of the other guy's hands into their own?"

Samir shrugged, "I have no idea. Maybe we should ask him?" he suggested, smiling.

"I think it's time we give Dujana a visit."

"By the way, speaking of copycats, here," Samir pulled up the Daily RP newspaper front page. The headlines read, *More MetalGhost CopyCats Arrested,* with pictures of police taking in handcuffs masked men and women.

The heavy dark feeling returned to Kashif, upsetting him. He stared at the news story in anger.

"But check this out," Samir turned to X-Bot and played a CCTV footage. The scene was outside of RP Police Precinct at night. Everything seemed quiet as officers hung around the doors chatting, as others made their way in and out of the building. One officer looked upward and panicked, dropping his coffee. Other officers looked up and began to yell and point upward.

"What are they looking at?" Kashif asked.

Samir switched to another camera and what he saw made Kashif gasp. The same woman Samir had shown him earlier, the ninja in purple and black, had tied up a police officer and had tied him up to a light pole. She was quickly taping something to the man's chest, and she jumped to the ledge of the roof as the gunshots fired her way from the officers below. Realizing the shots might hit the tied-up officer, they stopped firing. The woman stood on the ledge and spoke, "Too many of our city's police are corrupt. Take a look yourself," she pointed to the file taped to the man's chest. "I will find all of you corrupt officers, believe me." She jumped back on the roof and disappeared.

Kashif stood staring at Samir in shock. Samir stared back with a satisfied smile. "Ninjabi," he proclaimed proudly. "And again, she's a ghost."

"Looks like I have something else to talk to Dujana about too."

He waited until after Maghrib salah when the sun set, then suited up and headed out to The Heights.

It was a cloudy and dark night in the corner of RP City known as The Heights. Usually a place of life and activity, even late at night, tonight seemed almost calm. Dujana Awam was in his work apartment across the hall from where he lived in a five-story building on Sadiah Street. The work apartment was full of tables and shelves with different and various science experiments and gadgets. The walls were plastered with news clippings of Dujana being labeled a neighborhood hero, while other clippings of news articles claimed him to be a nuisance. That night, he was thoroughly indulged in working on his table with bifocal lab glasses, leaning in close with full concentration on brazing two metals together. He suddenly paused, looked up, and turned around. Noticing the dark and quiet room behind him, he returned to work. A few moments later, he calmly put down the new metal piece he was working on, then suddenly reached into his pocket and threw a rope cuff toward the dark side of the room. A blue shield blocked the rope cuff, and as it hit the ground, MetalGhost stepped forward from the shadows. Dujana, already with raised fists, loosened up and stood up straight.

"Well, well, well," he said in a cheerful yet surprised voice. "You really do work in the shadows." He sounded impressed. "I was hoping I would get to meet you, finally," he said with a genuinely friendly smile. "How uh... how did you get past the security guards and all?" He said, looking past him.

"Who said I went *past* them?" responded MetalGhost in a serious voice.

Dujana shook his head and let out a little laugh. "I shouldn't be surprised." The two men stared at each other for a moment. Dujana was a tall man, almost 6 feet 5 inches, with broad shoulders and a muscular build.

"You're a lot taller than I thought," remarked MetalGhost, trying to buy time by looking around the room he was in.

"And you're a lot shorter than I thought," he quipped back.

MetalGhost looked at him sideways. "But I bet you get that a lot."

"There are a lot of bigger guys than me out there. And for some reason, I tend to attract them," said Dujana.

"I'll let you handle them then," Kashif responded in jest.

Dujana laughed, "Well, to what do I owe this pleasure, MetalGhost? Why don't you sit down?"

"You sit. I'm good," he replied, continuing to look around.

"Am I your prisoner here?" Dujana asked, sitting down.

MetalGhost glared at him. "Not at all. This is your house."

"Well then, let me get you something to drink. I've got the best Moroccan mint tea from back home," he replied happily, getting up from his chair.

"Why don't you just sit right there," rebuked MetalGhost, raising his hand in front of him.

Taken aback and realizing the sudden harshness in his tone, Dujana responded, "Looks like I'm a prisoner then." He let out a loud sigh and sat down again. Both men looked at each other, the friendliness giving way to a tense air between them.

"Have you come to tell me not to go out fighting the filth of this city like you've told the others?" asked Dujana, still in a calm and pleasant tone.

"Will you do that?" asked MetalGhost, already knowing the answer.

"If you're asking me not to protect my people, you know I can't do that," said Dujana, folding his arms.

"I didn't think so. No, I'm not asking you to stop protecting people. But I do know you're helping these other... copycats. Why?"

"Because they want to help. And so I let them help," Dujana shrugged. "There's enough evil in the world; if some people want to do good, I'm down for that."

"By breaking the law and becoming vigilantes?"

"I think you know better than anyone that sometimes you need to take the law into your own hands. The police here, unfortunately they can't be trusted. It was you who brought that out into the light for us all to see."

"I think you're giving people weapons and telling them to go out in ways that can hurt others, including themselves. How do you know they won't use those weapons for evil?"

"I ask myself that all the time. And I hope you don't really think I give things to just anyone?" His voice sounded offended. "I vet them, make sure they're okay. And I follow their tracks. I, uh... have a guy who follows them to ensure they're not doing anything stupid. They're all good. Well, I mean, you have your fellows like McKenna." He laughed quietly. "But most of them are good." He continued, "You see, most people have grand ideas and noble intentions, but not everyone can do what we do."

The word "we" negatively struck Kashif. He didn't think these others were like him.

"See, everyone *wants* to do good until the time actually comes to act. Not everyone has the courage to fight. For those who do, well, maybe they win a fight or two. But more likely than not, they will get their bell rung a lot more often. I've had people come back and tell me they can't do it," recalled Dujana. "But the ones who are brave enough, the ones who are tough enough, the ones who can get beaten down but get right back up, now those people, I want to help," he said. "And to be honest, there aren't many of us out there, just a few. And I know you've been telling them to stop," he said with a side smile. "Can't blame you, I guess."

"But they don't listen." MetalGhost sighed.

"Because they admire you. You inspire them. They want to be like you, man. More than that, they want to help you," Dujana declared.

"I don't want anyone following me," snapped MetalGhost.

"So I've heard," a disappointed Dujana replied.

"What's so noble about breaking the law, beating up others, and all this violence? I'm not setting a good example. No one should want to be like me. I got thrown into this, and then it took over me like a... virus. Why would I wish this disease on anyone else?"

"That's how you feel, and no one can blame you. But despite all that, you provide one thing to others that no one else has been able to: a way out. You talk about violence. Well, we see violence on the streets here every day, man. And it's only gotten worse and worse. The police don't care, and they don't even come around here anymore. I'm not saying they're all bad, but we see that they're either corrupt or too scared to come around these areas. The truth is, they don't care about us. We're the forgotten. You call them and tell them you're calling from here, and they hang right up. For the longest time, things weren't good around here. But then you came along. You see, you've taught us one thing: we have no choice but to fight back against violence. You gave us hope that someday, all these senseless killings and crimes would end. But we'd have to take things into our own hands, do it ourselves. You showed us how."

MetalGhost listened to the words, and he felt them penetrating his chest.

"If you want to know if you're making a difference or giving us something, let me introduce you to a young girl named Jauveria. Or, better yet, in the house next door lives Ms. Johnson. Why don't you stop by there and ask her what she thinks of you? Not long ago, she was walking down the street with her two boys when she got robbed, and they took one of the boys—gone, just like that. But she's strong, even though you can see she's cracked, but she won't break. Why? Because of you. She believes in her heart that you will help her bring her boy back."

MetalGhost looked to the floor, not able to find the words.

Dujana continued, "She believes *you* will find her son... because I haven't." He paused, turned, and walked to the window. "Because he's out there, I know it. But I haven't found him," he said quietly, looking out. He turned back to MetalGhost, "Still, she believes that you will."

MetalGhost felt his breathing getting heavier and his mind racing, and it took him a few moments to gain control of it.

"I still don't want others following my path. It's not noble, and it leads down a dark path. Once you start, where does it stop? If you all want to help, well find another way. How many vigilantes can we have until there is no law? I know I have to stop soon before it fully consumes and destroys me because that's where this path leads. But you all need to stop before that. That means for you, no more helping them. It won't lead to anything good in the long run."

"That's a fair point." Dujana nodded in agreement.

"That's why I asked NightStrike to set up a meeting with all of you and me," declared MetalGhost .

The surprise on Dujana's face was apparent, "Now that's an interesting idea."

"Get them together for me. I'll tell them myself. Can you help her do that?"

"I can," Dujana said, folding his arms. "But what do I get out of this?" He said, raising his eyebrows.

"What do you want?" .

Dujana paused, staring at Kashif in his suit. "Who are you?" Dujana asked quietly.

"Really? I'm just someone like you," MetalGhost retorted.

"Yes," Dujana dragged out. "But really, who are you? Are you part of the black community? Do I know you?"

MetalGhost remained silent and continued to stare at Dujana, who was studying him.

"Is it Malcolm? Is that you? No, but it can't be," Dujana spoke thoughtfully. "Someone with more resources," he continued to think out loud. "Certainly not Iris Hill." He laughed at his own joke. He went through a few more names, but MetalGhost didn't respond to them. "Maybe you're one of the brilliant minds at Al-Fihriya University? Could it be the famous Samir Khan, or maybe... Nathan?" Nathan was a good friend of Kashif's and Samir's; he was a part of their group of like-minded friends at the University who would hang out together. "No, not Samir Khan," Dujana concluded. "He doesn't have the right or same physique, let's say."

"Ouch," Samir said from his earpiece. "That's it, man. I'm going back to the gym now."

Kashif tried not to smile behind his mask but stayed focused. "You can keep guessing, but it won't do you any good," he said.

Dujana sighed, "Fine. But... there is something else," he said. "What?"

"Well, your suit. It's incredible, a real work of art. I would love to have a real close-up look at it sometime."

"I'm blushing," Samir commented.

"I can introduce you to the one who made it one day," MetalGhost responded.

"Ahh, so it's not your invention. So, what? You have a team?"

"There's no team. And I tell you what, you get me all of the others together, and I'll give you this suit when I'm done. I told you I wouldn't be doing this for long. And when I'm done, you can have it."

A stunned Dujana stood up. He paused and hesitated as if not sure what he had just heard. "Really?" He was able to stammer out finally.

"Really," MetalGhost replied with finality.

"I think we have a deal. But I don't think I look forward to the day you won't be doing this anymore," Dujana confessed.

"It'll happen. And you're going to help me. See, one other reason I came to you. I noticed your rope cuffs." He pointed to the ground. "They're an amazing piece. I want to know if you can give me one."

Dujana looked genuinely shocked, "You want something of mine? Well, to be fair, those..." He nodded towards the rope cuffs, "That's the Burn Brothers' invention."

"Who are they?"

"They also work here," he said, looking around the room. "We all use this apartment to experiment and develop whatever we can. The Burn Brothers, now they're geniuses." Dujana went over to the rope cuffs on the ground and picked them up. He looked at them and then threw them to Kashif. "We're tired of guns. We, as a society, need to find an alternative. And that's why the Burn Brothers invented this. Keep it. I hope it serves you well."

"Thank you," Kashif said, putting it under his thobe. "And another thing, you have this way of... pulling guns out of people's hands. How do you do that?"

Before Dujana could respond, a giant piece of magnet shot out from the door and struck MetalGhost straight in his chest, sticking itself to him.

What?!

Staring at the door, the assailant appeared with raised hands: "Magnetize?!"

Dujana let out a small laugh. "Meet Ms. Johnson's *other* son, Akayden."

"But he... he's a bank robber!" Kashif protested.

"Oh no, Sir, Mr. MetalGhost! I... um..."

"He gave that money back, as it was not *his,*" Dujana finished with a displeased look at the young boy.

Akayden let out a small nervous laugh as he scratched his head. "Mr. Dujana told me to help the community and do good. I thought this would help, but I guess I only made things worse, and..." He spoke fast without taking a breath, "And I guess I messed up, but I gave all that money back, I swear!" Without his black suit on, Kashif could see he was just a young boy.

"What are you doing here, Akayden?" Dujana asked.

"I'm sorry, I didn't mean to just come in between your conversation, I know it's rude to interrupt two older people when they're talking, but I couldn't help it, and I saw you here, Mr. MetalGhost, and you asked about how the guns get taken out of people's hands, and…"

"Magnets," MetalGhost finished his rambling sentence.

"Magnets!" Magnetize responded excitedly.

"As I said, you've inspired a lot of people. Can I?" Dujana asked, pointing to the magnet stuck on MetalGhost's chest. MetalGhost nodded.

"But especially these youngsters, like Akayden here, need some guidance. That's where I come in," Dujana finished and took off the magnet. "And for you, go back home. And don't tell anyone what you saw here, understood?" He held out the magnet to Akayden.

"Yes, Sir. Bye, Mr. MetalGhost!" He took the magnet and ran back out.

Kashif shook his head. "Now, for this meeting, I asked NightStrike to bring everyone to the roof of the warehouses next Tuesday. You gather all your people."

"How can I find you to tell you when we are all ready for you?"

"I'll find you."

"Maybe I will be able to reach you through some sort of communication?" Dujana asked, turning and looking at something on his desk. When he turned around, he noticed he was alone in the room.

On his way out at the end of the hall, Kashif reached the window, scaled out onto the wall of the building, and then paused. His mind replayed what Dujana had just told him about Ms. Johnson, and he looked at her house next door. He jumped onto her roof and made his way down to the back porch. Ms. Johnson was sitting on the porch, gazing out, when she noticed the figure on her porch. She didn't flinch in fear or show any emotions; she just stared. After a few seconds, her eyes became watery as she smiled, "I've been waiting for you for so long."

"Hello, Ms. Johnson."

CHAPTER FORTY THREE

MEETING WITH THE OTHER VIGILANTES

Man, I'm telling you I'm going back to the gym," declared an annoyed Samir back in the lab the next day. "I'm a big-boned guy, that's all. Why did he think I'm not able to go out there?" He complained, recalling Dujana's comments.

Kashif tried not to laugh and just nodded at Samir in agreement to cool him down.

"I'm telling you, we get a bad rap for nothing, us bigger people. Big-boned and beautiful is all it is." Kashif nodded again, saying, "Yeah, you're right, man."And then you can go out there and fight while I help from here." Kashif smiled.

Samir thought for a moment, "No, I'll still stay here. You go out there and get beat."

Kashif laughed. "Can we focus on tonight, please? It's *the* big night."

"Ah yes, you get to meet your most tried and tested followers."

Kashif gave Samir an unamused look.

"What are you going to say to them?"

"I don't know."

"Do you have your speech ready?" He poked.

"No speech. Just going to tell them to stop."

"So, the shortest speech ever. And the most boring. Perhaps not the most convincing, either."

"Let's see how it goes."

It was finally time. What he had been looking forward to but also dreading at the same time. Time to meet the other vigilantes.

The night was clear with a full moon when Eva made her way up to the warehouse northeast of the central city, near the river, far away from the neighborhoods and the industrial areas. When she reached the warehouse roof, she found two men already there, Dark Coat and McKenna.

"Asalaamu alaikum sister!" Dark Coat joyfully greeted, black hospital coat and green scrubs. A green mask was hanging off of his face.

"Walaikum asalaam," she responded, looking around and realizing it was just the three of them on the rooftop.

"Where's your boyfriend? Thought you guys might come together," McKenna slyly commented.

"Boyfriend?! Woah, what did I miss?!" Dark Coat shouted.

Turning to McKenna, an unamused Eva rebuked, "You're not funny. In fact, you have no class."

"Easy there." McKenna laughed, clearly enjoying getting Eva upset. "All I'm saying is our friend here has really changed her tune on MetalGhost of late. I'm wondering what's going on, that's all," he said, speaking to both, but addressing mainly Dark Coat.

"That's why we're all here then, aren't we? To talk to him, maybe you'll change your tune too," Eva said coldly.

"I doubt that. I'm not much for talking," replied McKenna.

A few moments later, MetalGhost made his way up to the rooftop and found he was the last one to arrive, and a group had been anxiously awaiting him. Walking to the center to where the rest were standing in a semicircle, the small chatter that had been taking place came to a stop. All eyes were on him now. Looking around at each of them, he was able to recognize most of them but not all. Dark Coat, McKenna, NightStrike, Magnetize, Dujana, two others he did not recognize, and finally to his surprise, the ninjabi woman in purple and black. What Kashif had thought would be an easy meeting suddenly turned into a nerve-racking one where he was unsure of what he wanted to say.

They're all here, he thought. For the past few years, all of these people have found the courage to mask up and fight the corrupt, the oppressors, and the bullies and help the weak, the poor, and the oppressed. They each looked at him and found strength, courage, and motivation. Many had tried to follow him, but most had failed or given up; only these few were left standing.

"Your followers," Samir had called them.

"You'll soon have followers," he fondly remembered Aliya saying.

If only you could see me now, Alz. You were so right, he thought.

An unexpected sense of awe and admiration started rising up in Kashif as he looked at each of them one by one. That sense of admiration, he found, was broken as soon as Dark Coat spoke.

"Muslim standard time, much?" Dark Coat chided, speaking to MetalGhost. "I tell you guys what, it's a beautiful night. I can get the bar-b-que grilling up in a few minutes; what do you say?" He laughed. Even though he joked, there was a sense of seriousness in his voice.

"We don't want to give away our location, brother," Dujana replied calmly, stepping forward in front of the crowd and giving Magnetize a cold stare for nodding at Dark Coat's idea. Dujana wore a dark blue sleeveless Moroccan shirt with white borders, loose red pants, and silver body armor underneath. One of his muscular arms was bare, holding a bow staff with blades on each end. Tied around his head was a red bandana, the ends of which flowed gently in the wind. He looked around at everyone and then at MetalGhost, standing in front of them. "MetalGhost called this meeting, so we'll let him speak. But I don't think you've been introduced to everyone here?" He asked. Kashif shook his head. "I think you've had the *pleasure* of meeting who they call 'Dark Coat,'" he said, looking at Dr. Karim.

Dark Coat took a dramatic courtesy bow. "Fun fact, it was MetalGhost himself who gave me that name."

"And I believe you've met NightStrike and McKenna," said Dujana, moving on. "As well as young Magnetize." He gave Akayden a pat on the back, who raised his hand in a shy wave to MetalGhost.

"These two here, well, I'll let them introduce themselves." He turned to a man and a woman dressed in black and white long cloaks, with white shirts underneath and black conical sedge hats which covered their eyes. Both carried two swords holstered behind their backs. The two gave each other a look before nodding and removing a white mask covering their faces up to their eyes. The man stepped forward first, gave a slight bow, and raised his hat to reveal his face. Both Kashif and Samir gasped when they saw the faces.

"Oh my God, Kashif!" a shocked Samir yelled into his earpiece. Kashif put his hand to his ear upon hearing his sudden loud voice. "That's Li-Ming and Won! Our students!"

A deep, sinking feeling came across Kashif, and he felt his heart drop. Samir was right. The two vigilantes in front of him were his own students, whom he knew well. They were his brightest students, after all. *How could I not have recognized them?!*

"It is a great pleasure to meet you," Won stated. "We've come from Japan to study at Al-Fihriya University, but you have given us a reason to practice our swordsmanship here. I am who they call The Swordsman- Kenshi, and this is my wife, Kage Doku."

"The 'Shadow Venom,'" MetalGhost translated. They both examined MetalGhost in surprise, *"Watashi wa nihongo ni seitsū shite imasu,* I am familiar with Japanese." Kage Doku stepped forward and bowed as well.

The two stepped back, and Dujana spoke up, "And the last one here is Lady Nusaybah." He turned to the woman next to him in a black and purple abaya, with a mask covering her face, with slits revealing her brown eyes. She held a long brown bo-staff in one hand, planted against the ground. Her eyes had a fire in them, and Kashif experienced a fleeting moment where he felt he recognized her from somewhere.

"My daughter," Dujana continued with a smile. *Daughter?* Kashif thought, suddenly dismissing any ideas that he may know her.

"Or she might as well be, as I trained her myself. Of course, that's not her real name. But she takes her name after the famous Sahabiyat, companion of the Prophet (ﷺ), Nusaybah, who was one of the few women who fought in battles."

"I've seen you, you have been going after corrupt police officers," Kashif turned toward her. "You sure know how to fight."

Lady Nusaybah looked up and right at MetalGhost as if looking into Kashif's eyes and then nodded and looked back at

Dujana.

"That's all of us," Dujana declared. Giving the signal for Kashif to speak now.

Kashif had no idea what to say at that point, and so many thoughts were running through his mind. "Speech time," he heard Samir whisper, and he looked up at them all.

"I thank you all for coming here tonight. And for all you do, you've made a difference in many people's lives. But you're all just getting started now. I've been doing this for a long time, and if you want to know what you'll look like if you keep doing this, look at me. Suiting up, being a hero: it's a virus. And I'm sorry I've infected you all. You don't want to do this for long; it... gets to you and affects you. Mentally, emotionally, spiritually." He continued to look at each of them. "Now that I know who each of you are, I know you're all good people, family men and family women. So, I beg you all, go home, and be a family man and family woman. And make the changes you want to see from within our system, not outside of it."

"You expect us to work with and trust the police? You know they're infiltrated with crooks. You're the one who revealed that," sneered McKenna.

"You expect them to trust us, vigilantes, who disregard the law and take it into our own hands? Have we worked with *them?* Trust goes both ways. What's the point of having laws if we keep breaking them?"

McKenna paused, continuing to listen.

"There's no doubt that the police need reform, and I'm going to take care of that, I assure you. That process has already started with the new police chief. What I need from you is to work with them. There are... there are good people in the force," he said, remembering Zara. Suddenly, a warm feeling of hope came from within him. "I know good people in the police force who are trying their best to make the changes. Work with them. They're on your side, but they're doing it the right way: from within."

He turned to Lady Nusaybah, "Going after them is a dangerous game. You're only going to make them find more ways to hide. We should try working with the police, while getting to the source of the corruption: the gangs." Kashif could tell they were all contemplating his words. "This lifestyle isn't good for you, nor is it good for the city. Trust me, all I want is a normal life back. I will take out all of these mob leaders and the head of the snake, the one at the head of all the problems in this city, Iris Hill. And after I do, I'm done. Until then, I need you all to promise me that you will not get in my way, and you will not go out."

The group stared uneasily, an evident tension rising in the air, but no one spoke. Then, Dujana spoke up, "That, I'm afraid, we can't promise you. As you said, we're all helping others. That can't just stop."

"Help those around you, but stay out of the big war. Stop trying to go after the mobs and the big guys. It's too dangerous," MetalGhost responded, looking at McKenna. "You would've gotten killed quickly had you gone into that bar."

"I would've been fine," replied a defiant McKenna. "In fact, I would've come out of it cleaner than you."

"Watch it." Kashif wagged his point finger at him as a warning. "As I said, you're done."

"To hell I am," spat McKenna.

"I'm warning you, get in my way again, and it won't end up well for you. Let me handle this, and then when I'm done, if you still want to suit up, you work within the law," MetalGhost fired back. McKenna stared right back at him but gave a weak, unconvincing nod.

"What I need from the rest of you is what you know. These kidnappings, can anyone give me any information?"

"Mad Scientist," Dujana responded. "Kenshi and Kage Doku worked with the Burn Brothers. They got into his lab, and well... they can tell you."

"Experiments. Horrible experiments like I've never seen before," cried Kage Doku.

"He's experimenting on humans with some kind of serum that he injects them with. It...I don't even know how to describe it, it transforms them into something almost inhuman. You saw the monster that was unleashed. What we saw was worse," Kenshi stated with fear in his voice. "He calls it Echo Mas, whatever he puts in them."

"Echo Mas? That was also the name of the trafficking ring I

busted at the docks. So this is all related," said MetalGhost, trailing off into his thoughts.

"But he's not really the only one you should be after. Everyone knows it's Iris Hill at the top of all this. Get to him and stop the source," Kenshi pleaded.

"The head of the snake I mentioned."

"But when we went again, it was all gone. Wiped clean as if nothing was there at all. They moved the lab."

"To where? How do you just move a lab?"

Kenshi shrugged, looking worried.

"Thank you, anyone else?" When no one responded, he continued with a sense of finality, "So until I'm done, none of you should get in my way in the big war. Stay in your areas, don't come across me; I don't want any of you getting hurt. And when I'm finished, I'll give all this up. No more MetalGhost, no more vigilantes. I'll work with the police force and ensure the safety of this city that way. So you all won't have to suit up, too. If you trust me, then please, do not continue doing this."

"Where are you going to go after… you're done?" NightStrike asked.

"To try to get back to a normal life. I'm finished with this," he replied gloomily.

"MetalGhost, remember what I said, you've given us hope, and a way to help. The truth is, this is how we know to help, this is who we are. I don't even know how to work with the police." NightStrike continued.

Lady Nusaybah stepped forward, "Why not lead us? We can all use our skills to help the police, but you can lead the way. I don't think we are ready to abandon suiting up, and I don't think you need to either. You can help them as MetalGhost. But why not lead us, and show us the way? Show us how to work within the law and work with the police."

The thought stunned Kashif. "I..." he looked down and thought. His gaze went to Dujana, who was smiling and nodded in agreement. Kashif never thought about leading the group in front of him. Everyone in front of him was a fighter, motivated to bring about good. Maybe they just needed some guidance, he wondered. A strange feeling passed over him, and to his own surprise, he heard himself saying, "Fine."

Everyone looked around each other in a moment of joy.

"When I'm done, we can work together," Kashif returned each person's satisfied look.

"Now we're talking!" Dark Coat jumped. "Now we just gotta come up with a team name! How about..." Dark Coat began saying, but he was broken off by the noises of footsteps and people landing on the roof.

On the far end of the roof, dark figures began appearing out of what seemed like thin air. One after another, until all the masked heroes on the rooftop were surrounded and outnumbered by dark figures in black full-body cloaks. They each carried swords on their back, and the only part of them that was visible were their eyes: red eyes. The heroes backed together and made a circle, no one moved, and the only sound that could be heard were the fast-beating heartbeats.

"Anyone invite these guys to the party?" Dark Coat asked.

Lady Nusaybah twirled her bow staff as McKenna reached into his coat, hand on his guns, and NightStrike released a small arrow from her wrist brace and placed it in the bow, ready to shoot. MetalGhost stood in front of all the heroes as they positioned themselves in a fighting stance. He counted about fifty of these dark attackers. A moment passed as each side stared at the other as if waiting for the other to make a move. The silence was broken by all the swords unleashing from their holsters.

"Uh guys, I think we have a situation here," Magnetize's nervous voice broke out.

One of the dark attackers spoke, "Iris Hill sends his regards," before they rushed toward them with their swords.

The fight started, and MetalGhost, clenching his fists twice and raising them to a fighting position, witnessed each of them in action in person. NightStrike fired arrow after arrow as the arrows formed from the metal band on her wrist, shooting them at a breakneck pace. MetalGhost noticed the metal band on her wrist was a device that kept creating arrows from thin air, so she would never run out of arrows. Even more impressive was her aim; her arrows didn't miss a single target. However, the dark attackers continued rushing forward even after being struck by arrows. The arrows did not kill the attackers. It only slowed them down.

Kenshi and Kage Doku fought with their swords in a spectacular fashion that Kashif had never seen before, moving swiftly and in unison, a perfect harmony as if they had practiced together for all of their lives. They sliced each of their attackers who tried coming close. Dark Coat had large twin scalpels, which he used as knives. He reached into his coat and threw scalpel after scalpel, and when in close combat, he could slice the attackers in a highly surgical manner while extracting his stethoscope into a nunchuk.

McKenna pulled out his assault rifle, shooting down each assailant who jumped at him. His aim was precise, not missing a single target, and he loaded and reloaded his rifle as quickly and easily as MetalGhost had ever seen. Dujana and Lady Nusaybah had taken out a bow staff each and used it with incredible precision. Twirling and striking their attackers and keeping them at a distance.

Magnetize threw magnets at each approaching attacker and used his magnetic force to push each one off the roof. And MetalGhost retracted his shield and super-punched each of the assailant's back. What seemed to be a winning formula, as each of the heroes had better weapons, the assailants were crumpling down with each hit but, shockingly, were rising right back up. It seemed that no matter what they were attacked with, they would jump back up.

"These guys can't be human!" Magnetize yelled out as he threw one of the assailants off the roof, only to see him jump right back up.

"They're not staying down!" shouted Dark Coat fighting off two fighters simultaneously, grunting and breathing heavily.

"Keep fighting!" NightStrike yelled as she shot two assailants back who fell off the roof.

No matter how many they seemed to kill, somehow, more and more kept coming at them until they were backed into a corner of the roof. Dark Coat let out a loud wince as he was stabbed and fell to the ground. Lady Nusaybah went to his aid, but she was kicked on the side of the head and fell unconscious. A loud cry was heard when Kenshi screamed in anguish. Turning to face him,

MetalGhost saw that Kage Doku collapsed on the ground, stabbed and bleeding. Kenshi was standing in front of her with his sword. With each hero struggling and fatiguing, the fight quickly turned from bad to worse.

"Get behind me!" MetalGhost yelled to them all. They all made their way as MetalGhost pulled out his shield and attempted something he had never done before: he tried expanding his shield to cover them all. He kept trying to expand his shield until they were all walled behind him. The assailants looked through the blue shield, and they all jumped at MetalGhost, who deflected them back with his shield. All that could be heard on the heroes' side were metal stabbings at the shield, trying to break it. With each strike and push, MetalGhost struggled to hold it together. One by one, the assailants threw, kicked, punched, and sliced at the shield until a loud scream was heard from MetalGhost. Realizing they were all at the edge of the roof, MetalGhost growled louder and pushed back, taking steps closer to the dark attackers, pushing them with his shield closer to the edge of the roof.

"Aaaaarrgh!" He screamed as he reached towards the center of the roof. The attackers were now backed up against the edge of the roof. The shield had absorbed the energy of each strike against it, so with a final push, MetalGhost punched the shield toward them, releasing the same energy back at them, causing them to fly off the roof. As they all fell off, only one was left remaining, but when he looked around and realized he was the only one standing, he stared back at the group of heroes huddled together and then jumped off the roof himself.

The heroes were alone again but with significant injuries. Dark Coat ensured he was okay and had already patched himself up. But Kage Doku was bleeding profusely.

"Get her to a hospital!" shouted MetalGhost.

"I have a ride around the block," Dujana responded hurriedly as Kenshi lifted her.

"Let me bring her to the hospital. Follow me," said MetalGhost, taking her in his arms and flying off. They rushed behind to the nearest hospital, and when they arrived, Dr. Karim was sure to see her quickly operated on.

CHAPTER FORTY FOUR

OIL AND WATER

And then I grabbed him by the neck and brought his face down to my knee, and POW!" Abdul Malik was in the middle of one of his stories, one Kashif was sure didn't exactly happen the way he was explaining it, but he let him have his moment. A few weeks ago, Kashif stopped by to give Gatekeeper a gift for his loyalty and for providing Kashif information whenever needed.

"Here's something for you," Kashif had said, handing him a little box.

"Oh wow, what's this, man?" he asked, opening the box. "Wow! Now that's nice! Look at that. It's a watch!" he said, putting it on and showing it off. "You know, this looks pretty expensive. I could probably get a good grand off of this right now, I tell you," he said, thinking out loud. Kashif was quick to stop him from going any further in this thought.

"Uh, no, DO NOT do that. Whatever you're thinking to do, don't do that," Kashif emphasized, putting his hand on Abdul Malik's shoulder, mainly to control him from moving around. "See this watch, well, it's special. Listen, you're an important part of this team, right? So, it's very, very important that no one else gets hold of this watch. If you ever are in trouble and you need me, you know, for *me* to come, just press this button right here," he explained carefully, showing him a button on the side of the watch. "And it's crucial you only press this button as a last resort if your life is in danger. Do you understand?

Abdul Malik's eyes lit up like fireworks. "You mean this watch will signal you?" He asked excitedly.

"Yes, but again, only if your life is in danger should you press the button, okay? I need to know you understand," Kashif asked, trying to reassure himself that he was making the right decision.

"Of course, man, I understand. Only in an absolute emergency. Got it!" Gatekeeper assured him.

"Good."

As Kashif walked out, he had a bad feeling deep inside about what he had just given to Abdul Malik. And the very next day, the fear was realized. Abdul Malik had tracked down and stopped a man from breaking in next door, but the man then came into his store and backed him against a wall, and drew a knife. Naturally, Abdul Malik pressed the button. The watch beeped and made a mechanical noise.

"Yeah, you're in trouble now, you *shaytan!*" Abdul Malik yelled at the assailant. But after a few seconds, when nothing happened, the man started advancing toward him. As he started coming closer, the watch opened up, and a metal suit retracted all around Abdul Malik. The last thing the assailant saw was a screaming Abdul Malik before the suit covered his face.

"Wooooaahhh! Oh my God, oh...my God!" Abdul Malik screamed first in shock, then in awe. "Wow, look at that!" He looked at the confused assailant who had started stepping back.

"Yeah, come fight me now, punk!" He ran towards the robber and punched him to the ground. When he got up, he wielded the knife at Abdul Malik. At that moment, MetalGhost barged through the door, "Are you okay?!" He found himself staring at his own suit back at him. He super-punched the robber, knocking him out.

"Yeah, man! This is so dope!" Abdul Malik screamed in excitement under his suit. They agreed that they'd let Abdul Malik take all the credit for saving the day.

The next day Kashif came to check up on him, and he caught Abdul Malik in the middle of one of his stories. He grabbed Kashif and used him as the bad guy while re-enacting the scene for reporters and the TV crew. As Abdul Malik was telling his story, Kashif's phone buzzed. He looked at it and froze.

One new message: Aliya.

His heart dropped, and each breath became harder and heavier to breathe. Kashif opened the text message while Abdul Malik was still talking in the background.

"Hi, hello, salaam. Can I talk to you, please? I need to say something," Aliya wrote.

He felt his face flush red and himself shaking. *Could this be real?* He kept staring at his screen, breathing hard, and unable to move. He re-read the text a few times. Kashif didn't respond, instead kept going back and forth between the message and the name above it: *Aliya.*

It was her. It was really her.

Abdul Malik's voice broke his trance. He caught his breath as different emotions started going through his body.

"Step here, Kashif," Abdul Malik took him by the shoulders and tried to move him to the stance he wanted for his story. Kashif felt frozen, so he let Abdul Malik move him, his eyes never coming off his phone. After a few minutes, he took a deep breath and finally responded,

"You have one minute."

He could see she was typing, so he finally excused himself from Abdul Malik's reenactment, stepped out of the store, and made his way to his bike. He rode back to his apartment; Aliya had sent a lengthy response by that time.

"I just want to say I'm so sorry for everything that happened and how it happened. I think about it every day, I think about you every day, and it's killing me; I can't do this anymore. I need to tell you this: I'm sorry for what I did. I'm sorry for hurting you, but it wasn't my fault. I hurt myself too. And I miss you. And yeah, I guess my one minute is up, huh?"

It is reported that the fastest a human heart has ever been recorded beating was 480 beats per minute. Kashif was sure he had set a new world record at that moment. He was nervous, pacing back and forth, starting to sweat, but he never took his eyes off the screen. Off of every letter, every word. *I miss you.*

He was lost for words, unsure what to respond or say. All he ever wanted was to talk to her again and understand what had happened. And here it was. He felt a mixture of happiness, nerves, and anger. The anger started winning over.

"It took you over five years to say that?" he wrote back.

There was a pause and no immediate response. But after a minute, she started typing again. "I know. I'm sorry. I want to explain, and I need to get this out. Can I call you?"

"No," He replied.

"Please."

"No."

"Are you angry with me?" she asked.

"Obviously."

"I'm sorry. I'm angry with myself too."

A pause followed as he gathered himself, and then he let it all out. "You ruined me. I loved you, and I still miss you so much. Every day, I think about you. I wonder what you're doing, how you are, why you did this to me. I thought you loved me? I thought you would wait for me. Why did you leave me? Why did you leave me like that?"

"I think about you every day too. You have no idea how hard it's been for me."

"For you?! Yeah, it must have been really hard when you made it look real easy."

"It's not like that. Look, can I please see you? We need to let this out for both of us. It's time we finally do."

"No."

"Please, Kash. I need to let this all out. I think we both do."

"Fine."

"Same spot?"

"I don't think we should be meeting alone. That was our mistake last time."

"I know, I agree. That's why we won't be alone. There's someone else who's also been wanting to meet you."

"Who?"

"You'll see. Same place?"

"Fine."

Kashif sat down on a chair and let all the emotions run through him.

Aliya stood by the window where she had texted Kashif and

stared out. A rush of fear yet excitement flowed through her. For the first time in five years, she felt alive.

A short while later, Kashif landed fully suited on the rooftop of Aliya's parents' house, with his heart pounding out of his chest. They would sneak up here to talk, away from everyone and in the outdoors. Countless hours of conversations happened right there. Where they truly fell in love. As Kashif landed on the roof, all their memories ran through his head, with the realization they shouldn't have met all those times alone. After landing, he noticed she was standing on the other side of the roof, looking out. As she turned around, another figure emerged from behind her running toward Kashif.

"Kashif bhai!" Zainab screamed, approaching him with her arms out.

Before Kashif could react, she hugged his suit tightly.

"I missed you! Wow, I finally get to see your suit!"

"Uhh..." Kashif was taken aback. Stepping back a few steps, he noticed how much Zainab had grown in the past few years, now almost ten years old.

"Zainab, I missed you too," he couldn't help but smile. "How have you been? Wow, you've gotten so much bigger!"

"I'm good, I'm always reading and watching all your news stories. Wow, I can't believe you're a superhero! I wish I could tell my friends I know you!"

"Uh, yeah I don't know about superhero but..." Kashif laughed not knowing what to say.

"All of my friends have your poster up on their wall. They think you're the coolest!" They both laughed.

"Anyway, I have to go do my homework. I come up here now and get my work done. It's so peaceful up here." She gave another wide smile and went to the opposite side of the rooftop where she had set up a desk. Next to the desk was Aliya, who slowly started walking to Kashif at the center of the roof.

After all those years apart, now face-to-face. Reaching the middle, she stopped a few steps away. It was a moment before either said a word. They only stared at each other at first.

"Are you really going to wear that?" She asked about his MetalGhost mask. "Take it off. Let me see your face."

Taking a deep breath, he slowly removed the mask, revealing a nervous and watery-eyed Kashif. Aliya smiled and sighed. "How I've missed that face."

"I've missed you so much," he was finally able to say quietly, pain evident in his voice.

"I've missed you, too," she said, breaking into tears. "You have no idea…" She began, but her sobs drowned her words. They both stood in front of each other, crying.

"They call you the ghost of this city, but these last five years, you've been my ghost. Wherever I go, you're there with me. In my thoughts and mind. You're my ghost."

Even after all these years, she still warmed his heart. "You're still the only place that feels like home," he said, stepping closer, but he knew not to touch her; it would be wrong.

"I've always wanted nothing more than just to be with you forever," she confessed.

Kashif turned away, a frown forming on his forehead. "Why did you leave me, then?" He finally asked quietly, closing his eyes.

"I made a mistake. I don't know what I was thinking," she recalled between sobs. "My family had put so much pressure on me because we weren't sure what you would do. How long you were going to make us wait, if you'd ever be ready, we didn't know. And I didn't have answers for them, and I couldn't tell them… what you were doing. I couldn't tell them about this," she said, looking at the suit. "And I told them to wait, believe me, Kash, but how long was I supposed to wait? Especially without giving any proper answers or timelines? And in the meantime, Sufiyaan's mom asked my aunt for my hand; my aunt can be very persuasive, and she was very persistent. I said 'no' in the beginning, and both my parents did too. But I ran out of time, and I didn't even know what you were thinking or feeling. We hadn't spoken in weeks. I even went to your house to see you, but you weren't there.

"And the longer you were away, the more I started realizing something, Kash…"

Kashif began breathing heavier, recalling those days when he was consumed with anger and with MetalGhost.

"I realized, I couldn't tell anyone about this," she looked towards the suit. "You were helping people, you were literally saving people. And so in that time it became clear to me, it was either MetalGhost or me," she looked at him with wet eyes.

"Alz, no..."

"Yes, it was always what it would come down to. How could I tell you to stop being a hero to people in need? How could I be selfish and only think about myself? So, I made a decision, I didn't tell anyone about this life of yours. I chose you being MetalGhost over being with me."

Kashif felt his heart hurt. "But I chose you. I thought you chose him over me..."

"I chose you to help others over just being with me. And again, it all started happening on its own. My parents liked him, his family, everything. And there was nothing wrong with him. I mean, we've known him our whole lives, so he wasn't a stranger. And before I knew it, everyone was planning our wedding. It all happened so fast that I couldn't keep up, and I didn't even realize what was happening. I kind of just went along with it, and everyone was happy. I thought this was the right thing to do." She finally looked up at him. "Sometimes I feel it was a mistake, but then I see you doing all this good. I've been following you since the beginning. When I look at how much good you've done, it eases any pain I feel being away from you."

Kashif didn't know what to say. He was only then starting to realize how his actions affected others, how much of an emotional and physical distance he kept from others. She was right. How long was he supposed to keep her waiting?

"But I chose you," he whispered again. "I came to your house that day..." He broke off, starting to cry. "I came, Alz! I came for you. And I saw what was happening... I couldn't believe it. I came with this," he lifted the flap from his fingers, revealing the wedding band, now meshed between his gloves.

Aliya put her hands over her mouth in disbelief. "You... were there?"

"I ran after your car. But you didn't hear me. I chose you," he whispered.

"I'm so sorry. I wish you had come sooner," Aliya lamented.

They stood there in silence for a while, their hearts breaking in front of each other.

"Are you happy with him?" he finally asked, unsure what answer he was hoping for.

But Aliya didn't respond and looked him straight in the eye.

"Why not?" he replied.

"It's fine, but let's just say we're two totally different people. He's not interested in me, never was. He also just went along with the whole thing, went with his parents' wishes. And I've never been interested in him. I mean, we tried, but we're too different. And I can't get through to him, he does his own thing. That's how it's been."

She burst into tears. They both stood there next to each other, unable to hug or touch. Kashif looked into the sky helplessly as she looked to the ground. Not a word was said for a few minutes.

"But you're here now. You're here, and we're still…" he broke the silence, but Aliya started shaking her head now the tears came down harder.

"No, no…" She sobbed.

"What do you mean 'no?'" He asked.

"I have children now, Kashif. I can't do that to them." She wept.

"But you're not even happy!" He tried to reason.

"I make my own happiness; I have my kids, and he's good to them, at least. He's a good father to them. I can't do that to them."

"You're not happy with him, though," he repeated, hoping for a different response.

"We both do our own thing. Trust me, it's fine and better that way."

"How is that better? So you're going to give up your happiness for your kids? How does that make sense?" He questioned loudly.

"I'm not giving up my happiness, they are my happiness. And you're my ghost, remember. I always have you in my heart, which has kept me going."

"I don't just want to be in your heart. I want to be in your life, next to you every moment," he cried.

"It can't work!" She shouted while crying. "Are you going to give this all up now? Now when you're making a difference in the city?"

"I'll give up the whole world for you."

"And are you ready to be a father of two children who already have a father? Will that be fair to them or to you?" She demanded.

He paused, giving thought but then looked down.

"That's what I thought. And it's fine, and I know it's not fair of me even to ask you to do that," she said. "We might feel the same, but our worlds are not the same."

They both stared out at the sky and the city, standing next to each other. Both wanted the same thing but realized the world would keep them apart.

"I fear you'll always be on the other side of the glass," she finally said.

"What are we but oil and water?" He replied.

They stood together in the quiet again, looking out.

"I hate coming back to this city. Everything reminds me of you," Aliya whispered.

"I hate staying here because of the same reason."

They sat on the ledge for what seemed to be an eternity, each of them hoping the day would never end, hoping they could make this last forever. They talked about everything that happened in their lives.

"I have to get back," she finally said, looking at him with pain in her eyes.

He watched her go, feeling like he was losing her all over again.

Part III

CHAPTER FORTY FIVE

NATHAN

The student library at Al-Fihriya University was always a place where professors seemed to lounge more than students did. Surrounded by books, some of which the professors had written themselves, the most erudite of staff would congregate at the library center to discuss the latest news.

Kashif and Samir were sitting and grading papers while having an evening lunch. As they discussed school matters, a tall, dark, handsome man in khaki dress pants, a white shirt, and a green argyle sweater came to sit with them, as was their usual habit.

"You're unusually late, Professor Duncan," noted Samir.

"Got caught up with something big. Can't wait to show you guys," he responded excitedly. He motioned for the two to come forward as if to tell them a secret. "I've put together this design of MetalGhost's suit. I'm figuring out so much from these pictures. Look." Kashif and Samir exchanged nervous glances as they took the photos Prof. Duncan had pulled from his folder.

The photos were extremely clear and crisp, unlike any either of them had seen before. In an instant, Kashif knew where these came from: Ben and Mikaeel.

"Wow," remarked Kashif, genuinely amazed that the two amateur journalists who have been following MetalGhost for over a year were able to capture these pictures. The two had a unique ability to show up wherever MetalGhost was and take photographs. They would never get too close, but Kashif knew when they were there, hearing their *click, click* with each shot.

"Great shots," Kashif feigned excitement.

"You took these yourself?" inquired Samir, already knowing the answer.

Nathan chuckled. "I'm no photographer. I can hardly work my cell phone camera most days. It's those two students, Ben and Mikaeel. I've been paying them to follow MetalGhost around and take these pics. Boy, those two are hard to bargain with, too," he said, half-amused and half-annoyed.

"You've been what?" Kashif gasped.

"But check these out. His suit seems to be completely metal," said Nathan, ignoring him and animatedly pointing to a picture of MetalGhost at Jack's Bar & Ring.

That's why they were there, Kashif thought. The picture showed when the blue thobe had almost come off after ripping, revealing the metal suit underneath.

"And look at this here," pointed Nathan enthusiastically to the jetpack while keeping his voice low. "First-ever look at the jetpack running across his waist and under that thobe. That's a high-level piece of equipment, and it has to be just the right measurements for it to work. And it does, truly amazing." He awed at the jetpack Samir had designed for the suit.

Samir looked at the picture, attempting to show surprise while keeping his composure. Kashif could see Samir was trying not to seem too proud of his invention being raved at by another peer.

"Probably not a good idea to have it so openly around his waist, though," said Nathan examining the picture and rubbing his chin. "It's an easy target for others to hit his back and damage the jetpack, or worse, have it explode. Very high risk," he shook his head in disapproval.

"Well, where else could he have it?" Samir asked, sitting up straight, feeling offended. "I mean, what are the other options for him, right?" he quickly added, changing his stiff tone to a more casual one.

"Well, I was thinking he could lose the external jetpack altogether and instead have slits under his arms and sides, like fish gills, that could open only when he needs them. This way, they cannot be damaged easily by others," he said thoughtfully.

"Yeah, that's a great idea," Kashif poked Samir. "Poor design currently," he said with a straight face, enjoying messing with

Samir.

"I'm not so sure about that." Samir frowned at Kashif. "But hey, maybe you're onto something," he added, not to sound too off-putting towards Nathan.

Nathan continued showing them picture after picture of different angles of MetalGhost in the fight. Kashif had already confronted the two amateur photographers, almost threatening them to stop taking pictures. "Hey man, the world wants to see this!" Ben and Mikaeel had responded. "And we're just giving it to them!"

Looks like I need to pay them another visit and be more convincing this time, Kashif thought. As quiet and hidden as Kashif tried to be as MetalGhost, the more he was getting noticed. And these two weren't helping. *Perhaps not so amateur after all.*

Both Nathan and Samir had been going back and forth, exchanging ideas while Kashif was thinking, and his thoughts got broken when Nathan asked louder a second time, "What do you think, Kashif?"

"Uh, what?"

"Do you think he's a hero?" he asked with a sense of admiration in his voice.

Kashif paused, taken aback by the question. He felt as if Nathan was asking if he was a hero.

I'm not a hero. He had told Imam Dawood Murphy.

Samir and Nathan both stared at him, awaiting a response. After a long pause, Kashif replied, "I don't know."

"Oh, come on, what do you say?"

"He's a vigilante, Nathan. He's not exactly following the laws," stated Kashif.

"The law sucks, man. There is so much crime and corruption, and the police are all in on it, I tell you. I'm glad someone is standing up for us, the people. He's definitely a hero," stated Nathan, "a superhero." Samir stared at both of them, not wanting to be pulled into the conversation.

"He's inspiring," said Nathan in admiration.

"Yeah, well, how long can he do this, right? He's going to either get hurt or caught. He can't do this for too long," replied Kashif, almost as a self-confession. Samir shot him an angry look as if they'd had this discussion before. *You can't think like this,* Samir constantly told him.

When does this end, Samir? Kashif had asked him in the beginning.

When you're satisfied. When it's over.

I'm afraid it'll never be over. It's either going to consume me or kill me.

I won't let that happen.

Nathan had been taken aback by Kashif's comment, visibly worried while in deep thought. "Yeah, maybe you're right," he said solemnly.

"Come, it's time to get going," Samir said to change the tone and mood. As they got up to leave, Nathan was still thinking about that comment. *He can't do this for too long.*

In the following few days, Nathan continued bringing up MetalGhost, clearly becoming more venerated with him. "I tell you, he's what's right in this city. He's realized the problem, and he's solving it himself. It's what we need in this city," said Nathan one night.

Kashif countered with, "Well, that's what the police are for."

"You know they can't be trusted," exclaimed Nathan.

"They have a new chief, and I expect him to do the job," replied Kashif.

"Maybe," said Nathan. "But what about this old jerk, Iris Hill, making a statement against superheroes? As the wealthiest man in the city, certainly the most powerful, he should be helping this city. But no, he just hides behind his millions of dollars and his hotels and has the guts to make a statement against all vigilantes," an angry Nathan erupted. "Rumors have always followed this guy, and it's all but known he works with underground crime rings and different mobs."

"He's just making anti-vigilante statements for political points. We all know he wants to run for Mayor one day," replied Samir.

"One day, he'll get what he deserves," said Nathan fiercely, with fire in his eyes.

Kashif didn't like the tone or what he said but decided to change the topic and suggested they get some dinner.

CHAPTER FORTY SIX

NIGHTINGALE

I t was late at night when Nathan Duncan slid on long black gloves, tightly wrapping them around his fingers. He looked into the mirror, gazing at himself from head to toe.

Finally, he thought. It was the last piece of his outfit: a black shirt with a black vest, dark green pants and shoes, a ski cap on his head which he planned to pull down, and a large black coat with a hoodie around his body. He double-checked the backpack with him and the instruments he needed inside: rope, grappling hook, tear gas, hand ties, knives, and he had already loaded his gun, tucked into the back of his pants. He had been meticulously planning this for a while, and was now ready to go. He exhaled a deep breath and walked out the door. Today was finally the day.

The night before, Nathan, Samir, and Kashif were in the library after their classes, and Nathan had been in an unusually upbeat and happy mood. "You seem very happy, man," Kashif noted, smiling at Nathan, "What's the good news?"

"Have you ever had this dream, no, an obsession that you can't get out of your head?" Nathan asked.

"Yes, I know her name, and she lives in Kashif's head, actually." Samir elbowed Nathan as they both laughed. He winked at Kashif while the latter did not find it funny.

"My good friends, I've truly had great conversations with you all the last few weeks. And I must admit, you both have been very instrumental in my success. Well, upcoming success."

Iris Hill lived in the penthouse of the lavish Hill Hotel, which he owned. Very few people knew about this penthouse, but Nathan had spent time following Iris Hill. He had studied all the entrances to the hotel and knew where each guard was positioned and where all the cameras were. On that night, he made his way into the hotel and used the stairs to quietly sneak up to the executive level on the 10th floor. He scaled the walls to reach the security room. The door was locked, he picked it with a makeshift key to gain access into the security room. Slowly opening the door, he noticed a guard sitting in front of the giant screens, monitoring all the hallways on the above floors. He walked behind, wrapped his arms around the guard's neck, and applied pressure in a rear-naked choke. The guard struggled to fight back but was knocked unconscious within a few seconds. Nathan turned to the cameras, focusing on his path to the penthouse. He raised an emergency notification diverting most of the guards toward the other side of the building and away from the hallways he needed to go to. Then he turned off the cameras leading to Iris Hill's room.

"Oh, have we?" Kashif had looked at Samir in astonishment. "I hope we get some of the shares of your success then," he said, smiling and making the sign of money with his fingers.

They all laughed, "No, no. It's not going to be money, my friends. It'll be bigger than that. I'm excited because I'm finally ready," said Nathan.

Quietly sneaking around the hallways, he made his way to the private elevator, taking it up to the penthouse. The elevator was quiet; the only thing Nathan could hear was his heartbeat, quickening the higher the elevator climbed. When the elevator stopped, and the doors opened, he was ready. He threw tear gas into the hallway as soon as the doors opened and barged out with his ski mask down. Nathan ran towards a guard, punched him hard as he fell back into the second guard, and used the smoke to sneak behind and choke them both out. When the smoke cleared, Nathan was standing tall above both unconscious men. He tied them both up and taped their mouths.

Now, finally, he thought.

He took the guard's room access card, tip-toed his way to the door, quietly opened it, and slid inside.

He entered a large apartment. With the entryway dark, the only light shone through ceiling-level windows all around up ahead, displaying beautiful views of the entire RP City. Crouched behind a table, he scanned the living and side rooms. It was the most exquisite house Nathan had ever seen, with lush and expensive furniture, carpets, and curtains. But he didn't have time to marvel. Still crouched, he continued his way toward the kitchen. He noticed a doghouse and suddenly stopped. Taking out the gun from his back, he looked around carefully, scanning for any signs of a dog. He waited for a few moments but did not see or hear any animal. The penthouse was eerily quiet and still; not even the floor creaked as Nathan made his way past the empty kitchen. He heard the wind blowing outside against the large windows and the sound of birds chirping in the distance, but there was no sign of any person anywhere. Making his way down the hall toward the master bedroom, all he could hear was his heartbeat and the sound of the wind and birds in the distance. He carefully and quietly opened the master bedroom door and entered.

"Ready for what?" Samir and Kashif had inquired.

"You guys will find out very soon. I'm on the verge of doing something great. And not just for myself, but something great for everyone in this city. And I thank you both for giving me the courage and confidence." He gave them a warm smile.

Quietly closing the door behind him, the only light again came through the large set of windows looking out to the city. He stood still for a moment, scanning the room for any movement, but the room was empty except for a figure lying in bed up ahead. He pulled out hand ties from his pocket and made his move, quickly rushing towards the bed. Reaching the side of the bed, Nathan pulled the sheets back, raised his hands, and stopped in shock. Under the blanket lay a sleeping pit bull, snoring away. This shock was minor to what followed next. Nathan felt his whole body shake as he started feeling an electric shock run throughout his body. He couldn't see any wires, but he was being tasered. He began to scream, but only a whimper came out, enough to wake up the sleeping pit bull, who shot up and barked and growled at the frozen man now shaking on the spot.

A slow and deep voice came from the corner of the room, "You might be wondering why you can't move. Well, this isn't just a taser; it's a toy I've been working with. So glad you came by so I could test it." Nathan heard a beep, and he stopped shaking from the electricity and fell to the ground. He started to breathe heavily as he lay wrinkled on the floor. The pit bull had begun to bark louder, jumped from the bed, and brought its growling face in front of Nathan.

"Sit, boy. Let's enjoy the show we have here," said the voice menacingly. Turning to face the voice, Nathan could slowly start to see the silhouette of a man sitting in a maroon robe on a chair in the corner, covered in darkness.

"Let me guess. I don't know you, but you know me, and you came here to… what, seek some sort of revenge? What is it? Did I kill one of your family members? Do I owe you money? Hmm, no, looking at the way you're dressed…" He rose up and walked toward a limp Nathan on the floor, examining his bag. "You're another MetalGhost follower," he said the words in delight. Nathan felt his chest was on fire, worsening with each breath, and even more frightening, he could not move or feel the rest of his body. The figure slowly walked closer and hovered over him. He could now see the tall, aristocratic dark-skinned man with a bald head and a strong jawline. *Iris Hill!* Nathan stared into his dark black eyes, full of excitement as they stared back menacingly. "Oh, how I've been waiting for another of you to stop by," Iris Hill said in a slow, calm voice. It was chilling to Nathan how calm and leveled his deep voice was.

"I'm going to guess you didn't like my speech the other day about you vigilantes and wanted to talk to me about it? Of course, that's not the word you all use. What is that word?"

He threw his hands around and his head back as if to think. "Superheroes? But look at you, not very super, are you? None of you are. You all sicken me. Trying to take the law into your own hands? It has to stop somewhere, for God's sake. I've been enjoying bringing you, MetalGhost followers, down," he said while pressing a button on his watch. He smiled, looking at the wall across the room slide open, revealing the Black Dread suit. Nathan gasped in disbelief.

"That's right. Black Dread has been working very hard and

sending a message to all of you pathetic followers. And I think this is another perfect opportunity." He smiled a big hearty grin as he leaned in closer and pulled Nathan's ski mask off.

"How disappointing, another nobody," Iris Hill said dejectedly. Nathan felt a sense of feeling returning to his legs and fingers as he lay still on the ground. "See, you all have been messing around and damaging my work and business. Well, no more. And you walked right into a big opportunity for me." He leaned closer to Nathan on the ground, who felt he was able to move his arms. "Time to send a final message. This time, to MetalGhost himself," Iris hissed, bowing close to Nathan. With Iris Hill so close, he took his opportunity, turning to his side and reached for his gun. In an instant, he felt the electrocution run through his body again. "Not so fast. We're going to send a message to the rest of your kind: No. More. Playing hero," he said slowly, as Nathan continued receiving shocks on the ground. Iris took out a remote from his robe pocket and pressed a button to stop the shock as Nathan started to doze in and out of consciousness.

"I know you both don't drink alcohol, so I brought a little halal apple cider instead," Nathan had said, smiling.

Samir and Kashif looked on with delight and laughed as Nathan pulled out three glass cups from his bag. He poured each of them a glass and raised his glass. "Here's to a better tomorrow." He toasted them both, clinking their glasses.

When he finally awoke, Nathan felt the freezing wind slapping against his face. It took him a moment to realize he was sitting outside on the penthouse's balcony with his hands, feet, and torso tied to a chair. Four men with guns stood next to him, keeping watch. The same men he had knocked out earlier.

"Ah, you're back!" Iris cheered, sipping a drink. "Take a look at your city. Such a beautiful night, no? Are you willing to give your life for this city? Well, I guess you have no choice. You know, I will give you some credit. I almost didn't hear you coming in tonight. Very clever. But you must be wondering then, how did I know you were here?" he asked with a big smile. *"Uguisu,"* he said. "Nightingale. During my time in Japan, I became quite fond of the uguisu, a songbird. A nightingale," he took a sip of his drink and looked out into the night. "In Kyoto, Japan, there is the Nijo Castle, and legend has it the castle was a real safe house, indestructible from the outside and with unique architecture on the inside. The inhabitants were kept safe by many things, trap doors, secret hallways, weapons stored in everyday items, and… birds. Not real birds, you see. The hallways of the palace chirped with each step of an intruder who should not have been there. Chirp, chirp, chirp." Iris leaned in right in front of Nathan's face. "Ensuring no one snuck around undetected. See, you're my nightingale. And you have chirped your last. But don't worry. Your song will be played in front of millions." Iris started to smile broadly and laugh. That was the last thing Nathaniel Duncan saw.

By the morning, as Kashif walked into campus, he noticed the mood was tense, almost fearful. He passed by nervous chattering and students running back and forth, and he decided to turn and head to the professor's lounge. As he walked by the classrooms, he noticed each class had people huddled together. Opening the door to the professors' lounge, he found Samir and a group of professors had gathered together. The look of fear and anguish on everyone's face caused his stomach to turn, and before Kashif could ask what was going on, the T.V. blared loudly the voice of Iris Hill, who had been talking in front of the cameras, "This intruder thought he could intimidate me. Could intimidate Ridgefield Park City. See, this is the problem with vigilantes, it's a sickness and a disease, and they don't even realize it." Iris Hill's voice was different from his usual calm, deep voice, and it was that of a frightened elderly man.

Kashif's heart started to sink, and suddenly a strange taste came into his mouth as his breathing became heavier. Iris, on the T.V., continued, "This man was clearly diseased, talking of all sorts of nonsense, I tell you." He continued in his scared voice, "And who caused this disease? Who other than the intruder's hero, the criminal, MetalGhost. This is what MetalGhost has caused in this city! This madness! This is why he's dangerous, and so are all these lunatics who follow him. I call on MetalGhost, to turn himself in and stop his followers before this city gets destroyed by his disease."

The murmurs and shock of the fellow professors in the hall started growing louder and louder.

The news anchor reported, "Those were the words of the city's wealthiest man, Iris Hill, who caught an intruder in his own home last night. We're just getting information that this intruder was Al-Fihriya University's professor, Nathaniel Duncan. According to Mr. Hill, Professor Duncan broke into his building and penthouse, fought with Mr. Hill and his guards, and was killed in the skirmish. Afterward, Mr. Hill decided to do this, and we warn our viewers that what you are about to see is disturbing." The screen cut to a female reporter asking Iris a question, "Why did you decide to send this message?"

"So the whole world can see and know: the wonderful people of Ridgefield Park City will not be further diseased by MetalGhost. And to his ilk, a visual reminder that this is what happens when they do follow him," he said, pointing to the top of his building, where the body of Nathan was hanging from the balcony with his hands tied behind his back, a noose around his neck. His limp body swayed back and forth from the wind.

The whole hall screamed in shock and disbelief.

"I have a message for MetalGhost," Iris Hill's voice turned deep and confident. "Come meet me. I have something you need to hear."

Kashif stared at the screen with a scowl, breathing deeply. He was furious. The anger boiled up inside of him and was about to erupt. Kashif wanted to punch a hole through the TV, the wall, and through Iris Hill. Samir turned to Kashif, his eyes wet with tears. They stared at each other without saying a word. Both remembered what Nathan had said the night before. *I'm going to do something great for everyone in this city. And I thank you both for giving me the courage and confidence.*

CHAPTER FORTY SEVEN

IRIS HILL

'm going after him!" Kashif screamed, pacing back and forth in the lab.

"That's what he wants, man," Samir tried to reason with him, "Don't give in."

"He's a monster. He's what's wrong with this city, and now we know where to find him. We should have found him first. I've been putting it off for too long, and you know it!" he said, pointing his finger at Samir.

"Because he's too *dangerous*. He's connected to everything in the city. You're literally going to start a war."

Kashif stopped pacing and said, "He's already started the war." He glared at Samir in the eyes. "I can't believe you're telling me not to go after him now that we've found him. We cut off the head of the snake and deal with the body after. Trust me. I'm not leaving any of those scums that work for him alive either." He fumed.

"You're starting to sound like McKenna," Samir noted. "Attacking the rich and powerful, how are you different from him?"

Kashif resumed pacing.

"You're emotional, and I get it, but don't make decisions when you're emotional," Samir continued to warn him.

"I am, yes, because he's making it personal now. You saw what he did to Nathan… he…" Kashif couldn't finish his sentence. He lowered his head and bent down, exhausted, over the table. "No one else should have to be killed because I'm not doing what I should be doing." He sighed before speaking calmly, "I will go after him.

Tonight."

"Fine. But it'll have to be different from what you're thinking. Otherwise, you'll end up like Nathan. And trust me. I'm just as angry as you are. Let me make one more addition to the suit."

"Aahh," Iris Hill relaxed, placing his head on the pillow. The room was peacefully quiet where he lay. Finally, after a long day of interviews and statements with the entire penthouse full of buzzing people all day, there was quiet. The police had blocked off his room for the night as a crime scene, so Iris moved to the bedroom closest to the terrace. He had just fallen asleep when the sound of breaking glass woke him up. He shot up in bed, looking around, and before he could reach his side table lamp, a laser shot out from the corner of the room and hit his hand.

Aaahh! He screamed in pain.

"Don't touch the lights," a voice threatened from the corner of the room. Turning to look, up ahead in the dark corner of his room were bright blue eyes, seemingly floating in the air.

"MetalGhost," Iris Hill said calmly, not seeming surprised. He was still clutching and nursing his hand. "If you had told me you were coming, I could've put on something more befitting and offered you a drink," he said, looking at his pajamas in bed.

"Shut up. You knew I was coming," MetalGhost barked from the dark corner of the room, careful not to show his face or body. Only the light from his eyes was visible.

Iris gave a small laugh. "Well, yes, I did. Thanks for accepting my invitation," he confessed.

"It's no secret you're behind all the crime and scumbags in this city. It ends now," snared MetalGhost.

"Hmm, not all, I'm afraid. But I do know of all that goes on. I'll tell you that," he said almost proudly.

"Tell me why I shouldn't kill you right now?" MetalGhost snapped, keeping his voice low, aware of Iris Hill's gunmen in the next room.

"Because that's not you," Iris responded calmly, "and my reputation, well, that's not me either. Well, not entirely," he looked straight at MetalGhost. "I've been trying to get your attention for some time now. You're a hard person to reach. Maybe leave a phone number or something?" he said, waving his hand. "You and I are long overdue for a talk. It seems you have the wrong idea of me. It seems like my reputation has taken a life of its own. I want to assure you that we're on the same team."

"Yeah, right," MetalGhost scoffed. "I've figured out that you're Black Dread, going after the other vigilantes. You tried to kill me on the rooftop too, and now we're on the same team?"

"Not kill, for I did ask you to work together, but I admit I acted irrationally then. But things have changed, MetalGhost, and I assure you that I am not your enemy. I know, you all think I'm a monster..." He paused, continuing to clutch his hand. "But I'm probably worse than that," he stated, looking straight at the eyes in the corner of his room. "But even monsters can become afraid. Afraid of bigger monsters." The determined look turned into fear in his eyes. "I've done things I'm not proud of, but I never wanted this. Things have gotten out of control. That's why I needed to talk to you. What you're chasing, *who* you are chasing, I'm chasing the same."

"I've been chasing *you.*"

"I know you think that, but it's not me. The man you are looking for is a man I once supported, but he has gotten out of hand. He's gone... mad. His name is Dr. Carson Daye. I take the bad rep in the media, but he's the man behind so many of the horrible things that have happened in this city—starting with the power outage five years ago to kidnappings, experiments, and the monster in the city. All of it. But he's not done. The worst, I'm afraid, is yet to come. But we can stop it."

Power outage five years ago, the words echoed for MetalGhost. "You have one minute, so you better start talking." He powered up the laser again.

Iris spoke up, hearing the sound of the laser. "It's true that in the past, I have supported him; he came to me with a fantastic idea, you see. The idea to enhance our human race, 'Why be ordinary when you can be extraordinary?' he had said. I had the resources, and he had the mind. And together, we were supposed to change the world. It was supposed to be a cure, really, for all types of sickness, giving us humans such immunity and strength that we would never get sick or hurt again. Think of that!" He said with a laugh. "Well, naturally, that's not how things turned out, not exactly. Not when he started to... let's say, use people for experiments without their consent."

"You mean *kidnapping,*" MetalGhost corrected with a growl.

"As I said, I do not support his behavior or method. It wasn't supposed to be this way. While noble and good-intentioned initially, his experiments started turning into something much more... morbid. What was meant to be a means of helping people heal had morphed into an unhealthy obsession with testing the limits of human pain. He kept pushing the boundaries and wanted to see how much the human body could take. He began turning people into monsters. I believe you have had some encounters with such experiments of his," he said, turning his face away.

"Of course, you would know that," MetalGhost sneered.

"Of course," Iris responded, looking back at MetalGhost, but this time with fear in his voice and eyes. "He showed me what they could do, what these monsters could do to you. See, he used you as practice. He wanted to see how advanced his 'experiments' were by putting them against you. Do you think it's a coincidence those monsters found you again and again? On the rooftop, at Jack's Bar, at the warehouses? No, that was not me. They were planted by Mad Scientist. He's been hunting you, waiting for you, wanting to see them in action against you. And when he found all of your friends together too, well then, that was his Eid, wasn't it? A million-dollar opportunity to see how good his experiments were, and make no mistake, he wanted to take all of you out. Now, I'm no fan of vigilantes, it's true, and I think you have come to know that," he said with a snicker as Kashif became furious while remembering Nathan. "But I don't think you all should be killed. Just controlled."

"You'll never control us."

"Yes, well, that opportunity won't even arise if we don't work together right now."

"Your one minute is up."

"He's going to release his monsters on the city," Iris blurted out quickly, holding up his hands. "You saw what those *things,* barely human, can do against you. Now imagine releasing those on others. On your friends, family, and loved ones. On this whole city. He's truly gone out of control, and he must be stopped. You have to believe that I have tried everything to stop him. But it's up to you and your friends."

"I don't have friends, and they're not going to be doing anything."

"Then just you and me," Iris responded emphatically. "I can tell you where he'll be tomorrow night. I can tell you where he's been this whole time."

Kashif remained silent, staring back.

Does he think I'm that stupid to walk into a trap?

"It's not a trap," Iris carefully continued, as if reading his mind.

"I don't trust you."

"And I don't trust you. But we have no choice. We will have to trust each other here. It's not a trap because I will go with you. You can't just enter and expect to get through all the security yourself. I'll clear the way for you."

"Why should I believe you? Why should I believe anything you're saying is true?"

"You're right. You don't have to. But then you can watch for yourself this city burn to the ground. The choice is yours." He paused. "And I can tell you what you've been looking for, where he is," he said with some pleasure. "I know the Mad Scientist's hiding spot, his experiment lab. So I ask you, will you stop him? Will you save this city?"

"Tell me where he is."

"The place where no one can look, the tallest place in the city. The top of Meridian Tower. I can help you get up there."

"I'm going there now."

"Tomorrow. Dr. Daye invited me tomorrow. He has some big reveal that I'm honestly deathly afraid to see. Who knows? Maybe he even intends to kill me."

"Wouldn't be the worst thing."

"Yes, maybe not, I suppose. But that will be your chance. Tomorrow. Fly up to the 40th-floor balcony, and I'll take you up myself."

"After I do this, I will come to find you again and make you pay for all you have done."

"If you survive what the Mad Scientist has in store for you," Iris said slowly. "And if I survive, then you can seek your justice."

"Justice and revenge. It's either I bring you down now or later. I'm starting to feel I should just do it now," MetalGhost glared.

Unknown to MetalGhost, Iris had pressed a security button under his mattress, causing ten armed guards to be stationed outside of his bedroom door.

"You're a wild animal," Iris said in awe, "and wild animals need to be tamed..." His guards came rushing in and surrounded MetalGhost with guns. As the lights turned on, instead of having their weapons pointed at MetalGhost, to their shock, there was no one in the corner of the room. The guards stared in confusion at an object on the ground where they thought MetalGhost was. A guard walked toward the object, noticing it to be a small object projecting light upwards, showing MetalGhost's laser eyes.

"Tomorrow, after the Mad Scientist, I will come after you," said the mirror-screen projector. The device clicked off and flew up in the air and out the window where it came from. A block away, on the rooftop of a building, MetalGhost caught the mirror screen in his hand and jumped off of the building into the night.

"I don't trust Iris Hill," Kashif said back at the lab, where he and Samir discussed their next move. "He's trying to set me up. I know it."

"Maybe, but he sounded genuinely scared. I believe his story, especially that Carson is out of control. It makes sense that he is behind the monster and all the strange people you have encountered. We've seen what he can do. If he has even Iris Hill spooked, then I can't even imagine what he has planned," confessed Samir. "I think either way, at this point, Carson is the problem, and he needs to be stopped. I say we go after him tonight. Right now."

"Tonight? We don't know what he has in store for us or what we can expect there, we need to think about this."

"Do we want to give him more time to prepare his plan to release those monsters? Kashif, Carson is clearly the problem, we need to go take him out now," Samir continued adamantly.

"Why are you so resolute on taking out Carson now? I need to see what he's up to first, I don't trust Iris Hill's story. I need to think about this."

"I didn't mean to push; think about it. In the meantime, let me make some final updates to the suit. I think we should keep the laser enabled for now."

I don't know what to do. Kashif fell in his chair, exasperated, as Samir went back to working on the suit. *Should I go tonight? Do I fight Iris Hill or trust him? What if Carson is really crazy, do I kill him?* When he started this, he only sought justice for his abu. Now, he was thrown into a whole different world. What was the right and just thing to do? He reached for his phone, and as if almost instinctively and without thought he sent a text. A buzzing on his phone had Kashif scrambling in his pockets, but his mood changed when he saw the name on the screen.

Aliya.

He opened the text, "Kash."

"Alz," he responded.

Alz... He stared at his text, and before he realized what he had done and began to unsend his message, Kashif sighed and smiled as he looked out the window at the moon.

Aliya stood on her balcony, smiling at the message on her phone. She sighed as she turned her head up, looking up at the same moon.

Neither of them responded, nor did they need to, for this had been their way of signaling to each other they were thinking of the other. Nothing's changed, they both thought. She knew how to warm his heart. And just the thought of him made her smile. He wished he could talk to her, but he knew that door was closed now. He fought back the urge to reach out and talk to her more.

His head was spinning from so many thoughts. "Ya Allah, guide me," he sighed. Sitting quietly in the chair, he noticed the moonlight was shining into the room and onto a bookshelf against the wall. Kashif spotted that the light shined on the Qur'an, and instantly, his ami's voice rang in his head, "Du'a is us speaking to Allah, but the Qur'an is Allah speaking to us." He went to the wall, took the Qur'an and sat back down. Opening it up to the last place he had stopped, he read the passage, and felt a lightning bolt striking his heart.

"Oh you who have believed, seek help through patience and

prayer. Indeed, Allah is with the patient." He paused and read the line again. A sudden calmness swept through him. Just as he had felt the night on the balcony when he heard the adhan, Kashif felt he was being given clear answers: be patient, and pray. *How could I have forgotten that prayer is the answer?* He went to his prayer mat and raised his hands to begin prayer. Afterwards, as Kashif settled down and quietly thought to himself, he felt clarity in his thoughts and the move he needed to make. Calmly walking to Samir, he confidently stated, "We'll do this tomorrow."

CHAPTER FORTY EIGHT

SOME KIND
OF MONSTER

Looks clean," Kashif said, impressed, standing in front of the suit.

"For the big day," Samir commented. Kashif had noted he seemed apprehensive since the day before, now doubting their plan to go to the Mad Scientist with Iris Hill. "I'm just not getting a good feeling about this," he admitted.

"Samir, I'm doing this. I have to end whatever is going on." Samir gave a half-hearted nervous nod.

It's finally time. Kashif had been thinking extensively about what tonight could lead to. He had no doubt he would put an end to this: an end to the Mad Scientist, to Iris Hill, and, he hoped, an end to MetalGhost. He was tired of it all. A small thought in the back of his mind and heart also had been bubbling up: to give everything up, accept Aliya and her children, do whatever it takes to get her back, and try to make it work.

He left for Meridian Tower, but on the way, he stopped at the rooftop of Hashmi Plaza on Northwood Street, next to the complex Aliya and her family had moved into. He looked down from the building toward Aliya's balcony's sliding doors and windows. Jumping to the balcony was not an option for Kashif as her kids and husband would be home. So he remained standing at the ledge, looking out towards the windows, hoping to catch a glimpse of her. A few minutes later, he saw her walking past the window while talking to her kids. His heart started beating faster. She picked up toys cluttered on the floor and disappeared from view. Kashif had never seen her children, but the thought of her being a mother saddened his heart. She walked back into view and, this time, went toward the sliding doors at the balcony. For some time, she looked out and then gazed up as if knowing Kashif was there. She looked out at him, and a warm, loving expression came across her face. Kashif removed his mask so she could see his face, causing her to smile. He returned a shy smile. Both could feel the distance between them was palpable. Her two children came running out and hugged her legs. The world was keeping them apart, and at that moment, the thought came to Kashif. How could he tear those children away from their father? How could he become a father himself? Would it be fair to ask Aliya to break up her family for him? Maybe he'll always be on the other side of the glass, looking in from the outside. And he realized this was his fate. Even though he wanted her, all the signs were pointing to keeping them apart. *This is what Allah has chosen for me,* Kashif thought. *And He is the best planner, so I have to trust His plan, since He is the All Knowing.* His heart was heavy, but he knew contentment lied in trusting Allah. Feeling his eyes becoming wet, he closed his mask and stood up. Looking back for one last time, he spoke into the night "Goodbye, Aliya."

Aliya turned to pick up her children. By the time she looked back, the rooftop was empty.

Meridian Tower, an elegantly designed skyscraper, was the tallest building in the city. Unlike the other towering buildings at the center of the city, Meridian Tower was located right on the river. The top floors of the Tower were often hidden in the clouds and out of view.

"The top of Meridian Tower! It makes sense why we haven't been able to find Carson." Samir sighed in anguish. Searching for him for five years, he was literally above the clouds.

Landing on the 40th-floor balcony, what Kashif found infuriated him. Two men were already present and seemed to be arguing with each other.

"McKenna! Dujana! What are you guys doing here?!" Kashif demanded.

"Well, well, the final member of our convoy. Welcome, partner," McKenna replied sarcastically.

"What are you doing here? How did you find this place?!"

MetalGhost roared.

He glared angrily at a fully suited Dujana as a sudden sinking feeling hit his heart. They both stared at each other as the realization became clear to them. "Iris Hill," MetalGhost whispered.

"He got to you, too, huh?" Dujana asked. "Looks like he wanted us to come here…" He turned to McKenna. "Together."

"No, this is all wrong. We're walking right into his trap," MetalGhost began pacing back and forth. Turning to both of them. "You guys have to go back. I'm doing this alone."

"Too late, cowboy, we're riding along. I have a few words to share with this Mad Scientist, myself. But don't worry. I'll leave his scraps to you," McKenna glared at MetalGhost with his hands in his coat, no doubt on his rifle.

"It's too dangerous," MetalGhost shook his head.

"That's why we're gonna have to do this together." McKenna pointed to the other two men.

"Look, he's as reckless as they come, but he's right on this. If I remember, you did say we would work together and help you. Let us help you," Dujana reasoned.

MetalGhost sighed, realizing Dujana was right. He took a moment to let the realization settle in that working together would be better. "Okay, you're right."

"We can't risk just one of us going in. We've seen what this Scientist can do, and it might take all of us to stop him. We're all here for the same goal," Dujana continued, relieved. "To take out the Mad Scientist."

"Whatever it takes," McKenna growled, "…even if it means leaving one of you behind." He stared at MetalGhost.

Exchanging glares, they all nodded. "Let's go then," MetalGhost said, turning towards the entrance. He recited "Bismillah" as he led the way.

The floors above the 40th floor were off-limits to the general public, making the three heroes apprehensive about what they would find. "Who owns this place?" McKenna asked, walking up the stairs and looking through the windows to the luxuriant offices and rooms. As they approached the upper floors, the answer became crystal clear, as the giant letters 'IH' were lit up at the floor's entrance. They all exchanged alarmed looks, a sense of uneasiness at what was ahead.

It took them five minutes to reach the top floor, quietly sneaking up as they finally reached the last floor of the stairs, entering a large, dimly lit hallway.

"How can this place be this empty?" McKenna asked. Before the others could respond, they heard a noise from up ahead which surprised them.

Psst, they heard again, as a man in a suit stood halfway in between a door calling them over. The three men hesitated, giving distrustful looks at Iris Hill as he motioned them forward emphatically but quietly. Seeing their hesitation, he let out an annoyed sigh and came out of the door with his hands up. Without saying a word, he gave a nod of his head as if to say, "See?"

The three moved ahead slowly, and when they reached Iris, he quickly motioned them into the room. "You're probably wondering why this place is so empty," he whispered, closing the door as they all entered. "Well, as I said, I would make your path to the Mad Scientist clear. But I can only keep the guards away for so long."

"Where is he?" MetalGhost questioned.

Iris pointed to the floor above. "You could take the elevator, but going from outside the terrace would be a better surprise for him."

"So, what is your plan *exactly?*" Dujana asked with distrust.

Iris sighed, his forehead scrunched as if brooding in deep thought. He was visibly nervous, "I've been thinking about it, and I'm not sure." He looked at Dujana anxiously.

"I go in, and I take him out," MetalGhost replied in a straightforward manner.

"Not that simple, my friend. The guards, the gangs, the henchmen, I can keep them all away. But his… experiments are attached to his hip. And that's what I'm worried about. The only way is that I go in first, as he wants to show me his latest project. I will try to keep his attention, but you guys have to first shut it all down and then try to, I don't know, apprehend him," Iris went through.

"Kill him," McKenna corrected.

"Fine, at this point, it might be the only way of stopping him."

Iris sighed. "Then, let's go. I'll take the elevator up. You all enter from the terrace and remain out of sight for as long as possible."

Iris Hill took the elevator up one floor to what he once referred to Dr. Carson Daye a few years ago as "The most secure place in the city."

"You can run all your work here," an excited Iris had said, presenting the enormous hall with large windows looking out to the city on one side and the river on the other. "I will fund whatever you need. Just show me the results, Dr. Daye," he had said to the lean and scrawny yet tall man with a strong jaw and pointed nose.

"Oh, you will see results." The man let out a small laugh.

"Good. The start of a better world then begins now," Iris replied, shaking his hand.

"A better tomorrow, thanks to you, Mr. Hill." Dr. Daye smiled back.

As Iris now entered the hall, he realized that the "better world" never materialized. The hall had been turned into a full-blown laboratory. Tables stacked in rows of equipment, beakers, burners, and unusual tools were facilitated throughout the lab for various experiments. A unique mixture of smells enveloped the hall, which was bright with lights. Perhaps the most unusual and notable were the three enormous life-sized containers filled with water. The containers, which stood over ten feet tall, were filled to the top with a dark liquid, and three figures were floating inside, seemingly unconscious, with tubes and wires coming out of their sides and faces attached to the containers.

"Ah, there he is!" howled a loud, deep voice behind one of the three large glass containers. Iris slowly stepped closer, recognizing the familiar voice but could not see Dr. Daye. "Just in time for the grand reveal!" the voice exclaimed, laughing as Iris slowly walked closer. He stopped in his tracks as a figure appeared behind the glass containers.

"Dear God..." Iris shrieked, shocked at the image in front of him now.

Once, a scrawny, bony man had turned himself into a colossal figure that towered over Iris. Dr. Carson Daye, the Mad Scientist, was around six feet tall but appeared before Iris, over seven feet tall, with muscles protruding out of his sleeves, shirt, and pants. The veins on his neck and arms protruded out of his skin in a sickly manner.

"What have you done?" Iris asked in awe. The stench of something burning caused Iris to cover his nose. "And what is that smell?"

"That, my friend, is the smell of success. And what I've done, what you're looking at..." he said, raising his arms out and presenting his new form. "Is the start of the better world I had promised you." He repeated Iris's words back to him slowly with a crazed laugh that made the hair on Iris's neck stand.

Unknown to the Mad Scientist, three figures had crept into the lab from the outside terrace.

"This isn't what I had in mind when I said, 'a better world,' Dr. Daye," Iris spoke up, concerned. "Your experiments haven't proven to enhance human life. All I've seen is violence. I've told you, I want to see the results of humans being cured of diseases and pain, but all I've seen were... monsters. Look at what you've done to yourself. We're not supposed to change the world like this, but to save it."

"You don't think of this as 'enhanced' enough?" the Mad Scientist stared back. "Perhaps you liked me better before." He started trembling, his whole body shaking violently as he shrunk back into his previous self and body. The monstrous man had transformed back to his skinny self in an instant. Shocked, Iris let out a gasp. The Mad Scientist smiled and continued, "You see, the world will never be the same again. What you call *monsters*, I call progress. There are always learning curves, but each of my children continues to become stronger, and these three..." he said, pointing to the glass containers, "are the final results of all that experimentation. This city and the world will become better as a result of my work. The only downside is all the fog that my experiments have caused in RP City. I do hope you forgive me for that," he laughed.

"How are you planning to help this city?"

"Soon, everyone will benefit from receiving my Echo Mas potion. Look at what it has done for me."

"What potion? How do you even know it works?" Iris Hill asked.

"And that's what I want to present to you today. Thanks to MetalGhost, he's let me advance my work. I have learned and improved my work to incredible heights," he spoke, clearly pleased. "Now, let me show you one of my children." He smiled, presenting one of the containers and turning on the lights.

Hiding in the shadows, MetalGhost froze in shock. He recognized one of the floating bodies: *Fares!* His thought was broken by the sound of McKenna next to him, loading his sniper rifle. Before MetalGhost could stop him, McKenna fired.

Walking toward the containers, the hall's lights went dim, only leaving the light from inside the containers shining bright.

Clink, clink, crrkkk, the sound of bullets striking the glass containers one after another and, within a few seconds, the shattering of all three glass containers.

"Nooo!" The Mad Scientist let out a loud scream. As he started rushing toward the bodies in the containers, the deafening sound of gunfire caused him to fall to the ground. Looking up, bullet after bullet hit the three bodies all over. The bullets rained on the bodies, the tables, and the shelves, causing papers, glass, and tools to fly and fall all over the lab. After a full minute of nonstop gunfire, everything finally stopped. The lab was pin-drop silent. The Mad Scientist slowly rose up with his back to Iris. There was blood on the back of his shirt as he slowly turned around, Iris could see his eyes were red, and he had transformed back into his monstrous self. The Mad Scientist's face was that of the devil having gone mad. The veins were now ripping out of his face and head, forming a spider-like figure around his left eye, and he was quietly laughing to himself. The laughter became louder and louder until he was in a full-blown crazed howl.

Turning around, he saw three men behind Iris Hill.

"Ahahahahah," a maniacal laugh and expression caused an uneasy feeling for all the others.

"You," he said, turning to Iris, "you fool, you led your friends right to me as I knew you would. Oh, how wonderful it feels to have your plan work just the way you want it to." He continued laughing hysterically. The three looked at Iris, who shook his head, backing himself behind a table.

"It's over now, you maniac," MetalGhost stated to the Mad Scientist.

"Ah, my good friend. I'm so glad you are here! After all, this would not have been possible without you!" he said with a big smile.

McKenna and Dujana exchanged confused glances as MetalGhost stepped forward.

"For so many years, I needed a real match for my children, and you have provided a very noble training practice, I must say. Every time I sent one of my children after you, I learned what I needed to improve on and what adjustments to make," he explained with a satisfied look. "Oh, how I've been waiting for you. To show you the final product of all those years of adjustments. Let me introduce you to the start of a better world," he said, turning to Iris. The Mad Scientist reached into his pocket and took out a device, pressed a button, and the entire wall of the left side of the lab opened up. After a few seconds of silence, the sound of something pounding started growing louder, and the ground slowly started shaking faster and harder. Everyone took a step back as, from the darkness of the wall, in walked a giant fifteen-foot tall man with muscles protruding from everywhere in his body.

MetalGhost stared at the monster in horror. "Isiah!" he whispered to himself in shock, as the being in front of him was Ms. Johnson's missing son.

"No, not Isiah. The *new and improved* Isiah," Mad Scientist exclaimed. "This is Earthquake!" he said.

Earthquake looked at Mad Scientist with red eyes, then turned back and ran at full speed and force toward the three. McKenna reloaded and fired away all the bullets he had, but they bounced off Earthquake. He grabbed McKenna's rifle with one hand and shattered it while holding him up with his head with his other hand. He started crushing his skull until a giant rope cuff thrown by Dujana wrapped Earthquake's arms together, causing McKenna to fall to the ground. Earthquake simply spread his arms and broke the ropes easily, then punched with his giant fist, causing McKenna to fly backward and hit the wall. He landed with a crushing thud as he lay crumpled.

Turning to the other two, he punched MetalGhost back,

grabbed Dujana by his throat, and began to squeeze. Dujana reached into his pocket, extracted his bow staff, expanded it, and flung it into Earthquake's eyes. The monster screamed in pain and violently slammed Dujana to the ground and then threw him fiercely across the lab. The sound of body and bones crushing against the wall was followed by Dujana falling motionlessly to the ground.

With just MetalGhost in front of him, Earthquake stared viciously at him but walked back towards the Mad Scientist. "Ah, that was fun, but now we get to the real fun part. Oh, I can't wait," he exclaimed hysterically. Behind the Mad Scientist, the three bodies from the containers eerily rose, staring at MetalGhost. The look in Fares' eyes was nothing like Kashif had seen before.

"It's a shame that great achievements cannot come without great sacrifices, *Kashif*," the Mad Scientist turned to MetalGhost. "For Earthquake to be born, I had to perfect my formula... which caused the power outage a few years ago. I hear you have been looking for the one behind the power outage, and here I am," he spread his arms wide.

"You...," Kashif felt the rage rising in him thinking of Abu. He clenched his fist at the reminder of being at the hospital and watching Abu pass. At the darkness in the hospital room and chaos of yelling people on the floor. At the years of looking and searching for answers which had consumed him. Never realizing his old friend would be the one who actually caused it intentionally. "You're the real monster!" He leapt at the Mad Scientist.

The Mad Scientist nodded to Earthquake, and the monster jumped up toward MetalGhost and swung at him. Quickly jumping to his side at the last second from being crushed by the giant, MetalGhost took out his shield, clenched his fist twice, and swung at the beast. The beast winced and moved back as MetalGhost continued super punching and striking the monster repeatedly. Earthquake still stood after all the blows. MetalGhost then turned to the new enhancement to his suit: Laser's laser wristband. He charged his laser and struck the beast in the chest. After over a dozen blows and his chest and arms red from the laser strikes, Earthquake surprisingly ran forward, picked MetalGhost up, and began to squeeze him. Unable to escape, the monster squeezed harder, crushing him.

Ahhhhh! MetalGhost screamed as he felt his bones crushing. Shifting himself in an attempt to escape, he freed one of his arms from the monster's grip and struck a laser beam into his eyes. The monster yelled as he let go of MetalGhost, retreating a few steps back. MetalGhost jumped toward him to strike him again, but the giant fist of Earthquake punched him back. Getting hold of his bearings, Earthquake jumped on top of MetalGhost and started pounding away at his head.

Between each punch, the Mad Scientist spoke. "I see you have the laser beam of my associate, and I will gladly take that back. See, the secret to my success actually comes because of you, *my brother, Kashif,*" he proudly said.

"Kashif, get up! Get out of there!" Samir yelled through his earpiece.

Clang as the sound of the Earthquake's punch landed on the metal mask of Kashif. Again and again.

"You and I never did see eye to eye on our goals growing up, Kashif. And how sad, you could have joined me," the Mad Scientist continued. "But our friend, Samir, is different." He laughed.

The monster kept punching violently away, Kashif screaming out in pain.

"And so I have to thank Samir and you, too. See, *he* is the reason for all this. He showed me the way. He believed in me."

"Don't believe what he's saying… it's not like that, Kash!" Samir yelled.

Clang! Clang! The monster continued punching at his face mask. After taking blow after blow to the head, Kashif began to lose consciousness.

"It all started with our dear friend Samir, didn't he tell you? After all, he is the architect of all this," Mad Scientist pointed to the whole lab.

Clang, crrkk, the mask started to crack.

"None of this would have been possible without him. I wonder if you *do* know he is responsible for *everything?"*

"No! Kashif! Get up!" Samir screamed.

Clang! Each blow buried Kashif into darkness, his world

spiraling, and the only audible sounds in his earpiece were of Samir and the Mad Scientist, mixed together.

"Very fitting that he is the reason you're here with your suit. And he is the reason why you will be destroyed." The Mad Scientist proudly walked toward Earthquake who sat on top of MetalGhost. Kashif was barely conscious when Earthquake broke open the mask and ripped it off the suit, revealing Kashif's bloody and bruised face.

In the corner, hiding from all the action but watching, Iris Hill gasped. With all his efforts at finding MetalGhost's identity having failed him, he finally was staring at the man behind the mask.

"Enough!" Iris Hill screamed. "You have completely gone mad, and it's time I put this to an end." Iris removed his suit jacket and pulled down on his tie. A hissing noise came from him and intensified as his suit transformed into a blue leather material around him, with golden shoulder pads and forearms, and a red cape draped behind him.

"Ah, the Black Dread," the Mad Scientist smiled. "Hold him tight," he commanded Earthquake, holding the unconscious MetalGhost.

"You think you can use my own suit that I created for you against me?" questioned the Mad Scientist walking slowly towards the suited up Black Dread. "Nice touch of gold," he sneered with a smirk.

"It was your suit, I improved it. You want to talk about enhancements? Watch this." Black Dread slowly lifted into the air, floating, and then in a flash, flew towards the Mad Scientist with his fists out. In an instant, Fares and the two other monsters jumped in front of the Mad Scientist, protecting him. Fares caught Black Dread's fist in the air and threw him back to the other side of the room, right next to the unconscious Dujana and McKenna. Slowly wincing as he stood up, Black Dread reached into his pocket and took out two small yellow balls.

"You think you alone can defeat me?" the Mad Scientist scoffed.

"I'm not alone, I have my demons," Black Dread threw the balls and they exploded into bursts of fire reaching the three monsters. Unaffected by the fireballs, the monsters walked toward

Black Dread without any sign of pain.

Realizing he was not going to win this fight, Black Dread picked up Dujana and McKenna in each arm. "I regret letting you get this far, Dr. Daye," he walked toward a window, "and believe me, I will stop you." He flew out into the night with both men on his shoulders.

"I look forward to it," the Mad Scientist whispered, turning to Earthquake holding MetalGhost.

"I'm afraid I have no use for you anymore, MetalGhost. And so here we say 'goodbye' to you, old friend. It's really a shame you won't be around to see the result of my new world, *a better world.*" He smirked. Earthquake picked up the beaten and broken body of MetalGhost, took him to the window, and sat him up on his knees.

"Farewell," the Mad Scientist declared with finality as Earthquake kicked him in the chest. MetalGhost fell back violently, broke through the window, and started to fall down the side of the building. The monster stood with his feet on the ledge, looking down with the broken-off mask in his hand. He was about to toss the mask behind MetalGhost. "Leave it. I need to have a souvenir from this wonderful night." The Mad Scientist put his hand on his shoulder and took the broken-off mask. They both stepped back into the lab.

Kashif could not feel his body; he could only feel the freezing wind gushing past him. The fall felt as if he was moving in slow motion, and it lasted for a lifetime. Opening his eyes a crack, all he could see was the sky moving farther and farther away. A scream tried to escape, but no sound came out. The only thing he could feel was cold.

The wind is so cold, was all he could think. And everything went quiet all of a sudden. The last thing he remembered was seeing his life flash before his eyes: Abu, standing and smiling at him; Ami, how wonderful she looked on Eid, smiling as she gave him money as his present; the moment he threw his cap and gown in the air after graduating and letting out a loud cheer; the completion of Hajj and standing in front of the Kabbah, asking Allah to open the door to him in marrying Aliya; the baath paaki engagement.

"Kash..." He heard her voice. Kashif didn't feel the impact on the ground. He didn't feel anything at all.

CHAPTER FORTY NINE

FINALITY

Police Chief, Fahim Kazmi, stared in shock as Samir finished telling him the story with his head lowered. He moved toward the window, silently staring out into the night.

"God help us," Chief Fahim whispered. "It's unbelievable, what you've just told me," he remarked, turning to Samir. "Did you know where the Mad Scientist was this whole time?"

Both men looked at each other in silence, pain in Samir's eyes, fear in the Chief's. The air in the room had gotten heavy.

Chief Fahim let out a loud sigh and finally broke both of their thoughts with, "A witness said they saw him hit the side of the building next to the Meridian that he ricocheted off. Then he hit a small roof, which slowed him down, but he landed hard. It doesn't look good. I think you know that." He stared at Samir to gauge his response. Samir didn't return his look or respond, but there was anguish and sorrow on his face.

"I have to make some calls and handle the press. I think you understand that we're going to keep you here. There will be guards outside. No one in or out."

Samir nodded. Opening the door, Chief Fahim was surprised to find Aliya standing in the doorway, tears flowing down her eyes. "Where is he?" she cried out.

"I'm sorry, but how did you even get up here?"

"Where is he?! Is he dead?!" she demanded.

"No, but please stay here with Samir. I will return," he apologized as he walked past her.

"I want to see him," she said to Samir, sitting dejected and beaten.

She didn't wait for him to respond as she opened the door and went to the glass to see Kashif lying helplessly on the other side. The doctors had finished their procedures, and he lay alone in the room, intubated and wrapped in bandages. The guards looked at Aliya and Samir but decided to let them pass and enter the room.

Aliya rushed in and collapsed next to him, crying. "Don't leave me! Do you hear me, Kash?! Stay with me, please!" she broke down. A few moments passed before she raised her head and stared at Kashif lying unconscious, her weeping the only sound in the room, along with the beeping of the machines and the hissing of the ventilator. Wiping her tears, a somber realization came over her. *I always knew this was going to happen,* she thought. *MetalGhost was always going to lead you to this fate.* That fear was what kept her back all those years ago, and now it was forming a dark cloud above her again. The realization was becoming clearer: MetalGhost was always going to be in the way of her and Kashif. And looking at the unconscious Kashif now, she realized she couldn't have her kids around this. *This is why Allah kept us apart, and why we could never be together...* Taking a deep breath, she brought a chair next to Kashif and started reciting every prayer she knew.

Standing at the door and motionless the whole time, Samir slowly followed in and quietly sat next to Kashif on the other side of the bed. Looking at the unconscious Kashif, he was unable to hold back his tears. He let out a wounded cry looking down at his best friend, bruised from head to toe. He leaned in and whispered into his ear, "I'm so sorry, my friend. I have let you down." He looked at all of the wires and tubes running into him. Without Aliya noticing, he reached for the ventilator's power cord, grabbing it. "You deserve a better friend than me. I pray God forgives us both," he whispered.

Kashif didn't hear those words. Or any words that were said.

The End of Book 1.

AFTERWORD

A LOOK AHEAD...

Diary of Zara Rehman

April 3rd, 9:15 pm:

It's been three weeks since MetalGhost's fall. He remains unconscious. But the city is awake. And it's turned upside down. There's mayhem, and people are scared and hurting. The city is in mourning, and the uncertainty feels like a silent killer, but it's palpable. No one knows what to do or what will happen next. The result has been more and more vigilantes stepping up. I suppose there is a vacuum now that MetalGhost is gone, and every nut in the city has tried to fill it. We've arrested 36 vigilantes trying to take the law into their own hands. Arresting them has caused more upheaval and unrest. The Police Force has become an enemy to the public. I always had a fear it would come to this.

Throughout the years, MetalGhost's emblem had become graffitied on the sides of buildings. The "M" was a symbol of hope and peace for people. Today, while walking home from the precinct, I noticed some of the MetalGhost emblems had begun to be spray painted over. New symbols were painted across the "M." A "W" was the most common sight. W for War Drum. Was War Drum the new symbol of hope for the city? The thought causes a deep fear inside me.

April 9th, 8:00 pm:

As I walked across the street, a car exploded behind me, causing sheer panic as people ran for safety. The police do not have this under control. How can we when the city is against us? I opened my closet today and saw my black cloak. I have been hesitant and unsure of what to do for some time, but it is becoming more and more clear now, especially when I see my cloak staring back at me every time I open my closet door. Every day I hear people screaming outside and running in panic. Sounds of explosions are becoming a daily routine. Today, there was an explosion only a block away, the impact of it shook the ground beneath my feet.

This has gotten too close to home.

I cannot run or hide anymore. If I had been hesitant before, I could not be anymore. Maybe I can't help as a police officer, but I can still help my city. Help with the black and puruple suit that stares back at me daily. Lady Nusaybah. It's been a while since I've suited up, but I can't hesitate anymore. I know what I have to do.
Bismillah.

Lady Nusaybah and the heroes will return.

GLOSSARY

Abu: father, in Urdu and Arabic.

Adhan: the call to Islamic prayer (Salah).

Alhamdulillah: Arabic phrase meaning "praise and thanks be to God."

Ami: Mother, in Urdu.

Akhi: the term "brother" in Arabic.

Asalaamu alaikum: Muslim greeting, meaning "may peace be upon you."

Baat paki: a traditional Pakistani engagement of a bride and groom by their families.

Bismillah: short version of "Bismillahi Rahmani Raheem," one of the most important phrases in Islam, that Muslims use when starting any task. This translates to "I start in the name of God, the Most Compassionate, the Most Merciful."

Dhur: the second mandatory prayer of the day, at midday after the sun has passed its zenith.

Du'a: an invocation or prayer.

Dupatta: a long shawl-like scarf which covers the head and shoulders; traditionally worn by women living in the Indian subcontinent.

Ghadda: a donkey; meant to refer to someone as being stupid or foolish.

Insha'Allah: Arabic phrase meaning "if God wills."

Janaza: a Muslim funeral.

Jannah: heaven.

Masjid: a place of prayer for Muslims, also referred to as

Mosque.

Nani: maternal grandmother, in Urdu.

Nikkah: marriage contract in Islamic law.

Mutter ghosth: a delicious South Asian dish cooked in gravy with meat and peas.

Rabb: the term Lord in Arabic.

Salah: obligatory prayer in Islam, prayed five times a day.

Shaadi: wedding.

Shifa: a cure or healing.

Shaytan: devil.

Thobe: a loose-fitting, ankle-length, one-piece garment worn by Muslim men.

Tikka: a traditional piece of forehead jewelry worn by Pakistani brides.

Wali: guardian.

Acknowledgements

I want to start first and foremost by thanking Allah, God Almighty, the Creator, the Most Loving and Merciful. This idea of a Muslim superhero has been rolling around in my mind for years, and I never knew how to bring it to fruition. It is truly by the blessing and mercy of Allah that He has given me the ability, time, and health to be able to undertake this project. Alhamdulillah.

To my parents, my superheroes and role models. It was my dad who I told first about this idea and he encouraged me to write. After his passing I stopped writing, but it was also because of him I started again. He would want me to finish what I had started. I wish he were here to see the result but Allah had other plans. Please make a quick du'a for my dad.

To my wife, my biggest supporter, loyal friend, honest critique, and the one who kept pushing me to continue everytime I hit a wall. Thank you for wearing so many hats and doing so with a smile. I love you.

To my amazing publisher, Janan Sarwar. I am in awe of your commitment, dedication, and patience. You believed in me and this project from the beginning and this book would not have seen daylight without your guidance and leadership. I feel indebted to you for all your sincere advice and tireless hard work. I'm aware this book was a challenge for you and Global Bookshelves, but you took every bump in the road with stride, didn't let up, and kept everything moving along. May Allah continue to reward you for your incredible kindness and dedication. In many ways, you saved Kashif.

To Samir, yes *the* Samir, thank you for going through the book, ripping it apart, and providing honest feedback which was needed. Your advice and touch are what took this book to the next level. I can always rely on your sincere advice, which I will forever cherish.

To my sister, Jauveria, thank you for being the first person to read the finished book and for being part of the journey since day one. Your advice and feedback really added to the quality of the story.

Special thank you's are in order for Shantel, I love how genuine and professional you are. Your advice and marketing genius helped take this book to a global level, which I could not have done on my own.

Thank you to all the beta readers and editors, to Rumki C. To my illustrators Stanley and Ashiyam, thank you for bringing MetalGhost and the whole MetalGhost universe to life. Thank you to my community, to YM for keeping me grounded. Thank you, all.